CW01456928

THE ELFLAINE CHRONICLES

BALLAD OF DAWN

A NOVEL BY

HALEY HAMILTON

This book is a work of fiction. Any references to historical events, real people, or real places are used fictitiously. Other names, characters, places, and events are products of the author's imagination, and any resemblance to actual events or places or persons, living or dead, is entirely coincidental.

Copyright © 2024 by Haley Elizabeth Hamilton

All rights reserved.

No portion of this book may be reproduced in any form without written permission from the publisher or author, except as permitted by U.S. copyright law.

Produced by Softwood Books in London, England.

Book cover and all other art designed by Ida Thisted Jørgensen.

Edited by Courtney Hanan

First Edition

ISBN 979-8-9905785-4-8 (hdc)

To those who have known, all along, that there is magic.

PROLOGUE

SUMMER SOLSTICE

ELIDEH

E lideh Danu could not believe, after years of searching, she finally found it. It must have been fate, because one minute, she was browsing in a local, second-hand bookshop, and the next, it was there: the lost faerie Book of Straun. A beautifully bound book in supple, emerald leather, radiating magic. Elideh purchased it from the shopkeeper, who couldn't remember seeing it before, and had to stop herself from sprinting back to The Harbour Inn.

"Hello, Elideh. Productive day?" asked Mary, the innkeeper.

"Very much so," Elideh shouted as she ran past, quickly making her way to the staircase leading to her room.

She flung open the door, locking it behind her, and sat on the bed. She pushed her dark hair behind her ear, and took a deep breath.

Then she opened the book.

Even with all the research about the fae she had conducted over the past decade, and even though she knew that they had once resided in these lands long ago, she was genuinely in awe of what was written in this ancient tome. Not only was it overflowing with fae history, but, to her astonishment, it was also a grimoire. She flipped to a page with beautiful, gold calligraphy and her heart stopped.

It couldn't be.

There, written in gold, was a story that was strangely, eerily, horribly familiar.

Once upon a time, in a world where magic had to hide, there lived two sisters who loved each other very much.

The older sister, born of stars and chaos, and the younger sister, born of caution and light, were destined for greatness, but at a cost.

Their parents cherished them above all else, and would pay the price for the forbidden love they shared.

But destiny cannot be changed, and fate cannot be thwarted.

And the sisters could not hide forever.

The darkness waited patiently, searching for a way to them. Though forces beyond their control propelled them toward the inevitable collision.

But fate is not without mercy, and destiny is not without choice. Ancient threads began to weave together, connecting despite all odds. And the sisters could change the world, or damn it.

Although she had never been able to confirm it, she believed that her and her younger sister, Ailia, were connected to the faerie realm she had been trying to find for so long. And this story, written in gold, resonated with a story she barely remembered. A story her mother used to tell her. Hands shaking, she turned to the next page, and nearly dropped the book. Elideh shook her head and pinched her arm, making sure this wasn't a dream.

Holy shit. *Holy shit.* She found it. After all her searching, it was right there in front of her—a way to open an entrance to Elflaine. And if her suspicions were correct, if the story was true, she would be able to perform the spell. Today was Summer Solstice, one of the days when the veil between the realms was thinnest—one of the only days this spell would work. If she was going to do this, she had to act quickly.

Elideh wrote a note to Ailia, explaining everything she could. She would normally just call her, but didn't want to hear the inevitable "Wait for me before you make any rash decisions," or even worse, "Can you at least sleep on it, Elideh?" She couldn't afford to wait, and if she was being honest with herself, she knew this could be dangerous, and she had promised her parents, all those years ago, she would always keep Ailia safe.

Besides, she would only stay in Elflaine for a couple of days. But just in case she couldn't get back, she would leave the book at the inn for Ailia so that she wasn't left completely in the dark. Although Elideh tended toward spontaneous decisions, she liked to have a backup plan.

After writing the note and stuffing it into the Book of Straun, she carefully put the book on her desk, knowing Ailia would notice it immediately. Elideh traced her hand over the spine of the book and wished she could take it with her. But Ailia would need it if something went wrong, and ever since the night their parents had died, Elideh had sworn to protect her sister.

She texted Ailia to get to Portpatrick as quickly as she could, gathered some clothes and a notebook, and threw them in a small bag. She was sure Mary wouldn't mind if she left her things for a couple of days. Wasting no more time, she set off. She needed to be in a place where she could perform the magic without being found, and the ruins a short hike away would be perfect.

She slipped out of the inn without making a fuss over goodbyes and headed straight to the steep hill that would lead her to the crumbling castle. Elideh was not a runner like her sister, but she started jogging as quickly as she could through the mist toward her fate.

The wind was beginning to pick up, whipping Elideh's dark, silver-and-gold streaked hair around her face, the mist growing heavier with every step she took. She glanced toward the sea, the waves angrily crashing against the cliff, but quickened her pace. She wasn't going to let a little rain stop her.

The massive stone ruins of Dunsky Castle looked black against the pale gray sky, and Elideh walked toward the place where a door once stood, careful not to trip over the loose stones on the ground. She cautiously made her way through what must have been a grand hall at some point toward the back of the structure. It was strangely quiet, the stone walls blocking most of the wind.

Elideh unfolded the paper where she had written the spell, took a deep breath, and started reciting the ancient words. As soon as she had spoken the last word of the spell, a shimmery portal appeared not far from her at the edge of the treacherous cliff. She purposefully strode to the portal, sure of her choice, and walked straight through.

At first, there was a soft, still darkness.

And then starlight exploded around her.

And Elideh knew no more.

CHAPTER ONE

AILIA

Ailia stared at her open suitcase, wishing it would pack itself. She only had a couple of hours before she had to catch her train to Glasgow, and the rainy weather reflected her mood. Anxiety had truly settled in after Reed called her yesterday, asking if she'd heard anything from Elideh. Apparently, Elideh had not returned to the inn that Reed and his mother, Mary, owned, and Ailia hadn't heard from Elideh since she got the text telling her to drop everything and head to Scotland. Not that it was unusual to get these sorts of messages from Elideh, but it *was* unusual for her to just... disappear.

Luckily, Ailia had already contacted her doctoral committee and explained that although she had only been in Oxford for a couple of months, her sister had a lead for her to follow in Portpatrick. Typically things didn't happen that quickly in the academic world, but being Elideh Danu's sister came with some perks.

Elideh, despite her young age, was already a leading expert in her field, and a highly regarded researcher. She had been studying faerie folklore and how it fit into Scottish history for nearly a decade. She was convinced that there was more to it than scholars wanted to admit—that the faeries were real, and they just couldn't find them. She was currently a fellow at Oxford, making use of their resources to compile her faerie manuscripts and translations.

Ailia zipped up her suitcase, having packed her last sweater, and yanked her long, pale hair into a messy bun on the top of her head. She slung her backpack over her shoulder, looked around to make sure she wasn't missing anything, and headed out the door to the train station. Elideh had always been a bit reckless, so Ailia tried to ignore the apprehension slowly creeping into her thoughts. She was glad it was a short train ride from Oxford to Glasgow, and that Reed had eagerly agreed to pick her up from the train station and make the even shorter drive to Portpatrick. Whatever Elideh had gotten into, Ailia hoped it was less sinister than what she was imagining.

AILIA

"Good to see you, Ailia!" Reed greeted her with a warm, radiant smile as she stepped off the train. He was boyishly handsome, his dark auburn hair more wavy than normal in the humidity. She returned the smile, letting him take her bag and pull her into a hug.

"How was the train?" he asked, his dimple on full display as he looked down at her with his kind, brown eyes.

"Good, I got an entire section of my thesis done," Ailia said, falling into step beside him.

"Always the scholar," Reed teased. "Even with your sister missing."

Ailia rolled her eyes. "I'm sure Elideh is fine. You know her. She is always following some half-baked lead and forgetting things like her charger. Or common courtesy in this case."

Reed nudged her shoulder. "Aye, but you know how my mum is. And honestly, I can't help worrying about both of you either."

"Well aware," Ailia joked, jabbing him lightly with her elbow.

"So, any *developments*?" Reed asked, raising his eyebrows in the least subtle way possible.

"No," she sighed. "As usual."

"It's okay. Being a... you-know-what... isn't all it's cracked up to be."

Ailia smiled, but didn't meet his eyes. "Thanks, Reed."

The truth was, she was jealous. Reed was a witch. And so was Elideh, even though Elideh wasn't a very talented witch. Ailia and Elideh found out that the strange things that seemed to happen around Elideh ever since she turned sixteen were not just unlucky coincidences, but actually untrained magic. To their credit, magic was supposed to be make-believe. It wasn't until they met Reed that anyone had been able to explain what had been happening. Witches kept their true identities and their magic a secret—and Ailia, having studied the occult for the past five years, understood why, especially after the continued persecution of witches throughout history.

However, it was learning about her apparent magic that inspired Elideh to study the faeries. She had always been drawn to the faerie folklore in Scotland, reading everything she could about it when she was younger. But when she found out she was a witch, she decided that other supposedly mythical things could be real, too, despite Reed's insistence that the faeries hadn't been seen in hundreds of years.

Ailia, ever practical, decided to study the occult. To try to understand Elideh's powers, of course, but also to investigate how something so huge could have been covered up. All the while secretly wishing that she would one day develop her own magic.

"Are you hungry?" Reed asked.

"Yes, actually." Ailia's stomach chose that exact moment to growl loudly.

Reed shook his head. "Of course you are. Let me guess, forgot to eat again?"

"Maybe," Ailia hedged.

"Let's get you a sandwich, then. And you can tell me all your theories about where Elideh could be once we get in the car."

Ailia took a deep breath, but followed Reed to a sandwich stand just outside of the train station. She really didn't want to think about where Elideh could have gone, but she guessed there was no more avoiding it.

AILIA

Ailia was furious. And afraid. And maybe a little intrigued. But mostly really, really angry.

She paced the tiny room in the inn trying to decide what to do first. She read the letter for the tenth time. Then read it again.

Unbelievable.

She genuinely could not believe that her sister would expect her to just accept that she had gone off to *faerie land*. Ailia tried to calm her breaths and slow her racing heart. When she read those words—"this changes everything"—she assumed Elideh meant for their research. Not that Ailia was, in fact, a witch like her sister, despite not showing any signs of magic—ever. Or that the fae still existed, like Elideh had been claiming for years. There was just no way.

Deep breaths. Deep breaths. Deep breaths.

She read through the letter one more time. Committed it to memory. And then burned it.

Next step, skim through the supposed grimoire and read through Elideh's notes. Then she would make a list. Elideh's warnings be damned. Her sister may be an expert on the fae, but Ailia was an expert on the witches—two sides of the same coin, apparently. Ailia would stop at nothing to get to Elideh, even if it meant going to Elflaine and dragging her back herself.

But first she needed to figure out if what Elideh claimed was true. As much as she couldn't believe she was even considering this, she knew it was the only way to test her theory. She opened the grimoire and started searching for a spell.

CHAPTER TWO

TWO WEEKS LATER

AILIA

A ilia's pale braid bounced up and down on her back, and her breath came in sharp huffs as she ran down the cobbled street. The weather was unusually cold for June—even by Scottish standards. The breeze blew in from the ocean, pushing her along the path, as if the wind itself wanted her to fly over the loose stones. It felt nice to do something so normal after the past two weeks.

She tried not to think about her missing sister. Or that damn note. Or the fact that she actually performed magic. Instead, she tried to focus on the view and her breathing that was becoming more and more labored. She would never get over the beauty of this country. Scotland had always felt like home, but now it felt more like meeting her fate.

Ailia was coming up to her favorite part of this particular run. She knew that as soon as she made it up the steep steps and crested the hill, she would be able to see the beautiful ruins of Dunsky Castle.

The lush, green grass danced lazily in the breeze, but the black, craggy rocks along the coast looked like a place nefarious creatures might hide. Which, knowing what she now knew, she guessed there *could* be creatures waiting to drag her into the ocean. She shook off that unsettling thought and kept pounding away at the rocky path. The booming sound of the waves against the cliff combined with the dark clouds rolling in contributed to the ominous feeling that had been brewing inside her since Elideh disappeared.

Ailia kept up her pace despite the rugged path and the burning in her chest. She needed to outrun the rain and, more than that, she needed to silence the fear ringing in her ears. She couldn't believe Elideh had only been gone for two weeks. It felt like a lifetime ago that she got the urgent message from her sister to meet her in this tiny little port town. A lifetime ago she found the paper tucked into the damn *grimoire*. Leave it to Elideh to write an ambiguous note to decipher instead of just calling to explain the situation. She recited the note again in her head, which had become a habit since she found it on her first day at the Harbour Inn:

Ailia,

Just in case this works, I want you to know where I am. Please don't be mad.

My translations are complete and I've compiled enough stories to support what I have always known in my heart: the fae are real, and their realm still exists. The ancient ballads were not "faerie tales." They were oral history.

What I've found changes everything. The Book of Straun is a mythical faerie book that supposedly held all the secrets to Elfland (or Elflaine, as the faeries call it). I began searching for it half-heartedly—when the faeries don't want you to find something, you don't.

But I found it—or it found me. The Book of Straun is not just a faerie book, Ailia. It's a grimoire. It holds many secrets, but the reason I'm writing you this letter is I think I've found a way in. I think there's a spell that will open an entrance to Elflaine.

"But Elideh, you've always sucked at spells—how do you expect to use a grimoire?"

I'm glad you asked, sister. Here's what I think: I was meant to find this book. It's our birthright.

It's too complicated to explain it all right now, but what I've uncovered over the past year has convinced me I'm right. Don't trust anyone with this secret, and keep the book close.

If you're reading this letter, it means I've successfully entered Elflaine. The spell to open the entrance only works when the veil between the two realms is thin—Summer and Winter Solstice. Obviously fate led me to the book at the right moment, so I'm taking a chance. I need to know more about our heritage, about why our parents died and who we really are. And I promise I will find you.

Please don't come searching for me. I know more about the fae and their customs than anyone. I'll be okay. But I want you to let the book teach you its mysteries since I haven't had the time to fully delve into them. Study it. Learn its secrets. Fate led us both here, and destiny will reunite us.

Burn this after you've read it. I love you.

Ailia still couldn't believe it. Couldn't believe her sister was gone. Couldn't believe that Elideh actually found an entrance to Elflaine.

More than that, Ailia couldn't believe that after years of showing no signs of magic, she was able to perform a spell from the grimoire herself. Not that the magic was impressive, it was just a spell to light a candle. But still. It had worked. Not only had it worked, but it worked on her first try. Ever since Elideh disappeared, something had woken up inside of her. Something that felt ancient and dangerous and *intoxicating*.

Although Ailia was confident in her sister's knowledge of the fae, it didn't make Elideh's disappearance any easier. Once the fury that her sister abandoned her wore off, and she really started to process just how much her life—her world—had been altered, she hit a wall. She just couldn't believe, after all this time, that Elideh actually found an entrance to the faerie realm. She wallowed for several days, relying on wine as a crutch, barely getting out of bed.

Which is why she knew she needed to go for this run. Today was different. The sun shining through her small, latticed window woke her up for the first time since she arrived in this tiny village. Although she had grown accustomed to the constant rain, she recognized the sunshine for what it was— a sign to quit moping and get her shit together. So she decided to take advantage of the small break in the dreary weather to reconnect with the outside world and kick her ass into gear. She owed Elideh that much.

Being in the sun always made her feel more clear-headed, made her feel more like herself. Today was no exception. Despite the hangover that had been plaguing her for several days, she was already starting to feel recharged. The longer she ran, and the more sun she got, the faster she went, despite neglecting her daily exercise for over a week.

It had always been this way for Ailia. Ever since she was a child, being in the sun always made her feel as though she was being brought back to life. Ailia was the one to wake up with the sun. Elideh, on the other hand, thrived in the dark. She did her best work on clear nights, when the moon shined brightest. Ailia would never understand it, but then again, Elideh would never understand her sister's love of the sun.

Ailia finally crested the hill and was completely out of breath. But the view was worth it. The castle ruins sitting on a cliff overlooking the ocean had become one of her favorite places to escape to during their many visits to Portpatrick. There was something about the way the sunlight met the sea, and then collided with the cliff, that made her think of ancient, wondrous things. She wished she could linger, but the rain was rolling in. So she turned around and headed back to the inn.

She kept a fast pace in hopes that she wouldn't be soaked by the time she got back, but it seemed the weather was conspiring against her. The sky opened up before Ailia even hit the steps, and by the time she made it back to the inn, she looked like she'd swam there. She headed straight to her room—her sister's room—and showered off. The hot water beating down on her back washed away the remaining self-pity and left her feeling determined. She couldn't put this off anymore; the longer she waited, the longer Elideh would be in danger.

Ailia got out of the shower, dried off with one of the fluffy towels that smelled like lavender and mint, and put on real clothes for the first time since she discovered Elideh was missing. She assessed herself in the mirror, barely recognizing the girl in the reflection. Her protruding collarbones told the story of her habits from the past two weeks, her normally tanned skin nearly as pallid as Elideh's, making the smattering of freckles across the bridge of her nose seem too dark, and the purple under her eyes evidence of the nightmares that had been haunting her. At least the purple made her bright green eyes pop? She sighed, knowing she had been neglecting herself—a habit she was all too familiar with.

After dressing in tight-fitting jeans, a loose, white shirt, and her leather boots, she gathered all of Elideh's notes, took a deep breath, and headed down to the restaurant so that she could start making a list of all the potential entrances to Elflaine.

CHAPTER THREE

AILIA

Every time she walked into the quaint restaurant of The Harbour Inn, Ailia was enveloped by the mouth-watering smell of freshly baked bread, roasted meats and vegetables, and various herbs like sage, rosemary, and cinnamon. She pushed open the heavy, wooden door, the squeaking of the ancient hinges announcing her arrival.

She chose a small wooden table near the bar and settled into a tartan-cushioned chair, carefully stacking the papers she brought with her, and glanced out the window. The rain was pelting the thick glass, partially hidden by forest-green curtains, and she was thankful for the small fire that burned in the cozy stone fireplace in the center of the room. Her gaze lingered on the painting of Dunsky Castle that hung above the fireplace, wishing she could have stayed at the ruins longer. The rain had been relentless since she'd arrived, chilling the normally mild summer weather. The whitewashed walls of the restaurant reflected the light of the candles in the center of the tables, creating a cheery glow despite the turmoil that threatened to chase her back up to her room.

As usual, she was immediately ambushed by Reed's mother, Mary, the nosy owner and chef of The Harbour Inn, who was constantly fussing over Ailia's eating habits. Ailia had always been slim, but the stress of the past two weeks had taken its toll on her body. Her normally long, toned legs were starting to look skinny, her clothes fitting looser than she would have liked. She wasn't going to turn down the hot stew and homemade bread, but she could do without the commentary.

"I can't believe you are going to start running again when you're already wasting away to nothing," Mary shouted from the kitchen where she was surely preparing Ailia enough food for three people.

"Did you see her when she got back earlier? She looked like a drowned rat." Reed glanced over at Ailia, mischief shining in his pale, brown eyes. Ailia knew his mother would have a fit about her running in the rain.

"Can I just eat my meal in peace or do I have to endure the criticism?" Ailia mumbled grumpily from her table.

Reed walked past her toward the fire to stoke it, nudging her shoulder on his way. "We are just happy to see you out of your room."

Despite the teasing, Ailia had to admit that the saving grace of this whole cursed trip was Reed, and Ailia was leaning on their friendship more than ever at the moment. Ailia and Elideh had met Reed and his mother years ago on one of their trips. Reed was charming and handsome and kind, and there had been instant chemistry between them. Despite Ailia previously swearing off relationships for a while, she decided to try things out with Reed. They had an on-and-off relationship before Ailia realized that they would be better off as friends. She hadn't wanted anything serious in the first place, anyway.

Their connection with Reed solidified one night, though, when Elideh's napkin burst into flames after she lost a game of cards. Ailia and Elideh had both stared at Reed in shock when he explained what Elideh was—that she was a witch, and magic was absolutely real. Elideh had instantly latched onto the explanation, but Ailia, who had a very hard time believing magic existed, asked Reed to prove it. Which he did immediately, dismantling the wooden chair she was sitting in with a wave of his hand.

The revelation that magic was real had taken a while for Ailia to accept, but Elideh wasted no time adjusting to their new reality, moving quickly from "I suddenly have magic" to "so the faeries must be real too."

Reed explained that the faeries hadn't been seen in centuries and were as good as myth, emphasizing that it was a good thing the faeries were gone, as they allegedly had a very different set of values than mortals. Despite Elideh's relentless pestering, he wouldn't give them anymore details. To be fair, he did admit that very little was known about the faeries since their histories had been burned, along with much of the witch history, during the witch trials.

It turned out that Elideh's magic was rather unremarkable—she could barely perform simple spells. It seemed her magic was more connected to her moods than anything, and Reed promised to train her how to control it. Ailia had always wished she had magic, but now that she did, she wasn't sure whether to be excited or worried.

She stretched her arms over her head. Damn, she was really glad she went for that run this morning. Between the sunshine, the physical exertion, and the soreness that was starting to set in, she felt more like herself than she had in days. She desperately needed that dose of reality.

"Here's more bread—we are just trying to put some meat on your bones so you'll be ready for whatever quest you're about to go on," Reed said with mock sincerity.

"It's not a quest," Ailia said indignantly, rolling her eyes.

She never should have told them about her plans to look for her sister. She didn't want Reed involved because she wasn't sure how he would react to Elideh's involvement with the faeries. Obviously Reed and Mary knew the lore about the faeries, and probably more than they were letting on, but Reed had warned them over and over again to leave the folklore in the past. Elideh, of course, hadn't listened.

When Ailia and Reed had arrived in Portpatrick, Mary had given Ailia the key to Elideh's room along with a lecture about her sister's disappearance—as if she had any control over Elideh.

Ailia had trudged up the carpeted stairs, tired from the train ride and ready to take a nice, hot shower, but that was when she found the book. And the note. And all of Elideh's translations and manuscripts that she had labored over for years. And that was when Ailia knew something was very, very wrong. Elideh never went anywhere without her work. After reading the letter, Ailia was in shock for several days. She had never been good at hiding things from people, especially Reed, so she stayed in her room, trying to avoid the inevitable.

Finally, Ailia decided that the only thing she could do was to go find Elideh herself. She casually mentioned this at dinner with Reed and Mary the night before, and there was an uproar.

"You are not going to search for Elideh on your own, Ailia. She wouldn't want that." Reed had started pacing, kneading his forehead like the argument was giving him a headache.

"Definitely not," agreed Mary. "And let me tell you, next time I see your sister, we are going to have words. Abandoning you like this. It's so unlike her."

Reed was vehemently against Ailia searching for Elideh alone—especially since there was obviously something wrong. She knew what he really meant was that she needed a bodyguard, but that was typical Reed.

Ailia patiently explained that she was used to being on her own, but they wouldn't take no for an answer. In fact, they were still at a standstill on that particular detail. Although it felt nice to have people worrying over her, Ailia didn't want to get into it with them today. Today, she needed to focus on her list.

She quickly finished her stew and spread out Elideh's jumbled research on the rough wooden table. After cleaning up and getting them both a pint, Reed came over to sit with Ailia as she sifted through the vague faerie stories and her sister's muddled notes. Ailia was thankful there was no one else staying at the inn. She liked the peace and quiet.

"I still don't understand why you want to do this alone," Reed said carefully.

Ailia had to stop herself from sighing. "Why? Are you offering to come with me?"

Reed stared at her. "Of course I am."

At that, Ailia looked up at him and was met with nothing but sincerity in his light brown eyes.

"Reed, I promise I'll be okay. You know how independent Elideh and I are. I'll be smart and safe." Ailia paused, knowing he was not convinced. She reached across the table and placed her hand on his. "I'll even call to check in if that would make you feel better."

Reed looked her over and sighed. "You're so stubborn."

"It's a family trait." Ailia laughed and waved off the remark.

Reed sighed again and shrugged. "I guess I'll let you get back to planning for your quest."

"It's. Not. A. Quest." Ailia huffed.

"Okay, whatever you say," he said, lifting his hands in surrender.

Ailia shook her head as Reed headed toward the kitchen, but she couldn't stay annoyed at him for long, and he knew it. Although she knew that she and Reed were not right for each other, she found herself trying to remember why she had ended things between them. Reed was objectively handsome with his strong jaw, kind eyes, and charming Scottish accent, which she would absolutely never admit to him—he didn't need a boost to his already inflated, if not well-founded, ego. But he cared for her and had been a source of comfort and strength over the past two weeks as she had tried to piece herself together and form a plan.

She was so used to being on her own that it was almost disconcerting having people constantly checking in on her. Usually it was just her and her sister taking care of themselves. After their parents died, they spent most of their time in different foster homes all over the south of England. Since they constantly moved around, they never truly fit in, relying on each other for everything. They were lucky enough to get full scholarships to good colleges, and when Elideh started her research at the University of Aberdeen, Ailia decided that she would pursue her own path for the first time. They had been devoting themselves to their work ever since, and visiting each other as often as they could.

Reed returned from the kitchen and was sipping on a drink next to her. Ailia paused, redirecting her thoughts to her task. She liked to be prepared for all situations, and realized that she should probably have a paper map in case the magic she was sure to encounter on this trip disrupted her technology. "Actually, Reed, there is something you can help me with. I need a map of Scotland."

Rolling his eyes, he said, "Isn't that what phones are for?"

"Well," Ailia hedged, "I'm not sure if technology will work where I'm going."

Reed stared at her for a whole minute before responding. "You do realize that there is the same technology here as there is in your fancy university, right?"

Now it was Ailia's turn to roll her eyes. "Of course I do, it's just—never mind. I'll go buy a map at the corner store once the rain dies down. I'm not sure you would believe me even if I told you." She sighed, murmuring to herself more than Reed, "Hell, I'm not sure *I* believe me."

"Woah, woah, woah!" said Reed, frowning at her. "First of all, I will get you your map. Second of all, why wouldn't I believe you? Try me." His posture indicated she had already lost this fight.

She had debated telling him the true details of her plans, but decided it would be selfish of her to drag him into it. It was one thing to ask him questions about magic. It was completely different involving him in Elideh's drama. Especially given the amount of times he had warned Elideh to leave the faeries alone. She knew she could trust Reed, but she also knew he would insist on going with her if he knew the truth.

"Reed," Ailia said softly, "I know you would believe me. I just don't want you to get involved in case something goes... wrong."

Before Reed could respond, Mary shouted, "I knew it! I knew it was something dangerous. You cannot do this on your own!"

"Agreed." Reed crossed his arms, giving her a look that said there was going to be no arguing with him.

Damn. She really shouldn't have said anything.

CHAPTER FOUR

AILIA

After relenting to Reed and his mother's demands and promising to consider taking Reed with her, Ailia finally started on her list. The first place she was going to investigate was called Huntlie Bank. Although Ailia had read Elideh's translations so many times she could recite them, she couldn't help wishing Elideh was here to help her meander through the cryptic stories. But she could do this—it was in their blood.

Apparently.

Luckily, Elideh had been sharing her findings with Ailia for years, so she was already familiar with a lot of the work. Elideh's notes were maddening to sort through and made deciphering useful materials from personal quips extremely difficult, but Ailia was thankful she had something that might help her piece together an entrance to Elflaine.

There was no way she was waiting until the Winter Solstice to try to get to her sister—that was months away. And Ailia had a feeling that Elideh was in trouble. She had been having a recurring nightmare for the past week of a dark room and a general sense of despair that followed her into her waking hours. Ailia was convinced it was related to Elideh's disappearance, and she would not let her sister suffer.

She flipped through what Elideh called her "anthology," which was really just descriptions of different types of faeries. Ailia read through some of the more familiar ones—helpful Brownies that lived with families, mischievous Pixies that harassed livestock—and skipped to her sister's description of the "fae." According to Elideh, the fae were different in one major way: they looked like mortals. The fae were more beautiful, with pointed ears and flawless skin. They supposedly had magical gifts—like strength and speed—that humans could only dream of.

Of course, this was all speculation. Elideh's research had revealed that the last interactions between the fae and the humans had been hundreds and hundreds of years ago, and scholars of faerie lore had argued over the cause of the disappearance of the fae for many years. Was it a cultural shift? The result of religious persecution? Elideh, of course, had her own theories, and Ailia could practically hear her smug "I told you so."

Although Ailia was only two years younger than Elideh, and just as accomplished, she couldn't help but admire everything her sister had achieved at thirty years old. Elideh was already an expert in her field and highly regarded as a researcher. She had been obsessed with faerie lore for as long as Ailia could remember, making up bedtime stories when they were kids and charming Ailia to sleep. She became even more enamored with the faerie realm once they discovered she was not quite mortal. After completing her doctoral program in record time at the University of Aberdeen, Elideh was asked to teach at Oxford as a visiting lecturer. She applied to be a fellow to continue her research, meaning she was able to make use of their resources to compile her faerie manuscripts and translations.

Ailia, on the other hand, thought her time would be better spent learning as much as she could about witches, especially since they didn't understand Elideh's magic. She'd completed her degree in Celtic and Scottish Studies at the University Of Edinburgh and had been following a lead for her dissertation at Oxford when she got the text from Elideh—to get to Portpatrick as soon as possible. Hopefully her knowledge would help her now.

Her focus for her dissertation was witchcraft in the medieval time period. By luck or fate, the chapter she had been working on for the past three months centered around the events that led to the witch trials in Scotland, which, to her shock, frequently involved faeries. Many of the accused witches used faerie involvement as alibi, and even more surprising was the amount of times they were acquitted. So, lately, her studies and Elideh's research often aligned. When Elideh texted her and told her about a book she found that "could change everything," Ailia figured she meant for her manuscript. Now that she knew better, she was starting to wonder if ignorance truly was bliss.

Ailia mindlessly braided her long, pale hair and looked at the most recent documents she had from Elideh. Her latest translation was a ballad called "Thomas Rhymer." Based on the amount of notes in the margins, this story seemed to be important. Plus, it was one of the only stories that referenced a specific location. Ailia decided to read through it for the millionth time to make sure she hadn't missed some crucial detail:

True Thomas lay on Huntlie Bank

A wonder he spied with his eye
And there he saw a Lady bright
Come riding down by the Eildon tree.

Her skirt was of the grass green silk
Her covering of fine velvet;
And every strand of her horse's mane
Hang fifty silver bells and nine.

True Thomas, he pulled off his cap
And bowed low down to his knee—
"All hail thou mighty Queen of Heaven!
For I've never seen anyone like you on Earth."

"Oh no, oh no, Thomas," she said;
"That name does not belong to me;
I am but the Queen of fair Elflaine,
That has come to visit thee."

Ailia really hoped she wasn't following a dead-end lead by choosing
to begin her search at Huntlie Bank. There were a couple other places
that were referenced in different stories, but generally, the faerie lore
was vague about locations. She knew from her own research into the
witch trials that a lot of the interactions between the fae and alleged
witches were nearer to places like the Orkney Islands, Islay, and the
Highlands. Huntlie Bank was close by, though, and she had to start
somewhere. She glanced over at Reed only to find him frowning back
at her.

"What is it now, Reed?" Ailia asked sweetly.

"Why are you searching for your sister in faerie places?" Reed countered as the furrow of his brow became deeper.

"Well, first of all, Huntlie Bank is a real place," she said, dragging the papers toward her. "And secondly, if you want to read the stories, just ask."

After studying her for a minute, Reed crossed his arms. "If you're going to Huntlie Bank, I can definitely go with you. It isn't far from here. I'm sure my mum could spare me for a couple of days."

"That is true. I am perfectly capable of running this inn on my own," Mary said from somewhere in the lobby.

They were relentless. Ailia sighed deeply and looked up at the ceiling, mumbling about overbearing babysitters. After a staring contest between Ailia and Reed, she broke eye contact first. "Fine. If you want to follow me to Huntlie Bank, I won't stop you. Maybe it will prove to you that I am more than qualified to be traveling on my own. I'm not going to be in any danger, I'm just looking for my sister." She frowned at Reed. "Elideh does this all the time with her research. She will disappear with a backpack and a notebook and get lost in her work. She may even come back here while we are out looking for her. It's probably a fool's errand."

With a visible sigh of relief, Reed relaxed his posture. "Well in case it isn't a fool's errand, and in case it *is* dangerous, I would feel better if I were with you. I've warned you and your sister about the faeries, and if I know Elideh, she has probably found something out that she shouldn't have." He scanned her up and down. "Someone needs to make sure you eat. Besides, it couldn't hurt to have a little muscle to back you up, right?" And then he winked at her.

Ailia rolled her eyes and got back to her list. She had to admit, it would be nice to have a friend with her. And Reed might come in handy if they encountered anything... strange. Not only was he a powerful witch, unlike Elideh, but he wasn't joking about the muscle. She wasn't sure how running an inn equated to broad shoulders and a sculpted body, but she wasn't complaining. Plus, if her magic was truly awakening, she would need him more than he realized.

After she had successfully completed the spell that first night, she had been halfway out the door to find Reed when she stopped herself. If she told him about the spell, she would have to tell him about the Book of Straun. And Elideh had told her to keep it a secret. No matter how mad she was at her sister, she would always trust her. And if Elideh thought it needed to remain hidden, Ailia believed she had a good reason for it.

Plus, the magic could have been a fluke. She decided to see if it manifested more naturally before telling Reed. That way, she wouldn't have to tell him about the book. She felt like it was still too good to be true, and she wasn't sure she could endure Reed's pity on top of her own disappointment.

After another deep sigh, she considered how much she should tell Reed about her plan and why she was starting her search at Huntlie Bank. She decided that mostly the truth with a few omissions would do the job.

She looked up to find Reed alert and ready to play the knight in shining armor. Well, if this was a quest, she guessed he fit the role. "Through her research, Elideh was convinced that there are still entrances to the faerie realm." She waited for Reed to reprimand her, but he just patiently waited for her to continue. "So," she said slowly, "I think she might have gone searching for one of the entrances."

This, of course, was not true. Ailia knew her sister had found an entrance and was likely in Elflaine as they spoke, but Reed didn't need to know that yet.

Reed scoffed. "So this is the big secret that you didn't think I would believe? I have known you and your sister for a while now, and believe it or not, she was a little more forthcoming about why she was here and what she was looking for. Also, Ailia, in case you forgot, I'm a witch. I'm the one who told you and your sister the little we do know about the faeries. When do you want to leave?"

Brows furrowed, Ailia said, "Tomorrow morning."

"Okay, I'll go pack a bag."

And that was that. To say Ailia was shocked was an understatement. She had expected him to be more opposed. She stared after him as he left to go pack his bag.

She couldn't believe this was happening—that she was actually going to go look for a way to enter Elflaine. She looked back down at Elideh's translation and skipped to the part that worried her the most:

"Now you must go with me," she said,
"True Thomas, you must go with me:
And you must serve me seven years,
Through good or bad, as chance may be."

She mounted on her milk-white steed;
She's taken True Thomas up behind;
And yes, when her bridle rang;
The steed flew swifter than the wind.

Oh, they rode on, and farther on;
The steed went swifter than the wind;
Until they reached a desert wide,
And living land was left behind.

Even if she found Huntlie Bank, or whatever other entrances there were to Elflaine, what would she do once she got there? Had her sister been pulled into some sort of deal like Thomas Rhymer? Ailia sat back, rested her head against the seat, and closed her eyes.

Deep breaths. This was just a puzzle she needed to solve. And she was excellent at puzzles.

Ailia gathered all her papers and trudged upstairs. Although she was happy to have a plan, what she currently felt was pure dread. If Elideh was able to get into Elflaine, did that mean that the fae were able to travel here? If they were as dangerous as Reed said they were, there were so many ways this could go wrong.

Walking into her room, she carefully closed the door behind her and decided to start packing. She picked up the Book of Straun and wrapped it in a tartan scarf to keep it concealed. Then she got a notebook, her sister's journal, which she hadn't gleaned anything useful from yet, and all of her sister's translations and notes, and put them in Elideh's big travel backpack. She carefully folded three days worth of clothes and put them in as well.

She decided she would wear her rain jacket and rely on her hiking boots. After triple checking that she had everything she needed, she decided to head down for dinner—and to finalize her plans with Reed. At the last minute, she threw her running shoes in the pack. Running would keep her grounded and focused, even if it meant a bulkier bag.

AILIA

Ailia jogged down the stairs but paused when she saw Reed and Mary sitting together at a table, arguing about something in whispered voices. She couldn't make out what they were saying, so she loudly walked down the last couple of steps. They turned to look at her and plastered strained smiles on their faces. Mary immediately jumped up and declared she would get started on dinner. Reed just watched Ailia as she walked over to the table.

"Where are your bags?" Reed asked.

"In my room. We aren't leaving until the morning, right?" Ailia clarified.

"Well I thought I would pack the car tonight so we could get an early start."

"I only have one bag, but I can go grab it if you want. Getting an early start sounds like a good plan to me." Ailia had considered going for a run before they left, but the earlier they started this journey, the better.

"You only have one bag?" scoffed Reed. "The girl who packed three bags for a weekend trip to Ireland?"

Ailia quirked an eyebrow. "Ye of little faith." She stomped upstairs, snatched her bag out of her room, stomped back down the stairs, and practically threw her backpack at Reed, who caught it with better reflexes than Ailia anticipated.

Reed raised his eyebrows. "Wow, I'm impressed. I'll go get mine and put these in the car so we are ready to go first thing."

"Thank you," Ailia said with a little bow. Reed laughed and headed to his room. Ailia sat down at the table just as Mary walked over with three drinks and a basket of warm bread.

"Thank you, Mary. Do you need any help with dinner?"

Mary tucked a few strands of auburn hair behind her ear, giving Ailia a look that made her feel like she was in trouble. "Oh, no, dear.

I've got it under control. But I did want to talk to you while Reed isn't hovering."

Uh oh. Ailia wondered what Mary felt she needed to keep secret from Reed. The mother and son were very close—she hoped they hadn't fought about her.

"You need to be careful, dear," Mary said seriously.

Ailia sighed in relief and said with a soft smile, "Of course we will be careful, Mary. I will make sure Reed is only gone for a couple of days and comes back to you in one piece."

"I'm not worried about Reed," she said, waving a hand impatiently. "I'm worried about you. I know you're not telling us the whole truth—and I'm not asking you to. You have your own agenda with your sister. But Reed is a good son and a good man. He will battle between his sense of obligation to help me with the inn and his desire to protect you. Just try to stay out of harm's way."

Ailia blushed. She didn't know why, but the thought of Reed wanting to protect her made her heart stutter.

"I will be safe. Besides, I'm just looking for lost faerie lands that my sister might be trapped in—what dangers could I possibly encounter?" Ailia joked, trying to lighten the mood.

Mary looked at her in a motherly, knowing way. "Just be careful. Of course faeries are real—even if they haven't been seen in a long time. The Scottish people have always known that, witches even more so."

Mary gently squeezed Ailia's shoulder as she turned back towards the kitchen. If faeries were so obviously real, why had they been so difficult to find? She would have to think on it more another time because right now, she was tired and hungry and wanted to enjoy her last night at the tiny inn that had begun to feel like home.

CHAPTER FIVE

REED

After Ailia had gone to bed, Reed stayed up to talk to his mother in case he didn't see her in the morning. Although, knowing her, she would probably wake up extra early to make sure they had coffee and bacon rolls before they set off.

"Okay—lay it on me. Tell me this is a stupid idea," Reed said, knowing his mother was feeling very conflicted at the moment.

"It's not a stupid idea. You and I both know we can't let her wander off alone. I'm just worried she will actually find a way to get to the faerie realm." She paced back and forth, betraying her true level of concern about the journey.

"Mum, we don't even know if there are still entrances to the faerie realm. No one has traveled there in over a millennia," he said, stretching back in his chair. "I'm just going to follow along and make sure she doesn't get herself into trouble."

They had been having versions of this conversation for the past two weeks. The night Ailia arrived, unfamiliar magic had woken both Reed and his mother—the signature of a spell neither of them recognized. Since Ailia was their only guest, it had to be her. But in all the years they had known the girls, only Elideh had ever wielded magic. Since magic almost always manifested by a witch's twenty-first birthday, they assumed that Ailia had not been gifted, especially since Elideh's magic had always been unremarkable. Now Ailia had somehow performed magic and Elideh was gone. What a mess.

Reed and his mother knew the dangers of the faeries—had warned Elideh, in fact. But these girls were stubborn, and they didn't want to leave Ailia to her own devices now that her sister was missing. Even though the fae had disappeared from the mortal realm long ago, there was a deeply buried history that should remain that way.

Other faeries were actually the least of their concerns: brownies, sprites, pixies, and the like had resided in Scotland peacefully until the witch trials began in the 1500s. Once the mortals started burning witches, the faeries had disappeared. What they were really worried about were the fae. The fae were humanoid—and the subjects of Elideh's ballads that she relentlessly investigated. They disappeared over a thousand years ago, though, their realm sealed off completely.

The fae, which were the rulers of all faeries, might as well have been the things of legends and myths, so much about them lost or forgotten. But it would be naïve to think that they were gone completely.

Elideh had been acting very secretive the day she went missing. Reed wished that he and his mother had been more forthcoming with what they knew about the fae. They had hoped that Elideh's research would stay academic, and had overtly discouraged her from seeking to uncover the secrets of the faeries. They should have known better than to underestimate her. Reed knew Ailia had tried to downplay her worry, but he also knew that this was going to be dangerous—more dangerous than Ailia realized.

"How do you know for sure Ailia won't accidentally perform magic? What if she exposes both of you?" his mother asked.

Reed wished he could ease the worry in his mother's eyes. Witches had become experts at blending in with the mortals after centuries of persecution. He was confident he could handle this. Although Reed looked like he was in his late twenties, he was actually close to a hundred years older than that.

As much lore as there was about witches, a lot of it was wrong—the biggest myth being that witches were just humans with magic. It was not in the best interest of witches to advertise their immortal life spans, so they kept it hidden from the mortal world. In fact, it was something they hadn't even told Elideh or Ailia yet, since only full-blooded witches were blessed by the goddess with longer lives.

Over the past week he and his mother had argued about confronting Ailia about the magic they were confident she'd performed, but decided if she wasn't being forthcoming, it must be for a good reason. Their longer lives had taught them patience, and they knew they needed to trust in timing.

"Mother, I will be careful," Reed assured her, pulling her into a hug. "It's going to be okay."

His mother leaned into him. She pulled back and stared at him for a minute longer. "I trust you. Just please, please stay safe. And keep that girl away from the faeries."

"Don't worry, I will." And Reed meant it.

It was dark and cold, but it was the silence that unnerved her. Not even a trickle of water or the low hum of a fly penetrated the quiet that surrounded her.

She reached out, trying to see her fingers, but she was completely enveloped in darkness. The stone she was laying on was cold and damp, almost like a cave. But she knew somehow if she reached out farther she would find iron bars trapping her inside.

She tried to keep her panic at bay, but soon anguish overwhelmed her, and she let her tears fall before sleep consumed her once more.

***

AILIA

Ailia woke suddenly, the ghosts of tears still on her cheeks. She was soaking wet from sweat as she tried to remember where she was.

The inn. She was at the inn. Safe. Not trapped in darkness.

These thoughts did not give her much reassurance, since she was convinced her recent nightmares were somehow connected to Elideh.

As her breaths slowed to a normal pace, she sat back in her bed, trying to remember any details. Even as a child, Ailia had always had vivid, fantastical dreams. However, her vibrant dreams also meant she had terrifying nightmares. Nightmares that now kept her from sound sleep, and had ever since her sister disappeared. The haunting images of her sister alone in a cold cell, or of creatures so abominable that she prayed they were inventions of her imagination. She would be giving up on sleep for the night.

She tried to push aside the nightmare, wishing Elideh was there to cuddle up under the quilt with her like they did when they were children. Ailia would wake up from a nightmare, crying for parents that weren't there, and Elideh would hold Ailia close, quietly singing songs or making up fantastical stories until Ailia calmed down. Every memory Ailia had, the good and the bad, had Elideh in it. They had grown up learning that the only people they could rely on were each other. By the time they made it to their teenage years, Ailia noticed that the bond between her and her sister was much deeper than other siblings.

Where most sisters bickered, Ailia and Elideh fiercely defended each other and always took each other's side. Sometimes, it meant Ailia sneaking Elideh back into their house. Even though Elideh's magic didn't manifest until she was sixteen, strange things had been happening around her since she was a small child. Because Elideh didn't understand her magic until they were much older, it was always causing inexplicable issues. Their foster parents were quick to blame Elideh since she wasn't exactly easy to start with, so Ailia frequently hid Elideh, huddling close together in Ailia's bed and hoping she would go undiscovered.

Even more often, their devotion to each other resulted in Elideh starting, and usually finishing, fights with their peers after Ailia had been taken advantage of by parasitic, toxic boyfriends or relentlessly bullied by jealous girls. Despite their poverty and instability, they were confident and pretty—easy targets. But they always kept each other safe. Ailia *had* to find her sister. She was the only family Ailia had in this world—the only thing keeping her grounded and making her life brighter.

Ailia turned on the lamp beside her bed, needing the light after that nightmare, and opened the window, letting the breeze wash over her.

The sound of the waves gently crashing in the harbor helped soothe her as she breathed in the salt air, but the shadows that danced around the room did little to put Ailia at ease. She pulled out her list and Elideh's notes, settled into the fluffy pillows, and tugged the quilt up to her chin.

She took a deep breath, inhaling the scent that clung to the papers, making her feel closer to Elideh. Even though it was very unlikely, she was really hoping she would get lucky and find an entrance to Elflaine on her first try. Huntlie Bank seemed like the perfect place. She hadn't elaborated on her list, but figured she could regroup if this first destination proved to be a bust. Maybe she should start manifesting some of Elideh's belligerent confidence if she was going to start blindly looking for an entrance to the faerie lands.

Huntlie Bank was supposedly near the village Earlston in the Scottish Borders, just south of Edinburgh. From the pictures she found online, it looked absolutely enchanting—just the sort of place you would expect to find faeries. There were a lot of debates, according to her sister's notes, on the actual location of Huntlie Bank and the Eildon tree referenced in the ballad. Apparently, there was some sort of memorial to Thomas Rhymer, as well as a tower. Both were close by each other, so Ailia figured it would be a good starting point.

As luck would have it, Ailia had actually come across Thomas Rhymer in her studies on medieval witchcraft. Thomas Rhymer was a real person—he had been a Scottish laird that supposedly had the gift of prophecy. If the ballad was to be believed, this supposition would ring true since the Faerie Queen had gifted him a "tongue that can never lie."

Soon they came to a garden green,
And she pulled an apple from a tree—

"Take this for your wages, True Thomas;
It will give the tongue that can never lie."

Although Thomas Rhymer was frequently associated with the faeries, he was just as often associated with magic. Some even believed his powers rivaled those of Merlin. The most interesting thing about Thomas Rhymer, however, was that after he spent his seven years in Elflaine, he was returned to the mortal realm. Suspiciously, there was no record of his death. He supposedly disappeared; many believed he was either taken back to the faerie lands by the queen herself, or that he found a way back.

There were two places linked to this mythical figure: Rhymer's Stone and Rhymer's Tower. Rhymer's Tower, or Earlston Castle as it was once known, was believed to be Thomas Rhymer's home. Although it had little to do with the ballad, Ailia thought it deserved a place on her list of potential entrances to Elflaine. She was more hopeful about Rhymer's Stone, which was near Melrose, just south of Earlston. Rhymer's Stone was linked with the bank that True Thomas was laying on when he first saw the Faerie Queen.

It would take about three hours to get to Earlston from this sleepy town. Unable to stay in bed any longer, she threw the quilt back and started pacing around her room. Mary had agreed to let Ailia keep her things at the inn and had even told her not to bother with paying for the days she would be gone, but Ailia had insisted, and planned on leaving enough money for at least two weeks before they headed out.

Even though it was barely dawn, Ailia couldn't stay in her room any longer and decided to go down to the kitchen and search for food. She quickly dressed in jeans and a gauzy, long-sleeved, green shirt, threw on her rain jacket to guard against the drizzle she could see through her window, and laced up her hiking boots. She took one last look around her room, made sure everything was in order, and headed downstairs.

CHAPTER SIX

AILIA

Reed and Mary were already awake, sipping coffee.

"Good morning," she said in a cheery voice that didn't reflect the anxiety bubbling inside her.

"Well, isn't someone excited about their adventure," Mary joked. At least it seemed like Mary had come around, or was at the very least pretending she had.

Reed rolled his eyes and said to Ailia, "Do you want some coffee and breakfast before we head out? Mum made us bacon rolls."

Ailia's stomach grumbled at the mention of food. "Yes, please," she said, grabbing a bacon roll as Reed poured her coffee. "Then we won't have to stop for lunch."

"Just because you think you only need two meals a day doesn't mean it's true—or that the rest of us subsist on nothing more than coffee and bits of wind. We will be stopping for lunch. And dinner. Just so you know," said Reed, sounding exasperated already.

Ailia just nodded her head, thinking it best to not be contrary so early in the morning. Reed looked a little surprised that she didn't have more of a retort, but went on. "It should take us a little over three hours, although it is supposed to rain all day so it may take us a bit longer. Where will we be staying when we get there?"

Ailia stopped mid-bite. Shit. Twenty-eight years of fending for herself and the thought of finding a place to stay had not even crossed her mind. Normally, she was the over-planner to compensate for a lifetime of Elideh's recklessness. But when it came to traveling, Elideh always took care of lodgings, while Ailia took care of everything else. That was how they worked—like they shared one mind. She was already feeling her absence in the little things. What did she think was going to happen—that they were going to camp out?

"Now that you mention it, booking a place to stay may have slipped my mind," she said picking at her nails in an attempt to avoid eye contact with Reed. She knew she would never hear the end of this.

"Ah, I see. You mean to tell me the experienced traveler didn't book a place to stay? Interesting." Reed scratched his chin, reinforcing the sarcastic quip.

At least he was predictable. Before she could defend herself, he was up and putting her coffee in a take-away cup. She guessed she could deal with his sarcasm in exchange for coffee. She murmured her thanks and Reed smiled at her.

"There are loads of hotels scattered about that area. I'm sure we can find something when we get there." He put her coffee in her hands and ushered her towards the doors. "Let's head out before the rain really starts coming down."

Reed turned to his mother and swallowed her in a big hug. Mary turned to Ailia, holding her shoulders and pulling her into a comforting embrace. "Be safe, dear. And keep your wits about you." She gave Ailia a wink and walked them to the door.

Before they left, Ailia turned to Mary, suddenly emotional at leaving. "Thank you. For everything." She gave her one last hug before they walked through the door. Ailia could swear she felt a shift in the air as her steps carried her to the car. Her intuition was telling her change was coming, and it wasn't just about her sister. After studying witchcraft for so many years, she had become more in tune to the energies around her. Change didn't always necessarily indicate something bad. Like the cycles of the moon, change was a part of life. She prayed to whatever god was listening that what she felt brewing would be a good thing, although she couldn't help but feel the apprehension that accompanied the unknown.

Ailia and Reed quickly made it to his car—an old, worn, hunter-green Land Rover. It was obvious that Reed loved this car because despite its age, it was in pristine condition. They both jumped in and Reed pulled up the navigation app on his phone.

"Any place in particular I should search for or are we just going to drive until we find the faeries?" Reed teased.

Ailia sighed. "Yes. I do have a specific destination at least. There are two locations associated with Huntlie Bank—Rhymer's Stone and Rhymer's Tower. Both are near Earlston. I figured we could start with the tower since it should be easier to find. The stone is apparently off some random road."

"Earlston it is, milady," Reed said with a slight nod of his head, as if he was actually bowing.

Ailia laughed, nudging his shoulder. "I could get used to being called 'milady,' noble knight."

Reed's eyes twinkled as he typed in the destination, barely holding in a smirk. He pulled onto the road and headed away from the ocean, towards what Ailia hoped would be a way to get to her sister. She settled into the car and looked out the window, drinking in the beautiful, old, stone houses. The morning mist had settled over the lush green hills like a blanket, and although she still felt anxious, the dread from her nightmare still lingering, she also felt a wave of peace wash over her. At least she was finally doing *something*.

REED

Reed glanced over at the woman sitting in his passenger seat. For the first time since she'd arrived, she looked relaxed. He wished that she would trust him with whatever worries were pinging around in her head, but he understood better than most needing to keep secrets. Being a witch with a long life span meant that he rarely made friends and never confided in anyone other than his mother. It was too difficult to get close to people when they had to move around so frequently, lest people notice their lack of aging.

Ailia turned and saw him looking at her. Furrowing her brow, she gave him a look that said "What?" He looked back at the road and then said, "I just noticed something interesting."

"Something interesting? Care to elaborate?" she asked, eyebrows raised.

"I had never really noticed it before, but you and Elideh have such similar eyes."

Ailia laughed it off. "Yeah, that's about the only similarity we share."

That was not exactly true. Reed could understand why she would say that though. On the surface, the two girls were opposites. But on closer inspection, they were more like reflections of each other. Ailia had long, pale hair that sometimes looked like pure light in the sun, and he knew from experience that it was soft as silk. She was tall, reaching his shoulder, and considering he was a little over six feet, that had to make her at least five foot eight. Her long, toned legs went on and on, and her slender body was sculpted from all the running she did.

Elideh, on the other hand, was like a dark mirror image of Ailia. Elideh was slightly shorter than Ailia, but had the same long legs and slender build. Her rich, dark brown hair seemed to absorb the light instead of reflect it, and had gold and silver strands throughout like starlight. Her pale skin was the opposite of Ailia's sun-kissed complexion. Both girls had the same ruby, bow-shaped lips. Then there were those eyes. Ailia's eyes were a light, bright green, and Elideh's were the darker version—a deep emerald. But what made their eyes otherworldly was the golden ring that surrounded the green, and seemed to make them glow.

Reed hadn't seen Ailia in about a year, and he had forgotten how beautiful she was. There had always been something that had drawn him to her, but when she decided to end things, he knew it was probably for the best. They really were more suited to friendship. It didn't keep him from worrying over her though. Especially with Elideh gone.

They hadn't been in the car long, but Reed asked anyway, "Do you want to stop to get something to eat?"

Ailia turned to him and chuckled. "Considering we have been on the road for less than an hour and we ate before we left, I think we can make it until lunch."

This girl and her sass. At least he found it charming.

"As you wish, milady," he replied with a reverent nod of his head. But Ailia just giggled, and damn him if he didn't find it adorable. He'd missed her laugh.

"So tell me more about your research. Have you learned anything new about witches?" Reed had been wanting to bring up witchcraft without asking her outright how she had performed magic, and now seemed like as good a time as any since they had a long drive ahead of them. He wasn't sure why she hadn't told him about it yet, but he would respect her silence.

Ailia's eyes lit up as she started explaining her doctoral thesis. "So far, a lot of my research has been examining tapestries, epics, and ancient stories like Beowolf and the Arthurian legends. But the section of my dissertation that I have been working on most recently is about events that led to the witch hunts in Scotland. I wanted to see if there was some sort of cultural shift other than the obvious religious implications."

At that, Reed looked over at her. He carefully said, "And have you uncovered anything interesting?"

Ailia sighed in frustration. "No. Nothing that makes any sense, anyway. It's like it just happened completely out of the blue." She looked out the window, retreating back in her mind where Reed could tell she was lost in her thoughts.

Reed continued to drive but let relief wash over him. If she found out how the witch hunts started...

He wished he could steer her away from those subjects, but it seemed like she was on a sure course to collide with a deeply buried and bloody history. It was one of the reasons he so badly wanted Elideh to stay away from the faeries.

"Well, if anyone can figure it out, I believe it will be you and your sister. You're just stubborn enough," he said with a slight smile.

"I sure hope so," Ailia replied distantly. Since Reed had last seen her, she seemed more reserved. He let her think in silence and hoped they would find her sister, and that they could return to the safety of their quiet, academic lives. But in his experience, things were rarely that simple.

CHAPTER SEVEN

AILIA

The drive to Earlston was uneventful. Beautiful, but uneventful. As much as Ailia had traveled in Scotland, she had never really traveled by car through the countryside, mostly sticking to trains or bus tours.

They passed quaint little villages nestled in valleys, busy city centers with people rushing around, and finally stopped at the loveliest garden center in a town of about fifteen houses. Ailia devoured her chocolate chip scone and latte while Reed just looked at her over his black coffee, the corners of his mouth twitching upward every time she took a bite.

"Why do you always look at me like that?" Ailia asked in between mouthfuls of scone.

"I have no idea what you're talking about," Reed responded, smirk firmly in place.

"Like that—with that smirk."

"Hmm. I wouldn't say I always look at you with a smirk. It's usually only when I've had to convince you to eat and you proceed to inhale food like you've never had a decent meal in your life." He paused. "Or when you're sassy."

Ailia rolled her eyes but slowed down on the scone. She guessed she could be a little more ladylike with her eating habits since there were currently crumbs falling out of her mouth and chocolate smeared all over her fingers.

"I'm not sassy," she responded unconvincingly.

At that, Reed barked a laugh and just nodded his head placatingly. "You're right—never *sassy*," he said, emphasizing the word. "So what are we going to do first when we get to Earlston? We are only about half an hour away."

It was still morning—Ailia was glad they had started their journey so early. She thought for a second and took a sip of her latte. "I'd like to see Rhymer's Tower first, and then probably find a place to stay. I think Rhymer's Stone is going to be more promising, and that is closer to Melrose than Earlston. I'm pretty sure the Tower will be a waste of time, but I want to rule it out."

Reed nodded. "Okay, we can start at the Tower and then head to Melrose. It's only about a thirty minute drive. I think you'll like it there."

"You've been before?" Ailia asked, picking at the chocolate stuck under her fingernails.

After taking a sip of coffee, Reed nodded. "Melrose has a famous abbey that was founded in the early 1100s. My mother went through a phase of touring old abbey ruins about fifty years ago. We found out that many accused witches had hidden their grimoires and other heirlooms in the stonework of abbeys and kirks, believing their accusers would never think to look there. We were able to recover a couple of spell books as well as some valuable stones."

"That's incredible," said Ailia, shaking her head. "I can't begin to imagine how much was lost. I'll never understand the blind hatred that fueled the persecution."

Reed nodded. "Hate will always find its company. But that's why it was important to my mother to salvage the things our ancestors treasured."

Ailia smiled at him and squeezed his hand.

"Anyways," said Reed. "Melrose is a beautiful little town. I believe the construction of that abbey falls on a similar timeline as your Thomas Rhymer. Maybe if the Stone and the Tower don't pan out, we could visit the abbey and see if you find anything interesting there."

Ailia grinned at Reed. "Seems like my escort is also my tour guide."

Reed grinned right back and said, "Not just a pretty face, am I?"

Ailia laughed. "Humble, too."

Finishing their coffees, they headed back to the car.

AILIA

Reed was right. It had only taken them thirty minutes to get to Rhymer's Tower. She stared up at the ruins in front of her with her hands in her pockets. Frowning at the drizzle that was threatening to turn into outright rain, she pulled up the hood on her jacket hoping they would have time to investigate this tower—or what was left of it. There was barely one wall left, the highest point maybe three times Reed's height, the exposed stones smooth from years of wind and rain.

"I thought it would be... bigger," she said to Reed, who had just walked up next to her.

He put his hands in his pockets as well, squinting up at the tower. "It's definitely not the most impressive ruin I've seen."

Ailia glanced at Reed and then looked back at Rhymer's Tower. "Do you think we can go inside?"

"I don't see anyone here to stop us," he replied.

Ailia was about to ask how they could get in since it was fenced off, when Reed walked up to the fence and didn't even hesitate before easily scaling it, landing gracefully on the other side. He gave her a boyish grin. "Your turn, milady."

Ailia balked at the challenge in his voice. Reed had always pushed her to try things outside her comfort zone, but she had never hopped a fence. Or trespassed—illegal activities were Elideh's forte, not hers. She eyed the fence suspiciously and then looked around to make sure there was no one there.

"Hopefully there's not a fence blocking the entrance to the faerie realm, or this will be a shorter trip than I thought," Reed taunted. "Are you scared?"

Ailia frowned, annoyed that he knew her so well. "No. Just making sure there isn't a gate that I could easily walk through."

"Here, I'll help you," Reed offered. He stretched up onto his toes to reach his hand over the fence, and she figured, what the hell. If she wanted answers, she was going to have to take some risks.

She could barely reach his hand, but managed to grab on. He pulled her as she clumsily tried to find foot holds in the metal links. She got to the top but then slipped as she attempted to climb down the other side. She fell straight into Reed as she tried, but failed, to keep her balance. Thankfully, he caught her.

"You okay?" Reed asked, trying to hold in a laugh.

"I'm fine," she said, batting him away with her hands. "It's okay, you can laugh at me."

"I wasn't going to laugh. I just thought you'd be a little more... graceful... with all the running you do," he said, his eyes twinkling with mischief.

"Easy for you to say when you're almost as tall as the fence," Ailia grumbled.

She brushed off her hands and started walking across the sodden ground towards the ruin, Reed following closely behind.

"Anything in particular you're looking for here? If you wanted to tell me a little more about these 'entrances' you're searching for, I might be more useful," he said casually.

She couldn't tell if he was joking or not, but decided he was right and it wouldn't hurt to give him a few more details.

Ailia blew out a breath. "As my sister began translating the ballads that referenced the fae, she started to notice some similar themes. For example, in many of the ballads where someone is actually in the faerie realm, the person describes it as being "like night" but not too dark to see. There were also similarities in the places that humans entered the faerie realm. Most of the entrances were near hills or caves, and there was usually some sort of specific tree in the area, like the Eildon tree, which many believe to be a Hawthorn tree."

Ailia paused to gauge Reed's reaction, but he seemed unsurprised by the information so far. She continued, "Elideh was convinced that not only were these places connected by various trees like Rowan or Hawthorn, and a natural entrance like a cave or hillside, but that the locations would emit some sort of noticeable energy."

At that, Reed grinned. "Well, you're in luck. I happen to consider myself sensitive to energies *and* connected to the earth, you know—" he gestured at himself, "being a witch and all."

Ailia was really starting to appreciate that Reed was not most people. She was frustrated at how little she actually knew about witches. While her research definitely gave her an edge, she had very little hands-on experience with magic. Since Elideh was the only one between the two of them that had ever been able to perform magic, Reed had only worked with Elideh whenever they visited. Ailia, on the other hand, had been too focused on the history of witchcraft to learn anything practical. In fact, she had actively avoided Reed and Elideh's lessons because she knew she would be disappointed that she couldn't participate.

"Okay," she said slowly. "Maybe together we actually can uncover these secret faerie entrances."

Reed smiled sincerely, and Ailia found herself smiling back. For the first time in weeks, she didn't feel so hopeless.

CHAPTER EIGHT

AILIA

The ruins of Rhymer's Tower cast shadows over Ailia and Reed as they carefully walked around the perimeter. They searched for a way inside, but it seemed like they were out of luck. There wasn't much of an inside to be seen, anyway. They both sat with their backs against the ancient castle's wall, Ailia drawing her knees close to her body to keep the chill away.

Reed placed a comforting hand on her shoulder. "At least your instincts are right. I don't think we are going to find anything here."

"Agreed," Ailia said. "Let's head to Melrose to find somewhere to stay—and something to eat. I'm starving."

Reed stood and then offered his hand to help her up. She took it and stood, looking past him at the fence.

"That damn fence," she mumbled.

Reed just laughed and said, "Let me go first." He reached up and grabbed the fence with both hands. "It's easier if you use your momentum rather than trying to climb."

"Easy for you," grumbled Ailia, unconvinced.

Then, he gracefully pushed off of the fence, his back flexing, and landed in a crouch on the other side. He stood up and brushed his hands off.

Reed smiled at her. "You can do it, Ailia. And don't worry, I'll catch you if you slip."

Ugh. He was so damn nice.

She tried to do as he said, but predictably struggled gracelessly, and slipped right as she got to the top. Her stomach dropped as she fell off the fence, but instead of hitting the rocky ground, she fell into strong arms and a hard body. He did, indeed, catch her.

She looked up to find Reed's face tilted back in a laugh. "Are you really this clumsy, or do you just enjoy falling into my arms?"

She slapped his chest and he put her down, still chuckling.

"Next time, just let me hit the ground," she muttered.

She turned to trek back to the car, Reed following closely behind her. Luckily, they made it without her embarrassing herself any further. Reed opened Ailia's door for her, and once she was inside, he got in the driver's seat and pulled onto the road.

"I know you're used to... witchy things," started Ailia. Reed looked over at her and raised an eyebrow.

"Witchy things? Seriously Ails?" smirked Reed.

Ailia blinked at the nickname he used to call her, a nickname that Elideh normally used as well, but continued. "Yes, Reed, witchy things. I wasn't done." She huffed out a breath. "I know you're used to witchy things, but you seem to be relatively unphased by all of the faerie things as well."

"Ah, faerie things." Reed said, raising his eyebrows like they were sharing a secret. "Faeries used to be as much a part of our culture as the changing the seasons. There are a lot of things people don't understand, and a lot of history that was lost. It would be unwise to discount mysterious things."

"Protector, tour guide, and mystic—you really fit the bill for this quest," Ailia joked.

Reed smiled. "You have no idea."

***

AILIA

The short drive to Melrose finally brought the rain, and it was coming down in sheets. They found a hotel in the main part of town, parked, and sprinted inside with their bags. The lobby led to a restaurant with a small bar and several wooden tables. Before Ailia could shake the rain off her jacket, Reed was striding up to the hostess, asking for a table.

"Certainly. Just the two of you?" she responded politely.

"Yes, thanks," he replied. "We are also looking for a room for the night. Do you have any available?" Ailia had finally caught up to Reed and tried to take her bag from him, but he held onto it.

"We do," nodded the hostess. "Will you be needing one or two?"

"Two," Ailia responded at the same time that Reed said, "One."

They both looked at each other, frowning. Ailia lifted a brow and turned back to the hostess.

"We'll be needing two rooms, please," she said firmly.

Reed smiled at the hostess. "Give us a minute."

"Ailia," he said quietly as he gently tugged her by the elbow away from the hostess stand. "We are on the road looking for your *missing sister*. You don't know what happened to her, and both of you have an exquisite talent for finding trouble. Until we figure out where Elideh is, I'd like to stick close by. And that includes sleeping arrangements."

He turned them back to the hostess who looked unsure of what to make of the two of them. "We'll take one room, preferably with two beds."

Ailia gaped at Reed. He couldn't be serious. The hostess looked to her apologetically. "Sorry, but our single rooms only have one bed."

Damn it. It wasn't as if she hadn't seen everything before, but this wasn't some sort of couple's getaway. Reed simply stared back at her with his arms crossed and eyebrows raised, waiting for her verdict. She could practically feel the determination vibrating off him. This was clearly something he was willing to fight over.

The hostess looked nervously between the two of them. "I can ask the manager to put two beds in one of the single rooms?"

"Fine," Ailia sighed, admitting defeat.

"Very good." The hostess seemed grateful to have a resolution. "I'll show you to your table and bring you your key to your room." Reed grabbed their bags with a look of triumph and followed the hostess to their table.

After they sat down and placed their drink orders, Ailia rounded on him. "Seriously, Reed?"

"What?" he asked, feigning innocence.

"Sharing a room?" asked Ailia, gesturing awkwardly with her hands.

Reed laughed and waved it off. "It'll be fine—unless you think you'll be tempted by my charming personality and bulging muscles."

"For fuck's sake, Reed," laughed Ailia, unable to take him seriously after that comment. "You don't think it'll be weird? Considering we used to… date?"

She knew she was stating the obvious, but she couldn't help it. Being around him for the past couple of weeks, and maybe the vulnerability she felt at Elideh being gone, had transported her back to when they first met. It had been passionate and sweet and fun. Now seeing him staring at her, the thought of sharing a room with him was making her forget why they ended things in the first place.

Ailia shook her head. She needed to quit falling back into old habits. Even before she dated Reed, she had sworn to herself that she wouldn't get seriously involved with anyone until she learned to be at peace with being alone. Ever since she was little, she had wanted to belong. But by the time she had become a teenager, that desire had turned into her wanting to belong *to* someone. Her string of toxic boyfriends was legendary, according to Elideh, and Ailia finally realized she needed to make some changes. It was one of the reasons she had ended things with Reed—it was too easy to get lost in him.

Reed looked at her knowingly and gently reached for her hand. "Ailia, the last thing I want is for you to be uncomfortable. I will sleep on the floor if I have to." Then, after his moment of sincerity, he said jokingly, "You're practically like a sister to me now."

Ailia scoffed, knowing that was definitely not true, but said, "Okay, Reed. Whatever you say. Hopefully you'll be able to find a soft spot on the floor."

The waitress brought their drinks and they ordered their food.

"Apart from having to share a room, I think it's been an okay day," Reed said.

Ailia appreciated the change of subject. "I guess so. Even though I knew Rhymer's Tower was an unlikely spot, I can't help but feel a little disappointed we found nothing there." She tried to remind herself that Elideh had been looking for an entrance for years without any success, so she was going to have to be patient.

"I still don't really understand what we are looking for," said Reed.

Ailia didn't know how to respond without being caught in a lie. Since she had already given him several details about what she was looking for, she didn't know if she should go ahead and just tell him the truth.

"How about we eat first and settle into the room," Ailia hedged.

Reed's eyes swept over her. "You know you can trust me, Ails."

He had always been able to see right through her. "I do trust you. I promise. It's just really complicated."

Reed paused. "I understand. Whenever you're ready, you can tell me. Either way, I will help you however I can."

Ailia released a breath. "Thank you for understanding. I'm really glad you're here with me."

"Me too," he replied with a small smile.

The waitress brought their food, and they started talking about other things to pass the time. Ailia knew she would need to explain things to Reed, but was worried about how he would react. She guessed she would just have to wait and find out.

CHAPTER NINE

REED

Reed was fairly certain Ailia was going to tell him the truth. The battle in his head between keeping her safe and being honest with her was waging, and he wasn't sure which side to take. He didn't want to burden her with the truth—that the fae were more dangerous than she knew. But he also didn't want her to be blindsided in case they were able to find an entrance to Elflaine.

After eating lunch, Ailia decided to go through some of Elideh's notes. But when Reed started to see the anxiety take over after a couple of hours, he insisted they stop and have an early dinner. It wouldn't hurt to turn in at a decent hour.

They had been enjoying their dinner, and maybe enjoying their drinks a bit too much. Ailia had insisted on drinking Scotch since, according to her, they were in *Scotland*, after all. Obviously, that was a mistake.

"Okay. I think we've had plenty," Reed insisted.

"You're probably right," giggled Ailia. That was confirmation enough for Reed. He'd known Ailia long enough to know when she had over-indulged. She was always more of a lightweight than she wanted to be. "Let's go upstairs and check out our room." They stood, Reed grabbed their bags, and they headed to the spiral stairs.

"I can carry my own bag," Ailia said in between hiccups.

"I know you can—just trying to earn my keep on this journey," joked Reed.

They got to the top of the narrow staircase and found their room. Reed unlocked the door, and to his horror there was, in fact, only one bed.

"I'll go downstairs and see if there is a way they can sort this out."

"I'll wait here," said Ailia, still hiccupping. "That staircase made my head spin." She proceeded to slump down to the floor.

"Right, definitely the staircase, not the Scotch," he said with mock sincerity. "I'll be right back."

He heard a half-hearted "fuck you, Reed" as she leaned her head against the wall and closed her eyes. He should probably hurry.

After arguing with the hostess over the room, and her insisting she had done everything she could, Reed headed back upstairs trying to decide how to break the news to Ailia. He guessed he would actually be sleeping on the floor. However, when he got to the room, he found her passed out against her backpack. This was probably easier. No awkward conversation.

He opened the door and carefully moved Ailia aside to lean against the wall before bringing their bags in. The room was small but quaint, similar to the rooms at his own inn. He pulled the sheets down on the bed and went back to the hallway. Ailia was still fast asleep, so he scooped her up and carried her to the bed. After unlacing her hiking boots and setting them by the door, he tucked her in and sat in the chair by the window. He had slept in less comfortable places.

He glanced over at her, noticing how her pale hair seemed to shimmer in the darkness, and wondered how she had become such an integral part of his life. He had to remind himself that she truly was just a friend—maybe not quite a sister, though. He sighed and settled into the chair. It was going to be a long trip.

Ailia

Ailia woke up to a relentless pounding in her head. It took her a couple of minutes to remember where she was, half expecting to roll over and see Elideh passed out next to her. She slowly looked around the small room, taking in the old wooden furnishings and tiny window with eyelet curtains letting in a few rays of morning sun. Her eyes landed on Reed's imposing figure asleep in a small, sparsely padded chair.

Despite the sun settling on his handsome face, Reed was sound asleep, his eyelids fluttering, clearly in the midst of a dream. In the morning light, his normally dark auburn hair shined with bronze and fire-bright highlights, and his posture was relaxed despite his long arms and legs sprawled out over the tiny chair. There was no way that was comfortable, but she was thankful he was such a gentleman.

Come to think of it, how had she actually gotten into bed?

The last thing she remembered was sitting in the hallway, waiting for Reed to come back upstairs, and even that memory was a little murky. She must have fallen asleep, which, given the nightmares that had been plaguing her since Elideh disappeared, was a miracle. Luckily, or perhaps unluckily considering the nausea that was currently threatening her, the Scotch had at least afforded her one of the first full nights of sleep she'd had in a long time.

Banishing the thoughts of her frequent nightmares, and taking in her surroundings once more, she realized her boots were off and that the duvet was carefully wrapped around her. Which meant he must have carried her into the room and tucked her into bed like a child. Reed had always been that way—considerate, kind. She had forgotten how nice it was to be cared for like that. It didn't make it any less embarrassing. She stared at the ceiling, dreading the moment he would wake up and she would have to thank him for his chivalry. Knight indeed.

One of the last things she remembered, and the reason she had so much to drink, was that she decided that she was going to tell him everything. At this point, she either had to ask him to leave, which she knew he wouldn't agree to, or she had to trust him. And if she was being honest with herself, she did trust him—always had. More than that, she wanted him to stay.

She had made up her mind. Now if only the room would stop spinning. Ailia was trying to figure out how she was going to get out of the bed without vomiting when movement by the window caught her eye.

"Good morning." Reed yawned and stretched his arms over his head. "Hope you slept well."

"Morning, Reed," Ailia replied, sitting up slowly and propping herself against some pillows. For someone who had slept in a chair all night, he looked frustratingly well-rested and utterly unaffected by the drinks they had consumed the night before. "I slept really well, thanks to you, I'm assuming. You weren't joking about the knight in shining armor stuff, huh?"

"I aim to please," he chuckled. Reed stood up and pushed the curtains back. "At least the rain has stopped." He was right—it was actually a beautiful day, not a single cloud in the sky. One of the few clear days since Ailia had arrived in Scotland.

"Then we should take advantage of the sunshine," Ailia said eagerly. She got out of the bed without embarrassing herself—despite the room's relentless spinning—and headed to the bathroom to change clothes and freshen up. By the time she was done, Reed had changed as well and was waiting for her. She laced up her boots, grabbed her jacket just in case, and walked to the door. Reed opened it for her with a mock bow and, laughing, she said, "Let's get some breakfast and coffee. Then, we can make our way to the Stone."

"Sounds like a plan," Reed said as he followed her down the winding staircase.

It was so beautiful outside that they decided to take their breakfast and coffee to go and explore the town after some convincing from Reed. She was anxious to continue their search, but agreed that they could take an hour to enjoy their morning meal. As soon as they stepped into the sunshine, Ailia felt her headache and nausea start to wane. She sighed happily, tilting her face towards the sun. Scotland was always beautiful in a mysterious, ancient way, but in the bright sunshine, it was absolutely stunning.

It was like she had been transported into a fairy tale, walking around the ancient village with the lush hills as the backdrop. They fell into an easy, familiar rhythm of chatter, peeking into various shops and planning their day. Ailia appreciated the companionship she felt with Reed, and although she had fought with him and his mother about him accompanying her, she really did feel safer with him by her side.

She was used to relying on herself and her sister, but maybe having a friend she could trust was something she could get used to.

After spending as much time as they dared enjoying the morning, they got in Reed's car and set out to find the Stone. Ailia knew that if she didn't tell Reed the truth about where Elideh was, and that she had somehow cast a spell, she would lose her nerve, so once they had a general sense of where they were going, she took a deep breath and decided to confess.

"I thought about what you said last night, and you're right. It would make sense to give you more details about what we're looking for." Reed inhaled sharply, but waited for her to go on. "I don't really know how to say this, so I'm just going to be blunt. Elideh discovered that the tales of the faeries that have always been a part of Scottish culture are more than just bedtime stories. Faeries are real. Which you knew already, obviously." She said that more to herself than to Reed, to remind herself of her new reality. Reed nodded, giving her the time she needed to say it out loud. She took a deep breath, and then continued.

"Elideh believes that somehow we are connected to them." After a brief glance at Reed to gauge how he was taking all of this, she plowed ahead at the sight of his strangely calm face. "She has somehow found an entrance to the faerie realm. She wanted me to leave her there, but I absolutely cannot and will not do that. I am looking for an entrance so I can go after her."

The words tumbled out of her so quickly that she wasn't sure he had even understood her, especially because he stared at the road in silence for at least a whole minute before breathing out and saying, "I know."

Ailia whipped her head around at him, gaping, in utter and complete shock. Out of all the responses she had anticipated, that was not one of them.

"What do you mean, 'I know'?" she sputtered.

"Well, I didn't know for sure, but I guessed your sister's disappearance had something to do with the faeries considering how obsessed she is with them. Which I'm still trying to wrap my head around, by the way." Reed blew out another breath and said, "Okay if we are being honest, I have something to tell you as well."

He gripped the steering wheel so hard Ailia wondered if it would leave an imprint of his fingers. "I know you performed magic. Which is the main reason I insisted on accompanying you. I figured you had only recently discovered your powers, and new witches can be volatile." He glanced over at her. "And about Elflaine—this is bad, Ailia. The fae are dangerous and can't be trusted. I can't believe Elideh actually found a way in." Reed shook his head.

Ailia's head spun with this new information. They sat in silence for a while before Reed spoke again. "Why didn't you just tell me? About Elideh? And the faeries? And your magic?"

"I could ask you the same thing," countered Ailia, suddenly feeling very vulnerable.

Reed ran his hand through his hair. "Honestly, Ailia, I was hoping that I was wrong about you performing magic. I was hoping you wouldn't be involved with this world. It's unpredictable and unstable. And I care about you." Reed responded calmly, but Ailia could tell that he was frustrated.

"Well sorry to disappoint you. I am a witch. Just like you. Just like Elideh." She realized that she sounded pouty, and probably looked pouty since she had crossed her arms and was staring out the window.

But she hadn't asked for this. She especially hadn't asked for her sister to fuck off to the faerie realm without her.

Reed reached over and grabbed her hand. "Ailia. I'm not disappointed. I just worry about you. I can't help it. I will help you learn about your magic, just like I did for Elideh. And we will find her, I promise."

Ailia looked over at him and saw how sincere he was. She never could stay mad at Reed for long. His heart was always in the right place. She nodded, still thinking about the faerie part of all of this.

Ailia sat quietly for a moment. Her whole world had been turned upside down in the past two weeks, and she was struggling to process everything. She had conflicting feelings about her new abilities.

"How did you know I had used magic?" Ailia asked.

"That first night you were at the inn, my mum and I felt someone cast magic. We assumed it was you, but since your magic hadn't manifested before, we weren't sure," answered Reed. Ailia nodded her head. She still didn't really understand that, but there were more pressing matters.

"So, now what?" she said, fully turning to face Reed. "I don't know what to feel. Relief? Excitement? Fear?" She looked down, not wanting him to see her struggle through her emotions.

Reed took her hand and gently said, "Ailia, I understand that you're scared and probably confused. But you can handle this. Fate has been leading you to this moment your whole life. We will figure this out together. You're not alone." She stared at their hands and then looked up into his eyes. He was right. She *could* do this. She had never backed down from a challenge before, and certainly wouldn't start now. Not with so much at stake. She didn't let go of his hand, a steady reminder that she had a friend with her through all of this, as they turned off the road to the path that would lead them to the Stone.

CHAPTER TEN

AILIA

Ailia was bursting with questions for Reed. As unsure as she felt about suddenly having magic, now that Reed knew the truth, she was itching to learn more about it. She had let her jealousy of Elideh's magic prevent her from studying it more practically, convincing herself there was no point since she couldn't use any of that information in her dissertation anyway.

But right now, she needed to focus on the Stone. It took them a while to find it since it was not clearly marked from the main road. They had taken a couple wrong paths and had to backtrack, making her thankful Reed had a car that could traverse the rocks and mud. Finally, they found the right path and saw the Stone at the top of a hill not far from the road. They parked and started their trek.

Ailia's boots were splattered with dirt, and several loose hairs that had fallen out of her braid were plastered to her face as they hiked the steep path. She soon shed her jacket, tying it around her waist. Reed, to

Ailia's utter annoyance, looked like he had barely broken a sweat. She definitely needed to keep her morning running routine. After what seemed like forever, they finally reached the top of the hill.

Reed looked over at her. "I'm sure you have a hundred questions buzzing around in that brain of yours, and I will try to answer whatever I can. I'm certain you already know a lot from your studies and from things I've told Elideh, but just to warn you, ever since the witch hunts, a lot of our knowledge has been lost." He turned and gave her a pointed look.

"What?" she asked innocently.

"I know how you are. You're going to want all of the information at once, and you're going to get frustrated when I don't know specific details. I'm just trying to manage your expectations," he said.

He had her there. She could already feel herself turning this into a research project. She shrugged, and he rolled his eyes, not believing her feigned indifference. "Since many of our sacred texts were burned, witches have relied on oral history and sharing stories among ourselves the few times we encounter each other. But I will teach you everything I know."

Grinning, Ailia said, "I'll take whatever you can teach me, Reed. I do have hundreds of questions, but they can wait." Finally, they made it to the stone. They both paused to read the inscription:

This stone marks the site
of the Eildon tree
where legend says Thomas the Rhymer
met the Queen of the Faeries
and where he was inspired to
utter the first notes of the Scottish Muse.

"My question is how do they know this is *the* Eildon tree from the ballad? Obviously this is the area the real Thomas Rhymer lived, but why this particular place for the memorial?" Reed asked.

Ailia raised her eyebrows. "First of all, I didn't realize you were so familiar with the ballad," said Ailia, impressed by his knowledge.

Reed smirked at her. "I keep telling you this, Ails, not just a pretty face."

She rolled her eyes. "From what I've read about the stone, it didn't even exist until the early 1900s, and the location of Huntlie Bank has been disputed for centuries. The Melrose Literary Society chose this as the site for the stone because it tied in with a prediction made by Thomas Rhymer that came to fruition in the late 1800s. Supposedly, he predicted that one day a river would be seen from the Eildon tree, and after a viaduct opened, a new river flowed past this spot."

They looked out and could see the river in question snaking below them, the brick viaduct curving gracefully, and the elegant arches drawing Ailia's eyes. The water sparkled in the early afternoon sun, and the soft breeze gently pulled at loose strands of her hair. Ailia couldn't help but feel a mixture of excitement and sadness, knowing that her sister's research was what had led them here. She wished Elideh was here.

"I wonder if he was perhaps related to witches in some way and had the sight," mused Reed. "The little we do know about faerie magic is that it has its limits, and prophecy has historically been a witch's gift."

She couldn't keep the questions contained anymore. "Okay, I already know a lot about magic between what I've studied and what both me and Elideh have learned from you. I know you don't need a wand, I know you brew potions, but there is a lot I can't remember. Do witches have familiars? How do you recognize other witches? How many elements can we wield—"

"Woah, woah, woah—slow down," Reed chuckled. "First of all, you're right in assuming you still have a lot to learn. Elideh's magic was always... sporadic. Also, since her magic was always relatively weak, we only ever covered the basics." Ailia nodded. She had assumed there would be quite the learning curve.

Reed continued. "Witches are connected to the elements of nature and are able to manipulate those natural elements. Typically, a witch will have a favored element. As you know, mine is Earth. I have never met a witch that was able to wield all the elements. Hell, even wielding two is rare. For example, I have no connection to air or water, and little connection to fire. My mother only has a connection to fire. Elideh could cast spells, and randomly erupted in magic, but she never could wield an element with any sort of control." Reed paused, but Ailia eagerly waved him on. If only she had a notebook to jot all this down.

"You are also correct about potions, but typically potions are used more for healing. You have to use dark magic to make potions for nefarious purposes—which, before you ask, is forbidden." He gave her a pointed look that really should have been reserved for Elideh. Ailia was a rule-follower through and through. "Witches can have familiars, but they are typically real animals that will seek you out and stick around. Most witches haven't had familiars in centuries, though. It seems many of those bonds were severed with the assault on witches during the witch hunts and trials."

Ailia just stared at Reed. "The fact that all of this is now my life is just—" She shook her head, trying to bring herself back to reality—except now, reality was that she was a witch and could wield magic. "Sorry, I got us distracted." Ailia turned back to the stone and walked around it, as if a magical entrance to the faerie realm would just appear because she willed it.

"So, as a witch, how would you determine if this is an entrance to the faerie realm?" Ailia asked.

Reed gave her an indulgent smile, clearly happy to play the teacher. "Well, there are several things we could do. First, we could—" but before Reed could finish, he was interrupted by a low growl coming from the surrounding trees. He whipped his head towards the sound, grabbed Ailia, and shoved her behind him in one swift movement.

"Don't. Move," he whispered. Ailia followed his gaze to the tree-line. She could sense something was there, like they were being watched by death itself. Slowly, meticulously, a massive hound the size of a small horse, with dark fur and eyes that glowed like fire, crept through the dense trees towards them. The skies, which had been a beautiful, crisp blue moments before, started to darken; the birds that had been chattering sweetly were silent, and even the wind seemed to pause, aware of the danger that was present.

Ailia had never known true fear before this moment. She couldn't believe what she was seeing, but she was sure she had encountered this terrifying beast in one of her nightmares, and she had definitely read about these creatures in one of Elideh's manuscripts. The cù-sìth was a legendary faerie hound that usually kept to the highlands—except when it was hunting on behalf of a faerie. The encounters with these beasts ended either in death from pure terror, or in capture.

Despite her acute dread, she eased around Reed to stand beside him. He didn't even glance at her as he put his arm out, blocking her path. The hound crouched, readying his massive legs to pounce. All of a sudden, a wall of dirt and roots and rock flew up in front of the creature, spraying her and Reed with dust. Ailia stared at it in shock, and then looked over to Reed. His hands were outstretched, and he had a determined look in his eyes. She had never seen him wield magic like this.

Ailia could hear the creature tearing through the wall, but before she could react, Reed grabbed her hand and started sprinting in the opposite direction. Ailia turned in time to see the beast leap over the wall.

"Don't look back!" Reed shouted. Thick hedges blurred past them as they ran, but the pounding of the creature's gigantic paws on the ground behind them grew steadily closer.

Reed occasionally turned, throwing his free hand behind him to try to trip up the beast. The earth seemed to help them along, Reed navigating the terrain like he was moving it himself, which Ailia realized he probably was.

The beast caught up to them and Reed stopped, pushing Ailia to keep running. "Go, Ailia!" Reed shouted as he built another wall. The beast scaled it easily. His steps started to falter as roots sprung out of the earth, tripping him up, but they could not hold his huge paws.

Reed turned to Ailia with pure panic in his eyes and screamed, "Run!"

"I'm not leaving you!" she shouted at him, grabbing his free hand.

"Fine!" Reed shouted back. He turned to look at her, drinking her in, and before she could stop him, he dropped her hand, shoved her back, and ran towards the beast, flinging dirt, rocks, tree branches, and roots at the hound with his magic as he ran.

"Reed, NO!"

To her complete horror, she watched as the creature tackled Reed to the ground. They slid across the dirt, and he had his paws on Reed's chest, swiping anywhere he could reach. The only reason he hadn't ripped through Reed's throat was the vines that were currently strangling the beast. As the vines started to snap, and his giant maw got closer and closer to his target, Ailia experienced a surge of fear and rage and power she had never felt before. She'd be damned if Reed died on the mission to save *her* sister. By some instinct, Ailia threw out her hands and released a primal scream.

And the whole world lit up.

Pure energy shot out of Ailia's hands towards the creature, flinging him off Reed. Ailia didn't have time to comprehend what had happened, as the beast landed with feline grace and snapped his head towards her. As soon as the creature looked into Ailia's eyes, he paused. After a minute that seemed to last an eternity, and to Ailia's utter shock, the beast sat down, never breaking eye contact.

Ailia was panting, adrenaline pounding through her. Once she was sure the creature wasn't going to attack, she raced towards Reed as quickly as she could. She threw herself to the ground next to him, scraping her knees in the process. The creature growled but made no move towards them. Reed was still lying on his back, his eyes wild, looking between Ailia and the creature.

"What the fuck just happened?" Reed gasped in between breaths. He laid his head back in the dirt, wincing.

"I have no idea," answered Ailia, shaking and checking Reed for injuries. Although she was truly in shock, she was almost positive that the burst of energy that came from her was not normal magic.

After making sure that Reed was going to live, she stood to face the beast. Reed sat up and grabbed her arm. "What are you doing? We need to get out of here."

She looked at the beast curiously. "Reed, I don't think he's going to hurt me."

"Have you completely lost your mind?" Reed whispered back. "Do you know what this is?"

"Actually, I do," Ailia retorted. She looked down at him, fear gleaming in his eyes. "Reed. Trust me." Ailia didn't wait for his response as she took three confident steps towards the hound.

The hound continued to stare at her, and she paused. She was barely breathing as he began circling her, sniffing at her occasionally.

On second thought, this was really stupid. Maybe she shouldn't listen to her instincts if they were going to lead her to a literal hound of death.

Just as she was really starting to regret her choice, and was trying to decide how to get away from the beast, he laid down, staring at her over his massive paws. She took that as a sign she could approach him, and the closer she got, the more natural his colors became. She was standing right in front of him when the beast reached his head up to sniff her—once, twice—and then, hell must have frozen over, because the hound started wagging his tail.

Ailia looked at Reed, who was staring at her in astonishment. She said, "I think we're safe." She looked back at the hound and he had completely transformed. His eyes were a rich, ruddy brown, and his coat was an ashy gray. Now, he just looked like a massive, noble, magnificent dog. Reed slowly limped towards Ailia. "I have no idea what just happened, but this is definitely not normal behavior for a cù-sìth."

"Explain," said Ailia, still speaking in a hushed voice as she flung Reed's massive, bruised arm over her shoulder, letting him lean on her.

"These beasts are not controlled by any master, but they sometimes choose to bond with one faerie for life," explained Reed. Although he was speaking calmly, Ailia could feel the tension radiating from his body.

"So, what does that mean?" questioned Ailia.

"I have no idea. Either you are also part fae, and that is what your sister meant by having a connection to them, or you are the target of the hunt, and the beast has decided you're not a flight risk. Based on that blast of energy, I'd say it's possibly the former."

"What?" asked Ailia, not understanding how what he was implying could be true.

"Ailia, I have never seen anything like that blast of magic from another witch." Reed paused, catching his breath. "We need to get out of here. The fae haven't been seen in over a thousand years. So if he is bonded to a master, and there are fae in this realm, it can't be good. The fae could be anywhere. According to legend, they can shapeshift." Ailia was starting to sag under Reed's weight. She really needed to learn more about the fae. Fast.

"How did I even conjure magic like that?" She was still reeling from the rage and panic that preceded the burst of light.

Reed studied her before wincing. "Let's figure it out later."

They tried to back away from the faerie hound, but at the movement, the beast stood suddenly, much too quickly for a creature his size. He had definitely shrunk, but was still huge, his head nearly reaching Ailia's shoulder. Ailia and Reed froze. The hound walked over to Ailia and nuzzled her side, nearly knocking her over in the process. Reed steadied her as she studied the beast. She tilted her head, and the hound mirrored her movement. Something was drawing her to the creature, as if some primal part of her was certain he was safe.

Ailia reached out to pet him, which earned her a glare from Reed. She shrugged her shoulders and continued to reach out to the hound. He started wagging his tail and licked her palm. Ailia laughed and looked at Reed. "I guess he likes me?" She wasn't sure why she was so calm, but she felt an instant kinship with the creature.

Reed continued to look between Ailia and the beast and said, "If I didn't know better, I would say he's acting like a familiar. Let's see if he follows us to the car." Sure enough, as they turned around to walk down the path, Reed still gingerly leaning against Ailia, the hound stayed a step behind her, like some sort of mythical bodyguard. Ailia turned to look at him as they walked and said, "I think I will call you Storm." The beast's ears pricked up at that, and he gave a brief wag of his tail. Ailia looked at Reed and he just stared at her as he muttered, "This can't be happening."

"Do you think he will follow us to town?" Ailia asked curiously.

"At this point, Ailia, I hope to the goddess that this is all some sort of vivid hallucination," said Reed, who seemed to be concentrating on walking.

Ailia frowned at Reed and then looked at the creature who was happily trotting along next to her. "Storm," she said, reaching down to touch his ears. "You're way too big to accompany us into the town." At that, Storm let out a small whimper, moving closer to her. Reed ran his hands through his hair and gave an exasperated sigh, muttering, "This is completely mad."

Ailia tried to recall everything she had read in her sister's notes about cù-sìths as they walked, and finally remembered a critical detail. She turned to Storm and said, "Can you make yourself invisible?" At that, Storm gave her a look and suddenly disappeared. Maybe it was the adrenaline pumping through her, but she grinned—she was starting to find this whole thing hilarious.

"Holy shit," said Reed. Storm reappeared with what Ailia would describe as a smug look on his face.

"Okay, Storm, you can come with us but you have to remain unseen. And you have to stay outside. Can you do that?" She choked on a laugh as Reed swore when the beast nodded at her, and then disappeared.

They slowly made it back to the car, and when they got in, Storm reappeared momentarily outside of Ailia's window as if to say he would follow them. Ailia broke out in laughter, and Reed soon followed suit, both of them shaking from a strange combination of adrenaline, fear, and astonishment.

"Well this trip just got extremely interesting," said Reed once they could both breathe normally again.

"I don't know if interesting is the word I'd choose," laughed Ailia, still reeling from the whiplash of feeling terror, relief, and shock in such a short time span.

"Let's head back to the hotel. I think we need to eat something and regroup." Reed gripped his side, trying to hide his grimace.

"And probably take you to a hospital," said Ailia, giving him a concerned look.

"It's okay, I brought a healing potion with me. It's in my backpack in the room." Ailia nodded, relief flooding her that Reed would be okay.

Now that the shock of the whole situation was wearing off, every single one of her muscles ached. It was like her whole body was screaming at her for the energy she had just expelled trying to save Reed's life. She needed to rest, and then she needed to read through the journal her sister had left behind. No more avoiding the inevitable. If anyone had answers for her, it would be Elideh.

As they drove, Ailia occasionally saw a massive, gray body sprint by them, easily keeping pace with the car. What had her sister gotten them into?

CHAPTER ELEVEN

REED

This was really bad.

As much as Reed was trying to play it off, he was on high alert the entire drive back to the hotel. There was no way a cù-sìth just appeared out of nowhere so far away from the Highlands without a faerie close by. To make matters worse, Ailia was clearly charmed with the beast and had no idea that the hound's behavior was something to be concerned about. Cù-sìths did not bond to people. They bonded to one fae. And if that beast was here, its master was here as well.

He knew so little about the fae to begin with, so he had no idea what the beast's connection to Ailia could mean. And the blast that came from her—he would have to think on it later because right now, he could barely stay focused on keeping his eyes open and not passing out. Adrenaline had allowed him to power through the walk to the car, but it was wearing off fast and he was becoming extremely aware of every cut and bruise on his body.

Reed pulled into the hotel, and they snuck in through the back entrance to try and hide their disheveled state from the rest of the patrons. He assumed the cù-sìth had obeyed Ailia and remained outside, still invisible, since he heard no one scream that death incarnate had arrived.

Ailia was supporting almost his entire weight by the time they made it to the stairs. His injuries were way worse than he was letting on. There was a cut to his chest and it was oozing blood, hidden by his dark shirt, and he knew the beast had torn through muscle. When they made it up the last of the ancient wooden steps, Ailia grabbed the keys out of Reed's pocket and unlocked the door. Reed practically fell onto the bed in their tiny room, unable to stand up any longer.

Ailia rushed to find his backpack where the healing tonic was hidden. Reed slowly peeled his shirt away as Ailia turned to him, backpack in hand.

She audibly gasped when she saw his chest. "Reed! You're gushing blood! Why didn't you tell me?"

"It's not that bad, I just need the potion and I will be fine." He tried to tell her where the tonic was, but when he tried to speak again, he just groaned as a searing pain shot up his side.

To her credit, she took a deep breath, grabbed a towel out of the bathroom, and handed it to him to staunch the blood flow. "Shit, shit, shit," she muttered as she got his backpack, methodically pulling everything out until she got to the pocket he had hidden his potions in. She grabbed all of the bottles and held them out, silently asking which bottle to use. "The blue one," Reed panted.

She carefully put the rest of the bottles back where she found them and turned to him, saying with more calm than he would have expected, "Tell me what to do. Do I put it on the wound or do you drink it?" Reed only had the energy to get out "Drink." She popped the cap off the vial and poured the entirety of the contents into his mouth.

"Is that it? Do I need to do anything else? Recite a spell or something?" Ailia asked, panic starting to creep into her tone. When he didn't immediately answer, Ailia said, "I swear, Reed, your mum is going to kill me if you die right now." Despite his aching body, he let out a choked laugh. The tonic was already starting to work. Reed loved magic. "We just wait," he said through gritted teeth. Although the magic healed, it did not take the pain away.

Ailia sat carefully on the bed next to him, "Okay."

Reed closed his eyes and they sat in silence for a few minutes, until Ailia gasped. He guessed his skin had started to knit itself back together already.

"That's incredible," she whispered, awestruck by the display of magic. He frequently forgot that Ailia was so young and that she had such little experience with magic. She always seemed older to him, but he guessed that was probably due to her growing up fast and relying on herself for so long.

After some of the stories Elideh had told him, he admired that she could still be so vulnerable and kind. It had only been a promise from Elideh that had kept him from going after some of the people that had hurt Ailia in the past. Elideh had told him the stories to warn him that if he hurt her, she would make sure he paid for it. But from the moment he had met Ailia, all he had wanted to do was protect her and take care of her and make her smile. He loved her laugh and loved that life hadn't dulled her contagious light.

"It's working. I'm already feeling much better," Reed assured her, keeping his eyes shut. Ailia inspected him, making sure there were no other injuries hiding from her, and when she seemed satisfied that

Reed was not, in fact, going to die, she carefully got off of the bed and headed towards the bathroom.

"I'm going to shower off, and then run down to get us dinner."

She didn't get far before Reed grabbed her hand to stop her. He pulled her to him, and looked her over.

"Wait. Are you okay?" He noticed a scratch over her eye and tried to sit up, immediately regretting that decision.

"Woah, woah, woah. Lay back down," she commanded. She saw where he was looking and felt her eye. "It's just a scratch. I'm fine."

He looked her over once more. "You swear you don't have any other injuries, Ailia?"

"I swear, Reed," she said gently, giving him a smile that settled him.

He kissed her hand and nodded his head. Ailia brushed the hair out of his face and then headed to the bathroom.

As soon as she closed the door and Reed heard the water running, he finally released a deep breath. Today was a disaster. There was no other way to describe it. Not only had they both come so close to death that he still wasn't sure how they'd made it out alive, and to make matters worse, Ailia had somehow connected with a hellish death creature.

Although there was still a lot to process, there was a feeling he couldn't shake. After the blast of magic, which he would have to think about later, something had changed between them. He had always felt protective of Ailia, but since that moment, even with his injuries, a primal urge had taken over him to protect her at all costs. In fact, he was fairly certain that was the only way he had managed to drive them both back to the hotel with such a clear head.

When the creature had first shown itself, Reed had instantly recognized it. The cù-sìth had been used by the fae to hunt the remaining witches after the humans had given up on the witch hunts. It was actually one of the few pieces of faerie lore that was well-known. The terror he felt had only been surpassed by his desire to get Ailia the hell out of there. After that damned blast, however, he had been ready to sacrifice himself to the beast without a second thought.

In fact, he couldn't stop thinking about her. Even when she was just ten feet away from him and he could hear her humming in the shower, he couldn't stop worrying about what would happen if she fell while she was washing her hair, or if she had an injury he hadn't noticed. He dragged his hand down his face trying to steady his thoughts. Taking deep breaths, Reed couldn't fight the sleep imposing on him any longer as the magic from the potion overwhelmed his body.

CHAPTER TWELVE

AILIA

After getting out of the shower and getting dressed in the bathroom, Ailia peeked into the room to check on Reed. To her
relief, he was sound asleep, his wounds completely gone. She had no
idea how the magic worked, but she was thankful Reed had thought
to bring the tonics with him. Ailia had always been pretty good in a
crisis, usually calm and collected, but when she saw the blood flowing
from Reed's chest, she almost lost it.

Although they had always been close, she couldn't help feeling
like there was something different between them now. Her trust in
him and her connection to him had turned into a tangible thing. She
wondered if she should ask if something had changed for him as well,
but decided to ponder that later.

She quickly and quietly put on her shoes, then slipped out the
door. She hoped Reed wouldn't be asleep too long because they had
a million things they needed to discuss and he desperately needed a

shower to wash away all of the blood. At the same time, she would throttle him if he tried to get out of that bed before he was fully healed.

After ordering the food, she sat at a table while she waited and tried to sort through the events from the past couple of hours. She had used magic. Powerful magic. Much more powerful than anything Elideh had ever done. She just didn't know what it was—and if Reed was right, if it wasn't witchcraft...

She needed to know more.

The waitress brought the food in bags for her to take back to the room. She grabbed them and headed up the stairs. She would figure this out. She was just thankful that whatever power had blasted out of her had saved Reed.

AILIA

It turned out that Ailia didn't need to worry about Reed getting enough rest, because when she got back to the room, he didn't even twitch as she tried to eat as quietly as she could.

Now would be a good time to look through the grimoire. She carefully unwrapped it and started to flip through the worn pages. There were a lot of spells, but every now and then, there was a story. Strangely enough, the stories revolved around the fae. It made Ailia wonder about the original owner of the book, as the handwriting was mostly the same. She paused when she came to a beautiful illustration.

The image was split, one side featuring the night sky, and the other featuring sunrise. In the middle was a tree, caught between summer and winter. On the night side of the image, the tree was bare, and icicles hung from the branches. The other side showed a tree in full bloom, with beautiful greens and stunning flowers she didn't recognize clinging to the limbs.

Next to the illustration was a poem:

Sister of frost, sister of life
They reign over the land.
But though they share
A love so deep,
Their fate is of the damned.

Sister of day, sister of night
The mirror of each they are.
But fate has made it,
Peace will come,
Though the seeds of darkness thrown.

Ailia's research had made her familiar with ancient poems and ballads, but this story struck her as something more. At first she thought it was a reference to the ancient goddesses Beira and Brigid, but they weren't typically described as day and night. Beira was the goddess of winter and Brigid the goddess of summer. Many believed they weren't even separate goddesses, but two different faces of the same goddess.

She copied the poem into her own journal, deciding to think on it more. She wanted to read through some of Elideh's journal, which had been pretty boring so far—mostly notes about Elideh's research, or theories she wanted to find evidence for. After about an hour, though, Ailia couldn't stay awake anymore. She carefully wiped some of the dried blood off Reed's arms, hands, and face, but there was still so much. He would just have to shower in the morning.

She contemplated sleeping in the chair, but for some reason felt like she needed to be near Reed. She curled up next to him in the small bed, trying to take up as little room as possible. But even in his deep, magic-induced sleep, he pulled her closer to him, wrapping an arm protectively around her shoulders. Ailia relaxed next to him, the feeling familiar and yet different, believing she would sleep soundly through the night.

AILIA

Ailia woke up with the sunrise and slowly moved Reed's arm off of her. She quietly got out of bed, realized she hadn't even changed into pajamas, and decided she might as well head downstairs to get coffee despite her rumpled clothes. Coffee in hand, she opened the door to their room to find Reed alert and halfway out of the bed, and noticed he let out a barely concealed sigh of relief once he met her eyes.

"Good morning, sleeping beauty," Ailia joked as she set the coffee on the table next to the bed. She sat in the chair by the window, sipping her coffee contentedly.

Reed just shook his head, trying to hide his smile as he sat back in the bed and took a drink of his coffee. "Morning," he said, his voice hoarse.

"We had quite the day yesterday," said Ailia.

"Indeed. How will we ever top it?" he countered, the corners of his mouth turning up into a small smile. Ailia was glad to see Reed joking—he had really scared her yesterday.

"When you're showered and ready, let's go down and get some breakfast. Then we can discuss things," suggested Ailia.

"I like that plan," agreed Reed. He finished his coffee and then headed to the bathroom. To Ailia's relief, he didn't even have a limp.

CHAPTER THIRTEEN

REED

Reed was trying to stay calm as he walked to the bathroom. When he had woken up and Ailia wasn't there, he immediately panicked. Luckily, she walked in the door right away. He had to control whatever this was. He knew Ailia, and knew she would not like him playing the overbearing, territorial babysitter, as much as she joked about him being her knight in shining armor. Reed took his time in the shower to gain his composure. The hot water hit his body, and he examined the thin scars from Storm's attack. The flesh there was pink and tender, the potion doing its job thoroughly enough.

Potions had always been tricky for him. They required a lot of patience and intuition that he simply didn't have. His mother, however, was very gifted with potions. It was really pretty simple—use the right ingredients at the right time and with the right intention. The difficult part was knowing when and where to find the ingredients. Potions could go very wrong if you plucked an herb during the waxing moon instead of the waning moon. But now, Reed was thankful that his mother was so skilled and that he had brought the healing potions with him.

He finished washing all of the dirt and blood off of his body, and then quickly dressed. Ailia had already changed into fresh clothes. He walked towards her and looked her over. Frowning, he said, "You're sure you're not hurt from yesterday?"

Ailia nodded. "I'm sure, Reed."

Deciding not to push it, he walked her to the door, checking the hall before letting her leave the room.

Reed glanced out the window in the stairwell. "I guess your beast stayed outside, then?"

"The beast has a name, Reed," sighed Ailia, "and I hope he's not lonely out there all by himself." She frowned, looking out the window as if she could see the damn creature.

Reed rolled his eyes. "I think *Storm* will be fine, Ailia. Cù-sìths are usually prowling around the Highlands alone."

"Is someone jealous?" Ailia teased.

For fuck's sake. "No, I'm not jealous, I just want you to be careful." Reed paused. "There's a lot you don't understand about our world, and I'm not sure you should be treating a faerie hound as a pet."

Ailia frowned at Reed's tone. "I'm going to give you a pass since the hound in question *did* try to kill you. But in case you forgot, I haven't exactly been a part of this world for long." She crossed her arms as they made it to the bottom of the stairs. Reed stepped in front of her, placing his hand on the small of her back as he opened the door, guiding her through it.

"It's not like Elideh and I have spent a lot of time living like witches. We only met you four years ago, and that was the first time anyone was able to explain what Elideh was." She frowned at the ground. "And I guess now what I am."

Reed backed off at her defensive posture and rolled his shoulders back. It wasn't fair for him to take out his fears on her, especially because she did actually already know a lot about their world, thanks to her studies and her sister's experiences, as if her path up to this point had been chosen for her by fate.

"You're right, Ailia. I'm sorry." He pulled out a chair for her at the table by the window and sat her down.

She frowned up at him. "You know I can sit in chairs and open doors all by myself, right?"

Maybe he was being a little overbearing. "Let's eat, and I will explain everything I can." He reached out to hold her hand, needing to touch her for some reason, and she squeezed reassuringly. He could see her posture ease and was relieved he hadn't fucked things up. Every now and then she glanced out the window, presumably looking for Storm.

"I have a couple of questions, but first tell me why you've been giving off possessive, alpha energy ever since yesterday," Ailia said with a smirk.

Reed frowned at her and said, "I have no idea what you're talking about." Ailia rolled her eyes and sat back in her chair, waiting for him to give her an answer. Reed sighed, caving to her question.

"Maybe it's because we were just attacked by a faerie creature that hasn't been seen in a very, very long time," he answered.

"Fair enough," she conceded. "Speaking of faerie beasts, tell me what you know."

This was the Ailia he knew. No nonsense, down to business. He took a deep breath.

"To preface all of this, I will tell you everything I can like I promised, but keep in mind that almost all of our knowledge of the fae has been forgotten or lost, so a lot of this is speculation." Ailia nodded, gesturing for him to continue.

"Let me start with the cù-sìth. You seem to know what it is, presumably through your sister's research, but here is what you may not know: if the cù-sìth choose to bond, they are bonded to one fae for life, and they are hunters—not companions—for the fae. They stick to the Highlands when they are not doing the bidding of their masters. I'm tense because I cannot think of a reason why Storm would be here unless his fae master is close by."

At that admission, Ailia sat up a little straighter. "But how would the fae be here?" she asked.

"That's why I'm worried," scowled Reed. Ailia stared at him for a moment then shook her head slightly.

"Let's deal with that later," she said. "Let me ask some of my questions."

Reed leaned back in his chair. "Go for it."

Before she could ask her first question, the waitress brought their food. Ailia predictably dug in, and Reed waited patiently for her to come up for air. Between bites of bread, she said, "Yesterday you mentioned that I was a 'young' witch. What does that mean? I'm not that much younger than you. You're around the same age as my sister."

Reed was caught off guard by the question and thought for a minute before answering. She was so damn perceptive. Once he was sure they couldn't be overheard, he said, "This is not something that witches discuss openly, but you need to know." After another pause, he said, "Witches are immortal." At that, Ailia gaped at him.

He continued before she could interrupt. "So I am not the same age as Elideh." He winced, unsure how she would react. "I am one hundred and thirty-two years old." Ailia's shock was written all over her face.

After what seemed like an eternity, she said, "How is this possible? I have been studying witches my entire life and immortality has never been part of the canon lore. Does that mean that all those witches that were burned during the witch trials actually survived? Also, why haven't you ever told me and my sister this life-altering tidbit of information, Reed?"

Fair enough. He and his mother had discussed this very thing. Elideh's magic was so strange, they didn't want to talk to the girls about immortality until they were sure that Elideh was a full-blooded witch. It would have been an immense burden for Elideh to know that she would potentially outlive her sister, and she hadn't gone through her staying yet. It wouldn't be obvious for a couple more years that she wasn't aging like a mortal.

"I understand that you're annoyed at me, but hear me out. Witches have kept our immortality highly guarded, and let me clarify—we are not impervious to death. And we *do* age, just very, very slowly. We can be killed the same way mortals can be killed—beheading, burning, wounds to the correct artery—but we do not die from age or sickness." Reed paused, trying to gauge Ailia's reaction, but her face was carefully blank. He figured it was best to just plow ahead.

"We go through a 'staying' just like the fae supposedly do. Back hundreds of years ago, most witches came into their powers when they were around sixteen years old, and then they would go through the staying sometime in their twenties. It's been different since the witch hunts. Something about magic changed, and it hasn't been the same since. I was born in the late 1800s, and my staying didn't happen until I was almost thirty. Apparently, it's happening later and later for modern witches."

Reed could tell that Ailia was in scholar mode by the way she bit her bottom lip and leaned towards him. That was probably a good sign.

"Okay, so witches can be killed, but live for a very long time and eventually grow old. That doesn't sound like immortality to me, just a longer life. What about the fae?"

"That's true. And I guess the fae are more truly immortal in that sense." Reed paused, trying to remember the stories he had heard about the fae. "All of the legends indicate that the fae also go through a staying. As far as I know, their staying happens around the same time as ours, but unlike witches, the fae do not age. They also can be killed, but have the ability to heal themselves without the use of potions. The fae are naturally stronger and faster than witches, and can shapeshift. But they cannot wield magic the way that witches can."

Ailia frowned. "What do you mean 'the way witches can'? Can the fae wield magic at all?"

"From what I know, the fae can only wield magic for battle. Witches can wield magic anytime. For example, the fae could use magic if they needed to protect themselves, like you did with the cù-sìth, but witches use magic for daily tasks by calling on the element they are connected with. There are obviously limits to all magic, though. Witches manipulate natural elements, but the magic the fae possess is more like pure energy that can be roughly shaped for their purposes. The fae in general are more brutal, more wild, so it makes sense that their magic isn't quite as refined." Reed still couldn't believe they were talking about the fae like they were real. He knew that they had once lived here, but it had been so long, and he knew so little.

Ailia took a deep breath and took a sip of her coffee. "This is a lot. And I still don't understand why you wouldn't have just told us." She looked out the window. "Let's go for a walk. I need to clear my head before I hear anymore."

"Fair enough. Want me to get you a to-go cup for your coffee?"

"Yes, please." Reed got a cup and poured Ailia fresh coffee from the pot sitting on the table. They had only taken a couple steps outside when Storm appeared and almost knocked Ailia over with his greeting. Ailia's face lit up. Reed tensed at the encounter, but Ailia brushed his arm in reassurance. He eased at the contact, but he knew it would be a long road ahead for them.

CHAPTER FOURTEEN

AILIA

Ailia was relieved to be out in the sun. She was still trying to process everything Reed had told her and was wandering aimlessly down the street when Reed said, "How about we visit the abbey? It's a short walk from here."

Happy to have a distraction, she eagerly agreed and let Reed lead the way. Storm, who seemed to have shrunk to the size of a Great Dane, trotted happily beside her, occasionally wandering off to sniff a plant or snap at a flying bug. He always stayed close to her, though, and frequently put himself between her and Reed. This seemed to annoy Reed to no end, but he left it alone and didn't do anything to stop Storm.

Ailia laughed to herself at the absurdity of it all—walking down a very normal street with a witch and a faerie hound, searching for an entrance to a magical realm. She wouldn't be surprised if she woke up, still in Oxford, and this was all just a dream.

But for now, she had to accept that this was her reality. She recapped everything Reed told her and decided the first thing she needed to do was figure out her magic. Obviously she had it, or she wouldn't have been able to cast the spell from the grimoire. She had never had an experience of her magic "manifesting" as Reed called it, apart from the energy that had erupted from her, and she certainly didn't feel any pull to a specific element. She guessed that whatever had woken up inside of her after Elideh's disappearance could be her magic, but she thought it would be more obvious.

Something was bothering her, though. Both hers and Elideh's magic was not like regular witch magic from what she understood. From Reed's descriptions, it sounded like there were some pretty specific divides in what the fae and what the witches could do. She believed that Reed was being forthcoming with everything he knew about the fae at this point, and she knew most of the history was shrouded in mystery. Since neither of them knew a lot about the faeries, she decided to work out that piece of the puzzle later.

Reed had been quietly walking by her side, letting her think. She turned to him and said, "I think we need to figure out my powers."

Reed nodded his head and said, "I agree. That would be a good place to start. There are ways to test your compatibility with the elements. And I am fairly confident your powers have manifested since you were able to do some sort of magic that first night at the inn."

Ailia looked over at him. "Actually, let me back up. I don't understand why my magic and Elideh's magic are so different. Elideh's magic was always so weak. And you said it wasn't tied to an element, but sometimes it seemed to just... react... to her emotions. And she could barely cast spells from a spell book."

They walked a couple of steps, then Reed said, "My mother and I couldn't figure out Elideh's magic. We assumed it was because of the way magic has changed. It's also the reason we didn't explain our immortality. We didn't know if she was maybe just distantly related to witches. Only full-blooded witches have the long lifespan."

Ailia nodded her head. If she was being honest with herself, that made sense. She was still a little annoyed they had kept something so big from Elideh, but she at least understood their choice.

Although Ailia did want to see the abbey, she knew that they should go back to Rhymer's Stone. She was avoiding it after what happened the day before, but they had to keep moving forward with their plan. She stopped and turned to Reed.

"I think we should go back to Rhymer's Stone. We can revisit the abbey another day. We obviously didn't get a chance to look around yesterday."

"As you wish, milady," nodded Reed, trying to lighten the mood.

He took her hand, laced it through his arm, and turned them both around. Ailia looked up at him and smiled to herself. She really was glad that he was here.

AILIA

The sun was still shining down on them by the time they made it back to Rhymer's Stone. The journey was much quicker now that they knew which path to take. Ailia told Storm to follow Reed's car, and as soon as they parked, Storm revealed himself and was bounding up the path ahead of them, forcing them to jog in order to keep up.

"I never was much of a runner," said Reed, his breathing slightly labored. "I'd much rather spar or lift weights."

"Come on, Reed, I've barely even broken a sweat," scoffed Ailia.

"It's not that I can't, it's just that I don't like it. And in case you forgot, my chest was ripped open by a vicious beast yesterday."

Good point. Ailia slowed her pace, and soon enough they were back at the memorial. Before they left, Ailia had stopped by the hotel room to grab Elideh's translation of the Thomas Rhymer ballad. She took it out of her pocket, and Reed leaned over her shoulder to read it with her.

"Psh." Reed's huff blew stray pieces of Ailia's hair across her face.

Ailia turned to him and frowned. "What?"

"It's just like the faeries to trick a mortal with something as simple as a kiss. See? Verses five through eight, the queen literally seals the deal with a kiss."

Ailia read the verses aloud:

"Play a harp and sing, Thomas," she said,
"Play and sing with me:
And if you dare to kiss my lips
Sure of you I will be."

"Whether good or bad becomes me,
Fate shall never frighten me."
Then he kissed her rosy lips
All beneath the Eildon Tree.

—"Now you must go with me," she said,
"True Thomas, you must go with me:
And you must serve me seven years,

Through good or bad, as chance may be."

She mounted on her milk-white steed;
She's taken True Thomas up behind;
And yes, when her bridle rang;
The steed flew swifter than the wind.

"I guess you could see it as dishonesty, but it's a pretty common pattern in the faerie ballads from what I've read," said Ailia. "Any dealings with faeries always came at a price. Thomas surely would have known the kiss wouldn't be that simple." She wasn't sure why she felt the need to defend the fae, but from what Elideh had told her, they weren't what you would call 'moral.' They weren't necessarily evil, but they weren't necessarily good, either.

"I'm just saying, a witch would never deceive a mortal like that," said Reed, disgust written all over his face. Ailia rolled her eyes.

"Just keep reading," Ailia said. This time, Reed read the verses aloud:

Oh, they rode on, and farther on;
The steed went swifter than the wind;
Until they reached a desert wide,
And living land was left behind.

"Lie down, lie down, True Thomas,
And lean your head upon my knee;
Abide and rest a little space,
And I will show you wonders three."

Reed stopped. "See! Why would Thomas listen to her? Obviously there is going to be some sort of cost. This guy's a fool."

"Reed! Maybe he loved her? Maybe he was sick of living in the boring mortal realm and wanted a change? Hell, this probably isn't even real, just some sort of story," argued Ailia.

Reed raised an eyebrow at her. "Seriously? With everything you now know, you think this is just a story?"

"You're impossible," Ailia mumbled. Before he could retort, she kept reading from the ballad. There had to be something that could help them:

"Oh do you see the narrow road,
So thick beset with thorns and briars?
That is the path of righteousness,
But after it, few inquire."

"And do you see that braided road
That lies across the lily pasture?
That is the path to wickedness,
Tho some call it the road to heaven."

"And do you see that bonnie road,
That winds about the wondrous brae?
That is the road to fair Elflaine,
Where you and I this night must go."

"But Thomas, you must hold your tongue,
Whatever you may hear or see,
For, if you speak word in Elflyn land,
You'll never get back to your own country."

"Bloody hell," Reed interrupted. "Again, a great example of faerie pride. You're telling me there are three paths, one leading to heaven, one leading to hell, and yet—surprise, surprise—the best path is the one that leads to Elflaine. Absolute bollocks."

"Reed. Shut. Up. I get it. You don't like the faeries. I'm just trying to find a way to get my sister," said Ailia.

Reed huffed, but held his tongue. Ailia continued reading:

On they rode, farther and farther,
And they waded through rivers above the knee;
And they saw neither sun nor moon,
But heard the roaring of the sea.

It was murky night, and there was no guiding light;
And they waded through red blood to their knees,
For all the blood that's shed on Earth,
Runs through the springs of that countrie.

"The last couple of verses say that the Faerie Queen gifted Thomas a 'tongue that can never lie' which Elideh thinks means the gift of prophecy," said Ailia. "It also said that he was never seen again, but we know that's not true. He did come back from the faerie lands. Elideh thinks that the last verse is actually referring to Thomas's alleged death, since they never actually found his body."

Ailia sat down and laid her head back against the soft ground. She let the sun shine on her face, absorbing the warmth and light. She felt Reed lay down next to her, resting his hand on top of hers.

"Ails, we will find Elideh. I'm sorry I'm being a jerk about the faeries, I'm just anxious," Reed quietly confessed.

Ailia kept her eyes closed, thinking through the verses. "I wish it wasn't so cryptic. It says they rode on and on, and there was no sun or moon, but they could hear the roaring of the sea?" Ailia shook her head. "It doesn't make any sense."

"Neither do the rivers of blood or the murky night. But it's a ballad, not instructions." Reed squeezed her hand reassuringly.

They both sat in silence for a while, when Reed suddenly sat up, his body tense.

"What's wrong?" Ailia asked. She looked over to see Storm looking in the same direction as Reed, his ears perked.

"We need to go," whispered Reed. He stood and easily pulled Ailia up from the ground, tucking her into his side. Storm was at her back, nudging her along, but occasionally pausing to glance back with his ears raised.

"At least the beast and I seem to agree on something," Reed mumbled as he led them to his car.

Ailia was trying to listen intently to see if she could pick up on whatever Reed and Storm were aware of, but she didn't sense anything wrong.

They made it to the car, Reed still tense. He spun the car around, rocks and dirt flying up behind them. Ailia looked over at him trying to gauge if whatever perceived danger had passed, but his knuckles were white on the steering wheel and a muscle in his jaw ticked. She reached over and touched his shoulder, trying to soothe him in some way. He glanced over at her and then looked back at the road.

"We need to be cautious when we are around the faerie locations." The stern tone of his voice put Ailia on edge. What happened back there? Or what would've happened...

"Okay," said Ailia carefully. Reed had always been protective, but he had never been one to act in fear. "Let's just go back to the hotel and eat. We can talk through the ballad and regroup."

Reed nodded, still serious. The trip may not have gone as planned, but maybe they were on to something. If only she could get Reed to relax a little bit. This journey was not going to come without risks.

CHAPTER FIFTEEN

REED

Reed wasn't sure what he had sensed, but he knew that something had been watching them. Or someone. Although Reed had always been aware of his surroundings through his connection with the earth, it had surprised him when he detected a presence through the trees. The warning had not come from the leaves, or the trees, or the rocks—it had simply been a gut feeling. A feeling he probably would have brushed off if it hadn't been for Storm's reaction.

After ushering Ailia safely inside the hotel and ordering their drinks, he went to the bathroom to collect himself. He splashed cool water on his face and stared at his reflection in the mirror. He had been alive long enough to not waste time with pep talks, but he also knew that something had definitely changed since Storm attacked them, and he wasn't sure if it bothered him or not. He shook his head, unwilling to leave Ailia alone any longer. He just needed to adjust to whatever this was.

As he sat down, he decided to brush off the uneasiness that was taking root in him and focus on his task: help Ailia and keep her away from the faeries. Which was going to be difficult since she was hell-bent on getting into Elflaine.

"Well, I know you and Storm felt *something* at the Stone. Do you think it could be a way into the faerie realm?" Ailia asked after they ordered their lunch.

"I'm not sure," Reed hedged. He didn't want her going back there, but didn't want to keep her from her sister if it was a way into the realm. "I didn't sense any magic if that's what you're asking. It was more of a... presence."

Ailia nodded slowly. "Well, we have been there twice now, and if it isn't an entrance to Elflaine, I think we should move on. No sense in checking the same place over and over again. We can look through Elideh's notes later to decide where to go next."

Reed couldn't stand how discouraged she looked. As much as he wanted to keep her from the faeries, he would rip open an entrance to Elflaine himself if it would cure the sadness that had settled over her.

"This is going to be difficult, Ailia, but I believe we will find a way to get Elideh back. And I will be with you every step of the way." She looked slightly less defeated and nodded her head. Reed blew out a breath.

"You're right. I knew this was going to be challenging, and I need to expect these setbacks." Her shoulders straightened. "I want to know more about my magic. You said there was a way to test it?"

Reed was relieved at the change of subject. "We need to be in a place away from others. One, so we don't get caught by the mortals, but two in case your magic acts unpredictably. Melrose Abbey is surrounded by pretty dense forest. How about we go there after lunch since you wanted to see it anyway?"

"Perfect. The sooner we can get started the better."

"Agreed," nodded Reed.

AILIA

Ailia felt better after a nice, hot meal, and decided there was no point wallowing. She would simply focus on the next thing. Moving past challenges was more of an Elideh quality. Ailia tending to be more cynical. But hopelessness wouldn't help her find her sister.

They left the hotel and started heading toward the abbey, gravitating toward each other as frequently as Storm would allow. Reed turned to her, frowning. "What *is* your plan? For entering Elflaine? Are you going to just charge in and ask the first faerie you meet to take you to Elideh?"

That was actually a fantastic question. Usually Ailia was not spontaneous—in fact, usually Ailia was convincing Elideh to slow down and make a plan. The last two weeks had truly turned everything on its head.

"Um, I honestly hadn't thought that far. Finding an entrance seemed so impossible."

Reed looked like he wanted to clobber her. "Ailia. You cannot just waltz into Elflaine without a plan. I don't know why I'm only just now realizing the flaw in this quest, to be honest, but you cannot go there unless you're ready to fight—with or without magic." While he was talking, he had moved close to her and tucked her under his arm. And she let him. She found herself wanting him closer to her more and more often.

Reed continued, oblivious to their change in proximity. "Based on the old stories, the fae are ruthless. They will either kill you or capture you before you are able to find Elideh. Obviously I'll be there with you, but you need to be able to defend yourself." He paused to take a deep breath, calculating something in that pretty head of his. Ailia couldn't even be annoyed at his outburst. Now that he was talking through it, he was absolutely right. What had she been thinking?

"Once we figure out your magic, we have to start training immediately. We can still keep looking, but we are not going to Elflaine until you at least know some defensive magic," he said, his tone leaving no room for argument.

Ailia was quiet for a minute, trying to decide if she was offended by Reed commanding her, but ultimately decided that he wasn't wrong. "Okay, Reed. I will train. I promise."

Reed blew out a breath. They continued walking in silence for a couple of minutes, Ailia slowly disentangling herself from him. She was about to apologize for her lack of planning when Reed looked over at her and furrowed his brows.

"What is it?" Ailia asked.

"I haven't noticed this before, but when you're in the sun, you almost glow," said Reed.

Ailia raised her eyebrows at him. "That's ridiculous. I don't glow. My hair is just really light and shiny," Ailia countered.

Reed shrugged as if glowing was a perfectly normal thing. "It's just an observation. Sometimes witches have outward signs of their magic, and if the glowing is new, it could be connected."

Interesting. Ailia stopped walking for a moment. "How would we know for sure?"

Reed stopped beside her. "Well, everyone is different, but if it's connected to your magic, I would imagine you would glow more when you're using your magic. We will just have to wait and find out."

Ailia wondered if her alleged glow had something to do with the bright magic she had conjured. "Do you physically change when you use your magic?"

"My mother says that when I use a lot of magic, my eyes and my hair tend to darken. I've always assumed it's because of my earth magic," Reed explained.

Ailia smiled. "Although I feel like I'm way out of my league, I have to admit this is all very exciting."

Reed smiled back. "I would imagine so."

They continued walking, and as they got closer to the abbey, Storm bounded away, disappearing before he got to the ruins. Reed tensed and Ailia turned to him.

"Should we go after him?" Ailia asked.

"No, he probably went off to chase an animal. But I wish he wouldn't do that disappearing thing. It's unnerving. Let's just hope there aren't unwanted guests around." Ailia could feel the shift in Reed. He instantly became more alert and on guard, and had even angled his body so that he was one step ahead of her. She wished she could ease some of his tension, but instead drew closer to him and laced her arm through his.

Ailia looked around at the magnificent abbey. "This is really beautiful." It was still largely intact for being nearly a thousand years old. The structure towered over them, the stonework painstakingly detailed. They could see where there once would have been a magnificent stained glass window, and the beautifully arched doorways begged them to come closer.

"It's one of my mother's favorites. She said she felt good energy from it," said Reed, following her gaze.

And that's when Ailia realized she could feel something too. It felt like an energy, connecting the stones, the ground, the river, and even the sky. "I can feel it too, I think—something connecting everything together."

"That's good," encouraged Reed. "It's important to start seeking out those energies. That's really how magic works. You find your connection to something, and then use it for your own purposes. It's why using magic for wicked reasons is forbidden—it corrupts the connection you have with the elements since you are using them in an unnatural way."

Ailia processed this as she continued to walk around the ruins. There was no sign of Storm, but she figured a gigantic faerie hound could take care of himself. They spent about half an hour wandering around the ruins, Reed a steady force at her side, and Ailia finally felt clear-headed enough to try to delve into her magic.

She told Reed she was ready, and he led them towards the forest. Apprehension crept in as soon as they were under the covering of the trees. They walked until they found a small clearing by a stream and when Reed stopped and sat on the ground, Ailia did the same. She found a spot where the sun had broken through the canopy of leaves and sat, waiting for instructions.

Reed looked her in the eyes and said, "You're sure you want to do this? There is no going back once we fully awaken your magic." Ailia held his gaze and nodded once, not trusting her voice at the moment.

"Very well," said Reed. "Typically when a witch's magic starts to manifest, we do a simple test to see which elements the witch favors.

Keep in mind, most witches only favor one element." Reed pulled out a tiny bag from his pocket and dumped the contents into his hand. He held a smooth, green, marbled stone, an inky-black feather, an ancient looking candle with whorls embedded in the wax, and a small, spiral shell. "These items represent the four elements: earth, air, fire, and water. I am going to place them in a line in front of you, and I want you to focus on them. Let each one speak to you and see if you have a connection to any of them."

Ailia looked at Reed, her eyes questioning him as she said, "That's it? I just... look at them? Can I touch them?"

Reed smiled at her and said, "You can touch them, but the initial connection will be felt internally—like a recognition in your soul. You will feel a pull, and you just need to follow it."

He placed his hand on her knee, and with a softness in his voice that made Ailia's doubts wash away, said, "There are other ways to test for magic, this is just the most traditional approach. Give it a try. We'll figure this out together."

Ailia released a breath and settled farther into the ground. She closed her eyes and tried to focus on the four items in front of her. After steadying her breaths and calming her mind, she opened her eyes to look at each item. She glanced up at Reed who was staring intently at her, and as she looked back towards the items, she did feel *something*. She put her hand above each item, but felt that energy consistently each time she focused on a different element. Ailia shook her head and sighed in frustration.

Eyebrows furrowed, Reed asked, "What's wrong?"

"I feel energy. But it feels the same for every item. Maybe I need to focus more," replied Ailia.

Reed looked at her thoughtfully and said, "Let's try something else. Take your shoes off and then place your hands and feet on the ground."

Ailia looked at Reed curiously, but started unlacing her boots. After removing her shoes and socks, she pulled her knees up, placed her feet firmly on the ground, and then flattened her hands against the dirt. She looked over at Reed, seeing that he had done the same. He said, "Try to imagine that you are pulling the earth into you. If you start to feel a deeper connection to the ground, go into your mind and pull at the dirt the same way you would if you were scooping it up with your hands."

Ailia closed her eyes and tried to do as Reed said. She had no idea what to picture, so she envisioned tendrils of energy, which looked like rays of sun in her mind, gently caressing the ground around her. To her surprise, she felt the life force in the earth rise up to meet her, and entwine with her own energy. Her eyes popped open and found Reed grinning at her.

She closed her eyes again and tried to pull at the earth like Reed had instructed. At first, she tried to gently tug, and then she tried to yank. But nothing worked. She cleared her head and pictured the energy again.

This time, instead of pulling, she merely suggested to the earth that it should obey her. Instantly, the earth sprang up around her, and she could feel it curling around her fingers and toes. She opened her eyes but didn't break her connection. Reed was looking at her with shock written all over his face. He cautiously glanced between her and the tendrils of dirt that were still winding themselves around her and said, "Are you doing that on purpose?"

Ailia replied and said, "Yes, am I not doing it right?" She started to feel a little deflated but Reed said, "I just have never seen earth act that way. It's so... graceful. It looks almost like a caress. Let me show you what I mean."

Reed then pulled his hands up from the ground and the earth came with him in strong columns. She understood his confusion. The earth she was interacting with looked more like silk.

She broke her connection to the earth and shook out her hands and feet. Reed did the same.

"This is so fascinating. I have never met another earth wielder like you. We will have to experiment more later to see what you can do." His excitement was infectious. "Although it is very uncommon to have an affinity for more than one element. I think we should test for the others, just in case. Especially since the earth reacted to you in such a unique way."

Ailia happily agreed. She had just done magic. Real magic. On purpose. This couldn't be happening. "What's next?"

Reed grinned. "Fire."

AILIA

"Since I don't have a strong affinity to fire, you will have to rely on your instincts for this. Unlike earth, I cannot manipulate fire to work with me. However, I am impervious to it. I will not burn when it touches me, and sometimes I can move it around. But I can't turn it into shapes or wield it for fighting," explained Reed.

He paused to make sure she was following, and stood. "The easiest way to see if you have a link to fire is to conjure it." He reached down to help her up, and she grabbed his hand, suddenly aware of the scent of earth that clung to him.

"Conjure fire? You're joking, right?" laughed Ailia as she found her footing. Although she had lit a candle, she had done it with a spell. This was much more intimidating.

"Just close your eyes and convince yourself you want or need it. Think of the way fire smells, the way it smokes, the colors it emits. And see if it comes to you," Reed shrugged. As if conjuring fire was just a normal, post-lunch activity.

Ailia huffed out a breath, glared at Reed, and closed her eyes. She could practically feel his smirk from where she was standing. Visions of fire began to form in her mind. She thought of small candle flames, of bonfires, of cozy fires in cozy fireplaces. She thought of the way the flames danced and how they changed colors. She recalled the smell of matches, and wet pine popping as it heated. Reed gasped, and she opened her eyes.

Goddess above. She was holding fire. In her hands.

A dainty little flame lazily moved with the breeze. And then it was gone. She was panting, trying to reel in her shock. Reed rushed over to her. "Are you okay? Did it burn you?" She looked at him and saw the worry clouding his eyes.

"No, it didn't burn me, just surprised me. I mean, I was holding *fire*." Ailia rubbed her eyes and ran her hands down her face. "I thought you said this never happened," she stammered.

Eyes wide, Reed said, "It *doesn't* usually happen—I'm just as shocked as you are, I promise."

Ailia sat down, needing to settle her thoughts that were threatening to become hysteric. "What does it mean? That I can wield two elements?"

Reed sat next to her and pulled her into his side. "It means that you have been gifted with a great privilege." He gently tilted her chin up to him. "It's going to be okay."

CHAPTER SIXTEEN

CALLUM

Callum Rhauner had tracked the man and woman into the woods. He didn't know why his hound, Torneach, was accompanying the woman, but as soon Callum called for him, he had obediently lumbered over. Callum decided to stick around to see who these people were.

He stretched his arms over his head and focused on his breathing. The transition from the faerie realm to the mortal realm was not easy, and he was still feeling pretty weak. It wasn't a feeling he was accustomed to, and was starting to get on his nerves.

After getting closer, he scented that the man was actually a witch, and the woman was something else—but definitely not mortal. Which is why he decided to follow them.

They paused in a clearing, and he sank into a crouch behind a large tree. He shifted slightly so he was in the sun. Damn, he had missed the sun. Torneach sat obediently next to him, his eyes trained on the woman. Callum scowled at his hound, wondering why he was so interested in her.

He watched the woman—or whatever she was—wield earth magic, and then, to his shock, fire magic. Being able to wield two elements was uncommon for witches, so she must have a powerful bloodline. However, it looked like the male witch was testing her, which meant she was very young and very inexperienced.

He started to walk away from them as he debated what he should do. He was here for a very specific task—retrieve the artifacts for the Faerie Queen—and could not afford to divert from those plans. But something was drawing him to the female. And clearly his hound felt the same pull since the beast had ditched him as soon as they crossed the boundary into the mortal realm the day before. Callum hadn't thought anything of it at the time since he figured the beast was simply hunting. Plus, the transition from Elflaine to the mortal realm was not easy, especially since he hadn't been here in hundreds of years. He had needed a full day to recover, and still felt disoriented.

Torneach kept glancing behind them, whimpering, like he wanted to go to her. Traitorous mutt.

Callum paused as a thought occurred to him—maybe the witch could help him find the items he needed. As much as he hated to admit it, having a witch could be useful with their skills in magic wielding. And Callum did not believe in coincidence. If fate was leading him towards this woman and this witch, who was he to question it? He had learned the hard way a long time ago that fate had a way of getting its way.

Since he was stuck in the mortal realm until he found the artifacts, he might as well try to find a way to bargain for their help. But the witches and the fae had not partnered together in over a thousand years, and weren't exactly on friendly terms.

The pause was all Torneach needed to make up his mind, apparently. The hound turned around and sprinted back towards the girl. "Damn it!" Callum hissed as he went to follow his treasonous beast. Well, it made his decision easier. He would just have to convince the witch to help him.

REED

Storm sprinted over to Ailia out of nowhere and stopped right in front of her, bowing his head. Reed was never going to get used to this creature acting like a puppy around her. Ailia happily scratched his ears and Reed swore the beast was grinning at her. Although Ailia seemed unbothered by the creature showing up out of nowhere, Reed was watchful, still convinced the beast would lead its master to them.

He scanned the trees, using his connection to the earth to feel any presence that might be hidden. After reaching out to every root, leaf, and rock in the surrounding area and detecting nothing threatening, he relaxed his posture slightly and turned his attention to Ailia.

Two elements. At least. They had stopped because he didn't want her to burn out or lose control. New witches were very unpredictable. Plus, it was nearly impossible that she had a connection to more than earth and fire. Witches wielding two elements was practically unheard of; wielding three or four elements was myth.

Reed hoped for her sake that her magic was unremarkable. It would put her in danger if she was powerful—not only from faeries, but also other witches. He stepped closer to her, needing to be in arm's reach for whatever instinct had taken over in the past day. To his surprise, she shifted closer to him, as if that thread connecting them had tugged at her too.

Ailia looked up at him, her expression shifting from amusement at Storm to seriousness. "Teach me everything you know. I want to start training immediately."

Of course she did. Reed admired her determination, but knew that she would need to pace herself. "I will. I want you to train your magic as much as you do. The more you know, the safer you'll be. Right now, though, we need to go back and let you rest."

She looked like she was about to argue, so he interrupted her, trying to appeal to her logical side. "Here is your first lesson in magic: it has to be replenished. All witches replenish their magic in different ways, and we will find yours, but the one thing that is sure to help is food and sleep."

Although she looked disappointed, Ailia nodded. "Fine. I guess I do feel a little drained. I still need our main focus to be on finding an entrance to Elflaine, so we will have to train as we search." She paused, frowning. "I'm frustrated that all of my years of research on the witches aren't more helpful. I feel completely blindsided."

Reed reached out to her and touched her shoulder gently. "If it makes you feel better, I have been a witch for over a hundred years and don't feel exceedingly helpful, either. We will just have to figure this out together." He smiled at her and was relieved to see her smile back.

They started to walk towards the edge of the clearing, but as if the universe wasn't willing to give them a moment of rest, Reed sensed someone and pulled Ailia towards him.

"What's wrong?" Ailia asked.

"We are not alone." Reed lowered his voice to a whisper as he scanned the trees.

Then, a deep voice from nowhere said, "Relax, witch. I'm not going to hurt you or the girl."

Shit. The faerie had found them.

AILIA

Ailia was frozen in place and Reed was practically vibrating with tension as they waited for the owner of the arrogant voice to reveal himself. To her surprise, Storm was sitting at her feet, completely relaxed, but looking attentively towards the trees.

All of a sudden, Storm bolted over to the treeline and ran straight into the body that had appeared out of thin air. Ailia gasped, taking in the scene, realizing that the person standing before her was definitely fae.

Even though Elideh had collected stories and manuscripts about the fae for nearly a decade, no one was quite sure what they were supposed to look like. Elideh had been pretty spot on in her guesses about their appearance.

His stunning, green-blue eyes went straight to hers, and her breath caught. She couldn't help but stare. Reed was tall, broad, and handsome, but this male standing in front of her was somehow... more. His dark, thick hair barely concealed the pointed tips of his ears, and he was dressed in various shades of the forest—greens, browns, and grays—the fabric doing little to hide his pale skin and toned, warrior's body. And he was beautiful. In a way that reminded her of marble statues or descriptions of gods.

As he slowly approached them, she realized he was slightly taller than Reed and had several visible weapons. This could not end well.

For the second time in less than two days, Reed shoved Ailia behind him.

"What do you want?" Reed asked with a lethal lilt to his voice she'd never heard from him before.

The warrior took several slow steps towards them before answering calmly with an accent that sounded Scottish, but somehow more ancient, "I want your help."

Ailia had been peeking around Reed's shoulder and glanced up at him, but his attention was focused on the warrior in front of them. "No. Now leave," Reed said as the earth around them began to stir.

The male stopped his approach, and with an animalistic tilt of his head, stared at Reed. After what seemed like an eternity, he said, "Again, I'm not going to hurt you. My name is Callum. And I need your help. I am willing to trade something in return. I overheard you speaking about an entrance to Elflaine. I will help you find one if you assist me."

Ailia sucked in a breath and moved to stand beside Reed. Reed tried to push her behind him again, but she stubbornly shoved right back. The fae male, Callum, seemed to tense slightly at the interaction, but didn't intervene. Reed turned to Ailia and scowled at her. After a brief staring contest, Reed relented. Ailia decided not to push him too hard, so she stayed next to him and grabbed his hand, reassuring him that she wouldn't go farther.

She turned to Callum and said, "Do you swear it? Will you take an oath?"

Reed rounded on Ailia and was looking at her like she had suggested Storm could eat her left arm for a snack, but she didn't look away from

Callum. If this male could help her get to her sister, she would sell her soul to him if that's what he wanted.

Callum glanced between her and Reed and relaxed his posture as he crossed his arms. Then, he smirked at her. What was it with these males and their smirks? "This, I haven't seen for many centuries."

"Care to elaborate?" Reed bit out.

But Callum continued speaking to Ailia as if he hadn't heard Reed. "Your knight doesn't trust me, Bright One."

Ailia squared her shoulders. "Do you want to take the oath or not?" she demanded with more bravado than she felt.

Reed put his arm on Ailia's shoulder and spun her around to face him. "Ailia, I do not think you understand the implications of a blood oath. Only death can break it. I will not let you take an oath with *him*," said Reed, practically spitting the last word. Reed turned to Callum and glared at him, all but baring his teeth.

Stunned by Reed's behavior, which was a far cry from his usual teasing and fussing, Ailia used a harsher tone than she had ever used with him. "Actually, blood oaths are one of the few things I *did* learn about the witches in my studies. I would gladly take a blood oath if it helps me find my sister. And since when do you get to make decisions for me, Reed? You are not my keeper."

Reed looked at Ailia and then back at Callum, straightening his shoulders as he said, "As you wish. I will take the blood oath. Callum, if you help Ailia find an entrance to Elflaine, I will help you with your task, but you need to give us more details. She will stay uninvolved. That is my offer."

Before Ailia could protest, Callum said, "So be it. I was sent here to collect three artifacts. Once I have collected those, I will return to Elflaine."

"What are the artifacts?" Reed asked.

"I will explain more details when you need them," Callum answered cryptically.

Reed crossed his arms. "Will the artifacts endanger us?"

"The artifacts are not dangerous," said Callum.

Reed squared his shoulders. "Do you vow to keep her from harm?"

Callum glanced at Ailia, then faced Reed. "I will not intentionally put her in harm's way, but my oath is with you, witch. If she chooses to involve herself, I will not stop her."

Ailia knew the warrior was choosing his words carefully, and could see that Reed was not wholly content with his answers. But the declaration must have satisfied Reed, because he nodded and strode over as Callum pulled a dagger from his belt. In two swift movements, Callum cut his own palm, then Reed's, and they clasped hands. Ailia could have sworn the energy around them stuttered, the forest quieting for a moment.

Ailia could not believe Reed had just made an oath on her behalf. She wasn't sure if she should be mad or honored. Reed turned around and was walking back towards her with an intensity in his eyes she almost recoiled from.

"Let's go," he said, no room for argument. He gently took her elbow and turned her away from Callum, but faster than she could register, Storm was in front of them, blocking their way.

"Slow down, witch. We made an oath," said Callum, his tone bored. "You can't just run away."

Reed spun around. "I'm not running. I'm getting her out of here because I don't trust you."

"Reed," said Ailia, "I'm not going anywhere. If he can help us find my sister, I am part of this." And then, more softly because she could tell he was riding a knife's edge, "I'm with you, I'll be safe."

"And with you is where I'll always be," he said, looking her straight in the eyes. Ailia could not wrap her head around the shift that had occurred between them, but she could read between the lines. She was not going anywhere alone anymore.

"Glad that's settled," scoffed Callum. "We leave in the morning. Meet me here at sunrise."

Reed kept his eyes on Ailia, but said to Callum, "She will decide when we leave. We will meet you here tomorrow, but if she doesn't like what you have to say, or isn't ready to go, we will stay."

Ailia looked at Callum in time to see him roll his eyes and mumble something about 'unbearable, sanctimonious knights' before saying, "Very well. Don't be late."

And at that, he disappeared. Storm whimpered in his direction, but sat at Ailia's feet, staying with her either on command of whom Ailia assumed was his master, or from whatever connection they shared. Reed didn't speak as he led her out of the forest, and didn't relax until they were back in his car.

Trying to lighten the mood, Ailia said, "Well that was an unexpected turn of events."

Reed just looked over at her and then returned his attention to the road.

Okay, still fuming then.

Ailia reached over to touch his arm and said gently, "Reed. Please talk to me. I'm sorry about the oath. But I couldn't pass up that opportunity."

Finally, Reed said, "You have nothing to be sorry for. I would take any oath to keep you safe. I just hope the fae bastard keeps up his end of the deal." Ailia just sat, sensing he had something else to say. He ran his hand through his hair. "I don't understand what is happening. The fae have not turned up in the mortal realm in centuries. And all of a sudden, *he* shows up. Right when your sister has disappeared. And you've manifested magic." Reed blew out a breath. "Also, ever since Storm attacked us, I have felt this intense drive to protect you. And then what the faerie said about 'not seeing this in many centuries.' Do you feel different too?"

Relieved that it was not just her who had felt the change between them and that Reed had brought it up, Ailia said, "Yes. I feel it as well. I can't quite figure it out, but it's definitely something. I thought it was strange what he said too. Maybe we can ask him to explain it. We will figure it out." Then, after a pause, she said, "For what it's worth, I am glad you are with me. I am used to doing things on my own and taking care of myself. But it's nice having someone else to rely on."

Reed smiled a true, genuine smile. "I am glad I am with you too, and whatever it is that is connecting us, please know it's not a burden to me."

She didn't realize that she needed to hear that until he said it. "Thank you, Reed. I know it seems like everything is happening at once. But maybe this is just fate." She squeezed his hand and he squeezed it back, his reassuring presence putting her at ease.

They sat in a comfortable silence all the way back to the hotel as Ailia was finally able to remind herself of what she had accomplished—she had done real magic. And Reed would train her. Although she was excited about the prospect of learning magic, she couldn't help but wonder what sort of assistance a fae warrior needed from a witch.

CHAPTER SEVENTEEN

CALLUM

C allum stalked off to the edge of the forest, still invisible, and extremely annoyed. Why had he agreed to that oath? He was more powerful than the witch—he could have just forced them to help. Plus, there was no way he was taking that girl to Elflaine. He shook his head, the girl's bright eyes still forefront in his vision.

Callum still wasn't quite sure *what* she was, but when he had moved closer, he thought he sensed something fae about her. Yet she had definitely wielded witch magic. It didn't make sense. He needed to focus on the task ahead. And right now, he needed to clear his head of her citrus, sea salt, and lavender scent.

He found a small stream and bent over it, dunking his head in the crisp, fresh water. He hated to admit it to himself, but he loved being back in Scotland. Something about the country made his blood sing. And gods, he had missed the sun. He tilted his head towards the light, letting the warmth wash over him, and closed his eyes. It was unlike him to feel off-balance.

The first thing he needed to deal with was the bond between the male and the female. At first, he was sure he was wrong, but centuries of living had taught him to trust his instincts. Although there hadn't been a bond like the one the two shared in a long time, it didn't mean it couldn't exist. Callum didn't even know that there were any knights of The Order left. Yet that was definitely what the witch was.

Long ago, the fae and the witches had lived in peace with each other, typically keeping to themselves, but occasionally coming together to partner against the darkness. The knights were of an ancient order of witches that had been bound to the fae, not by force, but by mutual partnership. When the knight bond formed between a fae and a witch, it was unbreakable and sacred. What was even more strange was that Callum was certain the witch and the girl didn't know they were bonded.

Although the knight bond occasionally chose for itself, it was generally a mutual decision. The knights had disappeared when the realms were sealed, so Callum knew very little about The Order. Unfortunately, he would have to wait to find out more until he returned to Elflaine.

Then, there was the girl. Her sunshine hair and strange, pale eyes had nearly stopped him cold, but her scent was what had made him pause. He still didn't know what to make of her—or what she was. He was right in his original assessment that she was young. She hadn't gone through her staying yet, but she was definitely not mortal. He still couldn't believe that Torneach had gone with her *again*. Callum huffed in frustration and mindlessly swirled his fingers through the frigid stream.

That damn oath. He still wasn't sure why he had agreed to it. At least the witch would help him with his task. Now, he needed to come up with a plan. And deal with the insufferable way the knights were with their wards. Perhaps he would go for a run—that always helped clear his head. Then, he would have the rest of the night to decide what to do.

REED

Reed was pacing back and forth in their room at the hotel while Ailia quietly snacked on the fresh pastries they had bought in town. A blood oath. He had sworn a blood oath. With a faerie. And there was something between him and Ailia that had him feeling completely out of control. He needed to clear his head.

Ailia had been patiently watching him pace. Occasionally she looked like she was going to say something, but then would stop herself at the last minute.

They had until the morning to decide what to do. He had no idea what sort of help the faerie needed, but if he was willing to make a blood oath with a witch to accomplish it, it couldn't be good. And Ailia was part of it. Reed considered asking Ailia to stay behind, but he knew that would just start a fight. So instead, he asked, "What do you think we should do? Should we follow whatever plan this faerie puts in front of us?"

Ailia licked the last bit of chocolate off her fingers. "I think we look through Elideh's notes tonight and come up with another list of potential entrances to Elflaine. Along the way, we can check into these entrances if they happen to be nearby wherever Callum takes us," she paused, shooting Reed a look of trepidation before saying, "I know you don't trust him, but for some reason, I do. I have been sifting through all of the events from the past couple of days, and I think fate has led us to him. I believe he will take me to Elflaine if we help him with his task. But just in case my instincts are wrong, I don't want to waste any opportunities to find an entrance ourselves."

Reed nodded, thankful for something to focus on, even if he definitely disagreed with her about trusting him. "Okay. Let's go through your sister's notes and make a list. I will go get dinner and bring it up here so we don't waste any time."

Ailia nodded and started to sift through her backpack for the materials. Reed stood there for a moment, trying to reassure himself that she would be safe while he was downstairs. He knew she was capable of taking care of herself—especially in a damn hotel room. This instinct to protect her was really starting to piss him off, but he couldn't shake it. Finally, he forced himself out of the room and started down the stairs.

AILIA

As Ailia flipped through the pages of Elideh's notebooks, she couldn't help feeling the pang of grief that ricocheted through her. What if she was too late? The only thing that consoled her was that she believed she would know if her sister was dead.

Ailia knew that Reed didn't trust Callum, but what choice did she have? She could spend the rest of her life searching Scotland for an entrance to Elflaine. Although Elideh had somehow conjured an entrance with the grimoire, Ailia was not sure she would be able to do it, and she certainly didn't want to wait another seven months to test it.

No, helping Callum in exchange for getting to Elflaine was the right choice. She had been hopeful that Elideh's translation of Thomas Rhymer would lead them to an entrance, and in a way, it *had,* since it led them to Storm and Callum. Now, she needed to decide what to look for next.

The most obvious things they could look for were "faerie glens"—bowers or hills that were known for their faerie connections throughout Scotland. But Ailia knew Elideh had checked these more obvious places with no luck. She continued flipping through Elideh's notes when she remembered one of the translations Elideh had written of a different ballad.

Although the story itself was a bit... unsavory... it was one of the only other ballads that mentioned a specific place. Ailia skimmed pages until she found it, and read through the first couple of verses to refresh her memory:

Oh I forbid you, maidens all,
That wear gold on your hair,
To come or go by Carterhaugh,
For young Tam Lin is there.

There's none that goes by Carterhaugh
But they leave him something treasured,
Either their rings, or green cloaks,

Or else their maidenhood.

Janet has tucked her green skirts
A little above her knee,
And she has braided her yellow hair
A little above her brow,
And she's away to Carterhaugh
As fast as she can run.

When she came to Carterhaugh
Tam Lin was at the well,
And there she found his steed standing,
But away was himself.

According to Elideh's notes, this ballad was one of the best known, the story captivating its audience for centuries. The mortal woman, Janet, decides she loves Tam Lin, a faerie knight, and chooses to be romantic with him. They fall in love in the brief time they are together, and she becomes pregnant from their one-time tryst. She goes back to find him and tell him of her pregnancy, and he says that she must rescue him from the Faerie Queen.

Through a trial worthy of Shakespeare, Janet rescues Tam Lin from the Faerie Queen and they live happily ever after. Although it was an interesting story, Ailia was mostly focused on the place mentioned throughout the ballad: Carterhaugh.

Elideh, amongst other scholars, believed Carterhaugh to be a forest near Selkirk, nestled between the Ettrick and Yarrow rivers. As luck or fate would have it, Selkirk was only about twenty minutes from where they were staying in Melrose.

Ailia thought of her options. She decided since they were so close, she would insist they visit the forest before they started on Callum's journey. She had to know she had done everything she could to find her sister. Once Reed returned, she would tell him her plan and then get some much needed sleep. Although she had used very little magic, she felt completely exhausted. It had been a long couple of days.

REED

Reed took the steps up to the room two at a time, careful not to spill anything. The restaurant at the hotel was slammed for some reason, so it had taken forever. He finally made it to their room and felt relief wash through him seeing that Ailia was right where he had left her. Ailia was pouring over various books, but when he walked in, she glanced up and smiled. She moved the books off the bed and made room for him to sit with her as they ate, since the only other option would be to eat on the floor.

"That seemed to take longer than normal," said Ailia, a big chunk of bread already headed towards her mouth.

"It was busier than I've seen it."

"While you were gone, I think I decided what I want to do."

"Explain away, milady." Reed had decided it would be best to keep things as normal as possible. He didn't want things to change between them just because of this new connection.

Ailia laughed and swallowed a massive bite of bread. "There is a forest called Carterhaugh near Selkirk where a faerie story took place.

Since it's close by, I think we should tell Callum that we want to go see it before we start on whatever journey he has planned for us."

Reed nodded. "Okay. We can tell him in the morning." They ate in quiet contemplation, then Reed said, "I'm guessing I won't get you to reconsider accompanying us? I could fulfill the oath and then summon you when it's time to learn where the entrance is."

Ailia choked a bit on her soup as she laughed. "Summon me? For fuck's sake, Reed. You could just say that you would call me. I get that we are on a quest with faeries and magic, but come on." She continued to laugh and Reed found himself laughing along with her.

Reed raised his arms in surrender. "Okay I guess *summoning* you was a little heavy handed. Either way, you get my point. You don't have to come. It would put you in unnecessary danger."

Ailia looked at Reed, and reached over to gently grasp his chin. "I'm coming with you," she said softly, "and I know it is going to be dangerous, but if there's any chance we can find an entrance to Elflaine and get to my sister during this journey, I have to take it."

Reed pulled her hand to his lips and chastely kissed it. "I understand. If you were trapped in Elflaine, I would not rest until I found you," he said sincerely. "And you're definitely not my sister." He winked at her and released her hand, letting her get back to her meal.

Ailia smiled and tore off another chunk of bread, but Reed could tell she was still brooding over Elideh. "Ailia. We will find her. I'm sure of it." She nodded, and he changed the topic, wanting to give her a break from her worry.

After they finished eating and cleaning up, Ailia went to the bathroom to change. Reed sat in the chair by the window, grabbing a pillow to prop behind his head. Ailia came out of the bathroom and turned off the lights as she made her way to the bed. Thanks to the moon, there was enough light coming in through the window to still see.

After a couple of minutes of peaceful silence, Ailia turned over to look at Reed. "You don't have to sleep in that chair. I don't mind sharing the bed."

Reed looked back at her. "It's okay. I can sleep here, and I want you to be comfortable."

Ailia smiled. "You're a good man, Reed. I'm lucky to know you."

"I will always try to live up to that compliment," he said, the corners of his mouth tilting up. "Goodnight, Ailia."

"Goodnight, Reed."

She turned over, settling into the pillows. Reed waited until her breaths were deep and even before he relaxed into the chair. He hoped he could get some sleep. It had been a long, exhausting day, and he had a feeling this was just the beginning of a long, exhausting journey.

CHAPTER EIGHTEEN

There was the voice again. Calling to her. Taunting her. Threatening her.

She put her hands over her ears, but it didn't help. The voice was in her head.

Silent, practiced tears streamed down her cheeks, and she shook with fear. When would the voice stop?

Or when would it claim her?

She tried to think of anything beyond this cell, but the darkness consumed her.

The voice whispered to her of all the things it wanted from her—of the things it wanted to do to her. She had tried to stay strong, had tried not to let the voice get to her. But she started shaking violently, finally at the end of her rope, and let out a guttural scream that banished the voice.

She laid on her side, slowly rocking, tears flowing freely.

Desperately wishing to give in to the void surrounding her.

AILIA

"AILIA!" She heard her name from faraway, but couldn't stop rocking.

"AILIA, please!" That voice again. She knew that voice. But the despair still surrounded her.

All of a sudden, a heavy weight was on her, and she heard a piercing howl that shook her to her core.

Ailia's eyes snapped open. Panicked brown eyes met hers, and a massive paw rested on her chest. She looked around, trying to take in her surroundings.

There was Reed. It had been his voice calling to her. But what had woken her was the beast curled protectively around her body, nudging her with his wet nose. She looked at Storm, and he laid his giant head on her chest. Ailia rubbed her eyes only to find that they were wet.

"Reed," she said, her voice hoarse.

His hands cupped her face, and he buried his forehead in her hair. "Thank the goddess you're okay," he said, fear making his voice tremble.

"What happened?" Ailia said.

Reed looked at her, unwilling to let go, like he was afraid she would be taken back into whatever nightmare had held her captive. He sat down on the bed next to her and pulled her into his chest despite the warning growls from Storm on her other side. Reed took a couple of deep breaths and glanced over her once more.

"One minute we were both sleeping, and the next minute I was jerked awake by a howl coming from the street. After I woke up, I saw you thrashing in the bed. I kept trying to shake you, but you wouldn't wake up." Reed closed his eyes for a moment, as if he could banish the image he had conjured.

"By the time you started screaming, Storm was at our door, scratching furiously to get in. I still don't know how he got into the hotel, but I rushed to the door to let him in before he could break it down. He ran over to the bed and jumped onto it, almost as panicked as me. You stopped thrashing, but started rocking. I kept calling your name." He was running his hands through her hair as he spoke, continuing to pull her closer to him.

"You wouldn't wake up." He paused, running his shaking hand down his face as if reliving it was rekindling his panic. "Finally, Storm got right next to you and let out the most haunting sound I've ever heard. That's when you finally woke up."

Ailia settled closer into Reed and put a hand on Storm's head. The nightmare had felt... real. She had felt greater terror than she had ever known, and worse, complete despair. Reed began to stroke her hair again, sensing her tension. She blew out a breath. "Thank you. For bringing me out of it." Ailia closed her eyes, still feeling the tears she had cried on her eyelashes.

"What happened?" whispered Reed.

After gathering her thoughts, she said, "I've been having nightmares since Elideh disappeared. I wake up in cold sweats, shaking, not knowing where I am. Tonight I had one of the nightmares that keeps recurring. I was in a cell, surrounded by darkness. Normally it's just me in the cell, wishing I could get out, knowing I'm trapped. But tonight there was a voice." Ailia shivered and shut her eyes, trying to disperse the fear that was rising. Reed pulled her closer and continued stroking her hair. "The voice wanted something from me, but when it realized I could not or would not obey, it got angry. And started telling me all of the things it would do to me once it found me."

As hard as she had tried to keep the tears away, they silently started falling again. Because she knew it hadn't just been a dream. For a while, she had suspected that this particular nightmare was more of a vision. Of her sister. She prayed to whatever god was listening that it was a vision of an avoidable future, and not a peek into the present. Reed remained a steady presence, and Storm softly whimpered as she tried to let the fear and sadness wash out of her.

"We will find your sister, Ailia. And I will find a way for you to sleep without these nightmares plaguing you. I'm so sorry you've been dealing with this on your own. I wish you would have told me sooner." Ailia held onto him, knowing he spoke the truth. "I will help you banish the monsters," he whispered against her hair.

"Thank you, Reed," she murmured into his chest. And suddenly, as if all the strength had been drained from her, she was exhausted. She tried to tell Reed, but he just kept stroking her hair and said, "Sleep, Ailia. I will be right here." And it seemed like Storm understood, as he curled up closer to her, guarding her other side.

So Ailia slept.

REED

Reed's heart was still racing even after Ailia had fallen asleep. He had never felt such palpable fear. It wasn't just that Ailia had a nightmare. It was that while she was suffering, he couldn't reach her.

He had done everything to wake her up, and nothing had worked. Although he still didn't love the hound that was currently curled around her like a giant, monstrous cat, he was beyond thankful that Storm had busted in and woken her. He'd have to think about how Storm knew Ailia was in distress later. For now, he was just grateful she was safe and asleep. And he pleaded to the goddess to be with Ailia in her dreams and *keep* her safe.

He rested his head against the wall and closed his eyes. Reed didn't care what Ailia thought. Or what Callum, or Storm, or anyone else might think. This is how they were sleeping from now on. He knew he couldn't follow her in sleep, but at least he could be with her if she slipped into a nightmare again.

Hell, if Storm hadn't woken him up with that first howl, who knows how long it would have been before he noticed anything was amiss. Reed knew he would not be sleeping again that night, or perhaps any nights in the near future. First thing in the morning, he would call his mother to ask about a sleeping potion. He would not let Ailia endure these nightmares any longer than she already had.

Reed stared out the window from the bed, thinking about their journey ahead, and held Ailia, praying it would be enough to keep her demons away until morning.

CHAPTER NINETEEN

ELIDEH

Elideh blinked her eyes slowly, trying to see through the darkness. She knew it was pointless, but she tried anyway. She wasn't lucid often anymore.

Whatever they were feeding her was forcing her to sleep. And when she was awake, that voice tormented her. Maybe the drug-induced coma wasn't so bad.

She occasionally thought about her regrets, and she frequently thought about her sister, but mostly, she thought of escape.

She didn't know how long she had been trapped, but she knew she had to find a way out—especially now that she understood why she was able to find the faerie realm in the first place.

She hoped that her sister would not come searching for her. Unfortunately, she knew that Ailia would stop at nothing to find her—they were all each other had left.

If only she could get a message to her sister. If only she could—

CHAPTER TWENTY

AILIA

A ilia woke up to the steady sound of Reed's breathing and Storm's gentle snoring. She lifted her head from Reed's chest, trying not to disturb him. Briefly, she wondered how all three of them fit on the bed. It seemed like Storm was smaller than usual.

Although she tried to move as little as possible to sit up, Reed snapped his eyes open, obviously not asleep in the first place. At least she tried.

After Reed scanned her over, he stretched his arms above his head, yawning.

"Sorry I woke you up," Ailia said. She gently stroked Storm's fur, and she could have sworn Storm purred at her touch.

"It's okay, I wasn't asleep, just resting my eyes," Reed replied, smiling tentatively at her. Dark circles marred his face, and his normally healthy complexion looked sallow. "I'm glad you were able to get some rest."

He ran his fingers through her hair, then started gently tracing her face with his thumb. She closed her eyes, relaxing into his touch.

"The nightmares stayed away, then?" he asked.

"Mmhmm," Ailia mumbled.

"Good," Reed said, kissing her forehead.

He stood up, and Ailia immediately missed his presence. He walked over to the window, stretching, but stopped and said, "Shit, what time is it?"

"I have no idea," said Ailia as she searched for her phone. "It's almost noon. We were supposed to meet Callum hours ago. We need to leave."

Ailia rushed to the bathroom, and after splashing water on her face, she got dressed. She definitely did not look well-rested, the nightmare taking its toll on her. Although she had fallen back asleep, she did not rest peacefully. She hadn't wanted to worry Reed, but the terrors from her nightmare had lingered. At least she hadn't been dragged back into that horrible room with the haunting voice.

Once they were both ready, they headed out to Reed's car to meet Callum. Breakfast would have to wait. She hoped their tardiness wouldn't set a bad tone for the rest of the day. She needed Callum to be willing to work with them.

Callum

Callum had been waiting since sunrise for the witch and the girl. Now, it was well past morning, and approaching the afternoon. He was already in a bad mood because of the spotty sleep he'd had. Something had woken him in the middle of the night, and he hadn't been able to go back to sleep. If they didn't show up in the next ten minutes, he was going to have to go into the town to find them. Which he really did not want to do.

He paced around the clearing, continuously assessing his surroundings out of habit. Callum always felt more in control in nature. Animals were predictable. Mortals were not.

He heard the distant slam of car doors. He could hear them arguing from a mile away. Although he couldn't make out every word, he caught pieces of the fight. The girl was mad about the witch being an "overbearing babysitter," and the witch was mad that the girl was not taking his concerns more seriously.

Probably nothing, but worth monitoring. He whistled for Torneach, and to his complete frustration, Torneach did not come to him. Callum growled at the disobedience from his beast, and from the general impatience of waiting on these two all morning.

Finally, they made their way into the clearing. Callum had been right in his assessment. Both the girl and the witch looked tense, the girl fidgeting with her long braid, and the witch glancing nervously at her every couple of steps. He couldn't help but let out a low chuckle at their spat. At that, the witch looked at him, frowning, and took a step closer to the girl. The girl rolled her eyes.

"Nice of you to finally show up," Callum said as he strode towards them. But as he got closer, he noticed the dark circles under the girl's eyes and the way that Torneach was at her side, very much on guard.

Callum stopped and crossed his arms. Frowning, he said, "What happened?"

The girl and the witch glanced at each other and at the same time, they both said, "Nothing."

Callum had to stop himself from rolling his eyes. "Tell me what happened. I haven't seen Torneach act as a guard for anyone but me. And I could hear you arguing as soon as you got out of your car."

The girl furrowed her brow. "Who is Torneach?"

"My traitorous hound that has been following you around like a love-sick puppy," said Callum.

"Oh, you mean Storm?" As soon as the girl said "Storm," Torneach looked up at her, waiting for a command.

Callum stared at her. "You named him? And he responds to it?"

"Yes," she said slowly, petting Torneach—*Storm*—on his head. "Is that a problem?"

This, Callum was not expecting. Recovering quickly, he demanded, "Tell me what happened. Now."

The witch tensed and looked like he was about to punch Callum in the face, which wouldn't bother Callum in the slightest. It would be a relief to release some of the frustration that had been building since his sleepless night. The girl put her hand on the witch's arm, and although he remained tense, he seemed to back down. He looked to her, letting her decide how to answer.

Finally, after assessing Callum for several seconds, she had made her decision.

"I had a nightmare last night. When Reed tried to wake me up, he couldn't. Somehow, Storm sensed my distress, came barging into our hotel room, and was able to wake me. We are arguing because Reed decided to call his mother and ask for a sleeping potion." At that, she shot a glare in the witch's direction. "I've dealt with vivid nightmares my entire life and have had *that* particular nightmare for weeks. If I wanted something to help me sleep, I would have asked." The girl crossed her arms in defiance, and Callum decided that he liked this side of her.

He wondered for a heartbeat if he had somehow been jarred from his own sleep because of this girl's nightmare, but quickly dismissed the idea. Torneach's reaction, on the other hand, was interesting.

"Sounds to me like the girl has made her decision, witch. If she wants to suffer through nightmares, that's her choice." Callum could tell the witch was fuming, but kept going. "Now that we have lost several hours to this... ordeal... we need to get moving—"

"Actually," the girl interrupted, "we need to do something before we start on your journey."

Trying to hide his surprise that she had not only interrupted him, but had also made such a request, he raised his eyebrows. "And what would that be, princess?"

The girl bristled at his tone. "I want to go to Carterhaugh. It's a forest not far from here."

Callum knew of Carterhaugh. And didn't particularly want to go there. After the faerie knight Tam Lin had tricked his way out of the Faerie Queen's service, that forest had been cursed.

"I don't think that's a good idea," he told the girl, ignoring the witch completely. "That forest has been home to insidious beasts for a while now, and I'd rather not get eaten before I complete my task."

The girl sighed, and Callum couldn't tell if it was from exhaustion or frustration. "Well then you will have to wait for us to return. I'm going to the forest. I thought we could save time by leaving from there, but if we need to backtrack in order to meet you here, we can." At that, she turned around and started to walk away.

This girl was unbelievable.

"Not many would be daft enough to turn their backs to me, much less tell me what to do," said Callum calmly.

The girl paused, looking over her shoulder, assessing him. "You're not as scary as you look. Are you joining us or not?"

The witch glanced at Callum, but shrugged his shoulders and turned to follow the girl, Torneach already by her side. Callum sighed deeply, very unhappy at the way the day was unfolding.

"I will accompany you. Even with your witch and my beast, you will need an extra sword if you encounter any of the creatures that dwell in that forest. And I need your witch alive to help me." Although he was reluctant to go into the cursed forest, Carterhaugh was a stone's throw from the alleged location of one of the first items he was seeking.

Dragons were not native to Scotland, but there had been a few that had found their way to the country over time. The Linton Dragon, as it was known, was considered to be the last dragon of Scotland, and after it was slain in the 12th century, it was said that its teeth were buried in a secret passage under the dragon slayer's castle.

A single tooth from this dragon was one of the artifacts he needed to collect for the Faerie Queen. He wouldn't tell the girl that her plans actually suited him, or that he had planned on going near Carterhaugh first anyway. It was better to keep them on their toes.

The girl looked over her shoulder at him, her expression weary. "As you wish." She continued to walk away, and he couldn't help but wonder what he had gotten himself into.

CHAPTER TWENTY-ONE

AILIA

Ailia was a little surprised that Callum agreed to go with them. She had expected more of a fight. All that told her was that somehow, this trip to Carterhaugh served his purposes. Which she didn't mind, as long as she was able to see if there was an entrance in the forest.

Her conversation with Reed about needing to train if she wanted a fighting chance to rescue Elideh was replaying in her head. Especially after that dream. She knew Elideh was suffering and that there was someone actively looking to harm her. Her training was going to have to be fast and efficient.

In fact, she wondered if Callum would train her how to fight. Although she was pretty fit, she definitely was not capable of holding her own in hand-to-hand combat—she didn't even think she would come out on top in a bar fight.

But she needed to start her magic training immediately. Since Reed was apparently very skilled at wielding earth magic, it made sense to start there. She was itching to learn more.

Ailia and Reed had not spoken much since getting back to the hotel to pack their things. Their argument earlier had not ended well, especially since Callum had technically sided with her. Reed's shoulders were tense, and he hadn't stopped frowning since they left the forest. She missed the more carefree, quick-witted, Reed.

She decided that the way he was acting really wasn't his fault. He was just trying to look out for her. "Reed, I'm sorry about earlier. I wasn't trying to get in a fight about the sleeping potion. As strange as this sounds, I don't want to sever the connection I have with my sister. Even if it pulls me into nightmares."

Reed stopped packing and looked over at her. "You don't get it, Ailia. This isn't about you getting sleep, although I should remind you that if you don't get enough sleep, it's going to be harder for your magic to replenish." He ran his hands through his hair, which was unfortunately becoming a nervous habit.

"I was terrified. You were stuck in a nightmare—crying, screaming, and shaking. Whatever has changed between us is driving me to protect you. I couldn't do anything to help you, and it scared the shit out of me." His shoulders slumped as if the weight he'd been carrying was too heavy.

Ailia walked over to him and gently grasped his shoulders. "Reed. You cannot protect me from everything. And that's okay. What I need right now is a mentor and a friend. So tell whatever it is that makes you want to shield me to back off. Let's focus on looking for an entrance to Elflaine and training my magic."

Reed nodded, seeming to mull over everything she'd said. "Okay. I can do that." He gave her a soft smile. "Let's finish packing so we can head out. Although I don't mind keeping Callum waiting, we probably shouldn't piss him off more than we absolutely need to." Reed winked at her like they were part of some sort of conspiracy.

Ailia laughed. "Agreed. He's grumpy enough as it is."

Maybe things wouldn't go back to the way they were, but Ailia felt confident that they could navigate these new circumstances together.

REED

Reed wasn't sure where they were supposed to meet Callum, but it looked like Ailia was a step ahead of him. She had seemed different after last night—more focused. Older, somehow. As if the nightmare had hardened her. Although he wished she could stay as she was, he knew what this world was like, and knew there was no keeping her from it.

Storm was trailing Ailia as usual, and she turned to him. "Storm, I need you to find Callum and lead him to Carterhaugh. Find me when you get there."

Although Reed had become more accustomed to Ailia's interactions with Storm, he still cursed softly when Storm nodded his giant head, gave Ailia a gentle lick on her cheek, and disappeared. Reed wondered if Callum could communicate with Storm the way Ailia could. He guessed he would get his answer if Callum managed to find them in Carterhaugh.

After getting in the car and setting their destination in his navigation app, they headed to the supposedly cursed forest, if they were to believe Callum.

As if she had read his mind, Ailia said, "Do you think the forest is actually cursed? Or was that just Callum's way of trying to convince us not to go?"

"It could be cursed," said Reed truthfully. "There are a lot of beasts that roam the forests in Scotland—even more that dwell in the waters. Hopefully we won't run into any of them. Although we do have a faerie hound, a fae, a witch, and whatever you are, so maybe that will keep them away." Reed winked at her, and Ailia smiled back.

"That sounds like a bad joke. 'A faerie, a hound, and a witch walk into a bar...'" They both erupted in laughter, even though it was only a little funny.

"Wow, Ails," said Reed, still chuckling, "I really needed that. Thank you."

Ailia's eyes twinkled as she said, "Anything for my noble knight."

Reed laughed again, feeling lighter than he had in days. It was another pretty day, and he wished the drive was a bit longer. He knew as soon as they got out of the car, their journey would not be the same. With Callum accompanying them for the foreseeable future, he would need to keep his temper in check. Ailia said she needed a mentor and a friend. He would give her that. Even if it meant being nice to the faerie.

AILIA

Looking out the window of Reed's car at the beautiful, green hills that were slowly becoming denser the closer they got to the forest in Carterhaugh, Ailia suddenly realized something. She snapped her head to Reed and said, "Where are we going to sleep?"

"I hadn't really thought of that." Reed furrowed his brow. "How are we both so bad at this?"

"Seriously. You'd think after I failed to book us rooms the first time around, we wouldn't make the same mistake again." Ailia looked back out the window, thinking through their options, before realizing something else.

"Wait," Ailia said slowly, "Where will Callum stay? When we start whatever journey he is going to drag us on? Even tonight, I don't think there are many places to stay near the forest, and it's already getting late. I don't want to keep wasting time, though, staying in places longer than we need to." Sometimes Ailia's verbal processing got her thoughts jumbled, but Reed seemed to follow.

"I agree. I don't want to waste time when we could either be training or fulfilling this damn oath. I guess we could camp out? In the forest?"

Ailia wasn't what she would call a "girly girl," but she couldn't help her repulsed reaction to Reed's suggestion. He glanced over at her and grinned at the face she was making.

"What, the noble lady can't sleep in a tent?" he teased.

Trying not to look as offended or put off as she felt, she said, "I can sleep in a tent. It's just that... I like showers. And don't like bugs." She paused, then said a little triumphantly, "Plus, we don't have a tent."

"Good point," said Reed and she was suddenly being thrown to the side of the car as Reed quickly swerved into a U-turn.

"What are you doing!" Ailia shouted at him, grasping onto the handle above the door.

"Getting a tent. We just passed a small town, and I would bet they have some sort of supply store. I wouldn't want my fair lady to have to sleep out in the wilderness under the stars with all the bugs." He turned to her with a smirk on his handsome face.

Arms crossed, looking anywhere but at Reed, she was very unhappy at this turn of events. She really did not like the idea of sleeping on the ground with the bugs, especially in the dark where she wouldn't be able to see them. Elideh would be giving her so much shit right now, and would be thrilled at the prospect of sleeping under the stars.

She simmered in the passenger seat before deciding that this was truly the best option. After huffing out a breath and ignoring the laugh that Reed was trying to hide, she said, "Fine. We will get a tent. I just don't want to make a habit of it."

"As you wish," said Reed with a mock bow of his head.

Ailia rolled her eyes. "You know, not all of us are a hundred years old and used to life without modern amenities."

Reed gaped at her. "I thought you were a historian! I was born in the late 1800s. Most public places had indoor plumbing by then, and by the early 1900s almost all homes had it. For fuck's sake, Ailia, did you think I grew up in the dark ages?"

Still annoyed, but slightly amused, Ailia said with a smirk, "Clearly your old age is making you grumpy."

Reed shook his head, but a smile started to tug at his pretty mouth as he muttered something about her being sassy.

REED

After buying a tent, Reed navigated them back to the path that would take them to the woods. He was trying, but failing, to keep from snickering at Ailia, which only served to sour her mood further.

It seemed the prospect of "roughing it" had not been part of her plans, but he knew she would move past it fairly quickly. If camping led them one step closer to Elideh, he knew Ailia would take it. Reed was actually looking forward to spending some time in nature. Since he wielded earth magic, he always recharged quicker and grew stronger when he was in his element.

"You know, Ailia, this will actually be good for our training. Your earth magic will become more powerful the more time we spend connected to the element. You'll see." Ailia gave him an unamused, side-eyed glance.

Okay then. Not going to be easy to convince. Changing the subject, Reed said, "We are almost to the forest. Any thoughts about where we should go once we get there?"

Ailia huffed a deep breath, obviously still annoyed. "Not really, to be honest. According to the ballad, Tam Lin would approach maidens that entered the woods and demand some sort of payment. Usually a treasure, but frequently their 'maidenhood.'"

Reed slammed on the brakes—again—eliciting a shout from Ailia. "What the fuck, Reed!"

"I'm sorry, but it sounded to me like you just suggested you would be bait for this faerie." He spoke calmly, but his tone hinted at violence.

Gaping, Ailia stared at Reed in complete shock. "Are you serious? I'm not planning on offering up my maidenhood, or anything else for that matter, to a faerie in the woods." Reed realized he may have overreacted. She squeezed his arm, but still looked pretty shocked at what he had suggested.

"Seriously, Reed, you can calm down. I thought you said you were familiar with the ballad. At the end of the ballad, a mortal woman rescues Tam Lin from his service to the Faerie Queen." Ailia looked over at him. "Although she really pisses the queen off, the mortal woman and Tam Lin live happily ever after. I don't think Tam Lin still resides in these woods."

Reed stared at her and then ran his hands through his hair. "I swear to the gods, Ailia. You are going to give me a heart attack." He continued driving, swearing quietly under his breath. Overreaction or not, he knew she was desperate to get to her sister and wouldn't put it past her to do something self-sacrificial.

"There are two places mentioned in the ballad," said Ailia. "A well where the mortal meets up with Tam Lin, and a place called Miles Cross where the woman encounters the faerie riders and rescues Tam Lin. There is a well, supposedly, hidden in the moss and ferns. No one can agree on the location of Miles Cross, but most scholars think it could be referring to a bridge that is near the well. We find the bridge, we find the well. And that is where we can start."

"Sounds like you have *some* idea of where to go, then," Reed said, trying to bring his voice back to a casual lilt.

"I have no idea where the bridge is, though, and I'm assuming if it's that ancient, we will need to find it on foot."

"That, we can do. We are close enough to the woods that we can find somewhere to park and then walk the rest of the way," said Reed, pulling over to find a place to park for the night.

Ailia sighed reluctantly, but nodded her head and squared her shoulders. Reed was barely suppressing a laugh. "You know we aren't going into battle or anything."

Ailia rolled her eyes. "Let's just go. If this brings us a step closer to finding Elideh, I can get past the bugs."

They got out of the car, and Reed shouldered his backpack along with the tent. He tried to take Ailia's backpack as well, but she gave him a look that said 'don't test me,' so he relented. And they headed into the woods.

CHAPTER TWENTY-TWO

AILIA

Apparently things were easier to find when you had a skilled witch that could track with his magic.

"How do you know where to go?" Ailia asked after the third time Reed paused and redirected them.

"The stones, roots, earth—all of it is connected. So I can reach out with my magic and sense where there are potential man-made structures."

Reed held a branch back for Ailia as they ducked through the trees.

"Can you show me?"

Reed turned to her and grinned. "Of course, but let's find the bridge first. Since you're new to magic, it will be difficult to engage with the element and move through the woods at the same time."

Ailia smiled, and happily followed Reed on whatever path he had found.

It had been about half an hour of what felt like wandering when they found the bridge. The stones forming the bridge were covered in moss, and several were missing. Vines had twisted around spindly, ornamental rocks that seemed to reach out of the walls of the bridge towards the sky.

After inspecting it to make sure it was safe, and Reed making so many jokes about trolls that Ailia was ready to push him off of it, they decided to set up their tent in a clearing close by since the sun was starting to set.

The sky was streaked with golds, purples, and soft pinks, the wispy clouds lazily floating along, ushering in the stars. Ailia thanked whatever god had been watching over them lately for the mostly clear skies and lack of rain.

Reed set up the tent with ease and presented it to Ailia with a ridiculous flourish of his arms. "Your humble castle, milady." Ailia laughed and peeked inside. It actually wasn't bad. Tiny, but not bad.

"You think Callum is ever going to show up?" Ailia asked Reed.

"Shh don't say his name, it might summon him," answered Reed in a conspirator's whisper. Ailia giggled and nodded like they were sharing a secret.

Reed opened his backpack and pulled out a loaf of bread, some cheese, and a couple of apples. Ailia couldn't help but laugh at the absurdity of this whole situation. She was camping out. In an enchanted faerie forest. With a witch. Eating bread and cheese.

It was like some sort of satirical version of the books her sister liked to read. The witch in question looked at her in confusion and offered her some bread. She gladly took it and sat next to him. She'd just have to accept this version of her life for the time being.

"It looks like we will still have some sunlight for at least another hour," mused Ailia. "How about we try to train a bit?"

"Okay," said Reed eagerly. "Let me think about where we should start. It's been over a hundred years since I came into my own magic."

Ailia quietly ate her bread and let Reed come up with a lesson plan, wondering what it would be like to live for that long and guessing that she might find out.

"Let's start by trying to wield it again. The most important thing you can learn right now is how to quickly connect to the earth and let that connection become a part of you. The more intuitive that becomes, the easier it's going to be to command the magic."

Ailia nodded and started unlacing her boots so that she could ground her feet. She noticed that Reed was not taking his shoes off, so she paused. "Should I not take off my boots?"

"You should," he said, nodding his head. "I don't need to since I have been wielding magic for so long. Eventually, you won't need direct contact and so much focus to call it up. But for beginners, it makes it easier."

She finished unlacing her boots and grounded her feet and hands. Then, she closed her eyes.

Reed's voice washed over her. "Good, now try to connect to the earth like you did last time. However you envisioned it. But this time, try to be more aware of the energy itself and how you feel about it. Is it a warm feeling, like coming home? Is it a calming feeling, like meditating? Is it a chaotic feeling, but maybe a little exciting? Once you determine your connection, lean into it. And let it in."

Ailia tried to clear her mind and focus on the earth like she did before. Just like the first time, she envisioned her magic like rays of light, connecting with the energy of the earth. She opened her eyes and, yet again, the earth was moving around her in gentle swirls. Ailia grinned, but then closed her eyes, trying to focus on the way the energy felt.

The earth felt like an extension of her hands and feet—solid, reliable, unyielding. Her magic seemed to caress the earth and burrow into it, trusting it wholly. In fact, the more she thought about it, she realized that it felt like Reed. She felt comfortable and safe.

She tried reaching out with her magic, pushing deeper into the ground, connecting to the roots of trees, finding tunnels created by small creatures. She kept pushing farther out, seeing how far she could go.

Suddenly, she felt vibrations in the earth. Her magic was not alarmed by whatever presence caused these tremors, but seemed to recognize it? She reeled her magic back into herself and opened her eyes. Before she could say anything, Reed was already standing and tense. "I felt it too," he said quietly.

Ailia stood as well, swaying slightly from the magic she had wielded. Reed was instantly there, steadying her. "I think we are safe. My magic did not seem threatened by whatever—or whomever—it is," she whispered.

Reed glanced at her before resuming his focus on the trees surrounding them. Just when Ailia thought whatever creature it was had lost interest in them, Storm came bounding through the woods, nearly knocking Ailia on her ass as he collided with her, and smothered her with kisses.

"Get. Off. Of. Her. You demented beast." Reed was unsuccessfully trying to pull Storm off of Ailia, but Storm was not moving. He did, however, finally sit at her side, giving Reed a smug look. Ailia choked out a laugh at the power struggle between the two of them, and tried to wipe off her slobbery arms and face. Callum appeared through the trees shortly after Storm's arrival.

"You need to keep your creature on a lead. He tackled Ailia," Reed demanded, fuming.

Callum merely glanced between the two of them, his eyes more green than blue at the moment, before plopping down on the ground by the tent and grabbing an apple. "He is a wild faerie hound, witch. Normally he obeys me, but he won't listen when it comes to her." He shrugged his shoulders as if to say he had come to terms with Storm's behavior and could care less about Reed's concerns.

Callum seemed even more imposing than earlier, his hulking figure taking up more space than any mortal man ever could. He was dressed differently, in various shades of gray—simple pants, a loose-fitting tunic, and a dark leather belt adorned with several weapons. He unstrapped the sword from his back but left the daggers in place around his waist.

Trying to break the tension, Ailia spoke up. "Nice of you to join us, Callum. And just in time to eat our food."

"Get used to sharing, princess. We are going to be doing a lot of that on this journey." The wicked glint in his eye had her shifting uncomfortably on her feet and had Reed taking a step in front of her.

"Let me make one thing very clear, Callum," said Reed, crossing his arms. "I do not share."

Ailia had to stop herself from gaping at Reed. Was he seriously staking his territory? Before she could intervene, Callum rolled his eyes and continued as if Reed hadn't spoken at all.

"I am willing to spend two nights in this forest. That's it. Then we will move on," Callum ordered lazily. He unrolled a sleeping mat from his pack and laid it next to where he was sitting. She guessed he wouldn't be using a tent.

Ailia bristled at Callum's tone but decided someone needed to be level-headed, and it certainly wasn't going to be Reed, judging by the tension that was radiating off of him. Plus, she needed something from Callum, and all of her dealings with Elideh had taught her that sometimes it was best to be the mediator. "Two nights should be enough."

Callum raised an eyebrow at her response. He must have expected her to argue.

"I have a request of my own while we are demanding things," Ailia said sweetly. Callum rolled his eyes and Reed looked over at her with a worried expression on his face. "I want you to train me. To fight. Reed is training me in magic, but I want you to train me with weapons." Callum and Reed were both staring at her as if she had suddenly grown horns.

Reed crossed his arms. "Absolutely not."

Then, Callum burst out laughing.

She glared at both of them. "Reed, this is *not* your decision. And what is so funny about me wanting to be able to protect myself?"

Still chuckling, Callum said, "Seriously? You want me to train you to fight? Look at you. You're tiny. It would take weeks just to build up your strength to hold a sword, much less wield it." Reed, to her utter annoyance, was nodding his head in agreement with Callum.

At that, Ailia clenched her fists. She stalked over to Callum before Reed could stop her and crouched down to the ground so that their eyes were level. "If it is building my strength to start with, fine. But you will teach me how to fight. Just because I'm smaller than you doesn't mean I have to be weaker." Then she stood up and snatched her water bottle out of her backpack, trying to hide her shaking hands. She was sick of everyone trying to protect her—that's all Elideh had done growing up. She would be the agent of her own fate, and she would not let these boys tell her what to do.

"I'm going to get water, and when I come back, I don't want to hear one word about how *you* won't train me," she pointed at Callum, "or how *you* won't let me train with him," she pointed at Reed.

At that, she stalked off to the river, Storm clearly choosing a side and obediently following her. The corner of her mouth turned up at Storm's presence, knowing it would annoy both Callum and Reed, albeit for different reasons.

She sat by the stream, needing a break from her infuriating company. She guessed they got the message because no one came after her. Ailia wasn't typically one to lash out, but she was sick of letting life happen to her. Elideh had been telling her for years that she needed to stand up for herself more often, so here she was, making her stand.

Storm laid down in the long, soft grass at her side and put his head on her knee. She absentmindedly stroked his fur as she looked out at the peaceful river, water happily flowing over rocks, creating bejeweled shades of blue.

Ailia decided to focus on her magic again. She still had her shoes off from before, so she dipped her feet in the refreshing water, touching the smooth stones at the bottom of the river to ground her. She closed her eyes and pictured her tendrils of energy snaking into the bed of the stream. She felt the connection right away, much quicker than she had before, and opened her eyes.

She must be seeing things. Tiny spheres of water were rising up out of the river, suspended in mid-air. Storm was staring at them, ears perked.

Holy. Shit.

She was wielding water.

She gasped, and the water droplets fell, splashing her legs as they hit the surface. This wasn't supposed to be possible. She hadn't even been trying to connect to water. Then again, her feet were in the river. And it felt more natural than either time she tried to summon earth or fire.

Heart racing, she tried again. Maybe it was a fluke. She dipped her fingertips into the river and made herself aware of the feeling of the silky, crisp water on her skin. Without closing her eyes, she cupped her hands and lifted her fingers up, focusing on bringing the water up with her. And sure enough, the water followed, looking like icicles gently clinging to each of her finger tips.

Ailia stared at the water, glistening in the light. She curled her fingers inward, willing the water to move to her palms. It pooled into perfect spheres in each of her hands.

This felt so natural. She wished she could stay by the stream and experiment with the element. She let the water fall from her hands and watched as it elegantly curled back into the stream without even making a splash.

She stood up, about to sprint back to tell Reed, but she hesitated. She knew she could trust Reed, but what if Callum found out? If wielding three elements was supposed to be impossible, there was clearly more to her bloodline than even Elideh knew. Maybe she should keep this to herself.

Ailia tried to push the adrenaline down before heading back to their campsite. She didn't know if the fae, or witches for that matter, could sense emotions, and she didn't want to raise any suspicions.

After her breaths had calmed to a normal rhythm, she started to head back to the campsite, taking a sip out of her water bottle as she went. Maybe she could find some excuses to be alone so she could explore her abilities.

She still hadn't really thought about that blast of energy that had erupted from her to save Reed. And now this? Three elements? If this was a research question, she would be able to approach it with all the habits and skills she had developed over the past six years. But she knew their time was precious and that she was going to have to figure this out as they went.

Reed and Callum had built a fire while she was gone, which she was thankful for since she was a bit wet, and it was starting to cool down now that the sun was truly setting. She sat on the mossy ground by the fire, Storm laying beside her once more. Reed kept casting nervous glances her way, but Callum was outright scowling at her. She met his stare and said as sweetly as she could, "Yes?"

"People don't tell me what to do, and I am not yours to command." Ailia didn't say anything, but maintained eye contact. "But if you're willing to put in the work, I will teach you how to fight. My way. That is my offer."

"Agreed," said Ailia, nodding her head once, trying to keep the surprise from her face. Reed looked like he was going to interrupt but stopped himself at the look Ailia threw at him. "I want to start immediately."

"Very well, hope you're a morning person," Callum said with a wicked grin.

Ailia grinned right back.

CHAPTER TWENTY-THREE

REED

It looked like Callum was just going to sleep on the ground under the stars with no shelter. Reed didn't really care, and if he was being honest with himself, he was glad to have an extra body looking out for potential dangers. Not that he would ever tell Callum that.

After night had truly settled over the forest, and there was nothing but starlight left to see by, Reed finally convinced Ailia to go to bed. He opened the tent flap for Ailia to go inside, but before he could follow her in, Storm shoved in front of him and sat on the second sleeping mat.

"Bloody hell. You are not sleeping in here," said Reed, annoyed that he was talking to an overgrown dog. Storm simply looked Reed straight in the eye, spun in a circle, and laid down.

Ailia laughed. "I can sleep outside."

"Absolutely not. You are sleeping in the tent."

"Are you sure? I don't mind," said Ailia, her voice teasing.

"Oh please, you and I both know that you don't want to sleep in the wild where there are no barriers to bugs. Plus, there is no way I would leave you out there by yourself with Callum. Just get inside and go to sleep." Reed knew that either way, he probably wouldn't sleep.

"If you say so."

Reed glared at Storm once more, but Storm snuggled deeper into the blanket.

Reed shook his head as he zipped up the tent. If Ailia had more nightmares, he would hear her. Plus, it seemed like Storm was playing bodyguard, so he would have to trust the beast.

He turned around to see Callum lounging on his back, arms crossed under his head, and eyes shut. "Torneach wouldn't let you in the tent?"

"Shut up," said Reed, kneading his brow.

Callum chuckled quietly. "Guess it's just you and me then, witch."

Reed, having no interest in late-night pillow talk with this irritating male, laid down on the soft ground close to the tent and stared up at the stars.

"We could sleep in shifts," suggested Callum from the other side of the dying fire.

"I probably won't sleep anyway," said Reed firmly.

Callum shrugged. "Whatever you say, witch. But you won't be any use to the girl if you're exhausted."

Reed let out a frustrated sigh. "Fine," he gritted out. "We will sleep in shifts. You first."

Callum didn't respond, but after a couple of minutes, Reed heard soft snoring coming from Callum's direction. He had to admire how quickly the fae male could fall asleep. Then again, if he was a warrior, which Reed suspected he was, he imagined his training included getting sleep when he could afford it.

Reed turned his head towards the tent, trying to listen for signs that Ailia was asleep. He sent his magic through the earth to find her and released a sigh of relief when he felt the steady rise and fall of her chest against the ground. He spooled the magic back into himself, noting that Callum was unfortunately right. Since he hadn't slept the night before, he was feeling the strain on his magic. He guessed he would wait a couple of hours, then wake Callum. And try to get some sleep.

CALLUM

Callum had decided he was going to sleep for exactly one hour. He didn't need any more rest than that. When he woke up, he could sense the unsettled, anxious energy coming from the witch.

Although he hated to admit it, he did admire the witch's willingness to defend the girl. Not many were prepared to square off against Callum, so it was rare to find someone he might respect. He didn't think that was what he felt towards the witch, but at the very least, Callum wasn't disgusted by this male. And might even be able to work with him. Probably.

He loudly yawned, indicating that he was awake. "I will take my watch, now. Rest so you aren't completely useless tomorrow."

The witch didn't say a word, but simply rolled over on his side and faced the tent.

So moody.

Callum waited until he was sure the witch was asleep before silently, effortlessly, slipping into the night, becoming the darkness itself.

Before finding his new travel companions in the woods yesterday, Callum had stopped by the site of Linton Tower to scout out the area, and to see how difficult it would be to search for the underground tunnels that allegedly existed under the knoll. It didn't matter that the tower had been destroyed in the 1500s, all he needed was one of the teeth that had never been recovered, and was hopefully still buried in the ground. Luckily, the witch had earth magic.

Invisible to the mortals, he had also visited the nearby kirk to see the Somervail Stone, needing to confirm the legendary details of the dragon that had once ruled the area. Indeed, the stone depicted the slaying of the dragon, but also revealed the whispered part of this particular myth. There were, in fact, *two* dragons engraved on the stone, even though the legend only mentioned the slaying of one. Which was why Callum needed to sneak away tonight.

Although Callum had not encountered any dragons in his long, immortal life, he knew all of the stories about the ancient creatures. The remaining, forgotten Linton dragon was most likely a shadow dragon. They were reclusive and kept to their caves, preferring the cover of night. However, they jealously guarded their treasure and were known to hold grudges. Callum was particularly uneasy about this last detail, since he didn't think the dragon would take kindly to its kin dying at the hands of man.

Dragons were also notoriously brilliant. Callum had briefly considered asking the dragon for the tooth, but being highly intelligent didn't necessarily mean it would be reasonable, and he didn't have a death wish. Hopefully they would be able to take it without catching its attention. It wasn't a great plan, but he had to start somewhere.

Maybe it was fortuitous that they were in these woods. From what Callum had seen at the site of Linton Tower, there were no caves nearby. This forest, however, with its lingering magic, would be the perfect place for a dragon to remain hidden. He just needed to find a cave. And hope the dragon was asleep.

Callum had already decided that in case the dragon was nearby, it would be wiser to search for the cave in a different body, so he took his favorite form, a massive Highland stag. He silently and swiftly made his way through the ancient woods, sensing everything around him thanks to his current form's instincts and his own fae gifts.

The forest itself seemed quiet. He heard an owl hooting in the distance and occasionally felt the stirring of small creatures scurrying under leaves and fallen branches. The stars were bright, illuminating the stream that wove in and out of his path.

So far, no signs of a dragon. He circled back to the campsite, saw that the witch was still asleep, and crossed the bridge. After meandering through the trees, he finally came to a small clearing. And there, at the base of a hill, hidden beneath the brush, was a cave. He padded towards it carefully, and got close enough to see the entrance when he froze, every cell in his body on high alert. He was not alone.

He could not see the dragon, but he sensed its presence nearby—its ancient, strange magic drawing him to it, and simultaneously telling him to flee hard and fast. Its attention was focused on him from whatever shadows it was hiding in.

Callum didn't know if the dragon would be able to tell that he was not simply a stag wandering through the forest, so he slowly, lazily turned away from the cave and bowed his head to the ground, nosing the lush grass growing there. He took small steps and eventually felt the powerful presence turn its attention from him. He didn't dare run, worried it would cause the predator to take chase. So he kept his slow, wandering pace, trying to steady his racing heart.

Once he was sure the dragon was gone, he started moving more quickly away from the cave. Callum had been alive a long time and had faced many terrors, but the power that had radiated from that creature had truly startled him. Although he didn't particularly like the witch, he didn't dare go back to the campsite, not willing to lead the dragon to his companions. So he meandered through the woods, staying aware of his surroundings.

After an hour of backtracking and taking various paths through the trees, he finally shifted back into his fae form and made his way back to the campsite. He needed to rest. The adrenaline from the near miss of encountering a dragon hadn't left his system, and shifting to different forms for any length of time was always tiring. He was stealthily walking towards the fire when he paused, noticing the witch standing in front of the tent, glaring at him.

Ah, fuck. He really didn't want to explain where he had gone. But he guessed he would have to tell them either way if he wanted their help. Hopefully the witch wouldn't be too angry at him for abandoning his watch. Callum hadn't planned on being gone that long, and he felt a brief wave of guilt before casting it aside. He walked towards the witch, prepared to share some of his secrets.

CHAPTER TWENTY-FOUR

REED

To say Reed was angry was a massive understatement. He hadn't been asleep long when he felt something stir in the earth around him. Reed had sat up, bleary eyed, looking to where Callum had been laying. Except Callum wasn't there.

Instantly awake and alert, he reached out to the earth, trying to figure out what had woken him in the first place. There was some sort of ancient power thrumming through distant trees, the forest itself holding its breath.

Reed had unzipped the tent flap and peered inside to make sure Ailia was still safe, then started gathering small twigs and branches to restart the fire that had been reduced to embers. If there was something lurking out there that made the forest pause, he would not be caught in the dark.

After stoking the fire, he had reached out again with his magic, trying to sense what had caused the disturbance. It seemed that whatever threat had emerged was once again hidden, because the forest was at peace again. He took a deep breath, trusting what his magic was telling him.

That relief was short lived, however, and was replaced with irritation and worry at Callum's disappearance. The presence he had sensed was definitely *not* fae—it was much more ancient and complex. Had Callum been drawn away by that same force? Or had he caused the force to emerge? He knew he had been right not to trust the male.

He had been simmering for over an hour before Callum finally returned. Although Reed hadn't known Callum long, he could tell there was something more rigid in his posture. Callum paused but then headed straight for Reed, his expression hard. Reed crossed his arms and braced himself, hoping Callum had a good excuse for leaving them so vulnerable. He wasn't as worried about himself, but Ailia had been completely exposed to potential threats. Reed had learned that sometimes silence was the best weapon, so he waited for Callum to speak first.

"I'm sorry. For leaving without waking you," said Callum. "I was gone longer than I expected."

"You shouldn't have left in the first place," Reed snapped. "And next time, maybe tell us there is potentially a dangerous, mythical creature waiting for us."

"You're right. I won't do it again, and I will disclose relevant details," said Callum.

Reed was so shocked by the apology, he simply nodded his head. It took humility Reed hadn't known Callum possessed to admit to being wrong, and it made Reed think that maybe there was more to the arrogant fae warrior than he originally thought.

Callum sat by the fire, and Reed thought that he seemed weary. Again, Reed waited in silence. Clearly he was preparing to share something, and by the grim look on his face, Reed wasn't sure he was going to like it.

After settling into his spot on the ground and running his hands through his hair a couple of times, Callum spoke. "I think I found a dragon's cave. And I think the dragon still lives there."

Reed sat, dumbstruck. Out of all the things he could have said, this was not even in the top one hundred of what he would have guessed. Callum glanced over at Reed, but continued on. "Although the girl—"

"Ailia," Reed interrupted him. Callum shot him an annoyed look.

"Although *Ailia*," Callum said, saying her name like he was testing it out, "was the one who decided to come here, this area was actually the first place on my list as well."

Callum paused, but Reed patiently waited for him to continue. "I was sent to the mortal realm to collect artifacts, like I told you. Which is why I asked for your help. They are not easy to find. Although the fae can do a lot of things, we cannot wield magic the way witches can."

Again, Reed was surprised at Callum's honesty. "So what are you looking for?" Reed asked.

"The item I seek here is a dragon tooth. According to the legend of the Linton dragon, when it was slain long ago by the master of these lands, its teeth were buried in a secret underground passage. Today, I found where the passage should be." Callum paused and blew out a breath.

"However, there was rumor of a second dragon that was never found. Since dragons zealously guard their treasure and tend to keep to caves, I thought I should first find out if this second dragon exists. Long story short, it does. And it has just made my task much more difficult." Callum stopped speaking and scrubbed his hands over his face, looking more tired than when he started his story.

Reed was trying to keep his face calm and douse his instinct to wake Ailia up and get her out of this dragon-infested forest. "Do you think the dragon tooth you are searching for is in the underground passage? Or do you think the dragon you encountered has it in its cave?"

"I'm not sure," Callum replied quietly. "I think the best option is to probe the tunnels with your magic to see if you can detect anything."

Reed nodded, but Callum went on. "My gut is telling me that would be too convenient, and if I were a dragon, I would have found the teeth for myself rather than let them fall into the hands of the mortals that killed my friend."

"Makes sense," agreed Reed. "We can start with the tunnels in the morning. It will be good practice for Ailia."

They both sat in silence. A dragon. Bloody hell, he didn't even know they were real.

"What is she, anyway?" Callum asked offhandedly.

Reed furrowed his brows, assuming he was talking about Ailia. "What do you mean?"

"I mean she obviously has some sort of witch magic, and she is related to the fae somehow, otherwise Torneach would not have bonded to her the way he has. But I can't figure out from her scent what she is. There is something... more. Something ancient." Callum trailed off, lost in thought.

"I don't know," Reed responded carefully. "And she doesn't either. She doesn't know anything about her heritage. Her parents were killed when she was very young."

At that admission, Callum snapped his eyes to Reed's. Some sort of emotion flashed across his face, but Reed couldn't tell what it was. He hoped he hadn't shared too much. It was Ailia's story to tell.

Callum laid back on his mat. "I should rest. Changing forms is always draining, and I want to have all of my strength if we are going to potentially encounter a dragon tomorrow."

"That's fine. I got enough sleep," Reed lied. His head was buzzing with all the information Callum had shared, and he knew he wouldn't be able to sleep anyway. Callum closed his eyes with one hand under his head. Soon, he was sleeping peacefully.

Reed hated to admit it, but after Callum showed him the respect of being so forthcoming, he couldn't help thinking that he might trust this fae male slightly more now. He knew at one point the witches and the fae had lived in peace. Maybe things were starting to change. And he had to wonder if that change involved Ailia and whatever her strange heritage was.

Ailia

Ailia woke up feeling more well-rested than she had in days. Storm was curled around her, and she smiled at the comfort he brought her. Through the tiny mesh window in the tent, she could see that the stars had not quite retired, and the sun was still stretching its rays toward the sky.

She sat up slowly, savoring the peace. Storm lazily stretched out his long legs, sniffed in her direction, and then plopped his head back down on the mat. He definitely wasn't going to be her running partner this morning.

After quickly changing clothes, she quietly unzipped the tent flap, preparing to sneak past Callum and Reed for a run. However, she appeared to be the late riser in their group. Both of them were already awake, sitting comfortably around the small fire. She noticed the lack of tension and wondered what had changed during the night.

"Morning, boys," she said lightly, stretching her arms over her head. They both frowned at her. She gave them a sweet smile and sat between them. "What's for breakfast?"

"Someone's in a good mood," Reed teased, forgetting his frown and replacing it with a small smile. "We have leftover bread and apples—breakfast of champions," he said with more enthusiasm than necessary.

What she really wanted was coffee, and the next time they bought supplies, she would figure out a way to make that happen. She took the apple and stood.

"Let's go, grumpy," she said to Callum, taking a bite of the apple.

He continued to frown at her. "I'm not grumpy," he mumbled.

Reed stood, crossing his arms. "Where are you going?"

"For a run. And to start my training. Callum said I'm not strong enough to hold a sword, so I'm going to fix that." She started jogging in place, not bothering to wear her running shoes, enjoying the mild weather that would soon turn cold. She thought running barefoot might help ground her and test out her magic, and the moss covering much of the forest floor felt as soft as carpet. She took a couple more bites of the apple.

"I seem to recall agreeing to train you *my* way," Callum said, frown firmly in place.

"Careful, Callum, if you keep looking at me like that, your face will get stuck," Ailia teased. And just to annoy him even more, she stuck out her tongue. "Try to keep up!" She threw what was left of her apple at him and sprinted off through the trees. She could hear him swear behind her and she grinned, keeping her pace.

Suddenly, with no warning thanks to his feline stealth, he was there. She tried not to let her shock show, but decided she definitely needed to learn how to keep her movements so silent.

Ailia slowed down, wanting to savor the run. The forest was beautiful in the morning light. Rays of sunshine shimmered through the trees, painting everything a soft gold. The birds were chirping happily, and she could hear the distant trickle of the stream. Callum was still silent beside her, letting her set the pace, his dark hair reflecting strands of the morning glow. She decided to focus on the earth and see if she could connect to it while in motion.

The soft moss and leaves beneath her feet covered most of the loose stones, and the scent of pine, oak, and crisp river water flowed through her. She pictured the tendrils of energy weaving through her surroundings, and wondered if she could go faster—if her magic would clear a path for her like Reed had done when they were running from Storm.

Ailia willed the energy into creating a path and commanded the stones under her feet to move aside. Slowly, her path became less bumpy. Callum glanced over at her, also barefoot. He must have noticed the small difference. She smiled at him and to her shock, the corner of his mouth turned up.

"Think you can go faster?" he challenged.

"Definitely," she said.

She willed her magic to clear a path, this time moving stones into Callum's path at the same time. And she took off at a sprint towards the stream.

Callum seemed not to even notice the stones in his path, but he did wince every now and then as she tried pushing bigger rocks in front of him. They made it to the stream, and Ailia slowed, putting her hands on her knees to try to catch her breath. Of course, Callum hadn't even broken a sweat and was leaning against a tree looking completely at ease in the forest.

"That was a nice trick, little witch."

Ailia looked up at him sweetly. "I have no idea what you're talking about."

Callum chuckled. "You seem to be catching on to your magic fairly quickly. Hopefully the physical training will come naturally as well."

Ailia could have sworn he just gave her a compliment, but decided to brush past it. She wasn't sure what she would do if this unreasonably handsome male started being *nice* to her. "What's next? Now that we've done our warm up?"

The impish grin he gave her should have made her nervous, but instead, she felt excited, ready to learn what she could if it would help save her sister.

He gave her a scrutinizing once over. "You actually have decent balance. I assume you have your running to thank for that. And your core doesn't seem too weak. So we start with your arms." Ailia was expecting more criticism, so took his assessment in stride.

"Very well. How?" she asked.

"Push-ups," he said, a smirk on his face.

Ailia frowned. "Seriously? Push-ups?" For some reason she had thought her training would be more... remarkable.

"Seriously," said Callum. "I doubt you can even do ten. Go."

Offended, and ready to prove him wrong, Ailia got into position and started. After thirty, she had to stop. She looked up at Callum, victory written on her face. "There. I did three times the amount you asked me to."

"I didn't ask you to do ten, I said I didn't think you would even make it to ten. Thirty is still not enough." Callum gave her a smug look. "Until you can do a hundred without stopping, we aren't doing any more training."

He had to be joking. So much for the camaraderie she was starting to feel with him. She cursed soundly and glared at him. "Surely you've heard of cross-training?"

"We will go running every morning, and you will practice your push-ups whenever you wish. Let me know when you can do them all without your skinny arms shaking like jelly."

"A hundred push-ups is unreasonable, Callum," Ailia argued. "No one can do that many."

"Oh really?" Callum lazily dropped to the ground, Ailia lost count after a hundred. No fucking way.

He stood and stretched, giving her a cocky smile, as if doing over a hundred push-ups was completely normal.

She desperately wanted to wipe that smirk right off his face, but she had agreed to do this his way. Fine. She would do his stupid push-ups. If Elideh were here she would be whispering a plan to eventually kick his smug ass.

He seemed to read her thoughts because he laughed, implying *in your dreams*. But Ailia stood and started to jog back to the camp. She didn't need him to stand over her and witness her struggle to complete his task.

He followed her, matching her pace, but every now and then had to duck because of a tree branch suddenly swiping towards his face. It might have been petty, but it made her feel slightly better.

To her surprise, he smiled, seeming to enjoy the little game she was playing. They made it back to the camp, and she decided maybe training with him wouldn't be too bad.

CHAPTER TWENTY-FIVE

REED

Ailia and Callum made it back to the campsite in one piece, so Reed guessed their first attempt at training hadn't been a complete disaster. They were both extremely stubborn, so it would be interesting to see who cracked first. He knew that the couple of times Ailia had yielded to Callum had served her own purposes, but Callum was definitely used to being in control. Reed was happy to sit back and watch it unfold now that he didn't feel the need to punch Callum every time he looked his way.

While they were in the woods, Reed began to pack up their belongings so that they could get started with their day. They needed to stop in town to get more food—he noticed that over the past two days, Ailia was back to her old eating habits.

Reed knew Ailia would want to find the well that Tam Lin had supposedly met his mortal lover at, and Callum wanted Reed to check out the tunnels beneath the site of Linton Tower. After they had both woken up, Callum and Reed had discussed how to proceed now that there was probably a dragon to contend with. They had both agreed, which was becoming an unnervingly recurring theme, that they should deal with the tunnels and investigate the cave during the brightest part of the day.

Callum was convinced the dragon that resided in the forest was a shadow dragon, which meant light was their friend. So the plan was set: first, assess the tunnels; second, get supplies; third, deal with the cave. Then they would find the well. Reed hoped Ailia would be on board.

"Before we head out, we need to go over the plan, Ailia," said Reed.

Ailia gave him a curious look, but grabbed her socks and boots and started to put them on.

He took a deep breath, not sure how she would take the news that their plans now included a dragon. "One of the items Callum is trying to collect is nearby. It's a dragon's tooth." Ailia stopped what she was doing and looked up at him, eyebrows raised and mouth gaping.

Reed thought it best to plow ahead since the news wasn't going to get any less shocking. He glanced at Callum, but Callum's gaze was fixed on Ailia.

"Last night, Callum was scoping out the area, trying to confirm the location of the tooth. He believes there is a dragon guarding it and—"

"You're joking, right?" Ailia interrupted. She was standing, hands on her hips, looking between Reed and Callum like they had lost their minds.

"Why would we joke about a dragon?" Callum answered, frowning.

She blew out a breath and shook her head. "I guess if witches and faeries are real, I shouldn't be shocked about dragons." Waving her hand in Reed's direction, she said, "Let's hear the rest."

Reed nodded. "Today, we want to go to the location of the tunnels and see what we can find with our earth magic. We want to be absolutely sure that the teeth are not in the tunnels before we unnecessarily take on a dragon."

Having quickly overcome her shock, Ailia nodded. Now, she just looked determined.

"The location of the tunnels is near the village, so we will get supplies and then head back here to either look for the cave or look for your well."

"Okay, then let's go," said Ailia.

Both Callum and Reed shared a glance, equally surprised by how well she was taking this news.

"We can walk from here, and keep an eye out for the well on our way," said Callum in an offer of compromise that surprised Reed.

"Lead the way," gestured Ailia.

Callum shouldered his pack, Ailia and Reed doing the same, and they set off. Storm had been observing the exchange patiently and was immediately at Ailia's side. Reed mused over their unlikely group, but found that despite the danger they were potentially facing, he was excited. This was the most fun he'd had in decades.

CALLUM

They arrived at the site of Linton Tower in under an hour, which Callum considered to be decent timing since they had diverted a couple of times to see if they could find Ailia's well.

He was pretty sure they wouldn't find anything in the tunnels, but he was anxious to rule it out so that they could move on and not waste any daylight. Since there were mortals nearby, he had altered his appearance to seem less fae. He noticed Ailia looking at him, but she didn't say anything about his newly rounded ears or that he was now the same height as Reed.

"We are going to have to be very subtle about the way you two search this knoll. I can put up a shield so that no one can hear us, but they will still be able to see us," said Callum.

Reed and Ailia both nodded and started walking around, getting a feel for the area. The sun hadn't yet evaporated the dew that coated the lush grass. Although Callum had grown used to the near constant darkness of Elflaine, he found himself craving the sun the more he was around it. Callum tilted his face towards the light in a gesture that immediately reminded him of Ailia.

"This will be part of your magic training today, Ailia. This is going to be a bit more complex than what you've done so far. Not only do you need to connect with the earth around you, but you also need to probe it for information." Reed paused and Callum glanced at Ailia. She was focused, and he could tell she was already concentrating on her environment.

"Let me put it this way, let's say you are searching in the dark through a drawer. There are many items in the drawer, but you are looking for something specific. You touch different objects, not necessarily wanting to move them because you would just be doing double the work, until you find what you're looking for. Make sense?"

"I think so," said Ailia, brows furrowed in concentration.

"Okay, let's give it a shot."

Callum could sense the magic as soon as they started wielding it, but he couldn't see any evidence of it. He stayed quiet and out of the way, letting them work. After about ten minutes, Ailia huffed and rolled her shoulders. Reed glanced at her, assessing her to make sure she was okay. Which she clearly was. This witch was way too fussy with the girl.

"I could sense the tunnels, but they seemed to be empty. I couldn't detect anything other than roots and loose stones," said Ailia.

"Me neither," Reed agreed.

"I was afraid of that." Callum ran his hands down his face. "Well, at least we know dealing with a dragon is our only option."

Both Reed and Ailia nodded at him, Ailia looking a little paler than normal. Reed seemed to notice as well, because he pulled out a water bottle from his backpack and handed it to her.

"Let's go into town. We can grab supplies and some lunch," said Reed. His eyes flicked to Ailia who was drinking deeply.

Callum nodded and took down his shield as they headed towards the town.

CHAPTER TWENTY-SIX

AILIA

Ailia was desperate to eat. She wasn't going to tell Reed, because he would be obnoxious about it, but that had really drained her. She wondered when it would become less tiring to use magic. Maybe she should try to use a little bit all the time to start building up her endurance.

The three of them walked into the only restaurant in town. It was strange to see Callum looking so human. His normally imposing energy was dampened, and he was more average looking—less otherworldly. But she still found herself getting lost in his ocean eyes or wanting to brush his dark hair out of his face. Elideh would notice the glances Ailia kept stealing, and would be teasing her relentlessly if she were here. It wasn't her fault he was so beautiful.

Storm had remained in the woods in order to draw less attention to their little group, but she wished he was with them. She would have to bring him a treat when they returned.

"Just three?" asked the hostess, who was openly eyeing Callum.

"Yes, thanks," Ailia answered loudly. The hostess reluctantly dragged her eyes away from her perusal of Callum's sculpted arms.

"Any preference on table?"

"By the window, please," Reed answered. Ailia noticed the table that Reed indicated was as secluded as it could be in a restaurant this size, but would mean they could talk freely as long as they watched their volume.

They sat down at one of the old, worn tables, the chairs groaning under Reed and Callum's weight. The restaurant was quaint, but a little dark for her taste. The windows were made of an old, thick glass that barely let in any light. The exposed wooden beams on the ceiling only added to the tavern-like feel of the place. But food was food, and she was starving.

They ordered chowder and cheese toasties from the woman that had shown them to the table, along with hot tea for Ailia. Although it wasn't cold outside, Ailia felt like she needed to be warmed from the inside out. Maybe it was the magic. After the woman walked back to the kitchen, swaying her hips as she went, Reed turned to Ailia. "What's wrong?"

"What do you mean?"

"I can tell something's wrong," he said, crossing his arms. "You used too much magic."

She saw Callum roll his eyes and almost mimicked the sentiment.

"Reed. I'm fine. Yes, I'm a little tired, but I'm still learning how to use my magic. It's just going to be like this until I build up endurance, I assume?"

Reed frowned at her. "I guess I've forgotten how difficult it is on your body when you first start learning to use magic. Please tell me if you're doing too much, though."

Ailia nodded her head but wished he would relax a little bit. Changing the subject, she turned to Callum. "Now what? If the dragon's tooth isn't in the tunnels, what do we do?"

"Well," Callum started, but just as he was about to answer, the woman brought over the steaming hot tea. Ailia thanked her, and immediately poured herself a cup while waiting for Callum to continue. "We need to go back to the cave. I want to see it during the daytime and try to figure out if the dragon lives in it or just keeps his treasure there. Then, we can come up with a plan."

Ailia couldn't keep the surprise from her face.

"What?" Callum asked.

"Treasure?" Ailia stammered.

Callum glanced at Reed like he was trying to figure out what was so confusing. "Yes? Dragons covet and guard treasure. Everyone knows that."

"No. Everyone does not know that." Ailia took a deep breath. "So you're telling me that we are going to try to steal treasure from a dragon's cave? Without getting eaten?"

"Or incinerated," nodded Callum.

For the love of god. She couldn't believe how calm both Callum and Reed were. As if this was just another ordinary task for another ordinary day. She took a deep, steadying breath. She was not going to let them use her reaction as an excuse to make her stay behind.

When Reed had first told her their quest now included a dragon, she had tried to recall if Elideh's research ever included the mythical beasts. Unfortunately, she could not remember ever reading anything about dragons—not even a footnote. She made a mental note to look into the history of dragon lore if she ever got a spare moment to examine the turn her life had taken.

Just then, the woman brought over their food, and Ailia used it as a welcome reason to avoid looking at either of them. After inhaling most of her chowder, which was delicious, and half of her bread, she finally looked up to find them staring at her, Reed barely containing a grin.

Callum turned to Reed. "Does she always eat like that? Like she spends most of her life starving?" Ailia rolled her eyes as Reed finally let his smile crack.

"Yes. You get used to it," Reed shrugged. Ailia went back to her meal, choosing to ignore them.

"Once we're done, we need to quickly get whatever supplies you need, then go straight to the cave. It is almost noon, and we need as much light as possible," said Callum.

Ailia sopped up the remainder of her soup with the last piece of her bread and practically chugged her tea. If she was being honest, she could have had at least one more bowl of soup. But time was of the essence.

The woman came back to clear their plates and take their payment. Reed asked if they could get three loaves of bread to take with them. The woman nodded her head and went back to the kitchen. Ailia could have kissed him for thinking of that.

They got their extra bread and headed to the town's grocery store. After buying some food they could eat that night and the following day, and Ailia convincing Reed to buy instant coffee and a small kettle they could heat over a fire, they split up all of their items between the three of them, shoved everything in their backpacks, and headed back to the woods to find the dragon.

REED

Reed was debating how angry Ailia would be if he suggested she stay far, far away from the cave, but decided it wouldn't be worth the fight. Plus, it wasn't a guarantee that she was any safer alone in the forest. As soon as they made it to the edge of the woods, Storm came bounding towards Ailia, his tail wagging furiously. Ailia grinned at him and threw her arms around his massive neck. Callum watched the interaction, his eyes narrowed, calculating.

Ailia rubbed Storm's ears and gave him a treat. Then, Callum led the way to the cave. He had explained on their walk over that he would shift into some sort of tiny creature and try to sneak into the cave undetected. He recommended that they stay far enough away to have a decent head start if the dragon sensed trespassing and started looking for someone to blame. Reed happily agreed, glad for an excuse to keep Ailia out of harm's way.

Reed had been working on trying to smother his instinct to protect her, and although it sometimes meant physically restraining himself, he thought he was doing a pretty damn good job. This would definitely be a test of his self control.

"You can wait for me here," said Callum. "If I'm not back in an hour, set up camp far away from the cave. I'll be able to find you if I haven't been incinerated."

"Good luck, Callum," said Ailia, reaching up to squeeze his shoulder. He tensed at her touch, but didn't back away.

"I don't need luck, princess." And then, he disappeared into the forest.

Reed and Ailia sat down in a small clearing of trees, Ailia basking in the sun like a cat.

"I really hope he doesn't get eaten," Ailia said after a few minutes. Reed wasn't sure how sincere her worries were since she was lying back with her face tilted towards the sun, propped up on her elbows with her eyes closed. Storm was lounging next to her, almost asleep. So much for a guard dog.

"Do you want to practice your magic? Are you replenished enough after lunch?" Reed asked.

"Definitely. I actually feel really good," replied Ailia, sitting up and turning to face him.

"You did really well today, by the way. It was a tricky bit of magic, especially since the tunnels were so spread out." Reed was sincerely impressed by how far Ailia had come in such a short amount of time. She was a natural, unlike Elideh who could barely light a candle.

Ailia beamed at him. "Thank you, Reed."

He returned her contagious smile. "You're welcome." Reed thought for a moment about what they should practice.

"Perhaps we should try some offensive magic since we might be attacked by a dragon any moment now," Ailia joked.

"First of all, not funny, since that is an actual possibility," said Reed. "Second of all, offensive magic is pretty advanced."

"Try me," she replied with a challenge in her voice.

Reed sighed. "Very well." Ailia's eyes were practically glowing with excitement. Or were they *actually* glowing?

"Offensive magic requires you to know a little bit of combat. So although I hate to admit it, maybe it's a good thing you are going to start training with Callum. Do you have any experience with any sort of fighting?" Reed assumed she didn't, but then again, she frequently surprised him.

Ailia thought about it for a moment. "Well, I wouldn't call it experience, but Elideh is obsessed with kickboxing, and she has dragged me to some of her classes before. She's amazing, but I was never very good."

"That's actually better than nothing," Reed said. "So you at least know how to hold yourself, how to stay balanced, and how to shift your weight?"

"I could probably use a refresher, but yes. In theory."

"Okay. Let's start with summoning the earth to your palms. One of the advantages the witches have over the fae is that we can shape our magic. It's a little more precise and elegant than the blunt brutality of fae magic."

Ailia looked focused but excited. And Reed couldn't help but feel the same way. When he was younger, he had actually gone through extensive magical combat training with an older witch he and his mum met. When Reed found out that the witch was well-trained, he begged the witch to teach him everything he knew. And he did. Although Reed kept physically fit and occasionally practiced his offensive magic, he didn't get a lot of opportunities to really work on it.

Reed stood upright, squaring his shoulders and pressing his feet firmly into the ground, raising his hands, his palms facing Ailia. Ailia copied his posture, her excitement replaced with quiet determination. Before they started, Reed reached out with his magic to make sure he didn't sense that ancient presence from the night before. Once he was sure they were safe for the moment, he turned his focus to Ailia.

"There are three parts to wielding offensive magic. Pulling the available pieces of the element to you, shaping it for your purposes, and then wielding it. This is a 'work smart not hard' situation, especially if you are actually in a fight. For example, if you need a weapon like a sword or dagger, you want to call branches to you since they are already close to the right shape. If you want to create a bow, you would want to use roots. If you want a shield, compact dirt until it is hard as steel. The only limit to your wielding is your natural well of power and your imagination."

Ailia nodded, soaking in all the information.

"Let's start with a shield. In a fight, being able to protect yourself is vital. Envision a simple shape that you could strap to your arm or hold in your hand. I'll show you how I do it, and then you try."

Reed started gathering the earth to him, slowing down what would normally take him less than ten seconds. He found stones within the earth and wove them in with the dirt to reinforce the shield. Soon, he had a small circular shield that he could hold in his hand. Ailia grinned at him, and he grinned back.

"Now you try," he instructed.

Ailia kept her eyes open, which was impressive. It was hard to focus on wielding magic with visual distractions as a new witch. She started pulling loose dirt, stones, and small branches towards her hand. Just like before, the earth seemed to swirl and flow like water. After a couple of minutes, she had crafted a shield that resembled his. He could tell that it was not quite as strong, but just getting the correct shape in the time it had taken her was a huge accomplishment.

"Brilliant," he said with a grin. "Now do it again."

The pride that was radiating from Ailia withered slightly. "Shouldn't we try a weapon this time?"

Reed chuckled. "Until you can conjure a shield in under thirty seconds and withstand a blow from my magic, we stick to shields."

She sighed at him and mumbled "fine" before breaking down her shield and starting over. Reed reminded her to be aware of the amount of magic she was using and to pace herself.

While Ailia worked on her shield, Reed reached out again to see if he could sense either Callum or the dragon. Still nothing. It had been half an hour, and he wasn't sure if he should start to worry or not.

After Ailia had made her fourth shield, Reed made her take a break. He had a feeling that she would burn herself out because of her stubborn attitude if he didn't stop her. She sat next to Storm, who was still napping in the sun, and was rubbing his ears when Reed felt something—a pulse—coming from the direction of the cave. The forest fell quiet and Storm sat up, ears perked, alert.

Reed stood, ready to fight or get Ailia out, depending on the threat. He felt the pulse again and this time noticed that it didn't feel like the ancient presence of the dragon—it felt fae. He was grabbing their bags and Ailia in the next second and started sprinting in the opposite direction. The pulse had to be a warning from Callum. Ailia must have felt it, too, because she didn't even question him as they ran faster, faster, faster, using their magic to make a clear path.

Storm quickly overtook them, and Reed trusted whatever instinct the beast had to keep Ailia safe. They ran and ran until both Reed and Ailia were gasping for breath. Storm finally began to slow in a clearing by the stream. He sniffed the treeline and then sat down by the water. Ailia and Reed both tried to catch their breath, Ailia plopping down beside Storm, splashing her face. Although winded, Reed was still on high alert, sending out pulses of his own magic to test for anything sinister that might sneak up on them.

Suddenly, Callum appeared at the treeline, undetected by Reed's magic. Although he wasn't wounded, he did not look well. He stumbled into the clearing, and before he fell to his knees, Reed felt a shield go up around them.

"What happened?" Reed demanded.

Callum crouched on the balls of his feet, catching his breath. "Can confirm. There's a dragon. It's mad."

Reed ran his hands through his hair. Goddess save them.

"Why is it mad?" Reed asked, clenching his fists.

Callum took a couple more deep breaths. "Because I found the tooth. And tried to take it. Apparently, dragons don't like it when you try to steal their treasure."

For fuck's sake. Up till this point, Ailia had been quietly listening. She stood and walked over to Callum, kneeling down to face him.

"Why are you so drained?" she asked quietly.

"Because I had to shift five times to lose the dragon. Shifting once or twice is okay, but shifting into different creatures several times in a row is exhausting. And I used a lot of magic to warn you both to run."

"Thank you for doing that," Ailia murmured.

Callum nodded and slowly moved to sit against a tree. He leaned his head back and closed his eyes. Storm came over and sat by Callum, clearly sensing his depletion.

Ailia brought Callum a bottle of water and went back to the stream to sit. "Now what?" she asked after a couple of minutes of silence.

Eyes still closed, Callum said, "We wait. I have to get that tooth, but we need to come up with a plan. At least I know the layout of the cave now. We can camp here and act first thing in the morning."

"Very well. I will set up the tent and then go get firewood," said Reed.

After he was done, he left the safety of the shield Callum was keeping in place and was glad Ailia didn't offer to come with him. He needed some time to think of a way to keep her out of this plan. He was not going to let her anywhere near that dragon.

CHAPTER TWENTY-SEVEN

AILIA

A ilia was trying not to be too concerned about Callum, but it was Storm's reaction that really had her worried. The male must be in a vulnerable state if Storm felt the need to guard him. She watched him carefully, which he must have sensed, because without opening an eye, he said, "Quit worrying. I can scent it from here, and it's not helping."

Now feeling a little self conscious that he could smell her emotions, she said, "Sorry, I just haven't seen Storm worried about you. You must be very drained."

He opened one eye and sighed. "Yes, the beast can be an overbearing, motherly nuisance when he wants to be. Just like your witch."

"Reed is not *my* witch. It is okay to have people worry over you every now and then. And that's coming from someone who hasn't had a lot of that sort of treatment," Ailia said in a snappier tone than she intended.

Callum closed his eye and continued breathing deeply. "You know he isn't going to let you come with us, right?"

Ailia frowned. "What do you mean?"

"As your knight, he is not going to put you in unnecessary danger. He's going to try to convince you to stay safely guarded in the camp while we deal with the dragon."

Ailia stared at him. "What do you mean, 'my knight?'"

Callum somehow managed to roll his eyes while they were closed and said, "Forget I said anything. It's the exhaustion speaking."

"No, you've hinted before that there's something between me and Reed, and now you call him my knight? Explain." Ailia was not going to give him a pass, even if he was exhausted.

Callum sighed deeply and massaged his forehead, leaning his head back against the tree. His dark hair blended in with the bark, and he looked like he was as much a part of the forest as the trees. "Once upon a time," he started, "witches and faeries lived in peace and harmony with each other."

Ailia thought he might be the most punchable person in the whole world. "Callum, I swear, if you're screwing with me—"

"Let me tell the story, princess."

Ailia huffed but let him continue.

"As I was saying, once upon a time, witches and faeries coexisted peacefully." Callum glanced at her and gave her a mischievous smirk before closing his eyes again. "The fae had a separate realm, and the witches lived alongside the mortals, but both the fae and the witches traveled between realms with ease." This wasn't news to Ailia from what Reed had told her.

"But a darkness, that had always been, started to rise up, corrupting magic and killing everything that stood in its way," said Callum. "No one knew where it came from, or why it sought destruction so dearly.

The Queen of Elflaine decided to partner with the High Witch of the North to try to combat the darkness, because the darkness could travel between realms as well. Together, they formed The Order." Callum opened his eyes and paused for dramatic effect, to which Ailia waved her hand, indicating for him to go on.

He closed his eyes again, relaxing back into the ground. "The witches were much more skilled in magic, but the fae were invincible and strong. Together, they would be powerful enough to combat the evil that had infiltrated their world. The witches that joined The Order became knights and were bonded to a fae warrior. The knight's primary objective was to protect their partner by using their magic, and in return, the witch gained some of the fae's invincibility and strength. The bond was sacred, and together the witches and the fae were able to quell the darkness." Callum opened his eyes and looked over at Ailia. "The end," he quipped, the corners of his mouth turning up.

Ailia was gaping at him. "The end?" she sputtered.

Callum shrugged. "Okay, that's not the end, but it explains the knights."

"So you're not going to tell me the rest of the story?" she asked incredulously.

"Maybe some other time," said Callum.

She walked over to Callum and punched him in the shoulder. "You're infuriating. What does that have to do with me and Reed?"

Callum mockingly rubbed his shoulder. "Obviously he is somehow a descendant of The Order and has bonded to you."

She glared at him. Obviously?

"Callum. It is not obvious. How would that even happen?"

"I am not a seer, I have no idea," he said, waving her off. "I really do need to rest if I am going to slay a dragon later. Leave me alone."

She was going to kill him. He couldn't drop a bomb like this on her and then *take a nap*. Right at that moment, Ailia felt Callum's shield flicker and turned to see Reed walking into the clearing, arms full of firewood. She guessed her fury was written all over her face because he dropped the wood and strode purposefully towards her. "What did he do?" Reed demanded.

Ailia didn't even know where to start.

"I didn't do anything," murmured Callum.

"Let's just say we have some things we need to discuss," said Ailia. Reed's look grew more concerned, but he let her lead him away, out of range of Callum's fae hearing.

Reed

No. Fucking. Way. There was no fucking way it was true. Reed had, of course, heard of the knights, but the story was so ancient that it was more of a bedtime story than history. He paced by the stream, trying to wrap his head around this.

A knight. Just—no. No way.

He released a deep breath. As insane as this sounded, he had to admit that it did explain their connection. The way he had been drawn to Ailia from day one, and how something had changed after Storm attacked them—the intense instinct to protect her that had been ruling him.

Bloody hell. How was this possible?

"Please say something, Reed," said Ailia, nervously picking at her nails.

"I don't really know what to say. Part of me can't believe it," said Reed, "But part of me thinks it could be true."

"Are you upset?" she asked.

Reed whipped his head towards her. He hadn't thought for one moment that she would be worried.

He walked over and tugged her close to him. "Of course not. If this is real, I am honored to be your knight."

He had said it with a little bit of a teasing tone, but he felt her sag with relief. She pulled away and looked up at him. "What I don't understand is that Callum said the knights willingly entered into the bond. It seems like our bond just... appeared."

"I agree. Maybe our ancestors were bonded at one time, and Storm's attack somehow triggered it."

"And I thought I was just a witch. Does that mean I'm fae as well?"

"Well you're not *just* anything, for starters," Reed said, nudging her shoulder. "I don't know, Ails. But we will figure it out."

Ailia shook her head. "This is so much to take in—not to mention the fucking dragon. Which, by the way, I am going to help with. The whole reason this conversation started in the first place was because Callum said you weren't going to let me go."

Where she had been unsure moments before, she was now determined.

"To Callum's credit, I did spend the entire time I was searching for firewood trying to think of a way to convince you to stay," confessed Reed. But at the look in her eyes, he knew it would be pointless. He sighed in resignation. At least now he understood why he felt so out of control when she was in danger.

"I won't ask you to stay. But please hear me out. Callum is a trained, fae warrior and is most likely hundreds of years old with hundreds of years of experience. I have been wielding my magic for over a century and trained in battle magic for over two decades." He paused to gauge her reaction, but her face was carefully blank. "All I am asking is if it comes to actually fighting a dragon—a real-life, fire-breathing dragon, Ailia—please run. If only so that I can focus on trying to make it out alive instead of trying to save you."

Reed hated trying to guilt her into fleeing if it came down to it, but he also knew that what he said was true. He would sacrifice himself for her without a thought.

She stared at him for a solid minute. "Okay. I promise if it turns into a fight, I will run."

Reed could feel his whole body relax as he sighed a deep breath of relief. "Thank you, Ails." He kissed her head, and she leaned into his embrace, resting her head on his chest, the physical contact soothing the nagging bond. "And I promise we will keep training your magic so that you can participate in future dragon slayings," he teased, trying to convey his appreciation.

She leaned back and batted at his chest, but was smiling as she said, "Deal."

Holy shit. A knight. He still couldn't believe it.

CALLUM

Callum felt Ailia and Reed pass through his shield, but he remained where he was, eyes closed. He was unhappy that it was taking him this long to recover. Being in the mortal realm always weakened him at first, but since he hadn't been here in centuries, he had forgotten just how inconvenient it was. The adjustment period should only be a day more at most, so he would have to endure until then.

He had wanted to take on the dragon tonight, but Callum knew better than to go into a battle unprepared. And that's what this would be. A battle. He wondered briefly how the witch had taken the news, but then decided it didn't really matter. What was done was done. The bond couldn't be broken. He slowly opened his eyes to find the pair building a small fire. He had to admit, what the girl said earlier about companionship rang a little true.

Torneach glanced at him, sensing his small movements, and after a couple of assessing sniffs, seemed to decide that Callum had recovered enough and trotted happily over to the girl. He still didn't understand Torneach's obsession with her, but he was about to slay a dragon with the help of a knight of The Order, so anything was possible.

Callum stood and stretched, then went to his pack to start assessing his weapons. The magic the fae possessed, which was primarily for battle, extended to things like weapons and armor. Which meant he was able to use his shapeshifting gifts to shrink his weapons, even though he wasn't able to shapeshift anything else. He started pulling out miniature weapons one at a time, carefully laying them on his unrolled sleeping mat.

Ailia walked over, and to his immense displeasure, crooned, "Those are so cute!"

By the gods, this girl knew how to get under his skin. He stared up at her, and she took one step back with the glare he was giving her. At least she wasn't stupid.

"They aren't cute, they're weapons," he said impatiently. Then, to prove his point, he waved his hand over the miniature sword closest to him and it grew to its full size.

Reed walked over as well. "That's impressive magic. I thought faeries couldn't shapeshift objects."

"We can't, ordinarily," said Callum. "But our magic lets us shapeshift anything we can use in battle." Callum continued shifting the rest of his weapons until he had a small armory laid out on his sleeping mat.

"That's useful," remarked Reed.

"Also, the fae are the only faeries that can shapeshift anything. Other faeries like pixies, sprites, and brownies have limited magic."

"Aren't you a faerie?" Reed asked. "Actually, aren't faeries supposed to have wings?"

Callum rolled his eyes. "Only in your bedtime stories, witch. Yes, I am a type of faerie if you want to get pedantic. We all belong to Elflaine, and the fae rule because we are the most powerful. Power is currency in Elflaine."

Ailia was reaching for one of the smaller daggers, but Callum swatted her hand away.

"Hey!" she exclaimed, grabbing her hand.

"Don't touch the weapons," he warned. "You are completely untrained."

Ailia frowned at him, and Reed was suspiciously silent next to her. "Looks like your witch agrees," Callum smirked.

Ailia rounded on Reed. "Seriously? You're on his side?"

Reed, to his credit, held his ground. "Yes, actually. You need to train before you use weapons." She walked away frowning and started to set up the tent, occasionally muttering something about "stupid, bossy males," but Callum just chuckled to himself.

"I take it you know how to use these?" he asked Reed.

"I do," the witch answered confidently as he picked up a throwing knife. "I trained for about twenty years with an older witch who had extensive knowledge in offensive magic, and now I'm wondering if he, too, was a knight, or at least the descendant of one."

"Anything in particular you favor?" asked Callum. The oath with the witch was proving to be more useful by the day.

"I always liked throwing knives and archery. I'm not too bad with a sword, either," Reed said as he looked over the weapons. "But I will need some practice. I haven't had a sparring partner in a while."

Callum nodded, appreciating his honesty.

"Very well, we can practice tonight. I wanted to try to take on the dragon before sunset, but I am still adjusting to the mortal realm. I won't be fully recovered until tomorrow."

"I'd like the extra time to re-familiarize myself with the weapons anyway," said Reed.

Callum handed the witch a set of knives. "Then it's settled. We can eat, then train. And tomorrow, we will find the dragon."

CHAPTER TWENTY-EIGHT

AILIA

Lounging by the fire after eating almost an entire loaf of bread on her own, Ailia couldn't help but enjoy the view. The glorious sun was beating down on them, and Callum and Reed had both shed their shirts after briefly sparring, revealing broad shoulders and sculpted muscles. Ailia noticed Reed had added several more tattoos to his arms and chest since she last saw him without a shirt. Years ago, he had explained that they were protective runes—they looked like randomly placed stamps, but they were actually intentionally placed for their various purposes.

Callum, on the other hand, again reminded Ailia of a sculpture come to life, his pale skin steadily gaining color. She had been shocked, at first, to see his body was covered in scars. When she asked about them, he merely shrugged like it was normal and told her that was what most warriors looked like in Elflaine. Once she moved past the scars, she was able to appreciate the tattoos that snaked across his chest, shoulders, and back. The designs were intricate, and the placement looked almost like armor. She decided that she would stick to admiring instead of questioning for now.

After briefly sparring, they quickly moved on to the weapons, and it was incredible to watch. Reed was a little rusty, but Callum was patiently giving him occasional tips to get his bearings. They started with throwing knives, and once Ailia watched them for a couple of minutes, she realized they were both right. Until she was stronger and trained longer, she should not be handling anything sharp.

Callum set up a makeshift target on the trunk of a large tree. Reed stood about twenty paces back and had already sunk three knives into the target, getting closer to the center with every throw. Callum nodded his head, the only approval he would show, handing Reed two more knives, which he promptly threw at the target without pause, landing them dead in the center.

Callum seemed to think that was enough practice with the throwing knives, and grabbed two different sized bows. Ailia stood up and walked over.

"I've always wanted to try archery," Ailia said, gently grazing the smaller bow with her fingers. "What's the difference between the two?"

Reed handed her the bow she was admiring. "This is a recurve bow. It's better for short range."

"It's beautiful," said Ailia. It was elegantly made of hickory, the wood bone-white, and inlaid with intricate carvings and whorls—whorls similar to Callum's tattoos. She handed it back to Reed, who then gave her the larger one.

"This is a longbow," Reed said. It was made of yew and had been stained an inky black with those same whorls painted in a light gray, as if smoke had permanently settled on the bow. "It's more useful for longer distances and is probably what you would think of archers using in ancient battles."

"Or not so ancient battles," said Callum, taking the bow from Ailia. "Some of our most highly trained warriors in Elflaine are our archers, and they all favor longbows."

Reed weighed each in his hands and decided to test out the recurve bow first since, according to him, it would be easier to manage in close proximity, which they figured would be a likely scenario with the dragon. Callum handed Reed a quiver of arrows, which Reed gracefully slung over his shoulder, like he had done it hundreds of times.

This time, Reed moved to the other side of the clearing, right at the treeline, and shot his first arrow. It pierced the center of the target with such force that the massive tree seemed to shudder. Callum gave Reed an approving glance, and Reed was soon firing more arrows.

"I want to try," Ailia said.

Callum laughed as Reed said, "Absolutely not. You'll snap your face with the string." Seeing her temper start to rise, Reed joked, "I know I make it look easy, but I promise it's not."

"Fine," Ailia glared.

"Shouldn't you be practicing your push-ups, princess?" Callum drawled.

Ailia rolled her eyes but knew they were both right. She had just wanted to try. Maybe Reed did make it look easy. After huffing out a determined breath, she decided her only option was to practice her push-ups. If that is what it was going to take to make Callum train her, she would do it.

So she started, and every time she felt like she was going to collapse, she sat up, took a deep breath, and started again. She was nothing if not determined.

Ailia

By the time the sun had nearly set, Ailia had made it to forty push-ups in a row. She could barely lift the tent flap, but she had made progress at least. Assuming that Storm would be taking Reed's place in the tent again, she sat his mat outside so he didn't have to sleep on the ground.

After briefly sparring with the swords, Callum and Reed went out into the dusky forest to gather some firewood and refill their water bottles, Storm staying behind with Ailia, and currently lounging in one of the remaining sunspots. Ailia was grateful Reed had suggested she stay here, as she would probably have just embarrassed herself if she had tried to carry firewood right now.

She was nibbling on some of the cheese when she suddenly felt a strange presence—an ancient presence—coming straight toward her. Storm sat up, alert, a low growl rumbling out of him as he stared at the sky. Before she could react, strong claws grabbed around her middle and yanked her into the air, knocking the wind out of her lungs.

She didn't even have time to scream as the beating of massive wings sounded above her, drowning out Storm's frantic howls.

CHAPTER TWENTY-NINE

REED

Reed was running faster than he had ever run in his life, Callum quickly catching up to him. They had been gathering firewood, Callum wandering a little farther off than Reed, when Reed heard Storm's ear splitting howl. He dropped the firewood and started sprinting to the camp, panic and adrenaline flooding his veins.

Reed and Callum burst through the treeline to find Storm pacing around the clearing, whimpering, and occasionally glancing up at the sky.

"Fuck. FUCK," Reed roared. "AILIA!"

"She's not here," said Callum, in a lethally quiet voice.

"AILIA!" Reed screamed again.

Callum grabbed Reed by his shoulders and shook him, trying to say something to him. But Reed couldn't hear over the pounding in his ears. Reed shoved Callum away and closed his eyes with his hands on his head. This couldn't be happening.

"Reed. Listen to me. If we want to find her alive, we need to think clearly and rationally," said Callum. When Reed didn't immediately look at him, Callum shouted, "Now!"

Reed shook his head. He needed to calm down. He needed to think. What the fuck had happened? What was Callum talking about—find her alive?

"Where is she?" Reed asked numbly.

Callum paused. "The dragon took her. That's the only explanation."

Reed felt his stomach drop straight out of his body.

He shoved Callum hard. "This is YOUR fault! You led the dragon straight to us!" Reed flung the accusation at Callum, as if finding someone to blame would ease his terror.

Callum squared his shoulders and straightened to his full height. "I may be a lot of things, but I don't break oaths. I would never willingly put either of you in danger." Reed and Callum glared at each other, but Callum looked like his anger was barely leashed. Maybe he was telling the truth.

"Where's the cave?" Reed demanded.

"You need to calm down. We cannot just storm into a dragon's cave without weapons or clear heads. There must be a reason the dragon took her. It must have known we were going to come looking for it." Callum started pacing, running his hands through his hair. "Dragons are highly intelligent. We may be able to bargain for her safe return, but we have to play this right. We have to be smart." Callum stared at Reed, daring him to argue.

"I will make any bargain to get her back. Tell me the plan. I will do whatever you want." He tried to keep the desperation and dread out of his voice, but the knight bond was burning through him, begging him to act.

Callum started methodically gathering weapons, Storm following him, waiting for his orders. Reed grabbed the throwing knives, attaching them to a belt he found in Callum's supplies. Then, he took the recurve bow, strapping it to his back and putting the quiver of arrows over his shoulder. He turned to Callum and gave him a nod. Callum merely said, "Let's go. We will come up with a plan on the way."

"Done," said Reed.

And they took off at a jog, straight towards the dragon's lair.

CALLUM

Callum had slipped into the warrior calm that had been trained into him, but despite all his experience, he was having a hard time shaking the panic that was pulsing through him. Maybe it was because of the oath he had sworn, or maybe it was his fae instinct to protect, but for the first time in centuries, he was *scared*. Scared of losing the girl that radiated light. Scared they would be too late. And he was trying his best to hide it from Reed.

After their spat at the campsite, Reed seemed to dismiss the fear that was radiating off of him and replaced it with a steely determination Callum had frequently sensed from soldiers on the battlefield. Carefully honed instinct told Callum that, although they were about to face a dragon, time was their enemy at the moment. They had to get to Ailia as quickly as possible. Callum was confident that this was a kidnapping, not an execution. But he had never dealt with a dragon, so he couldn't be sure.

The darkness that he had told Ailia about in his very abbreviated story had not, in fact, been defeated. Callum had been fighting against it along with the rest of the fae his whole life. Sometimes it was small raids, and sometimes it was destructive, devastating battles—but it irked Callum that none of those encounters offered him an edge against a dragon. All he had to go by were barely whispered legends and his own wit. It would have to do.

Reed was silent beside him, hopefully spiraling into his magic as the witches could do. The forest seemed to mirror their unease—it was silent, as if all of the animals had safely holed away. Even the breeze that kept them cool all day had died. Hopefully between Reed's magic and Callum's strength, speed, and experience they would stand a chance.

If only Callum could banish the unfamiliar distress coaxing him to *hurry.*

Callum stopped Reed about a mile away from the cave. Reed looked at Callum, determination in his eyes, waiting for instructions.

"I'm not going to shift. There isn't a creature in this world, or any other world, that would give me an advantage against a dragon, and it would only weaken me. So we are going to move as quickly and as quietly as possible to try to assess the situation. I believe that the dragon has some sort of purpose behind taking Ailia rather than just killing her outright, we just need to figure out what it is."

At the mention of killing Ailia, Reed had paled, and the ground beneath them rumbled. "She is not dying today."

"I didn't say she was," Callum replied calmly, trying to keep his own dread locked deep down inside of him. "I will try to speak with the dragon first. You just focus on finding Ailia and getting her to Torneach—he will be able to get her to safety while we deal with the dragon." Reed nodded and glanced at Torneach, who was sitting patiently and had inclined his head, indicating he understood what he was supposed to do.

"Let's move. When we get close enough to see the cave, we will split up, and you will find Ailia. Torneach will go with you." At that, they set off, Callum centering himself, ready to fight the dragon.

CHAPTER THIRTY

AILIA

The smell of damp rock and metal hit Ailia right before her eyes snapped open. She was surrounded by treasure—a massive hoard of sparkling jewelry, golden statues, beautifully made weapons, and artifacts from various centuries lining the walls. The small sconces of fire on the roughly hewn rock walls cast flickering light onto the gleaming piles of gold that made the jewels glow, but created eerie shadows that seemed to dance between every crevice. She was in the dragon's cave. Trying to abate the panic, she looked around, searching for an escape. Which is when she saw two glowing green eyes staring at her from the shadows. Ailia went still as death.

"Hello, Bright One."

The ancient, powerful voice had spoken directly into her mind. She continued staring at its eyes, not daring to speak, but something about the name it had called her reverberated in her memory.

The dragon must have sensed her confusion, or maybe it could read her mind, because it said, "Ah, interesting. You do not know your own history, or what you are meant to accomplish." It paused, but Ailia remained silent, not willing to provoke the dragon—waiting to see what it would do with her.

"You do not need to fear me."

Given that she was in a cave with a dragon that could undeniably turn her to ash at any moment, she guessed she had no choice but to trust the ancient creature. She nodded once, but never took her eyes off the glowing orbs in front of her.

"I have brought you here to make a request."

At that, Ailia straightened. What could a thousands-of-years-old dragon want from her?

"Wait, what do you mean my own history? Or what I am to accomplish?"

The dragon's eyes blinked once. "I will not burden you with that knowledge yet. But I will tell you that we have waited for you and your sister for a very, very long time. Which brings me to my request."

All of a sudden, a vision was cast into her mind—scraps of images almost too disjointed to make out, flashing before her eyes. Some terrifying, others filled with hope. The images continued on, getting more and more gruesome and hopeless. Visions of war and destruction—many featuring herself and Elideh, leading others into battle, or facing horrifying monsters. And many, many versions of their deaths.

Ailia could feel panic gripping her the longer the visions continued. Were these real? Could she prevent them?

The last thing she glimpsed was Elideh, with a crown of stars circling her dark hair, and herself, with a matching wreath of pure light, making her pale hair glow, the image vanishing as quickly as it had appeared.

Ailia blinked, tears rolling down her cheeks.

"What does this mean?" Ailia whispered.

"The visions show shreds of potential futures. I cannot tell you which will come to pass, but here is my request, and with it, I offer you a gift."

Ailia lowered her eyes, tears still falling.

"If the fates allow it, make a place for dragons to be free. We tire of hiding and want to live in peace."

Ailia snapped her eyes up to meet the glowing eyes now just paces from her, the dragon still hidden in shadows.

"There are more of you?" she whispered.

"Many more, Bright One," replied the dragon in its deep, gentle tone.

Ailia thought for a moment. "How could I make the promise you are requesting? I don't have the power or the means to guarantee your safety."

The dragon's eyes pierced her, like they could see right through her. "Depending on the threads you follow, you will gain the means, but you already have the power."

Before Ailia could ask any further questions, the eyes turned towards the entrance to the cave, revealing iridescent, black-as-night scales, but nothing more.

The dragon turned to face her. "Your companions have arrived. Leave, and do not return. We will meet again, in a time of need. Your heart is pure, Bright One. Trust it."

Shadows caressed her hands and face, and a name had been spoken into her mind before the dragon disappeared. She looked down and saw a single tooth hanging on a golden chain around her neck. She stumbled towards the entrance of the cave, no longer afraid, but overwhelmed by what had been revealed to her and the part that she must play.

REED

Out of all the scenarios Reed had mentally prepared himself for, Ailia walking out of the cave, unharmed and *glowing*, was not one of them. He sprinted toward her and pulled her into a bone-crushing embrace. He set her down and gently took her face in his hands, looking into eyes that seemed too bright, then scanned her body for any sign of injuries. He took a deep breath when he was convinced she was okay, and nearly collapsed from relief.

Callum was standing a step behind him, still tense, glancing into the cave and then back to Ailia. Storm had been trying to shove Reed out of the way, and Reed finally relented. Ailia sank to her knees and buried her face in Storm's neck. When she lifted her face, her eyes were wet from tears. Reed kneeled down next to her and pulled her into his chest, holding her, letting her presence soothe him, and hopefully returning the favor.

Her shoulders started shaking, and he realized she was sobbing. Before he could say a word, Callum asked, "What happened?" His tone had Reed pivoting his head towards him. Was that the command of a warrior, or was that genuine concern that laced his request?

Ailia looked up, took a deep breath, and sat back on her feet. She looked at Callum and furrowed her brows, like she was trying to figure something out, and mumbled something that sounded like 'bright one.' Then, her gaze hardened. "We have a lot to discuss, but we need to leave this place and never come back."

She pulled a necklace from around her neck that he hadn't seen before, and handed it to Callum. "The dragon gave me the item you sought in return for a promise."

Again, Callum beat him to the question that was racing through his mind, practically growling. "You made a promise? To a dragon? We could have found another way to get the tooth. You should not have taken that sort of risk."

"Skatos will not harm me," Ailia said.

"Skatos?" asked Callum.

"The dragon's name," Ailia replied.

She looked so sure and, at the same time, so burdened, that Reed held up his hand to Callum, daring him to ask more questions. Ailia stood and started walking back towards the camp, Storm close at her heel, and Reed at her side. He would not be leaving her alone again. Ever. And it looked like Storm felt the same way.

CALLUM

They made it back to the campsite, and Ailia started packing their things. Callum guessed she was serious about leaving. It had taken him the entire walk back to the clearing to steady his heart to a normal pace. When he saw her walking out of that cave, alive and unharmed, relief like he had never felt in his life had washed through him. When she started sobbing into Reed's chest, it was all he could do to keep himself from shoving Reed out of the way and pulling her into his arms.

The sudden onslaught of these emotions were unsettling. He had never felt this level of worry over someone before, and he was having a hard time understanding it.

But the tooth. At least that had gone right. Although, when Ailia said she had traded a promise for the object, he had wanted to punch something. This was all becoming very complicated and draining. He needed to stick to his purpose for being in these lands in the first place: find the artifacts. One down, two to go.

After shrinking all of his weapons, he carefully arranged them in his backpack, leaving Reed the throwing knives and keeping a couple of daggers out for himself. Reed and Ailia had been quietly arguing while they were packing, but Callum had blocked it out, trying to focus on the plans he needed to make. He heard Ailia huff, and looked over to see her frowning at Reed. Callum didn't envy her—he doubted Reed would be leaving her side after this incident.

Callum shouldered his pack and walked towards Ailia and Reed. "We need to get out of this forest and move on. The two objects I have left to find are in Islay and the Orkney Islands. We will go to Islay first by ferry from Oban. It is about a four hour drive, so if we leave now, we will get there by midnight."

"Actually," said Reed before Ailia could respond, "that is what we were just discussing." Reed shot a determined glance at Ailia. "I am trying to explain to her that she does not need to come with us and should wait back at the inn with my mother, where she will be safe."

"Reed, I swear on Elideh's faerie manuscript, if you try to cloister me away, you will regret it," Ailia responded with a wrath Callum hadn't seen in her before.

"Ailia, I already explained this," said Reed sternly. "Clearly the items Callum is searching for are going to attract danger. You could have *died* today. I can't let you come with us."

Callum winced. That was probably not the right thing for Reed to say judging by the change in Ailia's posture.

"You can't *let* me come with you? You can't *let* me?" she said, her voice lethally quiet. Despite the glow that was starting to surround Ailia, Reed did not back down. Callum couldn't decide if Reed was being very brave or very stupid, but he decided to step in before Ailia started shredding him with whatever power was leaking out of her.

Callum stepped between them. "Reed. I understand that you need to keep her safe. I understand the bond you have with her is demanding it. But you do not get to make choices for her. She is still in control of her own destiny, as are you of yours. If she wants to join us, she will join us. You will have to find a way to live with the instincts that are ruling you."

Both Reed and Ailia looked stunned at Callum's words, but Ailia turned to Reed with a smug look on her face, as if she had won this particular battle, while Reed crossed his arms and frowned back at her. This would not be the last time they had this conversation, judging by how stubborn Ailia was and how overbearingly protective Reed was bound to be after experiencing her in mortal danger.

Callum rubbed his eyes, wondering how he had become mediator, and wondering if he would come to regret giving Ailia a choice.

CHAPTER THIRTY-ONE

AILIA

Ailia was fuming. If Reed thought that he could make choices for her and lock her away in a tower for safekeeping, he was sorely mistaken. Still in shock that Callum had taken her side—again—but also still furious that it had even come to that, Ailia was not speaking to Reed. When they had packed everything in his car, she got in the backseat, followed by Storm who had shrunk to the size of a golden retriever, and left Callum to ride in the front with Reed.

The two of them did not look thrilled about the seating arrangement, but they got into the car, and Ailia thought it was fortunate that the car was so large, as Callum looked uncomfortably tight in the front seat.

After Reed had turned onto the road, headlights illuminating the path ahead of them, Ailia realized she was starving. She was still furious at Reed, so her hunger would just have to wait.

Ailia had no words left for Reed. She was done having to repeat the same conversation over and over again. Done advocating for her right to go after her own sister to a person who was supposed to be her friend. She really hoped he could pivot from this pattern and start supporting her instead of trying to force her to flee.

Reed's shoulders were tense as he checked the map to make sure he was going in the right direction, and ever in tune to her needs, pulled over at the first petrol station they came to so that they could get something to eat. Prick.

Before Ailia could open her door, Reed was there, opening it for her and reaching for her hand. She brushed past him, but before she could get far, he gently grabbed her arm, turning her towards him.

"Ailia," he murmured, speaking quietly like she was a skittish animal that needed to be soothed by soft words. "I'm sorry. I know I can't make decisions for you. I just want you to be safe."

Ailia crossed her arms. "I understand that, Reed, but we've been through this before. You can't protect me from everything."

Reed's eyes bored into hers, and as if he couldn't take it any longer, he pulled her to him and pressed his forehead to hers, his breathing heavy. He leaned down, and Ailia was sure he was going to kiss her, but he hesitated. Then, he gently tilted her face to his, and brushed a soft kiss to the corner of her mouth. Like he couldn't stand the distance between them. Like he had been wanting to do that for a long time. Like he needed to.

And she nearly kissed him back. He was so familiar and comforting and real. Unlike the visions. Unlike the magic. Unlike the faerie realm. Maybe this was what she needed. Maybe she could understand his fear.

Reed finally pulled away, but cradled her face in his hands, like she was the most precious thing in the world. Concern creased his brow, but he spoke softly. "We will train more. But I'm struggling, Ails. You know I love you. When you were taken... I've never experienced fear like that. And then you came out of that cave unharmed, and the relief I felt was palpable. But then you were sobbing, and again, there was nothing I could do. Whatever the dragon did that made you cry like that—"

"The dragon did not harm me," Ailia gently interrupted, as Reed bowed his head towards her. "It showed me visions. And many of them will haunt me for the rest of my life." She leaned her forehead against his. "I was overwhelmed. And it brought my fears for Elideh back to the surface. I am okay now. I will deal with it." She paused, unsure if she should push him right now. "Please, like I said before, just be my friend."

Reed nodded his head, but the concern remained. "I will try."

"Thank you," she said.

Callum had been observing the exchange from several paces away. Something flashed in his eyes when they met Ailia's, and she felt her heart jump. "You need to get your emotions under control."

Ailia frowned and started to defend herself, but Callum interrupted. "I was talking about Reed." Callum turned to face Reed. "Your instinct to protect her will ultimately help you, but you have to keep all of the other emotions that come with that drive in check. Enough of the coddling. And enough of the kissing. If you start to blur the line between you two, this will become much more difficult."

Callum didn't wait for a response as he strode towards the store. Ailia went to follow, finding herself agreeing with him more often than she would care to admit, and slightly embarrassed about the kiss for some reason. Storm happily trotted along beside her.

Reed had given her some space to walk ahead of him and was strangely quiet after being reprimanded by Callum. She guessed maybe he really was sorry and would try to make efforts to keep his feelings under control. But she hadn't missed the 'I love you' that had slipped out, and she wondered about the almost-kiss. Was it just a reflex?

Ailia and Elideh had always found family in odd places, and Reed and Mary had definitely made the cut. Of course she loved Reed, but she was pretty sure she loved him differently than he loved her. And if Callum was right about the bond, she would need to be careful.

After choosing enough snacks to last the four hour drive and probably longer, they were back in the car, the tension much lighter than it had been. Callum seemed to be avoiding speaking to both her and Reed, but maybe he was just tired. Storm laid half his body in Ailia's lap while she snacked, occasionally snatching fallen crumbs.

Although the silence was not what Ailia would call comfortable, she figured it would be a decent time to rest. So she leaned her head back against the seat and closed her eyes, letting the gentle sway of the drive and the warmth seeping through her from Storm lull her into sleep. Hopefully they would be at their destination by the time she woke up.

REED

While they were driving, Reed called several local hotels to see if there were any rooms available. On his third try, he found one with a suite available. After informing the hostess they would be arriving late, she told him they could ring a bell for service, and someone would give them their key. Ailia had been asleep for nearly the entire car ride when they arrived in Oban.

He was still reeling from their earlier exchange. He had desperately wanted to kiss her—to *really* kiss her. But he knew it wasn't what she wanted from him. He didn't regret telling her he loved her, either. He was pretty sure she knew, anyway. He knew that she was dealing with a lot, but he just hadn't been able to stop himself. Reed wasn't normally impulsive, but he had needed her close to him. And it was almost an instinct to pull her into a kiss. He would have to talk to her about it. He didn't want anything to come between them.

Reed opened Ailia's door and gently woke her up. Her eyes were still full of sleep as she clumsily got out of the car. Reed had tried to tell Storm to stay outside, but at the look both Ailia and Storm gave him, he knew that wasn't a battle he was going to win. Storm disappeared and Reed assumed he was following close behind Ailia.

They got their key and wasted no time getting to their room. Ailia went straight to the bathroom, quickly changed, and stumbled towards the biggest bed in the room where Storm had appeared, already nestled in the pillows. She flung herself down on the soft mattress and was instantly asleep, Storm moving closer to her before settling in.

That left a couch and a recliner. Callum was lounging on the couch, eyes closed, so Reed guessed the recliner would be his. He didn't mind. As long as Ailia was comfortable and could rest. After triple checking the doors and windows, Reed laid down on the worn recliner, turning off the lamp beside him. He needed to try to get some sleep if they were going to be training tomorrow.

On the drive, Reed and Callum had not talked much, but had at least discussed a plan for training Ailia. Reed had suggested that Callum train with her in the mornings, and they would do magic training in the afternoon. She needed to learn faster so she wasn't so vulnerable. Especially since they were one artifact closer to Elflaine.

Callum agreed and even hinted that he would start training Ailia how to wield a dagger—push-up requirement aside. Reed wasn't sure if he was imagining it or not, but he could have sworn that Callum seemed worried about her. Maybe her capture had insulted his fragile, fae pride. Whatever it was, Reed was glad that Callum was taking Ailia's training seriously, despite his initial reservations.

Reed shut his eyes and tried not to think about the way Ailia's lips would have felt on his.

CHAPTER THIRTY-TWO

AILIA

A ilia woke up with the sun. She started to stretch her arms but quickly stopped and winced, gingerly lowering her arms back to her sides. Stupid push-ups. She glanced around the room, barely remembering their late arrival last night. Storm was curled up against her back, snoring peacefully, and Reed was sleeping in the recliner. Callum, however, was nowhere to be found. She decided to go for a quick run before waking up Reed and getting breakfast, so she snuck into the bathroom, changed into leggings and a loose shirt, and headed out the door.

She had taken two steps out of the lobby of the hotel when she spotted Callum, jogging towards her. His shirt clung to his chest, and his dark hair curled around the sharp edges of his face.

He stopped in front of her, his ocean eyes bright in the sun. "Going out alone? You're sure your witch would like that?"

Although his tone was teasing, she still bristled at the implication.

"Reed is not my keeper," she responded, crossing her arms.

"I guess technically, yes. However, I don't want to start the day having to explain to Reed why I let you wander off in a new town by yourself, so lead the way. I will follow." He gave her a smirk and a mock bow. She smiled and started running in the opposite direction, towards the sea.

The harbor town they were in was quaint. It was built right on the coast in a natural cove, and was surrounded by beautiful mountains. She hadn't run along the beach in a long time, and was looking forward to the salty breeze and the peaceful sounds of the water.

Callum silently followed several paces behind, and although she wasn't thrilled to have an escort, at least he was staying out of her way. In fact, if she was being honest with herself, she found that she was beginning to look forward to being around Callum. He put her at ease and didn't seem afraid to challenge her.

She wondered if Callum knew anything about this town. Atop a hill sat what looked like a coliseum, and in several different places, she could make out castle ruins nestled in glens, or proudly overlooking the bay. She wished that they had some time to explore; she could feel the ancient energy of the area with every step she took.

After running for about half an hour along the waterfront, she started to slow down for a break, but mostly to take in the view.

Callum stopped beside her, leaning against the railing overlooking the water.

"It's so beautiful here," Ailia whispered. "Do you know anything about this place?"

"I haven't been back to the mortal realm in centuries. What do you want to know?"

Ailia paused. "What is the coliseum? I haven't seen anything like that in Scotland before."

"I'm not sure, but it's definitely not as ancient as you'd think. The castle ruins at the top of the hill are far older."

"Is there anything unique about the castle?" she asked, happy that Callum was in such a chatty mood.

Callum paused, seeming to sift through distant memories. "Dunstaffnage Castle is one of the oldest castles in Scotland. Even before it was a castle, it was a stronghold for the ancient Scots. It is said to be haunted by a glaistig, but I have never seen her personally."

Ailia was sure she had read about glaistigs in one of her sister's manuscripts. Something about how they were spirits that had been enchanted by faeries to be protectors of castles? She wondered if she would be able to convince Callum to see the ruin.

As if he had read her mind, he rolled his eyes but turned in the direction of the castle.

"We need to be quick. I'm sure Reed is awake and panicking at your absence. Don't want to provoke him too much this early in the morning," he teased.

Ailia couldn't hide her grin as she jogged at Callum's side. If the glaistig was a faerie spirit, maybe she could find out some information about her sister. Surely they could travel between the realms. And at the very least, she was getting in a good run.

"After we search for the ghost, we need to do some work. I'm assuming you're still intent on training after your blubbery conversation with Reed yesterday?" he asked.

Ailia glanced over at him, frowning at his tone. Was that jealousy she sensed, or general annoyance about the conversation? Callum continued. "I'll take that as a yes. We can do our training in the mornings, and you can do your magic training with Reed in the afternoons." Callum gave her a thoughtful look. "Unless you had any different ideas."

Pleasantly surprised by Callum's addendum to let her choose, she didn't see anything wrong with his suggestion. "Thank you. For asking my opinion. We can train in the mornings, and I will train with Reed in the afternoons. Although I don't think me struggling to do push-ups will really constitute as training."

"Actually, I've been thinking about that. Maybe a hundred push-ups is unreasonable for someone without fae strength. You should keep practicing, because it will strengthen your arms, but we can work on combat training and wielding a dagger. I think you could do both of those without seriously injuring yourself."

Ailia chuckled. "Thanks for the confidence." But she was actually very excited about the prospect of learning how to wield a dagger. And she hoped Callum would teach her how to get in a good punch.

"Listen," Callum said cautiously, his tone more serious than it had been moments before. "It is none of my business, but you need to be careful. With Reed."

Ailia had wondered if this would come up. And also wondered why Callum cared. "Thanks for the concern, Callum, but I can take care of myself. Reed and I used to date. I think it was just a reflex."

Callum looked her over once, then turned to face the road again as they continued jogging. "I am confident you can take care of yourself, which is the only reason I didn't shove Reed off of you last night."

Ailia turned to him, shocked that he had considered doing that in the first place, but he continued talking, ignoring her reaction.

"The bond you two share could make things confusing. I just wanted to warn you so that you weren't going into the situation blind. I have met witches in the past, and typically don't trust them. But I can tell Reed is decent. Just know that the more physical you are with him, the stronger his instinct to protect you will become."

"What do you know about knight bonds?" she asked. She was genuinely curious, but also desperately wanted any information about her new reality she could get.

"Not a lot. They were before my time. But I know bonds of any sort can influence or exasperate any existing attractions."

Ailia was starting to feel slightly embarrassed with the turn of the conversation. She definitely didn't want to discuss any intimacy between her and Reed with Callum, but she did appreciate his warning. "Okay, Callum. I'll be careful. Thank you."

Callum nodded, but looked slightly more at peace than he had before. Feeling like she should change the subject, and wanting to get back to the easy companionship they had earlier, Ailia said with a challenging grin, "Want to race?"

Callum grinned back. "Always, princess."

Happy about the way the day was unfolding, minus the awkward advice, she sped up her pace, Callum matching her, and ran the rest of the way to the castle ruins.

AILIA

As soon as they walked inside Dunstaffnage Castle, Ailia was tapping into her earth magic, seeking out anything that might be hiding from them. The stones seemed to sing in response to her, telling her she was safe. It was still early enough that they had to sneak in—which had caused quite the whispered argument between the two of them. But for the second time in less than a week, Ailia was hopping a fence to investigate a ruin. She had to admit that this time she had at least been a bit more graceful.

Maybe it was the too-quiet atmosphere of the early morning, or maybe it was their purpose for being in the ancient castle, but Ailia's skin was tingling with awareness, ready for anything. Callum seemed tense beside her as well. "We are only having a quick look around, and then we have to go."

Ailia nodded in agreement. This place was creepy. Beautiful, but creepy.

The wind was whistling through the windows and the cracks in the stone, creating an unnerving song as they carefully padded across moss-covered stones, peered through ancient, stone doorways, and avoided the jagged, collapsed walls.

They had made their way into the tower when Ailia felt it. The otherworldly presence. She instinctively reached out to grab Callum's hand and was surprised to find he had been reaching for her as well. They glanced at their hands, but didn't let go. Ailia held her breath as a figure in green appeared by the window staring straight at them, immediately redirecting their attention. She felt Callum's grip on her hand tighten as he tugged her closer to him.

They had found the Green Lady of Dunstaffnage Castle—or she had found them.

Ailia and Callum briefly turned towards each other. As they had been walking through the ruins, Callum told her that this particular glaistig was known as the Green Lady, and was usually benevolent. There were many mysteries surrounding glaistigs, but since they were connected to the faeries, Ailia was hopeful this spirit could answer some of her questions.

After studying the ghost for a moment, Ailia thought she looked curious, and maybe a bit sad. She slowly started to walk towards the Green Lady, and Callum must have sensed the lack of ill-intent because he let her, slowly releasing her hand.

The Green Lady stared with eerie, blank eyes as Ailia made her way towards the window, trying to decide what to ask. But before she could say anything, the Green Lady raised her hand, signaling Ailia to stop. She felt Callum approach her side, hand on the dagger hidden at his waist. Would weapons even work on this creature?

"I will not harm you, Bright One," said the Green Lady, her voice otherworldly. "Ask your question, but come no farther."

Ailia knew she needed to ask the right question—she had a feeling she would only get one chance. She knew from Elideh's research that the faeries usually found ways to speak in half-truths. There was no point asking about an entrance to Elflaine since Callum had vowed to take them. There was no point asking if Elideh was there, because her nightmares had confirmed that particular point. Plus, if Elideh was in this realm, Ailia was confident that Elideh's first course of action would be to contact her. More than anything, Ailia wanted to know if Elideh was okay—that they weren't too late. But how should she pose the question?

Finally, she decided that straightforward would be her best option. "Is my sister a captive of the faeries in their realm?"

"She is with the faeries, and is a captive, but is unharmed."

Ailia blew out a breath of relief and chanced one more question.

"Is she in danger?"

The Green Lady stared at her, and quirked her head to the side, discerning her true intent with her question. "You are stronger together, and you will both face many dangers before the end."

Callum moved closer to Ailia, barely brushing his hand against her arm.

As quickly as the apparition had appeared, the Green Lady was gone.

"We should go," Callum whispered. When Ailia didn't move, Callum gently tugged on her elbow, guiding her out of the castle. As if in a trance, she followed him. Once they were back in the morning sun, Ailia turned to Callum. Before she could get anything out, he said, "I can't." Ailia waited for him to explain.

"I already know what you're going to ask. I can't get you into Elflaine. Not until we find the items I was sent here to collect." Ailia felt any relief from knowing Elideh was alive deflate. Callum took her hand. "But I swear, Ailia. I will help you find your sister," he paused. "And I might have a way to check on her."

At that, Ailia's heart jumped into her throat. "How?" she breathed.

"Torneach—Storm—is able to cross realms. I will send him with a message to see if I can figure out what is happening."

Ailia dipped her head and cradled her face in her hands, the relief palpable, then looked up at Callum, determination and gratefulness shining in her eyes. "Thank you. You don't know what this means to me. If I can just know she is okay…"

Callum nodded, a flash of something like concern in his eyes. "Let's go. We need to do some training." They started to walk back towards the sea. "And Ailia, I wouldn't tell Reed. About what the glaistig said. It will only make him more obnoxious."

Ailia gave a small laugh. "Agreed."

Chapter Thirty-Three

Ailia

After making it back to the waterfront and finding a secluded bit of beach, Ailia endured her forty push-ups and then worked on some basic combat training with Callum.

Although he only showed her various ways to stand, how to shift her weight, and the correct way to hold her arms, she was sore. And tired. But the tiredness felt more like weariness. She couldn't stop thinking about what the Green Lady had told her— you will both face many dangers before the end. What did that mean? The end of what? Between the visions from the dragon and the jarring words of the glaistig, Ailia was thinking she should probably tell both Callum and Reed about the Book of Straun in case it contained any explanations.

She shook her head and tried to focus on her earth magic as they made their way back to the hotel.

She had been practicing small things with her magic like reaching out to the earth or calling to the water, but she had stayed away from fire so far because that seemed like it could easily go wrong. She probably needed Reed's guidance with that volatile element.

They were in view of the hotel when Ailia saw Reed pacing outside the front door. As soon he saw them, he stalked over, frown firmly in place on his handsome face.

"Ah shit," Ailia mumbled.

Callum smirked. "Someone's in trouble," he whispered in a sing-song voice.

"If I'm going down, you're going down with me," she whispered back.

"I can hear you both," Reed said, no hint of amusement in his tone. "What the hell? You just leave? No note, nothing? You were just abducted by a *dragon*, Ailia. You can't just wander off alone."

Ailia tried to respond calmly. "I wasn't alone." She gestured towards the haughty fae male next to her. "Callum was there."

Reed ran his hand through his hair. "I see that. But Callum doesn't have any reason to keep you safe. I do. You don't go anywhere without me."

At that, Callum crossed his arms. "She is safe with me."

Reed looked ready to argue with Callum, and Callum looked ready to fight back.

For fuck's sake.

"Reed, you cannot be serious. We *just* had this fight. I am done repeating myself. If I want to go for a run by myself, I will. If I want to leave in the morning to train with Callum, I will." He started to interrupt her, but she continued over him, "If I want to wander down the street to get a damn latte without you tailing me, I will." Ailia was sure that even her posture was defiant as she leveled her stare at Reed. She was not about to lose her independence over one tiny incident with a dragon.

Reed frowned at her for an entire minute. "Fine."

Callum remained tense beside Ailia, but Ailia decided that was good enough for her. "Let's pack up and head out. We checked the ferry schedule on our way back, and the first ferry leaves in thirty minutes. We need to be on it so we can move on to the next task."

At that, Ailia didn't wait for a response and headed straight to the room to take a long, hot shower. After years of only having Elideh to rely on, she had almost felt relieved that Reed was willing to share some of her burdens. But the relief was slowly turning to resentment, and that was not a path she wanted to go down with Reed. She cared about Reed, and appreciated how much he cared about her, but she wasn't going to lose her freedom just because some ancient bond demanded it. Ailia knew it wasn't entirely Reed's fault and that he was probably already feeling guilty, but he really needed to figure out how to deal with this situation.

She thought back to what Callum had warned her about. Maybe he was right. Maybe she should be more careful with Reed. They had always had a very natural chemistry together, and it was getting more and more difficult to fight against it. Right now, she needed to focus on Elideh. This was the second warning she had received in less than twenty-four hours about some sort of danger they were both in. If only these creatures were less cryptic.

She turned on the hot water, and got in the shower, letting the water soothe her as she processed what she had learned from the glaistig. Elideh was a captive, but was unharmed. They both would face danger before some sort of looming end. She tried not to think about the things Elideh could be going through and remain technically un-harmed, but it was difficult not to jump to the worst conclusions.

Trying to distract herself, Ailia focused on her magic, connecting to the water with the gentle tendrils of her power. Soon, the water was swirling around her, suspended in the air around her body. Could she shape it? Closing her eyes, she envisioned Storm, and willed his shape into the water.

She squealed in delight when she opened her eyes and saw a miniature Storm perfectly sculpted out of water sitting in the palm of her hand.

So. Cute.

She tried to make her water Storm move, but as soon as she tried to command the figure, it burst into droplets, streaming down her fingers.

Slightly disappointed, but also thrilled that she was able to make such a detailed shape, Ailia got out of the shower, dried off, and got dressed. She was toweling off her hair when she walked into the bedroom to find Reed, Callum, and Storm staring at her.

Pausing, she said, "Can I help you?"

Storm simply bounded over to her and nuzzled her side. Callum shook his head and grabbed his backpack, mumbling something about going downstairs before leaving the room. After scanning her body like she could have somehow gotten injured during her shower, Reed finally said, "Sorry, nothing, just ready to get out of here. I feel like Dr. Jekyll and Mr. Hyde these days." He gave her a small smile, and she returned it, knowing he was feeling bad about earlier, and that this was his version of an apology.

She set the towel down and started braiding her damp hair. "Reed. I understand you're adjusting. We will figure it out."

Reed's posture relaxed and he grabbed their bags. "Thank you," he said earnestly. He walked over to her and gently kissed her forehead. She couldn't help leaning into his touch.

"I wanted to apologize for last night," he said, looking into her eyes. "I don't know why I kissed you. But I won't do it again unless you feel differently."

Ailia wasn't sure what she wanted, but she knew that she found comfort in Reed and that despite Callum's warning, she wasn't sure if she wanted more from Reed. He loved her. He wanted her. Hell, he acted like he needed her.

"I'm not sure, to be completely honest. I want to be careful," she hedged.

"That's okay, Ails," he replied, cupping her cheek. "It's up to you. You know how I feel about you—how I've always felt about you. And no matter what, I will be here for you." He pulled her into his chest, and she breathed him in, letting herself relax for a moment. He could be so intoxicating, always drawing her into his orbit. But she pulled away, not wanting to get ahead of herself.

"Let's just take things day by day," she said.

"Deal," Reed grinned. He gave her a chaste peck on her cheek, making her blush. "We should catch up to Callum before he decides to leave us behind. Although, that may not be the worst tactic in the world," Reed mused.

Ailia shoved his shoulder. "He's not that bad, Reed. Plus, we need him if we want to find my sister."

Sighing dramatically, Reed groaned. "Okay, fine." Ailia laughed and followed him out of the room, Storm trotting happily at her side.

CALLUM

Callum had never struggled with self-control, which was why he was fuming by the time Reed and Ailia caught up to him at the docks. This entire morning had been an exercise in pushing down his feelings that were more frequently clawing their way to the surface.

First, that fucking kiss. He had wanted to rip Reed's hands off of Ailia as soon as he had grabbed her when she clearly did not want to be touched. Then, he had the nerve to fucking kiss her—even if it hardly counted. If she had made any indication that the gesture had been unwanted, Callum would have tackled Reed to the ground.

But it was almost worse that she had leaned into Reed.

He had planned on staying out of it, but he couldn't help himself. She had to know that there was bound to be some confusion with their bond. He knew she could handle herself, but he wasn't sure how much control he could exercise if they started doing that all the time.

Second, the glaistig. When she told Ailia that prophetic bullshit about being in danger before the end, Callum had been ready to throw Ailia over his shoulder and lock her away somewhere safe.

And Reed. Fucking Reed and his fucking knight bullshit. Implying she wouldn't be safe with him and telling her what she could and couldn't do. Callum had to muster all of his self control not to punch the witch right in the face, but luckily Ailia beat him to it and told him off.

By the time she came sauntering out of the shower, he knew he needed to get away from both of them. At least the ferry was a four hour journey. He needed some time to clear his head.

Since he had promised Ailia that he would send a message with Torneach, he had been dreading the actual writing of the note. He wouldn't risk sending it to anyone other than his sister. But that meant she would tell their brother. And Callum really didn't want him involved. He guessed he would have to risk it, though. He had promised.

Once they got on the ferry, Callum called Torneach over. Ailia and Reed were chatting quietly, and a little too close for comfort in Callum's opinion. Torneach begrudgingly left Ailia's side and sat obediently, waiting for instructions.

Callum folded the note and gave it to Torneach, who carefully held it in his giant mouth. "You know who to take this to. Hurry back, my friend," Callum mumbled under his breath. Torneach glanced over at Ailia and then back at Callum, as if to say *look out for her*. Callum nodded, and Torneach disappeared.

Callum put his hands on the railing and looked out over the water. He felt Ailia approach, her alluring scent of citrus, lavender, and sea salt reaching him despite the breeze.

Ailia stood next to Callum, resting her arms on the railing. Her light hair was shining so bright in the sun it was practically glowing. She turned her pale, green eyes to him. "You sent Storm? With the note?"

Callum looked down at the water. "Yes. I told him to hurry back, and he seemed not to like the idea of being away from you for too long, so hopefully we will get a response soon." He gave her a tense smile, but turned back towards the water.

Ailia nodded her head, and brushed her hand over his. "Thank you. For doing that for me." They stood for a moment like that, in peaceful companionship, and as she was walking away, Callum tried to calm the racing of his traitorous heart.

Chapter Thirty-Four

The ferry ride was relatively uneventful. Reed had watched the strange interaction between Callum and Storm, and Ailia seemed quiet after Storm disappeared. But since he was trying to be less overbearing, he decided not to ask about it. If Ailia wanted to talk to him about it, she would. Despite the issues they had been facing because of this bond, he knew that Ailia still trusted him.

Although he was slightly disappointed that Ailia didn't want something more with him, he wasn't surprised. For whatever reason, in the time that he had known her, she had never had any long-term relationships. Elideh, on the other hand, went through boyfriends like Ailia went through chocolate scones.

However, he was happy to have the intimacy she was comfortable with and would let her set the pace. She had always been so cautious, and Elideh so reckless. It was incredible that the two sisters, as close as they were, were so different.

Right now, whatever was happening between him and Ailia was the least of his concerns. Reed was trying to quell the anxiety that was slowly making its way through his system. Before the ferry had docked, Callum told them what they would be searching for, and Reed was not thrilled.

Kelpies were practically as mythical as the unicorn, and although their legends were time-honored throughout Scotland, they were extremely sinister and dangerous beasts. When Callum explained that he needed the golden bridle of a kelpie, Reed thought he was joking. Kelpies were seen in the modern world as beautiful, mysterious water horses. In reality, they dragged wandering souls to their watery doom.

No one knew where the kelpies took their victims, because no one had ever survived. Most witches believed that the kelpies worked in league with the underwater kingdom of Finfolkaheem and the corrupted beings that dwelled there—the Finfolk. Although the kingdom itself was supposedly beautifully stunning, with its crystal palaces and many riches, there would be no return for those that do not live beneath the sea. They were so reclusive, no one was even sure what the creatures looked like.

They still had not discussed exactly how they were going to get the bridle of a kelpie, and Reed couldn't think of a way that ended with them all safely above the water. But the first step was to find the ford of the kelpie. The lore surrounding the ford was vague at best, but after consulting Elideh's manuscripts, they decided the most likely location was the northernmost tip of Islay.

Unfortunately for them, or maybe fortunately since they would be away from prying eyes, there was nothing in that desolate part of the island except for the Rhuvaal Lighthouse which had been abandoned for many years. They hoped they would be able to take shelter in the keeper's cottage—that the building wouldn't be in complete disrepair.

Since they had to leave the car in Oban, they would be going on foot. Although it was still the early afternoon, there was no way they would make it to Rhuvaal by nightfall. After the ferry landed in the port village of Askaig, they had inquired about rooms at the hotel. Reed had made sure Ailia's room was next to his, and then they had ventured out into the untamed wilderness of Islay to practice Ailia's magic.

Callum was currently laying against a rock, arms folded, the picture of bored indifference. Ailia had just done a couple of warm-up exercises with her earth magic, and now they were getting to the heart of the lesson: fire.

Reed was glad they were on a secluded, boggy beach. He had no idea how much control she would have.

"Remember, Ailia, I can only wield earth magic, so I can't instruct you on wielding fire. However, I cannot be burned, and I can smother your magic if it gets out of control." Reed glanced at Callum, who frowned back. "And Callum heals fast," he said to Ailia with a shrug.

Ailia laughed, and Callum's frown deepened, but Reed was glad to see Ailia happy.

"Okay, got it." Ailia closed her eyes, and Reed could see the focus in her posture. After a few seconds, fire appeared in her palm. She snapped her eyes open, and although she had a small smile, she quickly resumed her attention, narrowing her eyes on the fire.

"With all magic, you want to remain calm and in control—especially with fire. It is the most dangerous element to wield." Reed thought for a moment. "Try changing the size of the flame in your hand. Start by making it smaller."

Ailia glanced up at Reed, acknowledging she heard his instructions, then looked back at the fire. Callum had sat up by this point, his arms resting on his knees as he focused on Ailia.

After several moments, Ailia blew out a breath and the fire disappeared. She looked frustrated, but she squared her shoulders and closed her eyes again. The flame reappeared in her hand. This time, she kept her eyes closed. Reed pulled his earth magic to him and took a step towards her—just in case. Callum had stepped forward as well. "You might want to back up," cautioned Reed.

"I am not afraid of her," said Callum quietly, keeping his eyes on Ailia.

Reed bristled at Callum's tone, but looked back at the flame in her hand and marveled when it started to shrink. Ailia opened her eyes, and looked up to Reed, then Callum.

"Now what?" she whispered.

"Do it again. Until it becomes second nature. Then we can try something else," said Reed.

Ailia nodded her head, and the fire winked out, then reappeared nearly as fast. Reed couldn't help but feel proud of her. She was determined to master her magic, and he believed she would.

AILIA

After several attempts at shrinking the fire, Ailia decided to take a break. She was distracted. She knew she needed to tell Reed and Callum about the Book of Straun, but she was really unsure how they would react. And she felt like she was betraying Elideh since she wanted it to remain a secret. After the dragon, though, and the glaistig, she needed to investigate the grimoire, and she couldn't do that without including Reed and Callum.

Ailia took a deep breath, and was about to confess, but Reed spoke first. "I don't want you involved with the kelpie, Ailia."

Callum gave Reed a hard look and then met Ailia's eyes. He sat down, running his hands through his hair, his blue-green eyes never leaving hers. "If she wants to get into Elflaine, Reed, we have to find the items on my list. That is the only way to get back."

"We will just find an entrance ourselves," countered Reed. "We were looking for one before you interfered."

Callum blew out a breath and looked at the ground. "Ever since the witch trials, the entrances into Elflaine have been sealed tight. There is no way to get in from the mortal realm unless you are allowed in by the king or queen."

Ailia let this new information wash over her. She was normally so thorough—so cautious. Her urgency to find Elideh had distracted her. Neither her nor Reed had asked Callum details about why he was here. Why had she trusted him so easily? Not that she regretted it—she did trust him. Wholly. But that didn't mean she knew all of his secrets. "Callum," she said quietly. "Who sent you here?"

Callum didn't break eye contact with her, and did not hesitate to answer her. "The queen."

Reed scoffed at him. "Why would the Queen of Elflaine send you to the mortal realm for some sort of demented shopping list?"

Callum swallowed. "I am... bound to her. And I can't explain any more than that." He lowered his eyes. "I don't want to put either of you in danger, but I have to find those items, and there is no other way into Elflaine." After a pause, he said, "In fact, that is one of the main reasons I sent Torneach to inquire about your sister, Ailia. I have no idea how she got there."

"Actually," said Ailia. "There is another way."

Both Callum and Reed frowned at her. It was her turn to blow out a breath. She guessed it was time for truths.

"Elideh found an ancient faerie grimoire. The Book of Straun." Both Callum and Reed paled at the mention of the book. "And she found a spell to open an entrance to Elflaine. That is how she got there."

Although Ailia had burned the note from Elideh, she eventually decided to rewrite most of what she could remember, worried she would forget the last words her sister had left for her. Ailia fumbled in her backpack for Elideh's journal and pulled out the rewritten note, silently handing it to Reed. Callum walked over, and they both read the letter as Ailia waited for their reaction.

Reed looked up at her. "Ails, why haven't you told us about this before?"

"I don't know. I didn't think it would be useful to what we were doing, and I wanted a chance to go through the grimoire myself. Elideh has... trust issues. She said not to show it to anyone." She saw the flash of hurt in Reed's eyes and quickly said, "But I was going to tell you both about it. I really was. I just never got the chance to look through it on my own."

Callum sat down and ran his hands through his hair. Reed was still looking at Ailia carefully. Quietly, he said, "Can I see the book?"

"Yes," she said.

Ailia pulled the ancient tome out of her backpack and carefully unwrapped the scarf that she had put around it. She gently handed it to Reed, not looking him in the eyes. But he didn't take the book. Instead, Reed tilted her chin up so that she was looking at him.

"Just know that I trust you. And it's okay that you didn't want to share this with me." She nodded, the guilt that had been churning in her stomach easing.

"Let's look through it and see what this legendary book is about," said Reed.

The three of them sat on the driest piece of ground they could find with the book in Reed's lap. Reed opened it and carefully flipped through a couple of pages.

"This is... insane," he muttered.

"What do you know about the book?" Ailia asked.

"Not much," admitted Reed. "It is practically a myth. There are many legends about it. Some believe it was the first grimoire ever compiled. Some believe it was written by an ancient faerie queen and a High Witch together. Some believe it is dark magic. But no one has ever found it. Not in thousands of years."

"We have heard those same stories," said Callum stoically. "Some claimed that there were spells in the Book of Straun that could vanquish the darkness, since the book was as ancient as the darkness itself."

Ailia's head was spinning. How had Elideh found a thousands-of-years-old grimoire?

"We need to keep this hidden," said Reed suddenly.

He closed it and wrapped it back in Ailia's scarf. "It's emitting magic. I'm actually surprised I haven't noticed it before now. If it *is* as ancient as the darkness, it could be a beacon." Reed tucked the book back into Ailia's bag. "Callum, I know you've been shielding us, but if you can put any sort of extra protections around the book itself, do it."

Callum nodded. "I can keep it hidden."

"Good. Let's keep practicing, Ails. We can look at the book tonight," said Reed.

Ailia nodded her head and rolled her shoulders. She was relieved that Callum and Reed knew about the book, and wondered when she had come to trust them so completely.

CHAPTER THIRTY-FIVE

AILIA

A ilia was exhausted, but excited. She had managed to shrink the fire in her hand over twenty times and was even able to expand it without losing control. Although it seemed like small accomplishments, it had taken a lot of focus to maintain the fire. Reed was right—fire was extremely difficult to control.

At first it had felt entirely too wild; like something that didn't want to be caged. But the more she wielded it, the more she understood it. Fire was not stable like earth, or lovely like water. It was bold and exciting and powerful. By the time they were done, Ailia felt like she was more connected with the element, and was looking forward to her next lesson.

They had already eaten at the tiny hotel, Ailia absolutely starving after wielding magic and the combat training with Callum from the morning, and she was more than ready to shower and get some sleep. Reed had repeated several times that if she needed anything to come get him, but she had a feeling she would pass out as soon as her head hit the pillows.

She wanted to get a little bit of reading in before she went to sleep, so after quickly showering, she grabbed Elideh's journal and settled into the fluffy pillows on her bed. Reed had asked her to keep the Book of Straun hidden until they all had a chance to look through it, and if it was emitting magic, that was probably the safest route.

Her room at the hotel was charming in the way most Scottish hotels were—wooden furniture, cozy duvets, and, of course, a beautiful view out of the small window. Ailia preferred to sleep with the curtains open, wanting the sunlight to kiss her face as soon as the morning came.

Carefully flipping through her sister's journal, she decided to choose a random entry in the middle. Ailia was hoping that Elideh had written more about her discoveries, but so far she hadn't found anything other than Elideh's musings on various faerie ballads, local stories she had collected, and the occasional theory on how she could get into Elflaine. The entry Ailia stopped on was dated sometime around Samhain from last year. As she read, Ailia's heart nearly stopped at what Elideh had discovered:

I think I have found them—our parents. Well, not actually found them. I was conducting interviews in a little town outside of Edinburgh and came across a strange story. Ailia has done a lot of research on the High Witch of Scotland, Niven, so I am familiar with the lore. But the story I found was about Niven's only son—who I have never heard of, and I am almost certain has been lost to time and history.

Apparently, Niven's son fell in love with a faerie from a prominent bloodline. At the time, witches and fae were allowed to marry, but it was very uncommon because any child that was born to the couple would only inherit the witch's bloodline. The fae are generally proud and vain, so most are unwilling to let their bloodline die. I guess true love overcomes many obstacles, though, because the witch and the faerie married and, after many, many years, had two daughters.

For some unknown reason, the family disappeared. I may be jumping to conclusions, but something tells me this could be mine and Ailia's story. I don't know why—it's just a feeling I have. But it feels right. There are a lot of gaps with this story, so I need to do more research to see if I can find out more about Niven and this lost family before I involve Ailia. I don't like keeping secrets from her, but I don't want to get her hopes up.

She was so young when we lost them. She doesn't remember the night they sent us away—I've asked her. And honestly, I'm glad she doesn't. I'm glad she doesn't miss them the way I do. I'm glad she doesn't have the memory of our mother's kind voice and our father's laugh. Even now, even after all these years, I don't like to remember the last time I saw them, as I pulled Ailia along through the woods away from them, convinced they would find us.

If this lead can explain what happened that night, I will follow it. I have to know.

Ailia stared blankly at the journal, nausea churning in her stomach. Every time Ailia had asked Elideh about their parents when they were children, Elideh had hugged her and told her that *they* were each other's family now. But she never told Ailia what happened to separate them from their parents. She hated that Elideh had carried this burden alone all this time.

But surely Elideh *was* jumping to conclusions. That story was so vague—it could be about anyone. It could be completely made up, considering Ailia had done extensive research on the witches in Scotland—specifically the High Witch—and had never once come across anything that even hinted that Niven had any children.

Maybe Elideh had found more in her research. And whether or not that was the true story of their parents, it was obvious that their family had a magical bloodline, given their powers. Ailia shook her head. If she was being honest with herself, she couldn't handle the enormity of this right now. She would have to explore the mysteries of her family once Elideh was safe.

Ailia put the journal away and tried to calm her mind as she settled into her soft bed for the night. Luckily, she was exhausted, so it didn't take long for her to fall into an uneasy sleep.

It had been hours. It had been days. It had been seconds. Ailia wasn't sure.

At first, she had been trapped in one of her old foster homes, searching desperately for Elideh. Then, she had been lost in an overgrown hedge maze, the silence unnerving, and the hopelessness suffocating.

Now, a thick mist swirled around her, caressing the trees, making it impossible to see.

She was walking through the woods in a twilight so dull, she wondered if there was any color in this hellscape at all. She was panicking. She couldn't use her magic here, and she felt empty. And she was scared. How was she going to get out if she didn't know where she was?

She stopped to catch her breath, panting hard.

Then she heard something—something that made her heart drop out of her body. She would recognize that scream, that voice, anywhere.

She sprinted towards the sound, panic threatening to choke her.

Suddenly, the screaming—pleading—stopped.

She turned around frantically, but was met only with silence. The screaming started again, and she spun around, running as fast as she could towards it. When she was sure she was getting closer, she was enveloped in silence again. She kept running, though, certain she was close. She made it to a clearing, but it was empty—apart from the blood splattered trees.

Sinking to the ground, she pulled her knees to her body, vaguely noticing that her arms and legs were covered in scratches from where she had crashed through trees and bushes.

Where was she? Where was Elideh?

She rested her forehead on her knees and prayed to whatever god was listening that her sister was okay, and she let the tears fall silently down her dirty cheeks.

CHAPTER THIRTY-SIX

CALLUM

Callum woke up suddenly—immediately alert. He scanned his room, his fae eyesight easily piercing the night, but could not detect anything that would have ripped him from sleep so thoroughly.

Apprehension was slowly coursing through him, something urging him to *get up, get up, get up.*

He stood, grabbing a dagger, not bothering with a shirt, and slipped out of his room. He paused in the hallway, trying to pick up on anything unusual. That was when he noticed it—the darkness—coming from the other end of the hall.

No. It couldn't be.

The evil that had been plaguing the faerie realm hadn't crossed over into the mortal world in centuries.

Go, go, go the voice urged him.

Shit. Callum ran to the end of the hall, banging on Reed's door before skidding to a halt in front Ailia's room—where the darkness was seeping out from under the door. He yanked the handle, but it didn't budge. Callum slammed his shoulder into the door, bending the hinges.

The door should have splintered with the force Callum put into it.

Reed was behind him, throwing-knife in hand.

"What's happening!" Reed demanded.

But Callum could barely hear over the roaring in his head. He put his full body weight into the door again, and this time, it crashed down. He rushed in, and his heart nearly dropped out of his body when he saw Ailia laying on her bed, shrouded in the swirling, smokey darkness that Callum had faced so many times.

It seemed to pause at Callum's and Reed's presence. Reed lunged towards Ailia, but Callum stopped him.

"Don't touch her," he commanded. Callum walked to the bed and bent down over Ailia without getting too close. He spoke her name, quietly at first. The darkness was swirling, pulsing around her. His own panic—and the terror rolling off Reed—was becoming unbearable.

"Ailia!" he shouted in a voice laced with power that he typically reserved for the battlefield.

Her eyes snapped open and found his. And then she started screaming.

Callum barely had time to put up a shield before light as bright as the sun exploded out of Ailia. Callum and Reed were thrown backward, and from the look of the room, would have been scorched if it hadn't been for Callum's shield.

They both jumped to their feet, rushing towards Ailia who had sat up, her eyes eerie and glowing. She slowly turned to face Callum, and he paused, unsure of the otherworldly energy still surrounding her.

Her eyes started to dim, and as they did, her body slumped back down to the bed.

Reed was at her side, pulling her into his lap before Callum could get there.

"What happened?" Reed whispered.

"I don't know," said Callum quietly, trying to reel in his thoughts. "It's like something yanked me from sleep. I'm not sure what. When I couldn't figure out why, I decided to check on both of you. That's when I saw the darkness coming from Ailia's room."

"Why couldn't we touch her?" Reed asked, not taking his eyes off of Ailia.

"Because the darkness is unpredictable." Before Reed could demand more details, Callum explained the evil that the fae had been fighting for centuries, and how it could manifest in different forms. Right now was not the time to explain everything, though.

Right now, Callum was trying to figure out how the darkness had infiltrated the human realm and why it had found Ailia.

"This is not good," Callum said after several moments.

"Obviously," said Reed, still stroking Ailia's hair and occasionally leaning down to make sure he could hear her breathing.

"No, you don't understand," said Callum, running his hands through his hair. "If the darkness has found her, it will return. I still don't know how or why she survived being surrounded by it the way she was."

Reed didn't respond.

"As soon as she wakes, we need to leave. We shouldn't stay here any longer than we have to. I will shield us, which might hide us from it for a time. But I have a feeling it will eventually find its way back to her," said Callum.

Reed nodded his head. "I could carry her. If we need to leave right away. Just tell me what we need to do."

Callum considered it for a moment. Even though the fae had been battling the darkness for hundreds of years, they knew very little about it. They knew it was a corruption of magic, and that it was able to corrupt other beings—to turn them into abominable creatures that were very difficult to kill.

It seemed like the blast of light from Ailia had incinerated the darkness, though. Which was new. So maybe they would have time before they were found again. But maybe not.

"We should leave. We can take turns carrying her. From here on out, we should stay armed. And you should do whatever you can to keep your magic replenished," Callum decided.

Reed nodded and gently moved Ailia onto the bed. "I will pack my things and come back to pack hers."

Callum understood the unspoken words—don't leave her alone until he came back. And for once, he was in complete agreement with the witch.

He sat on the edge of the bed, not daring to touch her. Her pale hair was limp, and her normally sun-kissed skin was sallow. This journey had just become much more dangerous, and if he could release Reed from his oath, he would. But they didn't have a choice. They had to see this out to the end. If the darkness found Ailia once, it would not hesitate to find her again. If he could get her to Elflaine, he was sure he could keep her safe. He just had to find the last two items on his list. And fast.

Reed came back into the room, propping the broken door up against the wall. Callum wordlessly went to gather his things. It would be better to be on the move, and to be in a place where Reed could more easily wield his magic. Callum just hoped that they could stay hidden long enough to complete his task.

CHAPTER THIRTY-SEVEN

REED

Although the hike to the tip of Islay was not technically far, it was going to take them a while to get there. Between carrying Ailia and carrying all of their supplies, they were moving as quickly as they could. The land was boggy in places—water-logged—and in others there were hills that led to small mountains. Since it was still the middle of the night, it was not ideal to be navigating the ever-changing terrain. Overall, not a situation Reed was thrilled about.

Reed carried Ailia for the first two miles before Callum made them switch. He was reluctant to let her go, but knew he needed to focus on recharging his magic. So he passed her too-still body to Callum, and started to reach out to the earth, letting his connection to the element ground and center him.

"Why do you think she hasn't woken up yet?" he asked Callum.

Callum glanced down at the girl who seemed too fragile at the moment. "I don't know. It seems like she has gone into some sort of deep sleep—maybe to regain stasis. But the darkness affects everyone differently." Callum paused, worry wrinkling his brow. "It could also be the burst of energy that came out of her. It was powerful."

That was an understatement. Reed had never felt that sort of power. If Callum hadn't shielded them...

Maybe she was just recovering. Sometimes when a new witch emitted too much magic, their bodies forced them into a type of hibernation so that their magic could replenish. Unfortunately, that left her extremely vulnerable. Reed scanned the area again.

They continued walking carefully through the dense trees, trying to stay away from the small streams that snaked their way through the ground. Kelpies were able to traverse even the smallest bodies of water, and they couldn't afford to take any chances at the moment.

"Tell me more about the darkness. Ailia mentioned it to me in the story about the knights, but I hadn't heard of it before then." Reed paused. "Plus, in the story she told me, she said that the darkness had been defeated."

Callum was silent for a couple of minutes. "I did tell her that. It was partially true." He glanced at Reed who was frowning back at him. "We were able to weaken the darkness, and when the realms were sealed, the darkness was trapped in the faerie realm. But we have been fighting it on and off since then."

Reed mumbled a curse. "So this darkness... no one knows where it came from. And it can shapeshift. And corrupt magic."

Callum nodded.

"So why is it in the mortal realm?" Reed asked quietly.

"I don't know." Callum shook his head. "What's worse is I don't know *how* it's here."

They continued walking, both lost in their own thoughts and worries.

After a while, Reed asked, "Does the darkness normally... act the way it did with Ailia? It didn't look like it was attacking her." Reed shook his head. "But I can't figure out what exactly it *was* trying to do."

Callum looked down at Ailia again. "No. It normally obliterates. Creatively."

Reed swallowed, his mouth suddenly dry. He couldn't believe they made it out alive—that Ailia was okay. Or at least she seemed okay. Reed couldn't get the image of her eyes out of his head. He prayed it was remnants of her power that had made them glow and not whatever evil the darkness came from.

"Let me know when you need a break," Reed said.

"I will be fine," Callum replied, looking down at Ailia with a softness that Reed hadn't seen before.

Reed tried to focus on his magic—replenishing it and spiraling into it as much as he could. But he couldn't stop thinking about Ailia, surrounded by that darkness, and wished she would wake up.

CALLUM

They made it to the lighthouse just as the sun was beginning to peak over the horizon. Callum carried Ailia the rest of the hike, unwilling to hand her off to Reed. He gave Reed the excuse that he should focus on his magic. Reed seemed to buy it. In truth, Callum had not wanted to hand her off, holding her close to his chest the entire time, occasionally breathing her in, reminding him she was alive.

They walked up to the keeper's cottage, which was abandoned like they had hoped, and Reed began to test the doors and windows. They were all locked, but after a couple of forceful shoves, Reed had the door open. He put their supplies down and held the door for Callum.

Callum looked toward the dawning sunrise. "I think we should keep her outside. In the light."

Reed gave him a puzzled look.

"I may be wrong, but she seems to become more alive in the sun. And she seems to almost shine when she's in the direct light. Have you not noticed?"

Reed looked from Ailia to the sunrise, squinting his eyes against the bright light.

"You may be right," Reed mused. "I wonder if that's some-how connected to her powers. All witches recharge in different ways—maybe that will help her wake up." He ducked into the cottage and came back with several blankets and a pillow. Then, he found a spot on the beach and formed a makeshift bed on the sand.

Callum walked over with Ailia and gently laid her down on the blankets, careful to set her head down on the pillow. He stretched his arms, and despite the soreness, he immediately missed her warmth. Reed settled in the sand next to her, brushing a loose strand of hair out of her face, and Callum flinched towards her. What was wrong with him? He didn't normally feel possessive like this—he was used to being on his own. He shook his head, trying to clear his mind, and strengthened the shield he had been holding around them all night. Now, all they could do was wait.

"We should eat something," Reed said. Luckily, they had refreshed their supplies in the tiny port village yesterday. Callum sat on the other side of Ailia, and Reed handed him a chunk of bread. They ate in silence, watching the sun stretch towards the sky, casting glittering light over the ocean.

"So what's the plan for the kelpie?" Reed asked, his tone serious.

Callum ran his hands through his hair. "Well, there is only one way to get the bridle. One of us will have to trick the kelpie into thinking we are lost. Then, it should offer to let us ride it. Once we are on its back, it will trap us. And we will have to get free and steal the bridle—and most likely kill the kelpie."

Reed stared at Callum. "Oh, that's all?" he scoffed.

Callum shrugged. "It is the only option. Kelpies are notoriously reclusive and mysterious. The only way to find one is to play its game."

"So what happens if the bait—because that is what we will be—can't get free?" asked Reed.

"That's why I needed help," Callum responded with a strained smile.

"This is insane," said Reed, shaking his head.

And maybe it was insane. But there was no other way. Callum was contemplating the various ways they could free themselves from the kelpie when he felt Ailia shift beside him, and relief washed through him. She slowly began to open her eyes, lifting her hand to shield her face from the sun.

"Ailia," Reed breathed. She turned to Reed and gave him a small smile. Callum tried to push down the pang of jealousy that flashed through him, but then she turned to him.

"You found me," she said, her voice hoarse. Callum couldn't stop himself from reaching out to hold her hand.

"Always," he whispered. She squeezed his hand before letting go, and he thought his stupid heart would combust.

She slowly sat up, Reed helping her, and Callum went to get her some water. She thanked him and drank greedily as she leaned against Reed's chest.

After she had eaten a couple bites of bread and drained the water, she said, "What happened? Why are we on a beach?"

Reed looked to Callum, so Callum told her what he had told Reed, trying to ignore the way Reed was stroking her hair, and explained what he could about the darkness.

Reed was frowning when Callum had finished. "Wait, when you said that Callum found you, what did you mean?"

Callum had been so relieved to hear her speak that he hadn't even noticed the strangeness of her declaration. Ailia looked between the two of them and took a deep breath.

"I was lost—trapped. In what you called the darkness." Ailia nodded her head towards Callum. "I was terrified. I couldn't find a way out and it kept changing. Sometimes it was one of the homes Elideh and I lived in. Sometimes it was like one of those old hedge mazes. Sometimes it was the complete wilderness, and all I heard was Elideh screaming. But every time I started to find a way out, it changed. It felt like I had been trapped there forever, and I was about to give up." She looked up at Callum. "But then I heard you call my name, and I didn't feel lost anymore. I knew if I opened my eyes you'd be there. So I wasn't afraid." Ailia looked down at the sand and hugged her knees. "What do we do now?" she asked quietly. Callum wasn't sure he was breathing. Thank the gods she had found her way out.

Callum and Reed glanced at each other, each reflecting the other's worry. Reed put his arm around her shoulder, and she leaned into him once more, soaking up the comfort he offered her. "Callum and I are going to deal with the kelpie. You need to rest."

"I want to help," she replied.

Callum tensed at her request, but to his shock, Reed said, "If there is a way for you to help, you will." Ailia looked at him suspiciously but nodded her head.

"For now, how about we have as normal of a day as possible? I understand we are on a time crunch, but let's do some training—make sure you're okay," said Reed gently.

Callum wasn't sure if training was the best idea, but maybe it could help them determine how she was recovering both   physically and mentally. He stood up and reached for Ailia's hand. "Let's go, princess," he said with a wink, trying to keep his tone light despite the warring feelings flooding his thoughts.

Ailia took his hand and rose to her feet, completely steady. "Lead the way," she winked back. And Callum found he wasn't faking the smile he returned to her.

Chapter Thirty-Eight

Ailia

Despite everything that had happened over the last two days, Ailia felt good. Actually, she felt better than good—physically, anyway. She was doing everything she could to stay away from the horrors the darkness had trapped her in. She may have given Callum and Reed an abridged version of what she was actually lost in, but she figured they would be annoyingly overbearing if she told them the truth. Plus, she really didn't want to relive it.

But her body felt great. She felt strong—like the air she was breathing was somehow better than it had been before and was giving her energy that felt more pure. After letting Reed fuss over her and make sure she was able to go on a run, her and Callum had set out at a frustratingly slow pace.

Every time she tried to speed up, Callum told her to slow down. To quit rushing. To make sure she was okay. But she knew she was okay. She just had to make Callum believe it.

"I think you want me to slow down because you're afraid I could beat you if I really tried," said Ailia.

Callum snorted. "Not a chance."

"Then prove it." She took off. She heard Callum swear behind her, but kept going.

Faster, faster, faster. Until she felt like she was flying over the sand.

The ocean on her right was a turquoise blur, the wind whistling a song in her ears that made her heart soar. She had never run this fast in her life. She wondered how long she could keep up this pace.

Suddenly, Callum was beside her, running at a full sprint. She tried to push herself harder, but when she looked over at Callum, she tripped. Before she hit the sand, Callum lunged for her, rolling so his body was under hers and pulling her head into his chest. They skidded across the sand like a stone, rocks flying around them, and when they finally stopped, Ailia lifted her head, her eyes wide in shock.

"What just happened?" she asked, breathing heavily.

He was still holding her tight against him, and she could feel every defined muscle the warrior had spent centuries honing—every frantic beat of his heart. His body dwarfed her's, and she had never felt more safe. Her traitorous body seemed to melt into his, but her brain finally caught up, realizing that she was lying on top of him. She fumbled to roll off and sat on her knees, grabbing his hand to help him. He winced, and she noticed small drops of blood trickling off of his elbow. She moved around to his back and gasped—it was shredded from sliding across the coarse sand.

"Shit, Callum! Your skin! We need to get back. I'm sure Reed has an ointment or something we can put on the wounds to fix them."

"Ailia, calm down," he responded. "I heal quickly. I don't need an ointment. It barely stings."

Ailia frowned at him, trying to decide if what he said was true or if it was some sort of alpha posturing, but as she took a closer look at the cuts, they were, in fact, already starting to scab over.

"Callum, I am so sorry. I don't know what happened. I just tripped, but I don't know why we slid across the sand like that," she paused, and then said more quietly, "and thank you."

Callum nodded, brushing off her thanks. "Well, you were running so fast that I had to use some of my magic to give me a burst of speed to catch up—which I have never had to do, by the way. I could tell that you had no idea how fast you were going, and I knew if you lost control at that speed, you'd get hurt." He paused to test his shoulder, and to Ailia's relief, all the bleeding had stopped. "At one point, I'm not even sure your feet were touching the ground."

"I'm not sure they were either." Ailia shook her head. "This doesn't make any sense. Why would I suddenly be able to run at such an impossible speed?"

Callum snapped his head up and tilted it, considering her. Then, before she could stop him, he grabbed a jagged stone and cut her arm.

"Ow! What the fuck, Callum?"

"Just wait. I have a theory," he responded calmly.

"A theory that you have a death wish?" she bit out.

Callum rolled his eyes and stared at her cut. Right as she was about to continue her shouting, he held up her hand. "Look."

She looked down at her arm, and her mouth dropped open in surprise.

Her cut was almost completely gone.

"This mirrors what the fae experience when they go through their staying. Maybe you have gone through yours. Or are going through it? Since we still know very little about your heritage, I have no idea how it works," said Callum.

Ailia's head was spinning. And then, to Callum's shock judging by the look on his face, she swore. Colorfully.

"Can I not just have one normal day?" She laid back on the sand, more forcefully than she meant to, and rubbed her eyes until she saw fireworks dance under her eyelids. She put her arm over her face and leaned towards the ocean, breathing in the salt air like it was a salve. Her life had become a whirlwind, and she felt like she would never stop spinning—never catch a breath. This wasn't supposed to be a quest to uncover whatever these new powers were. All she wanted to do was find her sister.

Callum barked a laugh at her. "Are you serious? Are you throwing a tantrum right now? Because you're possibly going through your *staying*?" He sat down in front of her and grabbed her hand, pulling her up so she was sitting. "Do you know what this means if it's true? You're stronger. You're faster. You're *immortal*."

She was still staring down at the sand, wallowing. Nothing had been okay since Elideh disappeared. What if Elideh *didn't* go through a staying? What if they couldn't get to her?

Callum grabbed her chin and gently lifted her face so that she was looking at him. "This is a good thing, Ailia," he said softly. "And it will make training a lot more fun."

She huffed a laugh at the glint in his eyes, knowing 'fun' meant 'dangerous,' and she knew he was right. There was no point dwelling on things that were clearly out of her control.

Callum stood and reached down his hand to her. "Let's go back. You covered a lot of distance at the speed you were running, so it's going to be a trek." She grabbed his hand and let him pull her up. Damn, her stupid legs felt wobbly. Too much too soon.

He let go of her but grabbed her shoulder when she immediately started swaying. Callum shook his head. "You've got to learn your limits. And you need to get used to your new gifts." Before she could protest, he scooped her up and started walking back to the lighthouse, which was, in fact, very far away.

"You don't have to carry me, I can walk," she grumbled.

"You really can't, though," he said with a smirk.

Well, he had her there.

Ailia tilted her face towards the sun and closed her eyes, settling into his arms as if it was the most natural thing in the world. She focused on the sound of the waves crashing against the shore and tried to imagine what Elideh would say about her new *gifts,* as Callum called them, and she could immediately hear her sister's reprimand for being pouty—and to embrace being a badass. A smile slowly formed on her face, and the more she thought about it, the more she couldn't wait to see what she could do.

CHAPTER THIRTY-NINE

REED

Reed saw Callum carrying Ailia and shook his head as he started walking towards them. Why was there always something?

"Is she okay?" he shouted as he got closer.

"She's fine," Callum shouted back. "She's just decided this is how she likes to travel now."

Reed could hear Ailia cursing Callum soundly, and Callum laughing at her. Reed jogged to meet them, unable to hide the smirk from his face. "Princess indeed."

"I'm not a princess," Ailia said, very unconvincing as she frowned but made no effort to move from Callum's arms.

"Whatever you say, milady," Reed said with a small bow. Ailia rolled her eyes, clearly sick of both of them.

"She ran so fast we are pretty sure she was flying for a couple of seconds, so her legs gave out," explained Callum as they made their way to the keeper's cottage.

Reed's jaw dropped. "You're joking."

"I'm not," said Callum more seriously. "I think she must have gone through her staying. It's the only thing that explains her speed. But even at that, I have never seen another fae run that fast."

Reed looked her over. "Shouldn't it have been more noticeable? If she went through her staying?" Reed wondered if going through a staying should make her appearance more... fae-like.

"Maybe whatever happened with the darkness triggered it. But yes, normally there is some sort of indication when it begins. And it is usually a longer process—not an instantaneous switch."

Reed shook his head. "So then maybe not a staying? Guess we can just add that to the growing list of things that don't make sense."

Ailia started fidgeting. "Okay, I think I can walk now."

Callum gently set her down and continued to hold her waist until she seemed stable. "I'm fine," Ailia said stubbornly.

Callum arched his eyebrows at her.

"Here, Ailia, come sit and eat something," said Reed.

She carefully walked over to the small table Reed had pulled out of the cottage. He was trying to hold in his laugh at the sight of her walking like a baby deer—her unsteady legs betraying her assertion that she was 'fine.' Callum, on the other hand, was outwardly smirking.

"Oh shut up," she said. "Both of you," glaring at Reed as well.

Reed held his hands up in surrender. She sat and began to eat. Tilting her face towards the sun in between bites.

"We'll deal with the kelpie later—depending on how you adjust to your gifts," Callum said to Ailia. Reed had to agree with him. This would delay their plans, but if she had truly gone through her staying, there was no telling what her magic would be like.

"I agree," said Reed. "After you rest and can actually walk again," he smirked, "we will test out your magic to see if it has changed too."

"Fine," Ailia said. "If you two want to coddle me, I can't stop you. As long as you keep feeding me. And as long as we start working on the kelpie soon. I don't want to waste any more time than we have to."

Reed was happy to continue coddling her, as she called it. If it meant she stayed safe just a little longer, he would do whatever he needed to do. He had considered arguing with her about helping with the kelpie earlier, but decided it would be pointless. He knew that she was going to want to help, so now it was his goal to make sure she was as equipped as possible to face whatever threats they would meet and to keep her out of the thick of the conflict.

As long as she wasn't the bait for the kelpie, he could live with her involvement in Callum's insane scheme.

"Wait, I'm confused," said Ailia. "I thought I already went through my staying when my magic manifested."

"Fair point," said Reed. "But witches don't go through their staying the same way fae do. Like I explained, witches aren't technically immortal. Our staying is more of a slowing. In our twenties, we stop aging as quickly as mortals."

"But I thought that I was already basically doing that since my magic manifested?" Ailia countered.

"Well, actually," hedged Reed. "To be honest, I had been avoiding this topic. Since only full-blooded witches actually have a longer lifespan, I didn't want to get your hopes up since I wasn't sure if you would go through a witch's staying. The only true way to tell would have been time—if you had noticeably stopped aging."

"Oh," said Ailia, frowning down at the sand. "So what about Elideh? Do you think she has gone through a staying?"

"I honestly don't know, Ails, but that's why I was hesitant to talk to you about it. I know it would be difficult to think that you could possibly outlive your sister. And I didn't want to burden you with that information," said Reed gently. "But with the way things have changed, I think Elideh will mirror your abilities in some way."

"Maybe Elideh entering the faerie realm actually triggered all of this somehow," mused Ailia. "So explain the staying the fae go through, Callum."

"Typically, once the fae are in their twenties, thirties, or sometimes forties, they will come into their powers and stop aging. Before that, we don't have any magic, and we can't shapeshift," explained Callum.

Ailia's eyes whipped up to meet Callum's. "Wait... so am I going to be able to shapeshift?"

"I don't know," answered Callum. Ailia's shoulders seemed to droop, but Callum said, "Since you apparently have a mixed bloodline, I have no idea what you'll be able to do. But it will definitely increase your strength, your endurance, your speed, and of course, give you immortality. And as we saw, your ability to heal."

"What do you mean, 'as you saw,'" interrupted Reed.

"Oh, Callum cut me with a stone," Ailia casually responded.

Reed rounded on Callum. "I'm sorry, you did what?"

"Fuck off, Reed," scoffed Callum. "You know I would never endanger her. I just wanted to see if she could heal."

Reed let his emotions simmer before responding. "Okay, well now that we have determined that Ailia is, in fact, going through her staying, let's not experiment on her powers, yeah?"

Callum chuckled, and Ailia rolled her eyes at Reed. He knew he was being ridiculous, but he couldn't help it.

"Of course, Reed," said Ailia placatingly, patting his hand as she shoved more food in her mouth. "Now back to the coddling," she said jokingly. "Someone grab me more bread."

She laid back in the sun, but winked at Reed. She had no idea that, even though she was joking, he would spend the rest of his very long life taking care of her if she let him.

AILIA

Ailia's legs were finally working again, and she didn't feel weak. After convincing Reed that she would be able to practice her magic without fainting, they made their way to a clear spot on the beach. Since they were surrounded by water, it seemed like a good opportunity to push her limits and work with fire again.

She still hadn't told Reed or Callum that she could wield water. She wasn't sure why she was keeping it a secret, but she knew she would have to tell them eventually. For now, she would focus on fire. She had been playing with her earth magic all afternoon—simple things like tracing shapes into the sand, or building small figures with the rocks. It was becoming easy to connect to the elements, and she hoped that she could form a more natural connection with fire.

Since she had proven during their last lesson that she had at least some semblance of control over the fire, Reed decided it was time to work on some magic that would actually help her fight. He had her craft her shield of earth in one hand, which she proudly adorned with some seashells. Once he was satisfied that her shield wouldn't fall apart, he told her to hold out her other hand and conjure fire.

Her hands started to shake as she struggled to maintain the shape of the shield and wield fire at the same time, but both held, and she took several steadying breaths.

He frowned at her shaking hands, but she shook her head once, daring him to comment.

Reed sighed and raised his eyebrows in a challenge. "Shrink and expand the fire."

Ailia loved the feel of the fire in her hands. It was warm but wild—begging to be set free. And it was beautiful—mesmerizing. The fire fueled her, while the shield of earth grounded her. After successfully manipulating the flame several times, and her shield only crumbling once, they finally moved on to something more exciting.

"Throw a fireball up in the air and catch it," said Reed. He had his arms crossed and a slightly bemused expression on his face. Callum was observing from her other side, his face carefully blank.

Ailia could tell that Reed thought she would struggle with this task. However, shaping the fire into a ball was very similar to what she had been doing with water droplets the past couple of days. So she easily made a ball, tossed it once into the air, and caught it. She gave Reed a smug look.

"Now throw it at me," he grinned. He had moved into a defensive position, his hands raised and ready to wield the earth to shield himself.

"Gladly," she grinned back. Ailia was reveling in the excitement she felt. Her and Elideh were highly competitive, and having Reed here, unbreakable and ready for a fight, brought back that familiar adrenaline of a challenge coursing through her.

Ailia threw the fireball as hard as she could right at his chest. To her complete disappointment, it was barely an ember by the time it reached him. Before he could comment, she had already conjured another one and was throwing it at his face. This time, she focused on the fire after it left her hand. And this time, Reed had to throw up his shield.

Callum's mouth turned up at the corners and mumbled, "Nice aim, princess."

"I'm just getting started," Ailia muttered back.

Keeping her shield in place, she conjured ball after ball of fire, throwing them in quick succession at different parts of Reed's body, her frustration from the past couple of weeks igniting her. She hadn't felt like herself since Elideh disappeared, but she felt like she was finally coming alive. She reached out to the earth, strengthening her shield and rooting herself in the sand, perfecting her balance, and although she was not using her water magic, she felt it calling to her like a siren's song.

Despite the power coursing through her, Reed's shielding and instincts were very fast, and she was getting frustrated that she hadn't landed one single hit. She wondered if she could remove his shield with her earth magic.

Making a snap decision, she dropped her shield to both Callum and Reed's immediate protests, and threw her earth magic at Reed's shield at the same time she hurled a fireball. Just as Reed's shield exploded into dust, the fireball hit its mark—square in his chest. His shocked look was mirrored on Callum's face as she ran over to Reed.

"Reed, are you okay?" she asked. "I'm sorry, I got caught up in the moment."

"No, I'm fine," said Reed, looking slightly shaken. "I just... was not expecting that."

"That was a really dangerous risk, Ailia," reprimanded Callum. "Dropping your shield can be deadly."

"It was the only way I could get past *his* shield, though," Ailia countered after she was sure Reed was fine.

"I didn't say you shouldn't have done it, I just said it was dangerous. If you were on the battlefield, it might have been a risk worth taking."

"I disagree," said Reed. "Stay on the defensive. Don't drop your shield. Ever."

"We can argue about this all day, but if you had been using any offensive magic against her, she wouldn't have lasted long, and you know that, Reed," said Callum.

Reed looked ready to argue back but Ailia interrupted them. "I just wanted to see if I could use my earth magic to interfere with Reed's. If I was fighting against someone intent on harming me, I wouldn't have dropped my shield. Plus, now that I know I can do that, I will work on maintaining my shield while wielding earth magic for other purposes simultaneously."

Reed nodded his head, but still looked unconvinced. "Other than dropping your shield, you did really, really well. You're learning very fast. I didn't notice a change in your magic, though. Did you sense anything different?"

Ailia thought about it for a minute. "I don't think there was anything significantly different. Since I have never tried wielding two elements at the same time, I can't be sure if I was able to do it because of a change, or if I would have been able to do it before. It did seem easier to do than I thought it would be."

"Well, we will keep trying new things and see how you progress. Let's take a break. You need to eat and rest. We don't want you burning out," said Reed.

Ailia was starving. Of course. But she didn't feel the exhaustion that normally came when she used her magic. Maybe that had changed?

She was just proud that she had managed to throw actual fireballs. And glad that Reed couldn't be burned by her magic.

Chapter Forty

Reed had to admit, he was impressed with Ailia. In fact, he was more than impressed. He was astonished. She was powerful. He could tell that Callum noticed it too.

Although he wanted to push her limits on her magic, he was worried that it would draw unwanted attention. Magic tended to be drawn to magic. And if there was some sort of evil force trying to find them, her power might just be a beacon.

While she was resting, he had asked Callum to make sure his shield was still surrounding them. Callum reassured Reed that he had kept a shield around them all ever since they left the hotel, and Reed realized that Callum might be more powerful than he was letting on as well.

Ailia stood up and was stretching, so Reed walked over to her, ready to start again.

"This time, I'm not going to tell you what to do. Just use your instincts. But I am going to fight back, so be ready," he said with a grin.

He knew the bond he had with her would never allow him to actually hurt her, so he had to convince himself that this was a game.

"Bring it on, Reed," Ailia said with a wicked smile.

Reed's smile grew wider, thrilled to see that spark back in Ailia. She had been withering under the stress of Elideh's disappearance, and if it took getting hit in the chest with fireballs to make her feel more alive, Reed was happy to play.

Once they got into place, he gave Ailia a chance to construct her shield, and then they started.

Ailia had conjured a fireball, but before she could throw it, a vine sprung out of the ground and wrapped around her wrist. Shock flashed across her face but was quickly replaced by fierce determination. The vine burned away, and she was throwing a fireball at him in the same instant. He easily shielded against it and threw his magic at her shield, crumbling it.

She rebuilt it, but seemed to struggle to conjure her fire while she was rebuilding her shield. Reed took advantage of her distraction and forced the ground under her to shift. She stumbled, but quickly regained her footing, her lithe legs having regained their toned muscles since the beginning of their journey. Now, she was starting to look mad.

Good. He needed to know how she would react under pressure.

Ailia squared her shoulders and threw a wall of earth up between them. Reed easily dismantled it, but it had given her time to strengthen her shield and conjure her fire. As soon as the wall of earth came down, he was defending against fireballs.

Reed copied her tactic and built a wall of earth between them. He continually reinforced it against her attacks while reaching out through the ground to find where she was standing. Then, he started encasing her legs in sand, silt, and rocks until he heard her cries of frustration.

He took the wall down to find her glaring at him.

"Not fair!" she shouted at him.

"Fighting is rarely fair, Ails," he said with a smile.

Ailia threw her hands down towards her legs, and the earth trapping her flew apart. The fire in her hands was starting to wrap around her arms, like lethal gloves. Her eyes were glowing with fury, as if the beast inside her had finally woken up. Reed blinked, realizing suddenly that her eyes were *actually* glowing, the fire now curling around her shoulders.

"Ailia," said Callum, coming to stand next to her. She turned to him, still tense, and very bright—like she was a fallen star, or a ray of lethal sunlight.

"*Ailia*," Callum said more forcefully. Her shoulders started to relax, and her eyes began to dim. She shook her head and glanced between the two of them, still not quite herself.

"Reed wasn't going to hurt you. You were practicing. You're safe," Callum said in a soothing voice, tracing her shoulder with the back of his hand. Finally, her body slumped, and the fire went out. She sank to the sand, and Reed strode over, Callum kneeling down beside her.

"I don't know what happened," Ailia said. "I was furious. It was like the anger had completely taken over. I've never had a temper like that. Normally Elideh is the more emotional one between the two of us."

"I'm sorry if I pushed you too hard, Ails," said Reed. It hadn't seemed like she was overwhelmed until he trapped her. Maybe some instinct had kicked in when she felt helpless.

"You didn't push too hard. It was like I was overcome by this feeling that I couldn't control. Maybe my magic *has* changed," she said more quietly.

Callum had stayed quiet, but was looking at Ailia intently. "Your magic was acting the way faerie magic acts in battle. Our magic rises up to protect us and others. It is more a part of us, more connected to our emotions and instincts, than the magic witches wield." He paused, considering something. "It looked to me like your elemental magic was instinctually getting ready to defend you. I don't think that is common amongst witches, but maybe your magic is different because of your other gifts."

Gifts none of them really understood. They were quiet. Reed had to admit, Callum's theory made sense. Reed wasn't sure what that would mean for Ailia, though. He had always been in control of his magic, so he didn't know how to help her if her magic started acting on its own.

"Let's stop for the night," Callum said.

Ailia nodded her head, looking tired, and Reed wished he could shoulder the burdens that were weighing on her. She stood up and started walking towards the cottage. They all needed a good night's sleep. Reed was really starting to feel drained from not sleeping the night before and using his magic today. Hopefully Callum's shield would keep the darkness away.

AILIA

Although she should have been exhausted, Ailia couldn't sleep. The keeper's cottage was tiny, but cozy. Callum and Reed were sprawled out on the soft chairs by the fireplace, since they insisted that Ailia take the single bed. Not that she was complaining—despite the state of the creaky mattress. But she did feel a little guilty about how tired they both seemed considering they hadn't slept the night before.

"Goddess save me," Reed mumbled.

"Seriously, Ailia, what the fuck are you doing?" Callum muttered from his chair.

Ailia turned to her other side, the mattress squeaking and groaning with every movement. "I can feel every single coil in this mattress."

"At least you have a mattress," Reed said, stifling a yawn. He had a point.

"Fine," said Ailia, trying to settle into the ancient bed. "I'll just read until I fall asleep."

Impatient sounds of agreement from both Reed and Callum coaxed Ailia into quietly retrieving Elideh's journal and crawling back into the bed as quietly as she could.

Reed fell asleep almost immediately, and Callum lit a fire in the small hearth since it started to rain. Although it was technically still summer, it was beginning to cool down, especially at night. Callum stayed awake, but after a quick argument, and assurances that she would wake him if she heard any strange sounds, Ailia convinced him to sleep. After he settled into his chair, his steady, slow breathing indicated he was asleep, which left Ailia awake and alone with her thoughts. She wished Storm was back.

The soft pitter-patter of the rain on the roof was beginning to lull her, but she felt restless. She had been reading her sister's journal by the firelight, hoping to find some sort of explanation for her magic. Elideh had mostly written about her research—various theories she had about the faeries, thoughts on stories she heard from locals. Nothing about magic, though.

She wanted to look through the grimoire, but they had all decided to keep it hidden in case *it* was the reason the darkness had found her in the first place.

It started raining harder, and the fire was beginning to dim. She tucked Elideh's journal next to the grimoire safely in her bag, and snuggled into the small bed. She had to admit that she was maybe a little afraid to go to sleep—afraid of the nightmares that could be waiting for her. But as she closed her eyes and let the sounds of the night relax her, she convinced herself that she was safe with Callum and Reed right next to her, and she finally slept.

Chapter Forty-One

Ailia

For the next week, they got into a routine of waking up at dawn, Ailia testing her limits with her new abilities that they still weren't sure were fae, then training in the afternoon with her magic. After Reed and Callum were satisfied that she was not going to be dragged back into the darkness anytime soon, and once she was feeling more confident in her magic, they decided it was time to pursue the kelpie.

"You are absolutely *not* going to be the bait for the kelpie, Ailia," Reed said sternly with his arms crossed.

"We've gone through the options a million times, and this is the only way, Reed," Ailia countered. Out of all the options they had discussed, Ailia and Callum agreed that the most likely way for no one to be dragged to a watery death was for Ailia to be the bait. Between Callum and Reed, they should be able to free her. Reed, however, was obstinately against the plan.

"She won't be in any real danger. We will be able to kill the kelpie and free her before she even hits the water," said Callum, kneading his brow.

"You can't possibly know that," said Reed. "No one has ever escaped a kelpie. What makes you certain we could free her? I have offered myself as the bait multiple times."

"And we have decided that my control over my magic is still too unpredictable, and it is too risky for Callum to go up against the kelpie on his own," said Ailia. "I still have my magic. I still have my shiny new strength and speed. Between the three of us, I will be okay."

Ailia knew there was a risk to this task. A huge risk. But it had to be done. She hadn't had any more nightmares, but Storm had not returned yet either. Everyone was starting to get antsy.

Reed was staring between the two of them and finally sighed. "Even if I keep refusing this insane plan, I wouldn't put it past you two to go behind my back. So I'd rather be part of it from the beginning."

And Reed was absolutely right. Ailia and Callum had, in fact, joked about just leaving Reed out of the plan altogether. Over the past week, all three of them had become close. Callum was always pushing her and testing her, and Ailia found that she liked the challenge. He didn't treat her like she was a fragile thing that would break. He let her take risks and encouraged her to push past her limits. Although she had always been the more cautious sister between her and Elideh, she loved this new side of herself.

It seemed to annoy Reed to no end since Callum's pushing typically ended in some sort of mild danger or mischief, but it was just the way of the faeries—he really didn't mean any harm. They had all come to a nice balance and seemed to switch off being the voice of reason. But with the plan for the kelpie, Reed was definitely on his own, and he knew it.

Ailia grinned at Reed and Callum clasped his shoulder, saying, "I knew you'd come around."

Reed rolled his eyes and muttered something about being ganged up on, but Ailia was excited about helping get the bridle. She still hadn't told them about her water magic and wondered if maybe now would be a good time, but didn't want them to delay their plans in case they decided she should train with it before going after the kelpie. It would just be her secret weapon.

One of the reasons they were adamant about attempting their plan today was because the rain had finally cleared up. It was a crisp, sunny morning, and they all agreed the less water involved, the better. Now, it was time for Ailia to get lost. And to hopefully be found by a kelpie.

REED

They had gone over the plan so many times that Reed was actually beginning to feel more confident, and less like he was going to throw up. Callum had been scouting out different places in the woods that might work. They had initially thought to lure the kelpie onto the beach, but Reed had pointed out that shallow water would be better. Plus, the more earth they were surrounded by, the stronger his magic would be.

Kelpies were known to track their victims through any body of water, no matter how large or small, so they figured it wouldn't hurt to start off with a small tributary inside the forest, but close enough to the sea to entice the creature.

They made it to the clearing Callum had chosen, and Reed grabbed Ailia before she walked towards the water. "Remember, touch the kelpie with as little of your body as possible. It will be easier to free you the less entwined with it you are."

"I know, Reed. We've been over this a million times," she said more patiently than he would have expected. He knew he was crossing into overbearing territory, but he couldn't help it. The thought of her being dragged underwater scared the shit out of him.

Before he let go of her, he gave her a quick kiss on her head. "Just make it back to me," he mumbled into her hair.

"I will," she promised. And at that, she smiled up at him and walked towards the water.

Reed crossed his arms from behind the cover of the trees as he watched her go. "We better pull this off," he muttered to Callum.

"We will," said Callum, tense at Reed's side.

Before they left the cottage, they had strapped as many weapons to themselves as they could. Reed had his throwing knives and the recurve bow. Callum had a variety of daggers, a hunting knife, and sword strapped to his back. Yesterday Ailia had trained with a dainty dagger and hadn't lethally wounded herself, so Callum let her keep it. It was currently strapped to her thigh, hidden by her jacket that was wrapped around her waist.

Once Ailia was in position, sitting by the water looking lost and forlorn, Callum disappeared stealthily into the forest, positioning himself opposite from Reed. None of them had seen a kelpie, so they had formed their plan based on legends they had heard.

The only thing they were absolutely sure of was if the kelpie got Ailia underwater, there would be no way to save her. So they had to strike immediately. The tricky part was going to be the timing. She had to be touching the bridle in order to take it. Otherwise, it would disappear into the water with the kelpie if they killed it.

Reed was starting to feel nauseous again.

He shook his head, focusing on Ailia and calling the earth magic to him, readying himself. Now, it was just a waiting game. A deadly, risky waiting game.

CHAPTER FORTY-TWO

CALLUM

Callum was really starting to regret this. The longer Ailia sat by the water, just waiting for a kelpie to show up and drag her to her death, the longer Callum had to decide how stupid this plan was. They had been waiting for over two hours, and although Callum had to get that golden bridle, he was relieved the kelpie had not come.

They had agreed to wait as long as possible. They didn't know how long it would take a kelpie to sense someone's presence, and they also didn't know if the person in question needed to be genuinely lost in order for the kelpie to find them. Usually, Callum's plans were thorough and well thought out. Since they were literally dealing with legends, this plan was much looser than Callum was accustomed to—and it was unnerving him.

He kept telling himself that between his experience and Reed's bond to protect her, Ailia would be safe. But he couldn't know for sure. So he remained tense, ready to attack at any moment.

Finally, after another hour, and after Ailia was trying but failing to hide her boredom, Callum sensed the forest still around him. The normal sounds of birds singing to each other and creatures crawling through the fallen leaves had ceased. Ailia must have felt it too, because she looked more alert, her hand casually going to the dagger hidden beneath her jacket.

Callum scanned the forest, but saw nothing. Then, Ailia's head snapped to the side, and he followed her gaze.

Striding toward her was the most beautiful horse he had ever seen. It was corporeal, but its silver mane and tail flowed like water, its white, muscular body shining in the light. It was dazzling. Callum had to shake his head, feeling entranced by just a glimpse.

He saw that Ailia had stood, but was also shaking her head, trying to fight off the lure of the creature. It continued to walk elegantly toward her, slowly, like it was a wanderer itself. Ailia shifted toward it, not breaking eye contact, and Callum couldn't tell if the shift was intentional, or if she was being drawn to the creature of death.

This was a bad idea. This was a really bad idea. He prayed to whatever gods were listening that Reed was ready with his magic, and that the bond that demanded he protect Ailia would burn through the creature's allure.

Ailia paused and tilted her head to the side, as if she was listening. But Callum heard nothing. He started to move swiftly and silently toward Ailia, ready to abandon the mission if he thought they wouldn't be able to free her. She moved toward the kelpie once more, but he saw the flick of her eyes in his direction and almost sighed from relief. She was in control of her actions. That, at least, was a small comfort.

When she was close enough to touch it, she stopped suddenly, tilting her head again. Then, she reached out and stroked its mane. To Callum's shock, she was able to pull her hand away. She stepped closer and touched its neck. The kelpie leaned into her touch. Callum was edging closer toward her, liking this less and less.

The kelpie nudged Ailia's side, inviting her onto its back. She hoisted herself onto the kelpie, and that is when the bridle appeared. As soon as she grabbed the bridle, vines shot out of the sodden earth and attempted to wrap around the kelpie's legs. At the same time, an arrow flew toward its side, and to Callum's horror, went straight through the beast as easily as it would cut through water.

That answered one of the questions from the legends. Although they looked solid, they definitely were not. Callum could see the silvery strands of the kelpie's mane wrapping around Ailia's arms. The kelpie turned, kicked away the vines easily, and began to gallop toward the sea.

No, no, no.

Callum was sprinting toward them, ready to tackle the creature. Ailia was trying to fight it, but couldn't get to her dagger.

"FIRE, AILIA! USE YOUR FIRE!" bellowed Reed from nearby.

Ailia's hands began to glow, and in the next breath, the kelpie cried out angrily, and Callum saw steam rising from the beast's neck. Alila threw herself off of its back and Callum was there before she hit the ground. He wrapped his body around hers, and they rolled until finally coming to a stop against a massive tree trunk. He sprang to his feet and shoved Ailia behind him.

The kelpie rounded on them, glaring at Callum with its too-intelligent eyes, but another arrow came from behind it, whirling straight through it again. Then, it disappeared into the woods, as fast as the wind.

Callum turned to Ailia and grabbed her face, her shoulders, her hands. She was okay. Definitely shaken, but okay. He could have collapsed from relief.

Reed was there in an instant, pulling Ailia into his chest.

"We are *not* doing that again," Reed said fiercely. "Are you hurt? Are you okay?"

"I'm fine," said Ailia. "I feel like I could run a marathon from the adrenaline pumping through me, but I'm not hurt," she said with a shaky laugh.

"Well, we definitely learned a lot," said Callum. He decided to wait to remind Reed that they would, in fact, have to try again. This time, though, he didn't know if he could handle Ailia being the bait either. That had been way too close.

Callum hadn't thought to use fire against it. Although he wasn't sure that it would deter the creature for long. If anything, it just seemed to anger it. They would have to think very carefully about what to do next time. But for now, he figured Reed would need at least a day to cool off before reconsidering a plan.

Reed finally released Ailia, but was still raking his eyes over her, scanning for injuries. Callum would be lying if he wasn't doing the same exact thing. He just couldn't believe she escaped. It was supposed to be impossible. Just as he was about to suggest they head back, he noticed something on her wrist.

He grabbed her hand and flipped it. "What is this?"

Ailia frowned at it and then looked back at Callum. "I don't know. Maybe it's a bruise?"

Reed was peering over her shoulder. Callum guessed it could be a bruise. It was a blueish color, but it seemed to be shaped like a teardrop.

"Let me see," said Reed, taking her wrist from Callum. Reed ran his thumb over the mark, and Callum noticed Ailia shiver slightly, which annoyed him for some reason.

"I don't think this is a bruise. I think it's a marking. I can feel some sort of magic from it—but it's strange," said Reed, frowning at the mark.

"Great," muttered Ailia. "Now I have a weird, kelpie tattoo."

Reed frowned at her. "It's not funny, Ailia. If it marked you, it might be able to track you." Reed ran his free hand through his hair. "Fuck. Have you ever heard of anything like this, Callum?"

Callum stared at Ailia's wrist, and couldn't keep himself from grabbing it out of Reed's hand. He turned her wrist to the left, and then to the right, then grabbed her other wrist and examined it. He rubbed his thumb over the mark, just like Reed had, and his heart jumped when her eyes shot up to his.

"I haven't," Callum said, not looking away from Ailia's bright eyes. "Sometimes, oaths are sealed with markings, but this obviously is not an oath." He dropped her wrists and immediately missed the warmth of her soft skin.

"We need to go back to the cottage. Maybe there's something in the grimoire or your sister's manuscript," said Callum.

Ailia nodded her head, looking down at the mark on her wrist.

"I agree. Let's get out of the woods before the creature comes back," said Reed, closely following Ailia and scanning the trees as he walked.

Callum picked up the arrow that Reed had fired and followed behind them. He thought that Ailia was unusually quiet, but then again, she had almost been drowned by a kelpie. He would probably be quiet too.

CHAPTER FORTY-THREE

AILIA

Ailia couldn't stop looking at the mark on her wrist. It seemed to shift with the light, but maybe she was imagining things. She still couldn't believe that the kelpie had spoken to her.

At first, she was surprised to hear its voice in her head.

"Why are you here, Bright One?" the kelpie had asked.

"I'm lost," Ailia had replied in her thoughts, "and can't find my way back to my friends."

"Lying doesn't suit you, child. Why are you here?"

Ailia had paused, but decided to tell the truth. She hadn't really had a choice. "I need to find my sister, because without her, I am lost."

The kelpie had nodded its head and shook its mane, snorting a small spray of water toward her face. "I see. But you would not be lost without the Star Kissed; you would be fine without your sister."

Ailia frowned, turning over the confusing names in her head. "But I love my sister, and I need to know she is okay."

"Very well," the kelpie said, swishing its tail and stamping one of its hooves. "I will take you, Bright One, if you trust me."

Ailia had nodded her head, and approached the kelpie, stroking its mane.

She was pretty sure she had burned through most of whatever strange trance had taken hold of her initially, but maybe some of its charm had lingered. She realized as they were walking back that she *had* possibly made an oath. The kelpie had told her it could take her, and she had said yes. That was when it nudged her to get on its back. She really hoped that whatever she agreed to was not binding, but the mark on her wrist suggested otherwise.

Both Callum and Reed were walking right next to her—like they were afraid the kelpie would sprout out of the ground and take her away. They made it back to the cottage, and Reed opened the door, ushering Ailia inside.

"I think we should look through the grimoire," Reed said as soon as they were all safely inside.

Ailia couldn't hide the surprise from her face. "Really? You're sure it is safe?"

Reed sighed. "Is anything we're doing safe? At this point, if it shows us a way to get rid of that mark, I think it's worth the risk."

"Good point," said Callum.

Ailia stood and got the grimoire out of her backpack, carefully unwrapping it. She glanced at Callum, and he nodded. "I've already strengthened the shield."

She handed the book to Reed. "You can do the honors."

Reed released a deep breath and took the book. "Typically grimoires are fairly unorganized since they are kept for generations. But most of the time, there is some sort of chronological order to things."

"I didn't have a lot of time to look through it before now, but from what I did see, there were pages of spells alongside stories about the faeries," said Ailia.

"Grimoires don't typically contain stories, so that's one immediate diversion from the norm." Reed frowned. "I guess we just start at the beginning."

Ailia nodded, and Callum crossed his arms as Reed began to flip through the pages carefully. "I don't recognize a lot of these spells."

"I don't recognize half of the *words*," said Ailia, reading over Reed's shoulder.

Reed nodded. "Definitely not English."

"It looks like it might be the old fae language. Only our most ancient texts are written in it, and we don't have any full translations," Callum said.

"So a grimoire with fae stories, written in both English and some sort of lost language? Fantastic," Reed said sarcastically.

"Wait," said Ailia. "Go back a page. I thought I saw something about kelpies."

Reed flipped back to the previous page. "There—" said Ailia. "Under the illustration of the castle."

"I'll be damned," whispered Callum.

Although the noble kelpies frequently adhere to the Finfolk, they can, on occasion, act of their own accord. The kelpie puts its herd above all else and is always in search of ways to increase its power—and for freedom. Similar to the dragon, the kelpie hoards treasure and zealously protects its own. Stay away from the kelpies, for they are many, and they do not forget.

She plopped down on one of the chairs and crossed her arms. This was not a comforting revelation, and she had a feeling that Reed was going to revisit what he had mentioned earlier—that they were not going to go after the kelpie again. She was ready to sit back and watch the fight that would surely ensue.

Reed shut the book gently and began to wrap it up in the scarf. "We are done. We are not going after the kelpie, and we are not finding the rest of the items on your list." He glanced at Ailia and then back at Callum. "Or at least *she* isn't." Ailia rolled her eyes. So predictable.

"It's just a book, Reed, it might not mean anything. And it didn't say anything about a mark," said Ailia.

"Did you not read the same entry as me? There's no way you're going after the kelpie again."

"Let's skip the 'can't put Ailia in danger' speech," Callum sighed. "I, for one, am exhausted. And we all know that you are not going to stop Ailia from doing anything."

"Plus," said Ailia, sitting next to Callum, "I am not waiting until the Winter Solstice to find my sister. We have to find the items on Callum's list."

Reed closed his eyes and kneaded his forehead, muttering to himself. "You two are insufferable."

"How about you play that guitar you found, Reed?" Ailia suggested, sure to plaster her sweetest smile on her face.

Reed rolled his eyes but picked up the old guitar by the fireplace. He had been rummaging through the wardrobe on their first day in the cottage and found it buried under some moth-eaten blankets. He'd managed to fix the strings enough to pick out simple tunes.

Callum glanced at Ailia and quirked his eyebrows. They'd been taking turns distracting Reed every time he tried to make the case to keep Ailia out of 'danger.' "Good idea, Ailia."

"Thanks, Callum. In fact, how about we sit on the beach and start a fire? Tomorrow we can go back into town to get supplies and then come up with a new plan."

Callum stood and grabbed Ailia's hand, pulling her up.

"I know what you're doing." Reed grumbled. "But fine. We can pretend we are normal for a night."

Ailia easily lit the fire with her magic and settled onto one of the driftwood logs that littered the beach. There was no point worrying about the kelpie. Worry would get them nowhere, and Ailia was tired of being scared.

Reed started picking an upbeat song on the guitar, and Ailia closed her eyes, breathing in the salt air and soaking up the last rays of dusk. She opened her eyes to find Callum smiling at her. Suddenly, he stood and reached out his hand.

Ailia frowned at him, but took his hand anyway.

Callum bowed to her. "May I have this dance, princess?"

Ailia grinned and sank into an awkward curtsy, absolutely delighted when Callum pulled her into his body. Her hand felt so small in his calloused grip, and he led her effortlessly, guiding her with his other hand on the small of her back.

"Didn't know you could dance, Callum," joked Reed as he picked up the pace of his song.

"What can I say, I'm full of surprises," said Callum, winking at Ailia.

Ailia laughed, feeling lighter than she had in days. Callum lifted her, spinning her easily, never missing a beat as he glided back into step.

"You like to spin?" he asked.

"It's my favorite part," Ailia said as Callum twirled her under his arm.

Every time Callum spun her back into his hard body, she thought she felt her heart skip a beat.

Eventually, Reed slowed the tempo of the song, and as he played the last note, Callum brought her hand to his mouth and brushed a kiss along her knuckles.

Ailia felt herself blush, but she didn't care. She couldn't wipe the smile from her face even if she wanted to.

"Thank you, Callum."

He kissed her hand once more, and his ocean eyes consumed her. "If I had known dancing made you that happy, I would have asked a long time ago."

Ailia let her hand linger in his, then smiled at him again before turning to Reed and walking toward the fire. "You're getting better at that, Reed."

Reed leaned the guitar on the stump next to him. "Think about how good it would sound if one of the strings wasn't a tiny little vine," he joked.

"Well, even with your makeshift repairing, it was lovely," said Ailia.

They sat peacefully by the fire, listening to the waves. Despite the distraction of the dancing and the warmth of the fire, Ailia's thoughts soon turned to the kelpie. She glanced at her wrist, the brand from the kelpie shining in the starlight.

Reed noticed her looking at it. "It'll be okay, Ails. We will figure it out."

"We will," agreed Callum.

Ailia stretched her arms over her head and yawned. "Well, I think it's time for bed."

Callum and Reed both nodded to her, but made no moves to follow her. She wondered if they would try to hash out a plan for the kelpie, but decided to let them figure it out. The kelpie was a problem for another day. Now, she needed sleep.

CHAPTER FORTY-FOUR

AILIA

They woke up the next morning, and the brief moment of fun they had the night before was a mere memory. The tension from the previous day had returned.

Ailia decided it might be best to just have a normal day... or as normal of a day as they'd been having for the past couple of weeks. After eating a small, quick breakfast, she asked Callum to train with her. Typically, Reed let them wander off and train together, but today, he followed them.

"Looks like someone is back on bodyguard duty," muttered Callum, smirking at Ailia. Ailia glanced back at Reed. "Let's work on combat training today. I think I need more practice with the dagger."

"Agreed," said Callum.

Ailia could not get the dance out of her head, and she really did not need the distraction if they were going to train with weapons. Ailia took the dagger that she had strapped to her leg and got in a defensive position in front of Callum. Reed was close by, arms crossed and looking very serious.

"Reed, I'm going to be fine. We're just training," said Ailia.

"And I'm just watching," said Reed sternly.

Ailia rolled her eyes and focused on Callum, trying to forget about her hand in his, twirling under the starlight. "Let's go," she said.

Callum winked at her. He whipped out a dagger so fast she barely tracked his movements, and all of a sudden, she was blocking a strike. He backed up slightly, giving her a couple of seconds to reposition, and struck again. This time, she was more prepared. She blocked his blow and spun, using her momentum to shove her shoulder into his chest.

He was a solid wall. Of course. She backed up, readying herself to strike. But Callum was too fast—he swiped her legs out from under her and she fell. Hard.

"What was that for!" she gasped. Normally, their training was more predictable.

This wasn't a fair fight. But maybe that was the point. He walked over and reached down to help her up. She took it, and as soon as she was standing, she sliced at him. He moved out of the way at the last second, a feral grin on his face.

Right as he lunged toward her, Reed came out of nowhere and tackled Callum to the ground. Callum quickly rolled them and was on top of Reed, holding the dagger to his neck.

Ailia ran over and sputtered, "What is with you two? Reed, why did you tackle him?" When it was clear that Callum was not making moves to get off of Reed, Ailia rolled her eyes. "Callum, get off."

Callum obeyed, but was tense. "Don't ever do that again, witch."

Reed stood, looking like he was ready to punch Callum right in his pretty face.

"You can't just attack her without teaching her how to defend herself. She'll get hurt," Reed said, fuming.

"Kelpies won't fight fair. Faeries won't fight fair. She needs to learn—faster," countered Callum.

Ailia finally understood. Reed, still on edge from the kelpie, was fully consumed by his knight bond. And it looked like the kelpie fiasco had shaken Callum more than he was letting on.

Ailia stood between them and touched Reed's arm, knowing that the contact would ease some of his tension.

"Reed. If this bond is going to prevent me from training with Callum because of your drive to protect me, you're going to have to leave. And Callum, I know I need to learn faster, but I'm starting with nothing here. I need to know some defensive strategies."

Both Callum and Reed were glaring at each other. And to think they had been getting along so nicely for the past week.

Realizing that she was getting nowhere with either of them, she said, "How about this—I finish training with Callum, and then we can all go back to the village for supplies. Maybe it would do us some good to take a break for a couple of hours."

Callum and Reed both nodded, but still didn't look too happy. Reed gave them some space but still stood guard. Ailia guessed she wouldn't fight it.

"Okay princess, get into your defensive stance. You *have* learned the basics, by the way. You just need to apply what you've learned from hand-to-hand combat to wielding a dagger," said Callum, back in instructor mode.

Ailia nodded, not wanting to argue that those were two very different things for her. She listened patiently while Callum explained the subtle ways to adjust what she already knew to include the dagger. The biggest difference being not to stab herself, and not to get stabbed.

Callum stood next to her and had her practice different positions. After she was beginning to feel more confident, Callum suggested they spar. Reed walked over to Callum with his hand out. "Let me spar with her," he demanded.

Callum rolled his eyes but gave up his dagger. "Fine, I can critique you both this way," he said.

Reed squared off in front of Ailia, face still grim.

"Don't worry, Reed, I'll go easy on you," said Ailia sweetly.

Reed's mouth twitched. "Ever gracious, milady."

Ailia struck quickly, and Reed blocked her easily. Damn it.

She tried again, but every time she got near him, he deftly moved away. After several frustrating minutes, she stopped.

"I'm not going to learn anything if you're just on the defensive. You have to come at me too, Reed," she panted.

Ailia could see Callum smirking out of the corner of her eyes but decided not to draw attention to it. Reed looked her over once and then got into a ready position.

"Very well," he said.

Ailia squared her shoulders, ready to deflect a blow. Right as Reed lunged toward her, the ground under her shifted. He barreled into her, knocking the wind out of her as she fell to the ground.

She looked up and saw Reed leaning over her while she tried to catch her breath.

"Holy shit, I'm so sorry, Ails. I didn't mean to hit you that hard."

"You're. Dead," she huffed.

Ailia shoved Reed back with a wall of sand and then stood, finally able to breathe again. Reed had already disassembled the wall and was walking toward her, his arms up in surrender.

"I'm sorry, I didn't mean—" but before he could finish, Ailia was throwing fire at him. He threw a shield up at the last minute, the fire turning the sand into glass.

Callum was watching in amusement, but looked like he was ready to interfere if he needed to.

Ailia took a couple deep breaths and calmed down. She was still getting used to her heightened emotions. She knew Reed hadn't tried to hurt her, but it had really pissed her off. Especially since he had just tried to stop her training for that very reason.

"You realize that it's just training, right? And that you didn't actually have to tackle me?" Ailia said.

Reed walked around the glass wall and said, "Are you going to throw fire at me again? Or is it safe?" He gave her a sheepish grin.

"Don't be so dramatic. I was just mad," she said.

"I really am sorry. I have no idea why I used so much force. It didn't feel like I was, and then all of a sudden you were on the ground. Maybe the training we've been doing has made me stronger than I realize," he said jokingly.

But Callum looked at Reed curiously. "Actually, witch, you might not be far off. Let's try something." He walked over to Reed and held up his hands in front of him.

"Punch my hands as hard as you can," said Callum.

Reed frowned at him. "Not that I haven't wanted to punch you since I met you, but why?"

"I just want to see something," Callum replied.

Reed stood in front of Callum and then punched one of his hands. The furrow of his brow was the only sign of surprise Callum showed, but said, "Do it again."

So Reed punched Callum again. "Interesting," muttered Callum.

"What?" Reed and Ailia said at the same time.

"Let's race," said Callum.

Reed and Ailia looked at each other incredulously.

"Callum, are you okay?" Ailia asked.

"Just humor me," he responded.

Reed and Callum walked a few paces ahead and then stopped. "I'm not a runner like you two, so I don't think this will end well for me," said Reed.

"Just go as fast as you can," said Callum. "On three. One, two, three."

And they both took off at a sprint, sand flying behind them. Callum easily outpaced Reed to start with, but soon, Reed was catching up. Callum was always slightly ahead, but Reed was not far behind.

They finally stopped, and started to walk back toward Ailia, clearly discussing something.

Callum looked smug, and Reed looked slightly bewildered once they came into view.

"Anyone going to explain?" said Ailia impatiently.

"I think this confirms that you did go through a fae staying. Reed has inherited some of your gifts, just like the knights of The Order used to."

Oh. She had forgotten about that part of the story. If Reed was stronger and faster now, that was definitely a good thing. Reed looked unsure. "We are going to have to test this out. But let's head back to the village to get supplies."

"Agreed," said Ailia. "I can't eat stale bread anymore."

At least Callum and Reed had seemed to come to some sort of temporary truce. Ailia really hoped this kelpie thing wouldn't force a wedge between them. She had enjoyed the companionship and camaraderie that had developed between the three of them.

They got their backpacks and boarded up the door. Although they would be back by nightfall, they didn't want any creatures settling in their little shelter. A real meal would make them all feel better. And maybe a couple of drinks. They had earned it.

CHAPTER FORTY-FIVE

AILIA

The walk to the village was a nice change of pace. Ailia used it as an opportunity to work on her magic in small ways—clearing the path for them, swirling fire around her wrists, occasionally sending an ember to Callum or Reed if they were annoying her. Reed was also using the walk to test out his new strength, grace, and speed. Although he seemed skeptical at first, he quickly started to enjoy his new skills.

After stealthily sneaking up on Callum for the second time, Callum easily twisted and shoved Reed hard to the ground. Reed laughed it off, and Ailia smiled at the interaction. She walked over to Reed and reached out her hand to help him up. He took it and grinned at her.

"This is fantastic. I feel the same... but more. It's hard to explain," Reed said.

"Yes, I know what you mean," she agreed. "It took me a while to get used to it, but it actually feels incredible."

Reed nodded his head eagerly, but before he could respond, Ailia was being tackled to the ground by a giant, furry mess.

"Storm!" Ailia shouted in delight. He was licking her face while she laughed, and she felt like everything was right in the world again.

After sniffing her to make sure she was okay, he finally moved away from her so that she could stand up. He sat by her side, looking up at her adoringly and nudging her thigh until she was rubbing his ears affectionately.

Callum walked over and gave Storm a quick pat on his head and then bent down to look him in the eyes.

"What did you bring me, friend?" he asked quietly. Ailia observed their interaction with interest, having rarely seen Callum speak so gently.

Storm lifted his giant paw toward Callum, and Ailia saw that there was a note attached to it with a thin, black ribbon. Her heart stopped. Maybe she would finally have some answers about her sister.

Callum untied the note and thanked Storm before standing up and unfolding the paper. Ailia held her breath as Callum's eyes flew across the letter. It must have been short because it only took him a couple of seconds to finish reading. He looked up at her and said, "Your sister is okay. Right now, she is with the Crown Prince of Elflaine. She will be safe with him."

Callum's tone was tense even though the news was good. Ailia asked, "Is the crown prince... good?"

Callum bristled. "Let's just say that we don't get along. But yes, he will take care of your sister."

"Does the note say anything else?" Reed asked.

"Just that I should hurry with my task because the queen grows impatient," said Callum, eyes darting back to the paper. "You can read it if you want."

He handed the paper to Ailia, and Reed walked over, reading it with her.

My dearest brother,

Yes, the girl is here. There were some issues with mother when she first arrived, but she is with Aydan now, at the cabin. You know how he is.

Anyway, please hurry back. The queen is becoming unbearable in her waiting, and I am bored.

All my love

"I wish she had elaborated on the issues," said Ailia, worry wrinkling her forehead.

"My sister has a flair for the dramatic. I wouldn't worry too much about it. If Elideh was hurt or in danger, she would have told me," said Callum.

Ailia mindlessly scratched Storm's ears as they walked. At least she knew Elideh was alive. She didn't know if she could trust the faerie version of "okay," but she guessed it was better than not knowing anything at all. At this point, she just needed to finish Callum's list or make it to Winter Solstice without getting dragged to her death by some sort of creature from hell. She really needed that drink.

"I hope the village is close. I'm ready to have a hot meal and numb my worries with alcohol," said Ailia. Both Callum and Reed looked at her and raised their eyebrows. She was normally the one pushing them to work faster to accomplish their tasks, but knowing that Elideh was safe made Ailia feel like she could breathe for the first time since she went missing. And maybe the near-death encounters were starting to wear her out.

They walked in silence the rest of the way to the village, Storm trotting along happily beside Ailia, occasionally romping off to chase a small creature. Ailia wasn't sure if Callum and Reed were both processing information or if they were just giving her some space, but she was thankful for the quiet.

The weather was finally beginning to truly move toward Autumn, and she was enjoying the beauty around her. The leaves were slowly dancing in the wind as they fell to the ground, birds were flitting around, busily preparing for the cooler weather, and the sun was kissing her face through the trees. She would make it to Elideh. And bring her back. And put all of this behind her. Somehow.

As they walked in the front door of the tiny hotel, Ailia was immediately overwhelmed by the smell of freshly baked bread and the memory of the darkness that had consumed her the last time she was there. She shivered, and Reed came to her side, sensing her distress.

He put his arm around her shoulder, and as he pulled her into him, she let his comfort chase the memory away. He must have been remembering the same thing because he kept glancing down at her and then scanning the small dining room, ready to fight some unknown enemy. Callum was also on alert as they sat at a table tucked away in the corner of the room. Maybe this wouldn't be a relaxing visit after all. Maybe they should just go back to their cottage. Or maybe they just all needed a drink.

REED

Reed couldn't stop thinking about the book. Or the kelpie. Or that Callum was bound to the gods-damned Faerie Queen and hadn't told them. He was really trying to keep it together because he knew Ailia needed the break, but it was becoming more and more difficult not to just drag her away from all of this. They ordered some food and drinks, but were sitting in a tense silence.

Ailia still knew so little of their world, much less the fae. Hell, Reed barely knew anything about the faerie world. Although he trusted Callum, he also knew that, ultimately, the fae lived by a different set of rules. He just hoped that it was truly in Callum's best interest to keep Ailia alive and safe.

And that fucking kelpie. There was no way he was going to let Ailia be the bait again. They had been lucky. And he didn't think they would get lucky twice. He was already halfway through his beer before he even realized he was drinking it. Ailia cleared her throat and looked between him and Callum.

"So…" she said tentatively. "Are we just going to sit here in weird, tense silence or are we going to talk about what's bothering both of you?"

At least she didn't beat around the bush.

Reed blew out a breath. "I'm not going to lie to you, Ailia. There isn't a lot that has happened in the past day that hasn't bothered me."

Callum nodded his head, but kept his vigil looking out the window.

"Look, I get that the kelpie ordeal didn't go as planned," Ailia started. Reed scoffed, but Ailia continued before he could interrupt. "But can we just forget about everything for an hour? We aren't going to solve anything tonight. We have been living off of stale bread and dried meat for two weeks. Let's get a good meal, maybe even a good night's sleep, and hope the alcohol numbs some of our worries."

The hopeful look in her eyes melted away any sort of rebuttal that Reed could think of, so he lifted his glass and said, "Sláinte."

Callum and Ailia returned the gesture, and Reed tried to lean into the companionship and the break that Ailia needed, He could do that for her. Even if it was only a couple of hours.

CHAPTER FORTY-SIX

AILIA

A ilia wasn't sure how many drinks she had consumed, but she was sure it wasn't more than a couple. Either way, walking back to the cottage was going to be a pain. In. The. Ass.

She slowly stood, already swaying. Why did she feel so drunk? They had only been there for a couple of hours. Reed steadied her, and asked her something, but she couldn't figure out what he was saying. She started walking toward the door, but Reed stopped her. He gently grabbed her face and was looking at her with alarm in his eyes.

"Your eyelashes are pretty," Ailia giggled.

Reed frowned at her. "Ailia, did you hear what I said?"

She shook her head. Did she hear him? She wasn't sure.

"I asked if you are okay to walk. You haven't had that much to drink, but you seem pretty stumbly," said Reed.

"I think I'm okay," said Ailia.

Reed and Callum glanced at each other, but Ailia was sick of worrying about everything. She turned around and headed out the door. Storm came up to her, wagging his tail.

She loved him so much. After stroking his head a couple of times, she turned around to see where Callum and Reed were. They were right behind her, watching her with their brows furrowed.

"I've never seen her drink, so I don't know if this is normal behavior for her," Callum whispered, speaking to Reed as if she wasn't right there.

"The last time we drank together, we were drinking scotch. For several hours. She was pretty drunk, but not quite this sloppy," replied Reed. He crossed his arms. "Do you think her coming into fae gifts could have anything to do with this?"

She should be offended that they were having a conversation about her in front of her, but she kind of didn't care.

Callum studied her. "Possibly. Either way we need to get her back."

Reed nodded his head, and Ailia took that as her cue to head toward the forest. It was very dark. How were they going to find their way back? Reed was next to her a moment later, grabbing her hand.

"This way, milady." The smirk on his face told her that she was probably not going in the right direction. Whatever. They were no fun.

She let Reed lead her to the path they would take, but when she thought about how long it was going to take to get to the cottage, she stopped and sat on the ground. She heard Callum sigh behind her.

"Can't we just stay here tonight?" she whined. The ground was so soft. Maybe she could lay down for a minute.

"No, we can't sleep in the middle of the forest," said Reed patiently. He scooped her up.

"Put me down," Ailia yawned. "I can walk."

"Of course you can," said Reed, not putting her down.

"You're not okay," Callum said from somewhere beside her and Reed. "Why didn't you tell us you'd had too much?"

Ailia nestled into Reed's arms and laid her head on his chest. This was actually pretty comfortable. She really did like Reed. "I'm fine," she said sleepily. Maybe she would just close her eyes for a minute. Then she could walk the rest of the way.

"Clearly," scoffed Callum.

"Shh, let her sleep," scolded Reed.

Ailia yawned again, relaxed into the comfortable rhythm of Reed's breathing.

REED

"Is she already asleep?" Callum asked.

Reed looked down at her. Sure enough, she was breathing deeply, already fast asleep.

"Looks like it," said Reed, brushing her forehead with a kiss.

"Unbelievable. How did we not notice she was so drunk?" asked Callum.

"I don't know. It's like she was fine one minute, and the next she was completely out of it," said Reed, shaking his head.

"We need to keep an eye on her. It could be something residual from the encounter with the kelpie. Or maybe her magic was too depleted," said Callum, worry lacing his tone.

Reed nodded his head, sure that Callum could see him with his heightened fae sight. Of course they couldn't just get a meal without something going awry. Reed glanced down at Ailia again, wishing they had more answers.

They walked together in silence for a while. Reed thought he would be more fatigued from carrying Ailia, but he wasn't struggling at all. It must be the strength that had transferred to him through the knight bond. He had to admit, it was reassuring feeling stronger and faster. It meant he would be more formidable.

Reed noticed Callum stealing quick glances at Ailia more frequently the longer they walked.

"Everything okay?" Reed asked.

"Are you sure she's just sleeping? That she's not hurt?" Callum questioned.

"I guess we can stop for a minute and see if we can wake her," said Reed.

"No, we don't need to do that." Callum paused. "Let me carry her."

Reed stopped and looked at Callum. "I'm not tired, I can keep going."

Callum crossed his arms. They stared at each other for a moment, and Reed thought he detected a trace of something flash in Callum's eyes. Jealousy, maybe?

"If I get tired, we can trade," Reed said. And he turned back to the path and kept walking. Callum was silent next to him, brooding.

Deciding that maybe they should change the subject, Reed said, "So what do you think about Ailia having the Book of Straun?"

Callum took his time responding. "I think there are things at play here that are beyond our control. That perhaps have been in motion for a while." He furrowed his brows. "And I don't know why Ailia seems to be at the center of it all."

Maybe Callum was right. Maybe Ailia *was* at the center of this mess.

Callum spoke up again, this time more quietly. "We need to keep her away from Elflaine. I know we made an oath, but if you can convince her to stay away, I will do everything I can to bring her sister back to this realm."

Reed tried to hide his surprise but held Ailia closer. "Why are you just now saying this, Callum? You promised her you would take her to find Elideh."

"I know, but if Elideh is involved with the Faerie Queen, it isn't going to be as simple as just waltzing into Elflaine and getting her back. We will have to play the queen's game of court and follow all of her rules." Callum blew out a breath. "I don't want Ailia mixed up in faerie intrigue. We should keep her out of it."

"Why would Elideh be involved with the Faerie Queen?" Reed asked quietly.

Callum winced. "Do you remember what my sister said in her letter?"

"Yes," Reed replied slowly. "That your mother found Elideh."

"My mother is the Faerie Queen," said Callum, looking resolutely in front of them.

Reed stopped and gently sat Ailia down against a tree. Callum turned to him.

"What the fuck, Callum?" said Reed, lethally quiet. "Don't you think that's something you should have told us?"

"I'm sorry," said Callum. "It's complicated, and I didn't think it would matter. Now it does, so now I'm telling you."

Reed started pacing, but Callum went over to Ailia and sat beside her.

"This doesn't really change anything, Reed. Either way I would have kept Ailia away from my mother. It is just going to be more difficult now. So if you can do anything to convince her to leave it to me..." Callum trailed off, moving closer to Ailia as he spoke.

"Obviously I agree with you, but you know Ailia isn't going to leave Elideh in Elflaine. If I could stop her, I would have a long time ago," said Reed.

Callum ran his hands through his hair. "Very well. You need to examine that book, and we need to prepare her as much as we can for what she will face. It will make the kelpie look like child's play."

Reed nodded his head. Of course he would do anything to keep Ailia safe. Even if that meant playing into whatever warped faerie politics he needed to prepare for. Callum gently lifted Ailia into his arms and started walking. Reed frowned at him, but followed, glancing down at Ailia as they made their way through the trees.

She looked too young when she was asleep. It scared him how much he was willing to do to keep her out of harm's way.

Callum visibly relaxed as soon as he was holding Ailia, and Reed wondered why. Maybe Callum was starting to care for Ailia. Reed felt a pang of jealousy course through him, but if anyone understood the helpless feeling that Ailia inspired, it was him.

They continued walking, and Reed decided that he would start looking into the book as soon as they got back. There was no time to waste anymore. They still had to find the two items for Callum and then deal with whatever they were going to face once they got to the faerie realm. Reed looked up to the stars, wishing there was another way.

CHAPTER FORTY-SEVEN

CALLUM

Callum had tried to downplay how agitated he was that Reed was carrying Ailia, but couldn't deny how relieved he was to finally be the one holding her. He had to keep this under wraps.

They actually made pretty good time getting to the cottage. He hated admitting it, but it was definitely making his life easier now that both Reed and Ailia were stronger and faster. When they got back, he carefully tucked Ailia into the bed, while Reed started a fire. Storm loyally curled around her and promptly fell asleep. She was breathing deeply, steadily. Callum was still not convinced that there wasn't something sinister at play with her behavior tonight, but so far it looked like she was okay. He would not be sleeping, though.

It looked like Reed had a similar idea because once he got the fire going, he pulled out the ancient Book of Straun. Reed looked at Callum, but Callum had already strengthened the shield around them. Reed nodded his head, acknowledging the magic of the shield.

They both settled into chairs opposite of the fire, and Callum let the warmth settle his racing mind.

They had been back for about an hour when Callum noticed Ailia stirring. He sat up right away, Reed looking up from the grimoire at the same moment. Callum was already at Ailia's side, still worried that something wasn't right. She was laying on her back, one hand resting on the blanket and the other above her head. He saw a slight shimmer on her wrist as the firelight flickered. He took her hand in his and examined her wrist more closely.

"Reed, you need to see this," said Callum, trying to stay calm. The mark from the kelpie was glowing.

"Shit," muttered Reed as soon as he saw what Callum was looking at. "What does it mean?"

"I don't know," said Callum. "But it can't be good."

"Should we try to wake her up?" asked Reed.

"Maybe," Callum said.

Callum looked over at Reed. He couldn't believe that between the two of them, they didn't know what to do. From the look Reed was giving him, Callum could tell Reed felt the same frustration.

Reed sat down on the bed next to Ailia and slowly drew her up the pillows so that she was leaning against his chest. He had his arm protectively wrapped around her shoulder, and Callum was trying very hard not to shove Reed off of the bed.

"Ailia, can you hear me?" Reed asked softly.

He started stroking her hair, and soon she was stirring.

"Ailia?" Reed asked again.

Suddenly, she sat up straight, and when she opened her eyes, Callum's breath was knocked out of him. Her normally pale-green eyes were white.

Reed and Storm jumped up from the bed and stared at her. Storm whimpered, and his tail was tucked. Not a good sign. She turned toward the door and tilted her head slightly, as if she could hear something they couldn't.

Then, to Callum's horror, she got out of the bed, walked straight to the door, and flung it open.

Reed was already racing after her, shouting her name, Callum right behind him. He grabbed Reed. "Wait! We don't know what's happening. If she is in some sort of trance, we could hurt her if we pull her out of it the wrong way," said Callum.

Reed's eyes were wild, and Callum had a feeling they were a mirror image of his own. They started walking after her, keeping some distance.

But when Callum realized what she was walking toward, panic took control of him, and he lurched toward her to grab her. She was heading straight toward the ocean, and was not slowing down.

Right before he reached her, she twisted around, and the next thing Callum knew, he was flying backwards, a jet of water slamming into his chest.

Reed

Fuck. Fuck. *Fuck*. Ailia just wielded water.

She just attacked Callum. With her *third* element.

Reed was trying to wrap his head around what had just happened when he heard Callum shouting his name, and saw him still reaching out to try to get to Ailia. Reed turned to her, readying his magic. Her eerie, white eyes like lanterns in the night.

"Ailia," said Reed, in what he hoped was a calming voice. "Where are you?"

Ailia tilted her head in an animalistic way he had never seen from her right as a jet of water blasted him backward. Callum sprinted toward her but was knocked back with shards of ice—of fucking ice.

Reed jolted to his feet and threw out his hands, building a wall of sand and shells between Ailia and the sea. A huge wave from the ocean crashed over the wall, knocking it over as if it was a child's sandcastle. The wave obediently pooled around Ailia's feet and started to swirl around her. She turned her attention back to the water, and Reed's heart dropped when he saw the kelpie waiting for her.

"AILIA!" screamed Callum. Reed could see the blood dripping down Callum's chest, arms, and face from the ice. This couldn't be happening.

Both Callum and Reed were running toward her, but Ailia was already wading into the water. Storm tried to follow her, but couldn't get close.

"NO!" Reed shouted.

Ailia turned to them and slowly lifted both of her hands. A thick wall of ice rose up from the waves, curling toward her, forming a cage—to keep them out or keep her in, Reed wasn't sure. Callum blasted magic at the ice, barely cracking it in a few places before it was reinforced.

Reed threw his earth magic at the wall, making as little progress as Callum. He heard Callum roar beside him and looked in time to see him shift into a hawk. Not a bad idea. Maybe he could get over the wall that way. But as Reed started to hope, Callum fell out of the sky with a furious screech, shifting back into his own body before he hit the sand. Reed ran over to Callum.

"I'm fine," Callum shouted over the sound of the crashing waves. "Just get to her!"

That was easier said than done. The cage of ice had completely cut off access to Ailia from the shore, and she was almost to the kelpie. The water had parted for her, and in that moment, she looked like an ancient goddess, untouchable and all-powerful.

Reed tried to build a bridge of sand and shells across the water, but every time he tried to sprint across it, a wave crashed into him and destroyed the bridge.

"I can't get to her!" Reed yelled.

Callum was on his feet, wiping the blood and sweat from his face.

They both stood on the shore, helpless. Reed was shaking from rage.

"Conjure the bow!" he said to Callum. Reed was pretty sure that Callum's magic allowed the summoning of weapons in a situation like this. Sure enough, Callum was throwing the bow to Reed, then the arrows.

Reed swiftly loaded the bow and shot the first arrow directly in the center of the wall. The ice barely even chipped. Then, he shot an arrow over the wall toward the kelpie. It landed right between Ailia and the creature, but she didn't seem to notice. The kelpie, however, snarled. This time, when Reed shot the arrow, it went straight into the kelpie's side—and all the way through.

"Aim for her! Maybe it will get her attention!" Callum shouted. Reed could barely hear him over the roaring of the water.

"No way! Are you crazy? What if I hit her?" asked Reed, shooting another arrow at the kelpie.

"Maybe it will wake her up!"

This was a bad idea. But it might be their only option. Reed aimed for Ailia, but at the last second, a boat crashed through the surface of the water—right next to the kelpie.

CHAPTER FORTY-EIGHT

CALLUM

C allum stood in stunned silence next to Reed, trying to figure out what the fuck they were looking at. A small, nordic-looking rowboat had just... appeared. Out of the water. With two creatures in it. And they were rowing straight for Ailia.

The waves began to churn more frantically, and ominous clouds formed around them. The kelpie charged the rowboat, but one of the beings in the boat lifted a staff, and bright light that sparked like lightning shot out toward the creature. It reared back, stamping its hooves angrily in the water.

Ailia was still slowly walking toward the kelpie in her trance-like state.

"What the fuck is happening?" screamed Reed.

"I don't fucking know!" Callum shouted back.

"Shift again and see if you can figure it out!"

Good plan. Callum quickly shifted into a hawk again, hoping this form would do better in the storm that was escalating around them.

As he got closer, he could see that Ailia had stopped and was watching the interaction between the dark beings in the boat and the kelpie. Well, maybe watching. Her eyes were still an eerie white. Maybe she was waiting.

As soon as he got close enough to see more clearly into the boat, he almost tumbled out of the air in shock. Those were the nearly mythical Finfolk. They typically stuck to their palace beneath the sea near the Orkney Islands, so what were they doing here?

The Finfolk blasted the kelpie again, and to Callum's complete surprise, the kelpie bowed to the Finfolk and then dove into the water. The storm began to subside, and Ailia's eyes started to return to their normal bright green.

Callum realized right before she slumped into the sea that she was unconscious. He dove for her, shifting back to his fae form as he fell from the sky. He felt a surge in his magic, strength, and speed that he had never felt before, urging him toward Ailia. He hit the frigid water, and, luckily, she hadn't drifted too deep down. He dragged her limp body to the surface, praying to the gods that she was still alive.

Suddenly, there was an oar in front of him. The Finfolk were saying something in a language he didn't understand, but he assumed from their gesturing that they wanted him to grab the oar. The waves were still huge and angry, so he decided to trust them in his moment of panic, worried he wouldn't be able to help Ailia if he didn't get them both out of the water soon.

The Finfolk pulled Callum and Ailia into the boat and started to row for shore. Callum dragged Ailia onto his lap and pressed his ear to her chest. He released a ragged breath, relieved to hear the faint beat of her heart and feel the slight rise of her chest. Reed was still on the shore, screaming something at Callum, and sprinting into the water as soon as the boat was close enough to land.

"Is she alive?" Reed asked, his eyes wild with panic.

"Yes," said Callum, still trying to catch his breath.

Reed tried to pull her out of the boat, but Callum cradled her body close to him and gave Reed a look that made him back away.

After carefully getting out and walking to shore, Callum turned to the Finfolk, who had not left the water. He didn't know if they could understand him, but he had dealt with enough creatures to know that Ailia's rescue would come at a cost.

"Let us tend to her, and then we can discuss what happened," said Callum, using the voice he reserved for the battlefield. The Finfolk nodded in understanding and sat back in their boat, whispering in the language of their people, the waves slowly dying down, but the wind still whipping around wildly.

Reed glanced nervously between Callum and the Finfolk, but didn't say anything as he led the way to the cottage. He immediately started a fire while Callum, still holding Ailia, sat down on the floor.

"Get blankets and towels. She's freezing," said Callum.

Reed quickly gathered all the blankets he could find and started gently covering her.

"Should we lay her down on the bed?" Reed asked cautiously, eyeing Callum warily.

"No. She needs to be by the fire."

Reed nodded.

Callum leaned back against the chair and propped his knees up, pulling Ailia between them and laying her head against his chest. He took a towel and started drying her hair.

He was shaking. And trying to calm down.

But she could have died. And he didn't even want to think about what the Finfolk would ask in return for their assistance.

Reed sat down on the floor next to them. Callum was relieved that Reed was giving him some space because he was riding a very sharp edge at the moment.

Finally, Reed spoke up, never taking his eyes off of Ailia. "Who... what are those creatures?"

"They are called the Finfolk," replied Callum, trying to steady his breathing. "They are ancient sorcerers. Sometimes they can appear as merpeople, but most often they are creatures of the dark. They dwell near the Orkney Islands, and they have an underwater palace called Finfolkaheem. It is supposedly very beautiful and filled with riches, but anyone that gets taken there does not return."

Reed blew out a breath and ran his hands through his hair. "For fuck's sake. I've heard of them before, but didn't make the connection. I thought they were *confined* to the Orkney Islands." He shook his head. "Just what we needed, mythical sorcerers whom I'm assuming we now owe a debt to."

Callum nodded, gently drying Ailia's face and hands. He willed some of his own warmth into her with every touch, lending his strength and healing into every brush of his fingers on her body. "They will wait in the water until we discuss our debt with them. I am more concerned about why they are here in the first place. Although they are nomadic and infamous for their boating skills, they aren't supposed to leave the islands."

Ailia's breaths were still shallow. "We need to check her for injuries." said Callum.

Reed nodded in agreement. "And we need to get her into dry clothes."

He glanced at Callum, but when Callum made it clear he wasn't going anywhere, Reed stood and found dry blankets. Then, he leaned over her, and started to peel off her jeans. Callum had to stop himself from growling. Reed was an ally. Reed was going to help her.

After inspecting her legs, he moved on to her shirt. Callum sat her up, her head lolling to the side, while Reed slipped the shirt off of her. She had a small cut on her neck, but was otherwise okay. Reed quickly covered her with the blankets and sat back.

"I think she is unharmed, apart from the trance she was under," said Reed quietly. Callum and Reed sat in silence for a moment, and then Callum asked the question that had been running through his head, "Did you know? That she could wield water?"

"I had no idea," said Reed. Callum was relieved by his answer. He didn't know how he would have felt about Ailia sharing something like that with Reed but not with him.

"How is this possible? I thought witches couldn't wield more than two elements," said Callum.

Reed shook his head. "Wielding three elements is practically mythical. I have never heard of anyone that has been able to do that—other than the High Witch."

Ailia still hadn't stirred. But her breathing was even. Callum didn't know what it would mean for her—that she was so powerful. So unique. If the Faerie King found out... Callum wouldn't let that happen.

"No one can know," Callum said to Reed, his tone giving no room for compromise.

Reed nodded in agreement. "I know. This puts a target on her back."

As much as Callum didn't want to leave Ailia's side, he knew that he needed to speak to the Finfolk. They would only stay patient for so long.

Callum shifted slightly to grab a pillow from the chair behind him and gently lay Ailia on the floor, still wrapped in her blankets. "Stay with her. If she wakes, do not let her out of this cottage. I am putting a shield around it. Only I will be able to enter."

"She will be safe with me," Reed assured, and Callum believed him.

Callum nodded and walked out the door, knowing he needed to deal with this, and then he could get back to her. Knowing for certain what he had suspected, and had been avoiding, for some time now.

They were soulbound. And it took all of his resolve to leave her in her vulnerable state.

CALLUM

Callum stalked toward the Finfolk. The elder of the two left the boat to meet him on the shore, seeming to glide over the surface of the water. The storm had mostly subsided, but lightning flashed in the distance over the ocean. A bad omen.

Callum dipped his head in greeting, and the Finfolk returned the gesture.

"I am Callum. Thank you for your assistance with the kelpie. I owe you a debt."

The Finfolk observed Callum for a moment with his dark, haunting eyes.

"We can give you what you seek," said the Finfolk, his voice guttural and deep.

Callum stilled. The Finfolk were renowned seers, so he wouldn't question how they knew he needed the golden bridle. "You do not wish to collect the debt you're owed?"

"We will collect on the debt, but there are more important things that must happen first. Things have been set in motion. The prophecy is coming to fruition, and we must play our part in return for our reward."

Little was known about the Finfolk, but one thing was certain—they were great sorcerers. It was likely that the cryptic words he spoke were, in fact, divined in the ways of their magic. Callum wondered about the prophecy he spoke of, but decided that could wait. He needed to know what they wanted from him, and he needed to make sure the burden of the debt did not fall on Ailia.

"Very well, how do you wish to proceed? My only request is that the debt is fulfilled by myself alone," said Callum.

The Finfolk nodded his head, acknowledging Callum's request. Callum's shoulders loosened slightly in relief.

"You and your companions will meet us in our homelands by the next new moon. There, we will give you the golden bridle."

Callum tensed again. He knew that it was important to clarify details anytime a deal was made with creatures like these.

"We will meet you in the Orkney Islands, at a place on land of your choosing. There, we can take the golden bridle. We must continue our search for the items we seek, and once we have retrieved them, I can find a way to repay my debt to you."

The Finfolk's mouth upturned in a gruesome smile. "Very well, faerie, you have made your demands known. We will not ask you to come to our true home under the ocean. We will meet on land as you request, but you will take one of our boats to travel to the Orkney Islands."

Callum nodded his head and reached out his hand to seal the deal.

"One last thing, your father has a message for you, but perhaps he should be the one to tell you once you reach us."

Callum stumbled back in shock as the Finfolk gripped Callum's hand and lightning sparked between them, snaking up Callum's arm, burning a mark in its path. The Finfolk left him on the shore, speechless. He must have misheard. There was no way the Finfolk meant his father. But before he could call out to ask, they disappeared under the waves without a trace.

Callum ran his hands through his hair. His father was dead. Or that is what he had been told. If his father was truly alive, maybe he could somehow leverage that information to work in Ailia's favor. Maybe the Faerie Queen would grant a request. He had a couple of days to figure it out. But right now, he needed to get back to Ailia and prepare Reed for what they were about to face.

CHAPTER FORTY-NINE

REED

R eed had taken Callum's place next to Ailia on the ground by the fire, and Storm had curled himself protectively around her. She could wield water magic. This was really fucking bad. It shouldn't be possible.

How was she so powerful?

When Callum finally returned to the cottage, he looked like he had seen a ghost. He absentmindedly walked over to them and sat down next to Ailia, Storm moving to let him get closer. Reed wasn't sure why Callum had been acting so strange around Ailia since the kelpie attack, but something had definitely changed. Then again, Ailia did seem to bring out the protective instincts in people.

Reed let Callum sit and compose himself for a moment, but couldn't take the waiting.

"Just tell me. What are we going to have to do?" he asked, running his fingers up and down Ailia's arm.

Callum sighed deeply and looked down at Ailia, brushing a stray strand of hair out of her face in a gentle gesture that Reed hadn't seen from him before. Then he frowned and moved away, as if he thought better of his interaction with her.

"The Finfolk have agreed to give us a golden bridle. But they want us to come to the Orkney Islands to retrieve it. All of us," he finally said.

Reed furrowed his brows. "That's a good thing, right?"

"Well," said Callum. "Yes and no. They said they would call in their favor for rescuing Ailia at a later time. I ensured that I would be the only one to fulfill it and that Ailia would stay out of it."

"Thank the goddess," mumbled Reed. "Wasn't the last item on your list in the Orkney Islands anyway?"

"Yes," said Callum. Reed could have sworn that there was more that he was not telling him, but Callum looked exhausted, and Reed didn't want to push him.

"We have to be in the Orkney Islands by the new moon, which gives us a little over a week. And we have to take one of their boats," said Callum.

"One of those tiny row boats?" Reed sputtered. "They can't be serious."

"I guess we'll find out tomorrow. I'm assuming it will be waiting for us."

"Okay," nodded Reed. "You should rest, I'll watch over her."

Callum looked at Ailia again, something like longing in his eyes. "You're right." He laid his head against the back of the chair and was asleep in minutes.

Fuck. Take a boat? All the way to the Orkney Islands? That would take days. Reed glanced at Ailia but she was still fast asleep, Storm once again curled around her body.

Reed wasn't sure how many more surprises he could take.

REED

Reed and Callum took turns watching over Ailia, but two days had passed, and they were starting to get desperate. Not only did they have the deadline of the new moon from the Finfolk, but they were beginning to worry there was something more sinister about her deep sleep.

The Finfolk must have somehow known she was not ready to travel, because the boat they promised had not arrived. Reed was trying to stay patient with Callum, but the two of them had been at odds over Ailia, and it was beginning to cause some real problems.

They had moved Ailia into the bed, and Reed had sat next to her, uneasy about leaving her side. Storm had tried to push Reed out of the way, but eventually relented. Callum, however, had scowled at him when Reed made it obvious he had no intentions of moving. It had been so bad the first night, that they actually got into a screaming match over it; Callum making up some bullshit excuse about why Reed shouldn't be in the bed with her. Reed nearly punched him, but decided it would be better to keep the peace, so moved to his chair by the fire. Storm had given him a triumphant look before jumping up next to Ailia.

Reed didn't understand Callum's new, territorial behavior. Although Callum had become friendly toward both him and Ailia, he had made it clear that his interest in them extended to their usefulness for his task.

Finally, early in the morning on the third day of Ailia's seemingly endless sleep, she woke up. At the first sign of movement, Reed, Callum, and Storm were at her side.

"Ailia," whispered Reed, stroking her hair.

She leaned into his touch, and he sat on the bed next to her. Callum tensed at the movement, but Reed didn't care. Reed kissed her forehead, then looked down at her, willing her eyes to open.

"Ailia," said Callum, who had moved closer as well. This time, her eyes fluttered open. Maybe it was the light, but the gold ring around her eyes seemed like it was glowing. Reed tilted her chin up to get a closer look, but stopped when she smiled at him.

"What happened?" she murmured sleepily.

"We'll fill you in, but just take a minute to wake up first," said Reed.

All of a sudden, the door to the cottage slammed. Callum had stormed out.

Ailia frowned at the door. "What's wrong with him?"

"I'm not sure," said Reed. "I'll go find out. Are you sure you're okay?"

"Yes, I'm fine," said Ailia, stretching. When Reed made no move to get out of the bed, she nudged his shoulder. "Go check on him."

After one last chaste kiss on her forehead, he left her to figure out what had Callum fleeing the cottage.

Reed shut the door gently behind him and walked over to where Callum was sitting in the sand.

"What was that all about?" asked Reed.

"I just needed some air," Callum replied, staring at the sand.

"If there's something wrong, I need to know. You've seemed distracted ever since the kelpie attack, and distractions will put Ailia in danger." Reed crossed his arms, deciding enough was enough. He was done with Callum's behavior.

Callum looked up at him and squared his shoulders. "I said I'm fine, witch. Nothing I do will compromise her safety. Although now that she is awake, I would imagine we will have to leave soon."

At that, he stood and walked to the cottage, not giving Reed a chance to respond.

Reed ran his hand through his hair. They had enough to worry about without any extra tension between the three of them. Reed decided he would let it go for now, but if Callum still seemed off, he was going to confront him again.

When Reed got inside the cottage, his eyes went straight to Ailia, who was frowning at Callum from her place in the bed. Callum was packing his things, avoiding looking in her direction. Ailia looked over at Reed and silently seemed to ask what happened with a tilt of her head, but Reed shrugged his shoulders, not sure what was happening either.

He walked over to the bed and pulled her up so that she was sitting with her back against the pillows. "You're still feeling okay?"

"Yes, I feel fine," said Ailia, not letting go of his hand as she stood. "Now tell me what happened. And what happened to my clothes." She looked down, noticing that she was wearing one of Reed's shirts. It was big on her, nearly coming to her knees.

Reed took a deep breath, but went over to where they were keeping their dwindling supply of food and brought Ailia a chunk of bread. "After our dinner at the hotel, you seemed really drunk and fell asleep almost as soon as we got to the woods."

"That's embarrassing," muttered Ailia between bites.

"We both thought it was strange, considering how little you had to drink, but we think that you were actually under some sort of influence from the kelpie after what happened." Reed paused, not sure how to tell her what happened. Callum must have sensed his hesitation, because he picked up the story.

After finally turning to face her and scanning her body quickly, Callum said, "When we got back to the cottage, we put you to bed, but you woke up in the middle of the night in some sort of trance. Your eyes were completely white, and you walked out to the ocean where the kelpie was waiting for you."

Ailia's face was contorted in shock. Callum winced, but continued. "We tried to stop you, but you wielded water magic against us. We couldn't do anything."

"Oh no," said Ailia, with her hands in her face. "I'm so sorry. Did I hurt either of you?"

Callum turned back around and started packing Ailia's things. Reed guessed it was his turn to resume the story.

"You didn't," he said reassuringly, even though that was definitely not true. Luckily, they both healed quickly.

"You kept walking toward the kelpie—"

"Into the ocean?" Ailia interrupted, her brow furrowed.

"Actually, the water parted for you," said Reed. She gaped at him, and he decided to get the rest of the story over with. He finished telling her how the Finfolk had appeared out of the water and had saved her, but left the rest to Callum.

Callum told her that the Finfolk wanted them to travel to the Orkney Islands, but left out the part about the bargain he struck with them.

By this point, Ailia was sitting back on the bed, shaking her head in disbelief. "I can't believe that I have no memory of any of this."

Reed sat down next to her and pulled her into a hug. She didn't resist.

Callum seemed to have settled down a bit, and walked over to them. "The important thing is that you're okay. We will figure the rest out."

Then, he took her hand and flipped it over to look at her wrist where the mark of the kelpie was still shimmering. He frowned at it, but didn't say anything.

"Let's get you outside into the sun. And hope our journey to the Orkney Islands will be uneventful," said Callum, giving Ailia a tight smile.

Ailia nodded. But Reed wasn't naïve enough to think that anything they did from this point forward would be easy.

CHAPTER FIFTY

AILIA

Ailia stood and stretched. Reed had packed his things and then had given her some privacy to change clothes. Knowing him, he also recognized that she was overwhelmed and was giving her space. She really didn't deserve him.

Just as she finished getting dressed and was starting on her second piece of bread, Reed burst through the door, his eyes wild.

"What's wrong?" she asked, immediately alert.

"It's my mum. She just called to tell me the inn has been ransacked," said Reed.

Ailia stumbled back a step. "Is she okay? We have to go to her."

At that moment, Callum came in the door behind Reed, looking tense. "We have to go. The boat just arrived."

For fuck's sake. She looked between them, but before she could respond, Callum looked from her to Reed. "What happened? Tell me now."

Ailia answered before Reed could. "The inn that Reed and his mother own has been ransacked. We have to go to her."

"We can't," said Callum. "We cannot break a deal with the Finfolk."

Reed ran his hands through his hair. "Fuck," he muttered.

"Reed, is your mother okay?" asked Ailia.

"I'm not sure," he answered. "But we have all sorts of wards in place. The only way that anything was breaking into the inn was with powerful magic." He paused. "I have to go back and check on her. And help her get things back in order. You two can go, and I can meet you."

"The Finfolk were very clear, Reed. All three of us have to be in the Orkney Islands by the new moon. There is no way you can make the journey in time," said Callum.

"There is, actually," said Reed. He went over to his pack and pulled out a small, flat stone. "This is a talisman. My mother has one just like it. It allows us to travel to each other instantly."

Ailia stared at the stone. Magic was so fucking cool.

"But how will you get back to *us* in time?" asked Callum.

Oh. Good point.

"Well," said Reed, throwing a glance at Ailia before pulling out another, similar stone. "My mother and I made a stone for Ailia before we left."

Reed handed the stone to Ailia, and she turned it over in her hands. It was beautiful, and she could feel it vibrating with magic. Reed's stone was various shades of topaz, and Ailia's was its pale twin, with strains of clear crystal, milky white, and sparkling silver throughout.

"It's stunning, Reed," Ailia whispered. He and his mother really had thought of everything.

Reed gently grasped her chin and lifted her head up. "I've been wanting to give this to you, but didn't want to cross any boundaries.

The stone connects us. I will always be able to reach you as long as it's in your possession."

Ailia looked into his eyes, love and concern and desire staring back at her. She gave him a brief kiss on his cheek and felt his surprise at the gesture.

Callum interrupted them, loudly, asking, "How does the stone work?"

Reed dropped Ailia's chin, and Ailia took a small step back.

"The stones are crafted during the full moon, and are bound together through a spell. You only have to think of the person holding the other stone and turn it over three times in your hand. Then, the stone takes you to that person," explained Reed.

"That seems a little too simple. What if an enemy got one of the stones?" asked Callum. Ailia had to be honest, she was thinking the same thing.

"The stones are bound by blood. Ailia's stone is bound to my blood. Which brings me to the point of all this, actually," said Reed, turning to Ailia. "I will be able to get back to you, but you will have to offer your blood to my stone."

"Whatever you need me to do, Reed," said Ailia immediately. Callum had taken a step toward Ailia at the mention of blood but backed off after a moment's pause.

"It's not a lot, just a drop will do," said Reed, gently holding Ailia's hand. He grabbed a dagger at his waist that she hadn't noticed him wearing and looked at her again, asking for confirmation. She nodded so he pricked her thumb with the tip of the dagger and slid it over his stone. Ailia immediately felt the magic.

Reed rubbed the blood into his stone and wiped the dagger on his pants before putting it back on the belt at his waist. Ailia had already started healing, no trace of the prick on her thumb other than the dried blood.

"It's done," said Reed, releasing a deep breath. Ailia knew that this would put Reed at ease, and she felt confident about being connected to him in this way.

Callum had watched the ordeal with his arms crossed and a frown on his face. "So that's it? You two can travel to each other now?"

"Yes," said Reed.

"And no one else can use the stone?" Callum asked.

"Ailia's stone only contains my blood and hers. No one but us can use it," replied Reed.

"Very well," said Callum. "Go to your mother and figure out what happened. Just be sure you are with us by the new moon."

"I will," said Reed, turning to face Callum. "Do not let anything happen to her while I'm gone, or I swear to the goddess I will end you."

Well that took a drastic turn. Ailia had known the display of alpha nonsense would happen again eventually. Before Callum could respond, Ailia said, "We will be okay, Reed." She took his hand, reassuring him with her touch. "But I want you to take Storm."

Callum, Reed, and Storm looked at her like she was crazy. "I'm serious, Reed. If something nefarious is going on, and it wasn't just a break in, I want you to have Storm there. Plus, he can send messages if I don't have service in the middle of the ocean."

Callum looked amused, and both Reed and Storm were pouting, albeit for different reasons.

Reed sighed loudly, but said, "As you wish." Storm trotted obediently over to Reed, and gave her a sorrowful look.

She leaned down to kiss Storm's nose. "It'll be okay. You won't be gone long. Please look out for him and find me if something goes wrong." Storm nudged her cheek showing he understood.

"Well, that's that. Let's go," said Ailia, trying to shove away the uneasy feeling that was rearing its head.

CHAPTER FIFTY-ONE

AILIA

A ilia watched as Reed disappeared in front of their eyes. Before he left, he made sure that Callum understood that his death would be imminent if he let anything happen to Ailia, then turned to Ailia, pulling her into a bone-crushing hug.

This felt weird. Him leaving her. But it would only be for a couple of days.

Callum was already walking toward the boat, definitely annoyed by Reed's repetitive warnings if his posture and frown were anything to go by.

Great. Starting the trip with grumpy Callum.

She tilted her head toward the morning sun and closed her eyes. It would be okay. She was still going to work on her magic. She was still going to train with Callum. She would figure out a way to reset Callum's mood, and they would be fine.

Just. Fine.

She sighed, and after shouldering her backpack, followed Callum to the boat. To be fair to the Finfolk, the boat was actually very nice. It looked like a small, rustic yacht. She guessed if this journey was going to take several days, she was glad to have the extra space.

Callum stopped at the water's edge and was facing her. She finally caught up to him, and he wordlessly held out his hand to help her up to the ladder so she could climb into the boat. She smiled at him, but he was looking past her. Was he avoiding eye contact?

She made her way awkwardly over the side of the boat, Callum close behind.

"Well this is... nice," Ailia said, looking around. Callum merely nodded his head in agreement and started to head down the narrow stairs to the cabin below the deck.

Ailia hadn't been on many boats like this before. The only experiences she had with traveling on the ocean were the short ferry rides that she and Elideh took on occasion to different parts of England and Scotland.

This was definitely not a ferry. The boat was made of a rich, dark wood that she couldn't identify, and although it was simple, it was elegant and well made.

The more she looked around, though, she realized there was no helm. She knew enough about boats to know that the one thing they really needed was a way to navigate.

"Um, Callum?" she called down the stairs. "How are we supposed to steer?"

Callum's massive form appeared in the stairwell, and he looked up at her, his dark hair falling in his ocean eyes that seemed more blue than green today. She suddenly had the urge to brush his hair behind his ear and had to physically stop herself. She frowned, unsure of her reaction.

"It steers itself," he said as he walked up the stairs. She moved to give him space and realized she should have guessed that. With the boat belonging to ancient ocean sorcerers and all.

"Ah," she said. "Obviously." They looked at each other awkwardly for a moment, and Ailia wondered why it suddenly felt so strange between them. They had spent plenty of time alone together on their runs and during their training, but something felt different now.

"So how is the cabin?" Ailia asked, trying to break the awkward silence.

"It's fine," Callum hedged.

"What's wrong with it?" asked Ailia, seeing through his response immediately.

"Well," said Callum, shifting his eyes around the boat. "There's only one bed. And since the cabin is very small, it takes up almost the entire space."

Well, fuck. Ailia walked down the stairs to see the bed in question.

Shit. He was right. The bed filled the tiny cabin, leaving just enough space to walk in and out of the room. The ceilings were so low that even she was having to bend her head. She couldn't imagine how squashed Callum would be. Even worse, the bed was barely big enough for two people.

She climbed back up the stairs, willing nonchalance into her voice. "It's fine. It'll just be a tight squeeze."

"I'll just sleep up here," Callum said, still not meeting her eyes.

She walked over to him and reached for his shoulder. He tensed at her touch but didn't move away. "You're not sleeping on a ship deck when we can both be grown-ups and just share a damn bed."

Finally, he looked at her. She continued, glad she had his attention. "Please tell me what's wrong. We've already been through a lot together, and I have a feeling we are only just getting started. You can trust me."

She squeezed his shoulder, and he followed her hand as she drew it away.

Callum took a deep breath and then furrowed his brow.

"For fuck's sake, Callum. I'm not some fragile little girl. Just tell me what's bothering you," Ailia said, growing more impatient by the second.

"Nothing. Everything's fine." Ailia couldn't decide who he was trying to convince, but it wasn't working.

"Seriously, Callum?" Ailia crossed her arms. "Try again."

This time, he rolled his eyes and walked a few paces away from her, running his hands through his hair and muttering to himself.

"Fine," he said, turning to her. "There are several things. First, don't fucking keep secrets from me again. You say I can trust you? Well the same applies to you, princess. You should have told us about your water magic."

Ailia winced. That was fair. Before she could interrupt, though, Callum held his hand up.

"Second, you've almost died three times, Ailia. Three fucking times. You think you're going to keep getting lucky?"

"Third," he said, his voice rising over Ailia's response, "the Finfolk told me my father is going to meet us at our destination."

At that admission, Ailia stopped cold. Callum hadn't told them anything about his life. They knew he had a sister from the letter that Storm had delivered, but other than that, he was still very much a mystery to both her and Reed.

His shoulders were squared, and a muscle in his jaw ticked.

"We will come back to the first two things, Callum, but why is meeting with your father causing you distress?" Ailia asked cautiously.

"Because I was told that my father was dead. Hundreds of years ago," Callum answered tightly.

Ailia blew out a breath. She actually knew better than most how upsetting this news would be. She slowly walked over to Callum, him tracking each of her steps. Then, she hugged him. His body stiffened, like he didn't know what to do, but after a few seconds, he returned her embrace, pulling her into his body, timidly nuzzling his face into her hair.

"It's going to be okay, Callum," Ailia whispered.

She could feel him nod his head, and she continued to hold him, hoping that their closeness would ease some of his worry.

Finally, he pulled away and cleared his throat. He looked around the boat, and said, "I wonder why we haven't started moving yet."

Good question. "Do you think they're waiting for something?" Ailia asked.

Callum looked at her thoughtfully for a moment.

"Try using your magic to push us away from the shore. Earth or water should do it," answered Callum.

Ailia looked toward the land and decided it was worth a try. As soon as she reached out to both the water and the earth, she connected to them easily and pushed them away from the shore and into the open ocean.

She turned to look at Callum, grinning, to find him smiling back. "Well done, little witch."

Ailia curtseyed, and Callum laughed at her, his eyes sparkling in the sunshine. Good, maybe he was over his earlier mood, and maybe this voyage wouldn't be too bad.

CHAPTER FIFTY-TWO

AILIA

Wrong.

Wrong, wrong, wrong.

The voyage was bad. Very bad. They had barely made it out to sea, and Ailia had already thrown up over the side of the boat twice. Holy shit, she was so seasick.

Two or three more days of this?

Callum had helpfully held back her hair after the first time that she ran to the side of the boat, but he was definitely trying to hold back a smirk as she tried to steady herself against the railing.

"Why is my nausea so funny to you?" Ailia asked.

The corners of his mouth twitched upwards. "I wouldn't call it funny, just intriguing."

"And—" Ailia paused, covering her mouth and willing her body to stop what it was about to do. After a couple of deep breaths, she continued. "And why is it intriguing?"

He was definitely grinning now. "I've never seen anyone get seasick before," Callum said simply. "It just shows you haven't fully gone through your staying." He crossed his arms and tilted his head, eyeing her. "Or maybe it's a witch thing."

"Where is Reed with his potions when you need him," muttered Ailia, sure that he would have something that could cure motion sickness.

"Here," Callum said gently. "Lay down." He sat down against the railing and stretched out his legs, gesturing for her to lay her head in his lap. She wasn't sure how laying down on the *still-moving boat* would help, but what the hell. It couldn't get any worse.

She slowly lowered herself to the deck, trying to stay focused on anything but the sound of the waves and the unending sway of the boat. She laid her head in his lap, propping her knees against the railing to her side, and looked up at him.

"Close your eyes," he said softly. She did as he asked, still not sure how this was supposed to help.

He started stroking her hair, humming some sort of slow, haunting song that sounded like it could have been a lullaby. He moved his fingers to her forehead and gently traced the contours of her face. After a couple of minutes, Ailia felt relaxed. By the time he finished humming his song, the nausea was completely gone.

Callum was still running his fingers through Ailia's hair when she looked up at him.

"That was incredible," she whispered. "Thank you."

"Of course," Callum mumbled, occasionally twirling a strand of hair around one of his fingers.

"How did you do that? I thought that the fae didn't have healing magic." Ailia asked.

"We don't," said Callum, gazing out at the water.

Ailia waited to see if he would elaborate, enjoying the comforting feeling of his gentle touch.

"Sometimes, if we have a certain connection, we are able to help others heal," Callum finally said quietly.

Ailia frowned. "What type of connection?"

"It's complicated," said Callum. Ailia could tell he was unwilling to explain it any further and knew him well enough to know that she wouldn't be able to convince him to talk. Which was fine. She would just ask him another time.

Ailia closed her eyes again, reveling in the peace that she felt at that moment. They sat like that for a while, completely at ease, but when the sun started to set, Callum helped her sit up. They both sat with their backs against the railing, their shoulders occasionally grazing each other as the boat continued its back and forth across the frothy water.

"Seriously, Callum," she said. "Thank you. I feel amazing."

Callum turned and gave her a small smile, nodding his head. "I'll bring some food up here, and we can eat."

"Wait," said Ailia, reaching for his arm. She didn't know why, but she felt like she should share something with him. Like she should return his vulnerability. "I want to show you something." He looked at her curiously.

"Don't make fun of me, though," she said.

"Never," Callum said, frowning.

Ailia took a deep breath. It was silly, really. For her to be nervous about showing him a part of her magic. She looked down at her hand and focused, drawing water from the sea into her open palm. Slowly, carefully, she formed the water into the shape of Storm that she had been practicing. Once she was sure she got the details right, she looked up at Callum, raising her cupped hand so he could see the tiny water-Storm. Callum's eyes met hers right away, and she nearly gasped at the pride that was radiating from him.

She felt herself break into a smile, and as soon as she did, Callum returned it. His true smile that she so rarely saw. "This is incredible, Ailia. It looks just like him."

"Thank you," she said quietly, brushing a loose strand of hair out of her face with her free hand.

"Can I touch him?" Callum asked, quirking his head to the side.

"Sure," giggled Ailia. Callum brushed Storm's side with his knuckle, and Ailia manipulated the figure so that it nuzzled him.

Callum's smile grew wider and he laughed. "Really, Ailia. That's amazing. The details are so accurate. That must take a lot of control."

"It actually feels completely natural," said Ailia. "Like the water is an extension of me." She commanded the water-Storm to run in a circle on her hand, then released it back to the ocean.

"I don't know why I wanted to show you that," she said as she fidgeted with her sleeves. It was just a little trick—the magic wasn't that impressive.

Callum lifted her chin so that she was looking at him. "Thank you for sharing it with me." His tone was completely sincere, and she immediately felt relieved. "Too bad you can't make an army of water-Storms," he said with a grin. "That would be something to behold."

Ailia laughed as Callum stood and held out his hand to pull her up. After steadying herself and adjusting to the gentle rocking of the boat, Ailia looked up at Callum, half expecting the nausea to return.

He was still holding her hand, making sure she wasn't going to tip over. "You still feel okay?"

"Yes," she said, nodding her head. "Promise."

"Good. Then let's eat." He gave her hand a gentle squeeze before turning to get their food.

Ailia put her arms on the railing. What a strange day. She couldn't believe that just this morning she had woken up from a two day sleep. Although she was still very uncertain about what they were going to encounter once they got to the Orkney Islands, she couldn't believe how content she felt.

Callum made his way back up the stairs and sat a loaf of bread and some dried meat on the small wooden table that was nailed down to the deck. "Your provisions, princess," he said with a smirk that seemed a little sweeter than normal.

Ailia smiled back at him and walked to the table, happy that she could now enjoy her time on the sea.

Callum reached over to hand her some bread when she noticed something on his arm that she had somehow missed before now. She grabbed his forearm and turned it over, pushing his sleeve up past his elbow.

"What is this?" she asked, frowning at him. There were dark marks snaking up his arm from his wrist to his shoulder. It almost looked like lightning, or like he had been poisoned, but the marks weren't following the pattern of his blood vessels.

He quickly pulled his arm away and covered it with his sleeve. "It's nothing," he muttered.

She was going to punch him. "Callum, I swear. What did we *just* talk about? No more secrets."

Callum looked at her and rolled his neck, then his shoulders. "It's a mark from the Finfolk. To seal the bargain I made with them."

"Why didn't you tell me?" Ailia asked, trying not to shout at him.

"I didn't want you to worry. The bargain is for me to fulfill alone. I made sure to keep you uninvolved," he replied, avoiding her eyes.

Ailia wasn't sure why that upset her, but it did. She was sure that he had made the bargain in order to settle some sort of debt to the Finfolk. It was her responsibility, and he had taken it for her. "What will you have to do?"

"They haven't decided yet," he answered. "But whatever it is, I will gladly pay it."

Ailia looked into his blue-green eyes that seemed to shift in color throughout the day. "I will help however I can. You don't have to do everything alone, Callum."

"Just eat, princess," he said with a small smile. "The bargain with the Finfolk is very low on my list of concerns."

They finished their meal in silence that became more comfortable, and Ailia wondered how she had become so close to two people so willing to sacrifice everything to keep her safe.

CHAPTER FIFTY-THREE

CALLUM

C allum was so fucked.

He decided that he wasn't going to interfere with whatever Reed and Ailia had between them. Even if he was soulbound to her. Even if it felt like his heart was being ripped out of his body every time Reed touched her.

He would not force her into a life with him because of a bond if she wanted to be with Reed.

Ever since the kelpie, and the Finfolk, and her wielding her *third* fucking element, Callum had tried to create some distance between him and Ailia. He had to. It was becoming too instinctual to go to her. To touch her. To covet her.

But she was not a thing to be claimed. A creature to cage in the justification of love.

So he had been avoiding her. Until he just couldn't anymore.

The link between them demanded he help her. Protect her. Heal her.

When she was hurling up her guts, he had to do something.

She had asked why he had been able to heal her. It was one of the privileges of being soulbound. They were intrinsically linked; their souls connected by stardust.

Thank the gods she hadn't asked him to explain it further, because he wouldn't have been able to deny her. He would never be able to deny her a single thing. And he was strangely okay with that.

Just to touch her, to bring her comfort, to be near her—it was enough.

Although, he might throw all of his disgustingly romantic notions out the gods-damned window tonight if he was going to actually have to share a bed with her. The thought alone was fucking torture.

But he would not burden her with this revelation. Not now. Not when whatever fragile thing between her and Reed had been developing, and he had watched her carefully bloom over the past several weeks.

He could do this. He fucking better do this. Or he would hate himself forever.

They had been eating quietly, watching the sunlight reach for the sea until the light finally collided with the water, bathing the world in brilliant colors.

"Wow," breathed Ailia, looking toward the sunset. "I've never seen anything so beautiful."

"Me neither," said Callum softly, drinking her in.

Ailia turned to look at him, and he quickly shifted his gaze toward the horizon.

"Are you tired?" he asked.

"You know what? I am. You'd think that sleeping for two days straight would mean I was anything but tired, but I'm exhausted," said Ailia, accentuating her statement with a yawn.

"And you're still feeling okay? No more nausea?" Callum asked.

Ailia smiled at him. "No more. I'm okay."

Callum smiled back. "Then time for bed. I'll clean up. And seriously, Ailia—if you're uncomfortable sharing the bed," he said, nearly choking on the words, "I will happily sleep up here. I've slept in much worse places."

"Callum, it's fine. I think we can handle it." And then she winked at him. Gods save him.

She patted his shoulder as she walked by and headed down the stairs. Callum decided to take as much time as he possibly could cleaning up. The last thing he needed was to walk in on her changing clothes. Hell, maybe she really *was* exhausted and would be asleep by the time he got down there.

After casting out his power several times to make sure they were well and truly alone, and strengthening the shield around the boat, he couldn't put it off any longer. Besides, it was just a gods-damned bed.

Despite the weather growing colder, Ailia had cracked open the small, round window in the cabin to let in some air. There were no lights, and it had already become quite dark. Luckily, Callum's heightened vision allowed him to see everything clearly. Or, perhaps, unluckily, since Ailia's body, in her short night dress, was very visible in the bed.

"I thought you got lost," Ailia joked.

"Just making sure everything is safe. Sleeping is a vulnerable act," said Callum, readying himself for bed. Which, tonight, meant unstrapping his weapons, putting a dagger under his pillow, and leaving all of his clothes on.

He went to get into his side of the bed, but Ailia sat up, and even in the dark, he could see the frown on her lovely face. He guessed she had heightened vision now.

"Are you sleeping in all of your clothes?" she asked.

"Why? Would you prefer me to sleep without them?" he said in his practiced, cocky tone. Maybe teasing would be the best approach to this situation.

He heard her eyes roll more than saw it. "You can sleep however you want, but I personally would rather your dirty clothes not contaminate these soft, clean sheets."

For fuck's sake. "As you wish, princess." He walked over to his backpack and took off his shirt and pants, which weren't that dirty, and changed into soft, linen shorts.

Steadying himself, which he was annoyed about needing to do, he walked to the bed, pulled back the worn quilt, and got in.

Okay. This wasn't too bad. He could do this.

He started to relax into the pillow, his hands behind his head and his eyes closed, when he felt Ailia roll over to face him.

"Tell me about Elflaine," she whispered.

"I'm not telling you a bedtime story, Ailia," he said with a sigh, not opening his eyes. If he could just try to ignore her...

Ailia shoved his shoulder. "Please, Callum," she whined. "I want to know more about where we are going."

Callum sighed again. She was making it very difficult for him to ignore her when she was touching him and asking him for things.

He rolled over to face her, immediately regretting his choice. The gold in her eyes was sparkling, and her pale hair glowed in the moonlight.

She was so beautiful.

Before he could stop himself, he reached out to brush a stray strand of hair behind her ear.

Was it him, or did she lean into his touch? He pulled his hand away.

"I thought you were exhausted," he murmured.

Her eyes roamed over his face, and she adjusted her head on the pillow.

"You're right," she said quietly. "You can tell me about it in the morning." She yawned and snuggled into the quilt, moving slightly closer to him in the process.

He should move away, turn over—something. But he couldn't. He had to be near her.

He watched as her breathing slowed, and when he thought she was asleep, he stroked her hair one last time.

"Goodnight, Callum," she breathed, half asleep.

"Goodnight, princess," he whispered, thanking all the gods in all the worlds for this moment.

CHAPTER FIFTY-FOUR

REED

"Storm, I swear to the goddess, if you don't get off of me..." muttered Reed for the third time that night.

For whatever reason, Storm had decided that he was going to sleep *with* Reed. And Reed was very unhappy about it. In fact, Reed was unhappy about this whole situation. First, he was not with Ailia. Second, Callum *was* with Ailia. Third, Storm was with Reed. And to wrap it all up, the damage done at the inn had definitely been caused by the fae.

The most concerning part about the break-in, though, was that the room most destroyed was Ailia's.

He had been helping his mother clean up, not trusting the mortals to get involved in case they found something they shouldn't. It had taken nearly all day to put Ailia's room back together. They weren't sure what she had left behind in the first place, so they didn't know if anything was missing.

The anxiety of being this far from her, along with the knowledge that there were faeries that were surely after her, had Reed on edge. He knew she wouldn't like it, but he was going to have to check in on her as soon as the sun rose, especially because of the way Callum had been acting recently. He didn't like the way the male had become so possessive over her. And he realized that his frustration was very hypocritical.

If he could just hold her for a couple of minutes, he would be able to deal with their separation for the next couple of days.

Wow, he felt pathetic.

He had argued with his mother over whether or not he needed to stay. She had been furious that he left Ailia and had repeatedly told Reed that she could handle the repairs on her own.

But Reed wasn't worried about the repairs. He was worried the faeries would come back. He was going to make sure the wards around the inn were strengthened before he left. He wanted to be sure his mother was safe.

After pushing Storm off of him for what felt like the hundredth time, he cursed soundly and got out of bed. How the hell had Ailia been sleeping with the beast for the past few weeks? He was like a giant, hairy furnace.

Reed paced the length of his room. He had no choice but to go check on Ailia. If only to tell both her and Callum that she was now in some sort of danger from whoever ransacked the inn. He might have been annoyed by Callum's sudden territorial behavior, but he also knew that Callum would do whatever he could to protect her. He might even have some insight as to why—and more importantly, how, if all the entrances were supposedly closed—faeries might be looking for her.

Reed decided to go down to the kitchen to make some coffee. Dawn was still just a whisper, but he couldn't stay in his room any longer.

Unsurprisingly, Reed's mother was sitting at a table with a single candle lit, sipping a cup of dark, probably very hot, very sweet tea.

"Couldn't sleep either?" he asked from the kitchen, turning on the kettle. Tea would probably be better at this time of night... or was it morning? Whatever it was, tea would be better.

"No," his mother said solemnly, looking into her mug.

"It'll be okay, mum. We'll get everything fixed up, and I will make sure the wards are better this time."

His mother—his usually calm, steady mother—shuddered. "I don't really give a damn about the inn, Reed. I know it's our home, but this goes way beyond us. Faeries have not been in this realm for hundreds of years. Hundreds, Reed. This *must* have to do with the girls."

Reed sighed. "I was planning on going to see Ailia in the morning, anyway. I will tell her to be on her guard."

"And you're sure you can trust the faerie you left her with?" she asked, her tone lethally quiet. Reed knew his mother was furious with him for leaving Ailia alone, but he absolutely did trust Callum to keep her safe. And also wished Callum had heard his mother call him a faerie. He had a feeling the male would be offended despite it being technically correct.

"I'm sure," he replied. "I will spend the next couple of days making sure the wards are in place, and then I will return to her. I have to be in the Orkney Islands by the new moon anyway."

Reed's mother looked him over in the way that mothers did, seeing things that others did not. "You love her," she said after several moments. It was not a question.

Reed took a deep breath. "Can we not do this right now, please?"

"Reed, you should have known better. She broke your heart once. And she will do it again. From what you've told me about the bond you have with her, you are going to be connected to her for the rest of your life. Don't overcomplicate things."

She was right, of course. His mother usually was about these things.

"I wouldn't say she broke my heart, mother. That's a bit dramatic," he said, crossing his arms.

Mary scoffed. "You moped around for weeks after she broke things off with you. And to her credit, she made it clear from the beginning that she didn't want anything serious. You always fall too hard, my love." She reached out and stroked his hair in the comforting way that she had been doing since he was a child.

"I know," Reed said quietly. "I'm so fucked."

His mother patted him on the shoulder. "Yes you are, son."

She smiled at him, and he took another deep breath. "There has just always been something about her—something so magnetic. And now this bond... it amplifies all the feelings I've always had for her. But I know she doesn't want anything more from me than maybe an intimate friendship." He shook his head. "I need to get my shit together."

"Enough of this," said his mother, clapping him on his shoulder. "You're a brilliant witch, and being a knight is an honor. You know I have a special place in my heart for Ailia and Elideh, but you need to quit hoping for her to change her mind. It's not fair for either of you."

Reed nodded, taking a gulp of his tea. "You're right. Back to the plan. Fix the inn, fix the wards, and fulfill this fucking bargain with Callum."

His mother nodded her head encouragingly. "Just remember, my love, you are her knight. Nothing more. Try to move on."

"Okay," he said. "I can do that."

His mother grabbed his chin and looked into his eyes. "Of course you can. Besides," she said with a sad smile, "you don't have a choice."

CHAPTER FIFTY-FIVE

AILIA

Ailia woke up slowly, feeling more relaxed and rested than she had in weeks—maybe months. She realized that her face was in Callum's chest, his arm draped over her waist, and for some reason, it felt like the most natural thing in the whole world. She closed her eyes again, wanting to hold on to the peace that she so rarely felt. She listened to the steady rhythm of Callum's breathing, wondering why she felt this way.

Ailia's past relationships had been far from peaceful—some downright hostile. She didn't know why she always attracted men that were toxic in some way, but by the time she'd met Reed, she was over it. She had been hurt too many times. Which was why she had told Reed that she didn't want anything serious when they first decided to date.

After several minutes, Callum shifted, drawing her closer to his chest. She found herself nuzzling in on instinct. She heard Callum yawn, and he sleepily buried his face in her hair. Her body fit his like a puzzle, like she was always meant to lay here like this with him.

Suddenly, Callum pulled away from her. She immediately missed the warmth of his presence.

He looked flustered. "Sorry, Ailia. I didn't mean to get so..."

"Snuggly?" she interrupted with a giggle.

He looked down at her and seemed relieved that she wasn't upset. He chuckled, his eyes roaming over her face. "Sure, if that's what you want to call it."

Callum rolled onto his back, leaning his head against his forearm and yawning again. She didn't think she had ever seen him so.... cute. She also realized she had never been this close to him while he was shirtless. Of course she had noticed his sculpted arms and chest before, but damn.

Her eyes snagged on the strange marks left by his bargain with the Finfolk. After stopping herself from tracing the lines up and down his arm, she decided she needed to get out of that bed. Although the new feeling of familiarity that had overcome her was strange, yet somehow *right*, it was also making her think very inappropriate thoughts about what she and Callum could be doing at the moment.

She shook her head and stood, stretching her arms over her head as best as she could without hitting the low ceiling. She felt Callum's eyes on her and realized that her nightdress was pretty short. She normally would have felt embarrassed, but she didn't.

"What's on the agenda for today?" she asked, trying to shift the focus.

"Well," said Callum, dragging his eyes away from her, "We still have two or three more days until we arrive in the Orkney Islands, so we could—"

Callum stopped speaking and was instantly on his feet, barely avoiding hitting his head, staring at the ceiling at the same moment that Ailia heard the footsteps above them.

They both waited, completely still and silent.

"Ailia," called a familiar voice.

Ailia let loose a relieved breath. "Oh, it's just Reed."

Callum frowned, but Ailia answered, "We're down here, Reed!"

They heard him walking toward the staircase, and then Reed appeared, his smile faltering as he looked between Ailia, Callum, and the rumpled bed.

He walked over to Ailia, bending his head to fit in the room, and pulled her to him. "Are you okay?" he asked, holding her shoulders as he scanned her body.

"Of course I'm okay, Reed," said Ailia, confused by the question.

Reed glanced between her and Callum again. "We just woke up," said Ailia, hoping that would alleviate whatever dots Reed thought he was connecting.

That was apparently the wrong thing to say, because he rounded on Callum. "You couldn't find somewhere else to sleep?"

Before Callum could respond, Ailia stepped in front of him. "Actually, I insisted he sleep in the bed with me. Callum offered to sleep on the deck, but that wouldn't make any sense, considering the bed is big enough for two people." She crossed her arms. "Is that a problem?"

Ailia had made it clear to Reed that they were not together. She understood Reed being possessive, especially with this complicated bond, but she didn't belong to him.

Reed stared at her, trying to decide how to proceed. "Of course not, Ailia. I understand."

She sighed and squeezed his hand. "Thank you, Reed."

Callum had observed the interaction quietly, but was tense. He rolled his shoulders. "Now that's settled, why are you here, Reed? Just couldn't stay away?"

Despite the joking tone, Ailia thought she detected a bit of venom in his question.

Reed frowned at Callum. "Let's go upstairs and I'll explain. This room is way too small for all three of us."

The weather had turned pretty chilly overnight, so Ailia pulled on some long pants and a sweater and followed Reed upstairs. Callum was behind her, throwing a shirt on as they walked.

They sat down at the table, and Callum brought over bread and a couple of apples.

Ailia started to pick at the bread, looking at Reed expectantly.

"I have bad news," said Reed.

"Explain," said Callum, crossing his arms. It seemed like he was back to the normal, no-nonsense version of himself that Ailia had grown accustomed to.

"The attack at the inn was definitely fae," said Reed. Callum swore quietly, but Reed continued, running a hand through his hair. "And they targeted Ailia's belongings."

This time, Callum swore loudly and began pacing behind Ailia.

"Judging by your reaction," said Reed, his eyes following Callum's movements, "this is as bad as I thought it was."

"The only way the fae can access this realm is by receiving permission from the King or the Queen of Elflaine. As you know, I am here on the queen's orders. The king did not know about my mission, but I wouldn't be surprised if the attack on the inn was orchestrated by him."

"Wait, wait, wait," said Reed, holding up his hand. "Why would the king and queen not be working together?"

"Ever since the witch trials, their relationship has been splintered. They have only worked together when necessary to fight against the darkness," said Callum.

"So why would the king be looking for Ailia?" asked Reed.

"I don't know," said Callum, kneading his eyebrows.

"Well can you find out?" Reed asked with barely concealed impatience.

"Probably not," Callum stated honestly.

"For fuck's sake," muttered Reed.

Ailia felt so frustrated. And she was sick of being blindsided by conflicts. Then, a terrifying thought dawned on her. "If the king is looking for me, does that mean that Elideh is in danger as well?"

Both Callum and Reed looked at her, and she knew the unspoken answer was definitely 'yes.'

Callum rested his hand on her shoulder, easing the dread that was threatening to consume her. "We need to get back to Elflaine. As soon as possible. I thought that the mortal realm would be safer, but if the king is after you, we are better off there under the queen's protection."

"How can you be sure the queen would protect her?" asked Reed.

"One thing is for certain, if the king wants Ailia, the queen will interfere just to spite him." Reed nodded, but Callum kept pacing, trying to solve something. "If my suspicions are correct, I think there might be a way to get to Elflaine without finding all of the artifacts. We will have to wait until we get to the Orkney Islands for me to be sure though."

After a pause, Reed said, "Are you going to let us in on your plan or do we just have to wait?"

"You'll just have to wait, witch," said Callum with a tight smile.

CHAPTER FIFTY-SIX

CALLUM

Thank the gods that Reed did not linger after delivering his news. Callum was already riding a knife's edge after Reed showed up and implied something happened between him and Ailia in that bed. He couldn't understand why Ailia was always so patient with Reed's overly possessive bullshit. Especially since she had made it clear that she did not belong to him despite all of their outward affection.

It had already been difficult enough to wake up next to her and not do anything about her body being so close to his, especially with that gods-forsaken night dress. He was surprised that she seemed so comfortable. Maybe their bond was starting to reveal itself to her.

Not much was known about being soulbound—it happened so rarely. A soulbond was not instantaneous. It required trust and time to fully form. Of course, the fae still fell in love, and would promise themselves to each other. But a soulbond was unique. As if fate had woven two destinies together. As if their very essence was made of the same things.

Which is why it had taken Callum so long to admit it. No one he had ever met had a soulbond. He wasn't even sure Ailia was fae. Or if that even mattered. He had only ever read about them, but with him and Ailia, they checked every box: Torneach forming an instant bond with her, Callum sensing her distress during her nightmares and being able to reach her when nothing else could, the uncanny insight into her thoughts, the ability to comfort and heal each other—but the thing that finally convinced him was the most recent occasion she found herself in mortal danger.

He wasn't sure he completely understood it, but when the trance from the kelpie had fallen away and she sank into the ocean, his powers had transformed. He had felt faster, stronger, and if he had been thinking clearly, he would have recognized that he had more control of his magic than he had ever experienced. Those that were soulbound were so connected, that their natural abilities would become enhanced if their partner was in danger.

This was just another reason why he wanted to get back to Elflaine. The library at the Faerie Queen's castle definitely had books on how the soulbond worked. For now, he would just have to suffer through it. And it truly *was* going to be suffering every time he shared a bed with her.

He needed a new focus for the day. She had asked about Elflaine, maybe he could start preparing her. Or maybe he should tell her about his father. Or *maybe* he should just take her down to that bed and kiss her until she was breathless.

Callum sighed and ran his hands through his hair. Maybe he should just jump off the boat and let the frigid water knock some sense into him. Just as he was seriously contemplating leaping into the water,

Ailia walked up beside him, her citrus and sea salt scent nearly knocking him over.

"You seem tense," she said, resting her arms on the railing beside his.

Well, that was not far from the truth. "I'm fine," he said unconvincingly.

She gave him a look telling him exactly how unconvincing he was. "Look, I know Reed can get under your skin, but he really means no harm. He's doing what he thinks is best."

Reed was not bad—Callum had met much worse, actually. But it pissed him off that she was always making excuses for him. "Why do you feel like you need to justify his actions? What is he to you?" Callum hadn't meant to sound so terse, but he needed to know what was going on between them.

Ailia frowned at his tone. "I'm not sure what you mean. He's my friend."

Callum scoffed. "Well you certainly are not *his* friend."

Ailia raised her eyebrows and crossed her arms. "And what am I, then?"

Callum was really regretting this conversation. He looked out over the water and ran his hand through his hair. To his surprise, Ailia sighed and looked out at the water as well. "You're right," she said quietly. "I know I'm more than a friend to him. I know he's in love with me." She blew out a breath. "And I love him too, just not the way that he loves me."

Callum could have collapsed from relief.

"It's why he acts the way he does. Why he wants me to stay safe and doesn't want me to go to Elflaine." She paused. "Hell, I had to work hard to convince him just to train me... and to let you train me." She looked over at Callum, searching his eyes. "But it just isn't... right with him."

Before he could stop himself, he gently took her chin and tilted her head up toward his. "That's because what you're describing is not love, Ailia. It's possession. Reed wants you—to have you, to keep you. He needs you to stay, needs you to listen, needs you to be safe. And although it looks like love, it isn't."

Ailia was quiet for a long time, but never looked away from him. He wasn't surprised by a lot, but the words she spoke next shocked him. "Isn't that what love is? To be wanted? To be kept from harm? To be taken care of?"

Her confession nearly broke him. He still knew so little about her. What had happened in her short life that led her to believe that those things counted as love?

"No, it's not," he said quietly. "Love is empowerment. Selfless desire. Partnership." Callum paused, willing her to understand. "But most of all, Ailia, love is freedom."

Ailia looked down, but Callum gently tilted her head back up. "And you will have that one day, little witch."

She smiled softly, and damn him if it didn't make his stupid heart jump around in his chest. He knew Reed didn't mean any harm, and knew that in his own way, Reed was loving her. But he also knew that the love that he felt for Ailia was wildly different than the love Reed had for her. He knew that he would never keep her from growing, and learning, and *living* just to relieve his own worries. Maybe one day she would understand that.

Changing the subject, mostly because he would definitely kiss her if she kept looking at him like that, he said, "I want to teach you how to shield."

Her smile widened and she said, "Absolutely. Can you also teach me how to shift?"

He grinned at her eagerness. "You would have to fully go through your staying before you can shift. It takes a lot of energy and magic to transform into another creature. Some fae never do it. But if the time comes, yes, I will teach you."

Callum walked toward the middle of the boat, and she followed. He was thankful for the distraction. Plus, she really did need to learn how to shield. He hadn't wanted to make her or Reed any more anxious than they already were, but if the king's minions were after her, she would need all the help she could get.

CHAPTER FIFTY-SEVEN

AILIA

Damn—learning to shield was really fucking hard. Harder than it had ever been to wield her elemental magic. Ailia knew that Callum was constantly keeping shields up around them, but had assumed it was just a normal fae ability. Getting this raw power to do anything on purpose was difficult enough, but actually maintaining the focus to keep a shield around an entire boat, or cottage, or just more than one person, took mental strength that she definitely did not possess yet.

"Callum. I'm exhausted," she said, probably a bit dramatically. "Seriously, my brain feels like mush." She massaged her forehead, like that would help.

Callum smirked at her. "Do it one more time. Just around yourself."

"*Ugh*, you're so bossy." She was huffing like a petulant child, but she really didn't care. "Fine."

Once again, she reached into the part of her that was still very unfamiliar and commanded the magic to guard her. When she first learned to connect to the earth, she had envisioned the magic like tendrils of light. But this was different—it was pure, unfettered power. She felt the energy surround her like a small, protective bubble. Callum immediately struck out at her with a dagger and then a small blast of his own magic. Her shield held, and she would have cheered if she hadn't been so fucking tired.

The first ten times she had attempted the shield, Callum had instantly broken through it, not holding back with his attacks. She was sore, to say the least.

"Okay, can we stop now? Please?" she begged.

"Well, since you asked so nicely, princess," he teased.

"Thank god," Ailia breathed. She plopped down on the deck of the ship and turned toward the sunset. She had to admit, although she was not a fan of being confined to a small boat in the middle of the sea, the sunrises and sunsets were incredible.

Callum sat beside her, their shoulders barely touching. "You did really well. Shielding is very difficult. To be honest, I wasn't even sure you'd be able to do it. Not many can."

Ailia looked over at him and frowned. "Really? I assumed it was something all the fae could do."

"It's not. Although I am sure most wish they could. Elflaine is a ruthless place, and shielding would definitely be a valuable asset," said Callum.

"Tell me more about Elflaine," said Ailia. "If only so I have a distraction from my aching body."

Callum's nostrils flared, and something flashed in his eyes. "As you wish, princess." He glanced at her. "Once upon a time—"

Ailia shoved him and Callum laughed. "Not this again!" Ailia was laughing with him, but she really didn't want another half story. "Just tell me about the place, the way things work, what I can expect."

Callum sat up and smiled at her—a genuine, full smile that she rarely saw. Damn he was gorgeous.

"Very well. Where to begin..." he said tapping his chin.

"How about I ask you questions. Like this is a research project?" offered Ailia.

"Ask away," he said, nodding his head.

Ailia thought for a moment. There were a lot of things she needed to know, but trying to decide on the right questions to ask had always been a fun challenge for her. She decided to start with the basics.

"In the stories that Elideh has transcribed, the faerie realm is frequently described as dark—almost a constant twilight—but breathtakingly beautiful. What is it actually like?"

Callum thought for a moment. "It is beautiful, that is true—nearly a mirror image of Scotland, just... more. Ever since the darkness infiltrated our realm, the sun has not risen fully. It's not completely dark, but it is not completely light, either."

"Well that answer is cryptic," said Ailia, furrowing her brows.

The corners of Callum's mouth quirked up. "I don't mean to be cryptic, but it's hard to describe. You'll understand when you see it for yourself. Ask another question."

Ailia didn't hesitate with her next question. "Are all the fae like you, or are there different types of faeries?"

"Well, no one is like me," he said with a cocky smirk.

Ailia rolled her eyes. "You know what I mean." Callum grinned and nudged her shoulder with his.

"There are many different types of faeries—all the ones that are written about in your world. The ones like me are fae, and the way that you probably imagine faeries to be are called different things—sprites, brownies, pixies," explained Callum.

"So what is fae society like? Obviously there is a king and a queen. You've said you're a warrior. What else is there?" asked Ailia.

Callum huffed out a breath and crossed his legs in front of him. "There are healers, scholars, builders—just like in your world. But fae society is... complicated. Faeries do not have the same sense of morality as humans do. They—we—are ruthless. The king and queen stay in power because they hold the most influence and are the strongest, fastest, and most in control of their magic. Because we live for so long, the only time there is a shift of power is typically during some sort of coup, and that hasn't happened in centuries."

"I see," said Ailia, processing the hierarchy. "So power determines your place in society."

"Yes," Callum nodded. "Which brings me to an important point, actually. When we eventually get to Elflaine, you shouldn't advertise your magic."

Ailia frowned at him. "But it's witch magic. Surely that doesn't count?"

"Since you are also fae, or at least part fae, I think it will actually matter a lot. I don't know of anyone like you, or of anyone that has been as uniquely gifted as you. So I truly do not know what will happen." Callum had shifted closer to her, and she could sense the concern in his tone.

"Oh," Ailia said, suddenly very uneasy about going to Elflaine.

Callum took her hand in his and looked into her eyes. "I will be with you the entire time, Ailia. You will not be alone."

Ailia nodded, trusting him completely.

"So how do you fit into everything?" Ailia had been wanting to ask him this ever since they had received the response from his sister—who was apparently a princess?

Callum sat back again. "That, little witch, is very complicated."

"Try me," Ailia said.

Callum sighed and kneaded his forehead. "You need to know this anyway, since we are apparently going to be meeting my father in a couple of days." He paused and took a deep breath. "My father is Thomas Rhymer."

Ailia would have fallen over if she wasn't already sitting. "What?" she managed to sputter.

Callum released another deep breath. "My father is Thomas Rhymer. From the ballads. My mother, the Faerie Queen, fell in love with him—"

"Your *mother* is the *Faerie Queen*?" Ailia gasped.

Callum nodded, and Ailia shook her head in disbelief. Callum took her momentary silence to continue. "She had sent him away after he had served his seven years, but realized after he left that she was pregnant. With me. Time passes differently in Elflaine, and sometimes the fae can make strange choices. She decided to give birth before telling my father about me. Many, many years had passed in this realm by the time she decided to bring him back. But when she went to search for him, he could not be found."

"Wow," Ailia whispered. She was speechless. Callum looked her over and reached out like he was going to take her hand, but stopped himself. He looked down at the ground, continuing his story.

"My mother kept me hidden from the king as long as she could, but since Thomas had been in the faerie realm for so long, and she had gifted him with faerie abilities, I was more powerful than she thought I would be. The king actually threatened to kill me, but by that time,

I had already gone through my staying, and was a valuable asset on the battlefield. My mother swore that I would never challenge my half brother, the son she had with the king, for the throne, so he let me live."

Ailia shook her head. "Holy shit, Callum."

Callum shrugged. "I'd never want the throne, anyway. I am much happier away from the castle and the court."

Ailia took a deep, steadying breath. "So you have a half brother. Is your sister the daughter of the king and queen as well?"

Callum's eyes softened. "Yes. Morgan, my half sister, is the only saving grace of that entire gods-forsaken court. Aydan, on the other hand... I'll just say this: he lives up to his role as a fae prince."

Ailia wasn't sure what that meant, but she got the feeling that Callum did not get along with his brother. However, it was obvious that he loved his sister very much. Ailia couldn't believe that she had never thought to ask him questions about his life before now. She was also fairly certain that he wasn't normally so forthcoming with information.

"Thank you, Callum," said Ailia, taking his hand and giving it a soft squeeze. "For sharing all of that with me."

"Anything, princess," he said, his eyes earnest.

Ailia didn't know if it was the exhaustion truly settling into her, but she felt something new blossoming in her chest. She wasn't sure what she had done to earn Callum's trust, but she was thankful for it. He had always been transparent with her, but this was a different level of companionship.

Callum looked her over. "You're exhausted. Time for bed."

She nodded her head and stood on her shaky legs. He eyed her, clearly trying to decide if she could stand on her own, and she rolled her eyes at him. "I can walk just fine."

"Whatever you say," he said, smirking at her.

Ailia took the steps below deck slowly. What she wouldn't give for a hot bath to soothe her aching muscles. She quickly changed and fell into the bed, thankful for the soft pillows. It was much colder, so she kept a sweater on, and pulled the quilt tightly around her. She still couldn't believe that Callum's mother was the Faerie Queen—and that his father was Thomas Rhymer. Finally, she let her exhaustion consume her, falling asleep almost instantly.

CHAPTER FIFTY-EIGHT

CALLUM

C allum stayed above deck for a while longer. The sun had set fully, and since it was so close to the new moon, the stars were bright above him. He was thinking about his father, and how strange it would be to meet him, when he felt a ripple of power come from beneath the deck.

He was up instantly and sprinting to Ailia, moving so quickly that the boat was a blur around him, knowing that whatever happened couldn't be good. Ailia was writhing in her sleep, sweat pouring off of her, and then freezing almost immediately. That was when he noticed the temperature. Although the weather had cooled some, the room below deck was frigid.

There was no darkness seeping out of her like before. She must be trapped in some sort of nightmare—and the power he felt must have come from her. He tried to get close to her, but she was moving so violently that he couldn't get near her. If he could just touch her, their bond could maybe calm her enough that he could wake her.

"Ailia!" he shouted, but she could not hear him.

"AILIA!" he shouted again, this time finally grabbing her hand.

As soon as he touched her, he was no longer in the cabin under the boat. He turned around frantically searching for her, ripping through tree limbs and trying to get his bearings. Finally, he spotted her, and all rational thought left his head. She was being dragged through the trees of a dense forest by something he could not see, and she was covered in blood and bruises.

The sight of her captive elicited a guttural growl from Callum, but the scent of her blood and raw terror made him see red.

She kept trying to stand, but her captor was moving too quickly. She fell, over and over again; silent, frustrated tears staining her dirty face. He could see the determination in her eyes to put up a fight. Her fierceness fueled him and filled him with pride. His soulbound was not giving up.

Callum tried to run to her, but no matter how fast he ran, she stayed just out of his reach. He stopped, panting. Where the fuck were they and what the fuck was happening? He took several deep breaths, sinking into the lethal calm he had learned on the battlefield. He needed to assess the situation.

They were nowhere near the ocean. And Ailia was not wearing the clothes she had on in the bed. Maybe he had somehow entered her dream. Whatever the vision was, it was not confined to the normal rules of space and time. How was he supposed to get her out if he couldn't catch up?

He shouted her name over and over again until his voice was hoarse, but she didn't respond. He wasn't sure how long they had been there, but her blood was flowing freely, and he roared in frustration. Finally, out of ideas, he blasted all of the magic he could muster toward the captor he still couldn't see. The forest was instantly alight, and Ailia's eyes snapped to his.

She released a piercing, primal scream—and the vision was gone. They were back on the boat. Ailia was shaking, her lips and fingers blue. She leaned over the bed and heaved up blood, and Callum was immediately by her side, holding her hair and speaking in soothing tones. Once she stopped, Callum dragged her to him and wrapped her in his arms.

After several steadying breaths and reassuring himself that she was alive and they were out of danger, he started examining her, methodically scanning her body for injuries. He got to her delicate hands and froze. Gently, he lifted her arm, avoiding touching her wrists. At the movement, she winced, her first reaction to his presence since they left whatever hellscape she had been trapped in.

Her slender, perfect wrists were rich shades of purple, black, and blue; the bruises in the same places where she had been manacled. Callum wasn't sure why these particular injuries had followed them into their world, but the fact that she had actually been hurt during that dream made him blanch.

His rage was a tangible thing. When he found whoever—whatever—had caused this, he would end them. Slowly.

Callum carefully ran his fingers over her bruises, willing them to heal with his touch and the bond they shared. After a couple of minutes, the bruises lightened to sickening shades of green and brown, but would not disappear completely. He didn't understand. She should have healed.

"What happened?" she whispered between ragged breaths.

"I don't know," answered Callum, putting aside his fears and fury for the moment. He pulled her closer, as if his body could envelop hers completely, and protect her from this unknown threat. "You were trapped in a nightmare, and writhing on the bed. I finally managed to grab your hand, but I was pulled into your dream."

She was still shaking, still freezing. He settled them both into the bed and leaned his back against the headboard. Putting one hand under her knees and the other on her back, he scooped her onto his chest, cradling her head to his shoulder. He pulled the quilt up around her and held her tight. Once he was sure she was comfortable, he started rubbing her back, shoulders and legs, trying to give her body some warmth.

After a few moments, and after her shaking diminished to shivering, she asked, "What was that? Ever since Elideh left, my nightmares have always been like glimpses into her head. This was not like that. Could it have been a vision? Of the future?"

Callum thought his heart might have stopped at her suggestion. As long as he was living and breathing, that would absolutely not be any version of her future.

He kept stroking her back, and said quietly, "I don't know, Ailia." He hated that his long, useless immortal life gave him no edge to handle this. "I swear to you if that is a vision of the future, I will find a way to change it. And if I can't change it, I will find you."

Ailia released a deep breath and wrapped her arms around his chest. Silent tears soaked his shirt, and he held her even closer. "Nothing could keep you from me—not dreams, not visions, not realms, and not darkness. I will always find you," he whispered into her hair.

Eventually the tears stopped, and her body relaxed; her even, gentle breathing a gift, indicating that she had fallen asleep. Callum tried to force the very visceral fear out of his system, but he knew that he would never recover from what he saw. That Ailia being dragged, broken and bleeding, would be his new living nightmare. That he would be on

edge until they figured out why everything seemed determined to take
her.

CHAPTER FIFTY-NINE

AILIA

Ailia woke up, and her first thought was that she had never felt so warm. She was cradled into Callum's chest, but when she opened her eyes, she saw a fluffy tail curled over her legs. When had Storm arrived?

Although she hadn't moved, Callum must have sensed that she was awake because she felt him tilt his head down to hers and was surprised to feel gentle kisses trail along her forehead.

"Are you awake, little witch?" he whispered.

"Yes," she breathed as she nestled into his warmth.

"We will figure this out, Ailia," said Callum as he gently stroked her hair.

And she believed him. She guessed she could officially add Callum to the short list of people she could unequivocally trust.

They sat there in the tranquility of the early morning light, the gentle rocking of the boat nearly lulling her back to sleep.

"I'm going to get you some water," Callum said, finally breaking the blissful silence. "Plus, I don't feel like getting in a fight with Reed this early in the morning, and I am sure he will notice Torneach's—Storm's—absence and arrive shortly."

"Don't go," said Ailia before she could stop herself. Callum held her tighter, and she returned the embrace.

"Never, princess," he said gently. "I won't be far." Callum gave her one last kiss on her forehead and then carefully moved her to the pillows on the bed. Storm took Callum's absence as an opportunity to practically lay on top of her, showing her how much danger she had truly been in.

She rubbed his ears absentmindedly while she waited for Callum. That was when she noticed the bruises on her wrists. Ailia frowned at them, wishing there wasn't such a visual reminder of her nightmare.

Just then, Callum came down the stairs, and when he saw what she was looking at, his eyes darkened and he looked her up and down.

"Those were the only injuries you brought back with you. I don't know why you haven't healed from them yet," he said, handing her the water and helping her sit.

"It must be some sort of dark magic," said Ailia. She took a sip of the crisp water and almost moaned in relief. She didn't realize how raw her throat was until that moment. "Maybe Reed will know something."

Callum stiffened at the mention of Reed's name, but nodded his head. As if she had summoned him, they heard footsteps pounding on the deck. Reed was down the stairs swiftly, his hair ruffled having obviously just woken up.

"What happened?" he asked, rushing to Ailia's side. "When I woke up and saw that Storm was gone, I knew something was probably wrong."

Reed grabbed her hands, and she winced when his fingers grazed the bruises. He looked down, frowning, trying to understand her reaction. When he saw the bruises, his eyes snapped up to hers, and then he turned to Callum. Before Ailia could blink, Reed had slammed Callum against the wall and had his hand at his throat.

"You need to back down, witch," said Callum calmly.

"You hurt her," said Reed.

Callum shoved Reed hard in the chest. "Quit reacting to everything with your emotions. Of course I didn't hurt her."

"Someone better explain what happened right now," said Reed. His eyes had become a richer brown, and the wood from the ship was starting to groan. Since they were surrounded by water, the only connection he had to his magic was in the materials the boat had been built with, and it looked like he was ready for a fight.

"It was a nightmare, Reed. Or some sort of vision. We aren't sure," said Ailia, glancing nervously at the walls. "Calm down or you're going to tear the ship apart."

Reed took several steadying breaths. Ailia hadn't noticed it, but Callum was now standing at Ailia's side.

"We will explain what happened, witch, but above deck. I am suffocating from the reek of your bravado and jealousy," said Callum. He rested his hand on her back. Callum found his heavy wool jacket and placed it over her shoulders, ushering her up the stairs. Reed was fuming behind them.

The sun still had not risen, so they were bathed in dimmed starlight. Ailia had always loved the quiet moment between true night and dawn. But today she just wanted the morning to come.

Callum led her to one of the stools, and once she sat down, he brought her another cup of water. He stood behind her, and she could feel the heat from his body. She didn't know why, but she leaned into him, and he laid his hand on her shoulder in response.

Reed glanced between the two of them, noticing the interaction, but stayed silent, waiting to be told the story. Callum explained what happened, and once he was finished, Reed stood and started pacing.

After running his hands through his already ruffled hair several times, making it look even wilder, Reed said, "That must have been dark magic. Even seers are not able to interact with their visions." Ailia nodded her head, unsurprised. "If witches and the fae are working together to find Ailia, she is in more danger than we thought, especially since it seems they can access her in her dreams. I will have to ask my mother about any wards or spells we can use to protect her mind. I'll be back."

And to both Ailia and Callum's surprise, Reed simply pulled his stone out of his pocket and disappeared.

"Well that was very unlike him," muttered Ailia, who had been expecting some sort of lecture.

Callum frowned in Reed's direction and nodded his head. "Let the witch sort out the wards. We need to work on your shielding today. Maybe it can extend to your mind."

"Callum, it's still nighttime. And I haven't eaten anything. Can we just... breathe for a minute?" Ailia closed her eyes and rested her head against his hard chest.

Callum leaned down, his mouth grazing her hair. "We can breathe all you want, princess, but if you think for one minute that I'm going to leave you vulnerable again, you are sorely mistaken."

Ailia shivered at the feel of his breath on her ear. "You're right," Ailia sighed. She couldn't even be mad at Callum. At least he wanted her to fight. Storm had finally tromped up the stairs and sniffed the air before sitting down at Ailia's feet and laying his head in her lap. It looked like he was not leaving her side anytime soon, either, and she was fine with that.

Callum reached out for her hand, and she let him pull her up after giving Storm one more scratch behind his ears. She yawned and stretched, eyeing the dimming stars. She knew she should feel more urgency to train, but she couldn't help feeling like they were putting off the inevitable. So far, everything on this trip was pointing toward some sort of doom. She just wanted to get to Elideh. Maybe then they could figure it out together. Like they always had.

CHAPTER SIXTY

REED

As soon as Reed made it back to the inn, he turned to the wall nearest to him and punched a hole straight through it. He needed to get out of the building. He needed to bury his feet in the earth and ground himself before he truly lost it and did something he regretted.

For some reason, he felt like he was losing Ailia. He had only been gone for two days, but something had changed between her and Callum. He wasn't even sure she realized it, but Callum definitely did. And then this damn bond demanding he protect her—what was he supposed to do when it seemed like she needed protecting even in sleep?

He strode out of the inn and started walking toward the castle ruins. He needed to clear his head, but more than that, he needed a solution. If something had attacked Ailia in a dream, and had left real wounds, he needed a way to get to her if it ever happened again. If she could be bruised, she could bleed. And if she could bleed, she could be killed. He shuddered at the thought.

As he walked, he went through all of the options he knew of. Sleeping potions wouldn't help if the nightmares turned out to be visions. If Ailia was truly a seer, she would not be able to manipulate visions, she would just be an observer. The talisman stones wouldn't help since Callum said that she had been wearing different clothes than what she wore to bed, so Reed assumed she wouldn't be able to take anything with her.

His feet carried him up the familiar path as he thought through what could have caused this. If it was another witch, and Reed was fairly certain it was, he would need some of their blood to counteract any spell they might have cast on Ailia. But even at that, he had never heard of a spell that could drag another witch into a visceral dreamscape.

He finally made it to the ruins as the sun was beginning to rise. He sat down and took off his shoes, digging his feet into the soft earth. He let the energy of the grass and stones and roots soothe him. The sun had fully risen by the time he felt in control, and he knew he wouldn't find a solution until he consulted his mother. So he reluctantly got up, grabbed his shoes—not bothering to put them back on—and started jogging back to the inn.

REED

Reed was not surprised to see that his mother was already sitting at a table with a pot of coffee and two cups waiting for him.

"Tell me what happened, Reed," she said calmly.

Not beating around the bush, Reed explained quickly what happened to Ailia. His mother swore colorfully when he was finished, reinforcing that this was, indeed, very bad.

He ran his hands through his hair, hoping his mother had some sort of solution.

"I can't think of anything that would help her if she's being pulled into a vision or a dream or a gods-damned different realm and is able to physically suffer," explained Reed.

His mother stared at her coffee for several minutes. Reed let her think. She had been alive much longer than him. Hopefully she would know something he didn't.

She let out a deep breath and then looked up at him, her expression grim. "There is a solution, but it's very dangerous. And I don't think you're going to like it."

He waited for her to continue. She shook her head slightly and then stood. He figured she was going to get her grimoire. They kept it hidden away, so he waited as patiently as he could for her to lower the wards to retrieve it. She came back and gently set the heavy, old book on the table between them.

After flipping through several pages and muttering to herself, she finally found whatever it was that she was looking for. She looked up at him, and turned the book toward him.

Reed quickly read through the spell and then *he* swore colorfully.

"This spell links for life—there's no undoing it. And we don't even know if it will work." He stood and started pacing. "Ailia would never agree to this—hell, I don't even know if *I* would agree to it. The intimacy of linking your minds is a lot to ask."

"I know, Reed, but there aren't a lot of other options. I'm still not sure how Callum was able to enter her vision at all." His mother frowned down at the book like it would give her answers. "He shouldn't have been able to."

Reed shook his head. "And there is nothing else we can do?"

His mother's eyes softened as she looked at him. "I'm sorry, my love. There's nothing else."

Reed blew out a breath. "Very well. I'll give her the option and explain how much danger she will be in if she refuses. Hopefully she will agree."

Mary nodded and then stood, opening her arms to him. Reed engulfed her in a hug, her familiar scent comforting him. "It's going to be okay, Reed. While you are gone, I'll try to do some research. I think there may still be a witch living in the town over. I'll drop by and see if he can help."

Reed pulled away and nodded. "Please don't put yourself in danger. I can't be in two places at once."

His mother scoffed at him. "Reed, I can take care of myself. I am much older than you, and I've had much more time to practice my magic. Go to Ailia and convince her to agree to this spell. I'll be fine." She smiled up at him, and he kissed her on the cheek.

He went into the lobby to grab some paper so that he could write down the spell. Once he was done, he said his goodbyes to his mother and pulled out his stone. This needed to be done right away. He just hoped that Ailia would allow it.

CHAPTER SIXTY-ONE

CALLUM

Callum guessed it was only a matter of time before Reed was back with them permanently, but he had been expecting at least one more day alone with Ailia. So when Reed showed up later that morning, he was unhappy to say the least.

He was even unhappier when Reed explained the decision Ailia needed to make. To be fair, he had never seen Reed look so strained, so he believed that it was truly the only option.

Ailia blew out a breath. "So you're telling me that there is no way to prevent this witch from dragging me into another vision, and the only way to deal with it is for one of you to forge some sort of connection with my mind? Permanently?"

Reed ran his hand through his hair and nodded. "Unfortunately, yes. The connection is permanent because it is such an intimate decision. You can't offer your mind to someone without being sure you can trust them. The spell won't even work if you try to do it with someone you don't trust."

"And even if we do this, there is no guarantee that I could be pulled out of the vision? It just means that one of you would be there with me? And maybe be able to reach me the way Callum did? Or maybe not?"

Reed nodded again. "Yeah. That about sums it up."

"Fuck," said Callum. "This is not good." He started to pace. He had rarely felt powerless in his long life, and he did not like it.

"We are in agreement, there," said Reed grimly.

Ailia was also pacing and had re-braided her hair three times in the past ten minutes. "I can't ask either of you to do this," she finally said.

"I'll do it," said both Callum and Reed. They turned to each other and frowned.

Ailia rolled her eyes at them. "If I'm truly immortal, that is a very long time to have that link."

"The connection only works in dreams, and just because we have access doesn't mean we can use it," said Reed. "I think it works like a door, but the door only opens to your dreams, or your subconscious. You would be able to pull us in, but we wouldn't be able to enter on our own."

"If there is any chance that it could help release you from one of those visions, I will gladly do it," said Callum.

"Plus, you and I already have a bond that connects us forever, in case you've forgotten," said Reed.

"Of course, Reed. I know." Ailia sat on the deck of the ship and pulled her knees to her chest. "I'm just frustrated. I feel so helpless." Callum had been trying to give Ailia and Reed space, so he let Reed kneel down next to her.

"Ails, you aren't helpless," Reed said gently. "In fact, you're extremely powerful. Which is probably why you're being targeted. But everyone can use a little backup."

Ailia looked into Reed's eyes and nodded. "Okay."

Reed's relief was palpable, his shoulders relaxing as he released a deep breath. Before he could say anything, Callum said, "I want to do it."

Reed stood up and scowled at Callum. "It should be me. We already share a permanent bond."

"Well if you're willing, witch, maybe it should be both of us. We already know that I was able to get her out of the first vision. What if your magic doesn't work against another witch's spell? There are too many unknowns." Callum was not willing to back down from this. If someone was going to have some sort of access to his soulbound's mind, it was going to be him. And if Ailia agreed to let Reed perform the ritual as well, he would figure out a way to live with it.

Reed crossed his arms, trying to read Callum's motive. "Very well. Let's just get it done. I still don't know how this dark magic works, and I don't know if Ailia even needs to be asleep to be pulled away."

Ailia had watched the interaction curiously. "I don't know why you both want access to my dull dreams, anyway."

Callum could tell she was trying to lighten the mood, but her posture indicated that she was tense about the whole situation. She glanced between the two of them, but when she realized they weren't going to back down, she huffed a breath and squared her shoulders.

"What do we do, Reed?" Ailia asked.

AILIA

Ailia was shocked that they were both so willing to take this risk. What if their connection somehow trapped them in a vision as well? If she had more time to think about it, she might have insisted they just leave her to it. But she knew they wouldn't back down.

"It's actually pretty straightforward. The main requirement of the spell is complete trust. We will exchange blood with you and recite the spell. But that's really it."

Ailia and Callum both frowned at him. "How does the spell know if there is complete trust?" Callum asked.

"It's not that the spell would know, but because the result is so intimate, it simply won't work if the trust isn't there," shrugged Reed.

Ailia blew out a breath and muttered, "No pressure or anything."

Callum walked over to her and gently cupped her cheek. "You don't have to do this. I will find you no matter where you are. If you don't want either of us to have this access to your mind, just say the word, little witch."

Ailia touched his hand, leaning into it. She believed him—that he would find her no matter what. But why risk it? "No, I know I need to do it. I really don't want to be trapped in a vision like that again. As long as you're both sure you're okay with it," she said.

"We are," Callum assured her.

Reed took that as his cue to pull out the spell and a dagger. "Ailia, you will have to drink some of mine and Callum's blood, and we will have to drink some of yours."

"Drink it?" Ailia sputtered. "You didn't say anything about drinking blood, Reed. We aren't vampires."

Reed shrugged his shoulders. "Sorry, Ails, that is what the spell requires. A sacrifice of blood that is ingested. I don't make the rules."

"For fuck's sake," muttered Ailia, but she held out her wrist.

Reed gently took her hand, frowning at the lingering bruises. As he made a cut on her forearm, he muttered the spell. Then, he took her arm and drank from her, quickly giving Callum her arm to follow suit before her magic healed her.

He then sliced his own arm, holding it up to Ailia's mouth. She took it and drank the blood, trying not to gag. Callum took the dagger from Reed and made a clean cut on the inside of his hand, holding it up to her mouth. His blood tasted different than Reed's, which was a strange thought, but Ailia didn't have time to examine it.

The ritual was complete, and they all just stared at each other, waiting for something to happen. Suddenly, Ailia gasped. Both Callum and Reed's eyes widened. She could feel their presence in her mind. Reed's presence reminded her of the earth—stable, solid. Whereas Callum's presence felt wild, yet safe—familiar somehow.

As quickly as she had felt them in her mind, they were gone.

"What happened?" she asked, looking between them.

"Well, I think the spell worked. I definitely felt the connection," said Reed.

Callum nodded. "I also felt it. It was exactly as you described—like a door."

"So that's it?" asked Ailia. This felt too simple.

"I think so," said Reed, frowning. "But I guess we won't truly know how it works unless you get pulled into a vision again."

Callum scowled. "Hopefully we won't ever find out."

Ailia couldn't agree more.

Chapter Sixty-Two

Ailia

Ailia was ready to get off the boat. After they all swapped blood, Reed and Callum watched her anxiously, like they expected her to suddenly fall into a vision. She understood their trepidation, but she really needed some space.

After practicing her shielding with Callum for the rest of the day, and laughing at how twitchy Reed was from trying not to interfere, they all sat around the small table and discussed their plan for the next day. They were finally going to be arriving in the Orkney Islands.

Callum had filled Reed in on the surprise visit from his father, and despite the tension from the past few days, there seemed to be a level of peace settling over the three of them.

Ailia stood and stretched. "I'm going to bed. And before it causes some sort of fight, I'm sleeping with Storm. You two are just going to have to figure it out."

Storm, who had been laying at Ailia's feet, perked his ears.

"We will be fine up here, princess," said Callum, stretching his legs under the table.

Reed stood. "I'll walk you down."

"Going to check for monsters under the bed?" Ailia joked.

Reed rolled his eyes and followed her.

They got to the tiny room, Reed hunching his shoulders and standing at the door while Ailia changed for bed. He carefully avoided looking her way, and she wondered if she should ask about his sudden reserve.

"Listen, Ails. I don't know what's going on between you and Callum, but I don't want to interfere—"

"What do you mean?" she interrupted. "Nothing has changed between me and Callum."

Except... was that true? With everything going on she hadn't exactly had the time or energy to examine her feelings. Maybe Reed was right. Maybe he was seeing something she hadn't even admitted to herself. She did find herself wanting to be close to him more and more often. She frowned.

Reed gave her a knowing look. "You've made it clear from the beginning that you and I are not meant to be, so I just wanted to let you know that no matter what, I will always be here for you. As a friend." He spoke the last part quickly, as if he didn't want to lose his nerve.

Well, she had not been expecting that confession. She walked over to him and took his hand. Finally, he looked up at her.

"Reed, I hope you know that I care for you. And I am honored to be your friend," she kissed the top of his hand, and his shoulders relaxed slightly.

He pulled her into a hug. "I just worry about you all the time. Please be careful."

She wasn't sure if he meant to be careful in general, or to be careful with Callum, but she nodded her head. "Of course."

He pulled away and chastely kissed her forehead. "Off to bed, then."

She had to admit, she was glad that Reed cleared the air. And he seemed genuinely relieved by her reaction. She hadn't really thought of her interactions with Callum, and didn't feel like now was a good time to start.

Storm was waiting for her in the bed, and she snuggled up to him. Hopefully this would be an uneventful night. She really didn't want to test their theories with the spell.

CALLUM

Callum assumed that neither him nor Reed would be sleeping that night. Reed looked more at ease than he had in days when he came back above deck. Callum wondered what sort of conversation had transpired to change Reed's mood, but it wasn't his place to ask. Besides, now that their sea voyage was coming to a close, Callum needed to focus on the task at hand: deal with his father and get the golden bridle.

Reed sat on one of the stools beside Callum. "Anything I need to know before we get off this boat?"

Well that was straightforward. Callum definitely wasn't going to tell Reed about the soulbond. He didn't want Ailia to hear it from anyone but him. Once all of this was past them, and they got to Elflaine, he would tell her.

"Nothing that I haven't already told you, witch," said Callum.

Reed studied him, then squared his shoulders. "Just so you know, there's nothing between me and Ailia." He leveled a stare at Callum. "I don't know what's happened between the two of you over the past couple of days, but I know what it's like to be in love with her." Reed paused, crossing his arms. "If you hurt her, though, I will fucking kill you."

Callum hadn't been left speechless many times in his life, but he truly didn't know what to say. The witch was perceptive, he'd admit that much. Then again, maybe Callum hadn't been keeping his feelings as contained as he thought.

He took a deep breath and reached out his hand to Reed, a mirror image of the oath that had started this journey. "She is safe with me."

Reed grasped his hand, never breaking eye contact. This was an oath that Callum would never break and never regret.

They sat in easy silence for a while, occasionally taking turns to check on Ailia. Luckily, she was sound asleep, Storm practically wrapped around her body.

Eventually, Reed said, "Do you think the Finfolk are going to just give up the bridle?"

Callum shrugged. "That's what they said. Hopefully they won't ask me to fulfill their end of the deal right away. To be honest, I am more concerned about what my father has to say." He could at least give Reed that truth.

The night passed rather quickly, Callum's apprehension growing by the hour. Finally, right before dawn, they saw land. Callum was relieved the night had passed without any incidents, but he was not sure he was ready to face his father.

Reed walked over to the railing and was gazing at the cliffs that were quickly approaching. Callum joined him, watching the spray from the waves crash against the rocky bluff.

"I'm assuming the Finfolk are going to keep us from smashing to pieces against those very sharp rocks?" Reed asked.

Callum shrugged. "I guess we will find out."

Sure enough, the boat began to slow, navigating the waves effortlessly toward a hidden cove.

"I'll go wake Ailia," muttered Reed. It seemed he shared Callum's anxiety now that they had finally reached their destination. Callum just hoped this would be quick.

CHAPTER SIXTY-THREE

AILIA

"Time to wake up, milady," Reed announced as he walked into the room.

Ailia stretched her arms, glad to hear Reed in a good mood. "Morning," she said sleepily. She sat up in time to catch the clothes that Reed had tossed in her direction.

"Get dressed, Ails. I'll pack your things," Reed said.

At that, Ailia was wide awake. "We finally made it?"

"We are currently being navigated into a cove," he answered.

Ailia quickly changed clothes, eager to leave this part of the journey behind her. By the time she was finished, Reed had packed her bag and was carrying it up the stairs. "See if you can wake that sad excuse for a guard dog," he called behind him.

She turned to Storm, who was stretched out like a gigantic cat on the bed. She smiled and walked over to him, nudging him. "Up, up, up, you lazy beast." Storm opened one eye and then closed it again, nuzzling into the pillows. "Storm!" Ailia laughed. "Get up! We have to go."

Finally, after a lot of prodding and bribing, Storm got out of the bed and followed Ailia up the stairs.

Just as she made it above deck, she felt the boat shudder to a stop. Callum unfurled the ladder over the side and took two steps down, reaching over to take Ailia's hand. She followed him and sighed as her feet touched the sand. Reed threw the packs down to Callum, then climbed down the ladder. Storm simply looked over the side of the boat and made the jump, landing gracefully at Ailia's side.

After that, everything happened very fast.

She heard a shout from the cliffs above them, and Callum appeared in front of her, pushing her to the ground. She looked up to see an arrow protruding from Callum's shoulder. An arrow that had been meant for her.

"RUN!" he shouted, summoning weapons as he frantically looked around.

Reed grabbed her hand, pulling her up. He caught the bow that Callum tossed to him and started sprinting toward the shelter of the cliffs. They hadn't made it far when two massive fae males stepped out from behind the rocks. Ailia looked around wildly, trying to figure out what was going on. Storm was right at her side, growling at the males in front of her.

Callum caught up to them but was panting and bleeding from the wound in his shoulder. He had broken the arrow shaft off, but the tip of it was still stuck—probably the only reason he wasn't bleeding more. He stood at her back, and Reed took a step in front of her. In total, there were seven males surrounding them, all armed.

"What the fuck are you doing here, Alasdair?" spat Callum.

"We are here on orders from the king, Callum. Give us the girl," said the one closest to them.

"Orders from the king? You've got to be fucking kidding me. You're *my* fucking soldiers!"

"Give us the girl, Callum," the male said grimly, standing his ground despite the aggression roiling off Callum.

"Not a chance," growled Callum.

In the distance, Ailia could see the Finfolk running toward them. But they would never make it in time. At that moment, the males attacked.

Callum threw a shield around them at the same time that Reed built a wall of earth between them and the males. While the soldiers were trying to break through the wall, Reed and Callum turned to Ailia.

"When the wall breaks, you have to fight. I don't know why the king wants you, but it can't be good," said Callum quickly.

Ailia nodded as the wall shattered. She barely had time to conjure a shield before a dagger was thrown right at her chest. Now she was thankful that Callum hadn't taken her training lightly.

She struggled to keep up with the onslaught of attacks, and she was only fighting one of them. Three of them were engaging Callum, and Reed was managing the other two. Already, Callum and Reed had been forced to give up ground, Storm hurling his massive body toward the males in between attacks, but never going far from Ailia's side. The soldiers were relentless. There was no elegance or honor in this battle, just unforgiving brute force to get through Callum's and Reed's defenses and get to her.

She was holding her own against her opponent, but knew that was probably because they wanted her alive and relatively unharmed. Although Callum and Reed were standing their ground, they had both suffered some pretty serious injuries and were slowing in their attacks. They were both powerful, but strength and magic eventually ran out, and they were outnumbered. They couldn't keep this up.

She knew it would be a risk, because it would leave her completely vulnerable, but she was not going to let them die for her. Keeping her shield up, she called all of the elements to her and reached inside for that unfamiliar, raw power.

She took a deep breath, and unleashed it all.

Everyone flew back, some of the males hitting the ocean, some of them hitting the cliffs with a sickening thud. She hadn't shielded Callum, Reed, or Storm, hoping Callum had already been shielding them, but they were all lying on different parts of the beach, far away from her.

She sank to the ground, completely exhausted, when she felt strong arms lift her from the sand. She looked around, not understanding how Reed or Callum could have made it to her so quickly. When she looked up, though, she saw an unfamiliar, beautiful, cruel face smiling down at her. "Thank you, my dear. That little display made this much easier for me. I haven't seen a light wielder in many, many centuries."

Ailia saw a young woman with stunning red hair and dark eyes walk up next to the male holding her. The woman waved her hand over her head. Ailia tried to protest, to move—to do anything—but she was so weak she couldn't even speak.

"It's as I suspected," said the woman, her voice devoid of warmth and kindness. "She is strong. It will take a lot of power to bind her."

"Very well, witch, do what you must but make it quick. They are starting to stir," said the male. Ailia used her remaining energy to turn her head. She saw Callum trying to sit up. He lifted his head and made eye contact with her. The fear in his eyes made her blood go cold.

"NO!" Callum roared. He started to stand, but the witch waved her hand in his direction, commanding the wind to hold him to the ground. He struggled to his knees, fighting the magic, trying to crawl to Ailia.

The male holding her shifted her body to one arm, cradling her like a child, and reached out the other toward Callum. "I should have killed you when I had the chance. I knew you'd eventually be a problem," he said, venom dripping from every word as a blast of magic crumpled Callum's body into the sand.

"Ailia!" shouted Reed. She could barely see him from the angle she was at, but she felt the sand move beneath her and recognized Reed's magic.

"Why is the witch glowing, Caitriona?" asked the male impatiently.

The stunning redhead turned toward Reed, cocking her head. "A knight."

The earth around them quaked, and the male holding her cursed soundly. "We do not have time for this," he said as he blasted Reed, knocking him back into a rock. He didn't move.

The witch turned her attention back to Ailia and grabbed her head with both of her hands. Without warning, Ailia's head started to burn, and she screamed and screamed and screamed. It felt like it was burning straight through her mind, and she thought if it didn't stop soon, it would surely kill her.

She thought she could hear Callum shouting something, but she couldn't make it out over the roaring in her head. Finally, the burning began to subside, and she once again saw the cruel, cerulean eyes of the male before everything turned black, and she knew no more.

CHAPTER SIXTY-FOUR

CALLUM

This couldn't be real. As soon as the witch and the king disappeared with Ailia, and the magic holding him left with them, Callum stood, sprinting to the place they had been. The sound of Ailia's scream had nearly cleaved him in two.

Fuck, fuck, fuck.

Ailia was gone. And raw, furious power was thrumming under his skin, begging to be released. Begging him to find her. To save her. To destroy the ones that took her from him.

He heard a low moan and turned to find Reed, shaking his head and trying to stand. Callum quickly went to him, and grabbed his hand to pull him up.

"Where did they take her?" asked Reed, his voice sounding as hoarse as Callum's felt. Luckily, the other soldiers were still knocked out. It seemed that Ailia's magic had at least recognized Callum and Reed enough to keep them from unconsciousness.

"I don't know," said Callum. "I don't fucking know. FUCK!" Callum threw a dagger at the cliff nearest to them so hard that it cracked the rock. "What did the witch do to her? Why was she screaming?"

"Oh shit. Shit," said Reed, running his hands through his hair. "I couldn't see them, so I didn't know what was happening." All of a sudden, Reed stilled. "The witch," he whispered. "Fuck. Callum, the witch. She said something about binding Ailia." Reed looked at him, and the horror in his eyes reflected the feeling in Callum's chest.

Callum stood, his fury barely leashed. Trying to think rationally. "What could that mean? Binding her magic?"

Reed shook his head, his eyes wild. "I don't know. Binding her to someone else? Fuck. I don't know what that witch is capable of."

"Did the witch break the connection we have with her dreams?" asked Callum.

"No, I doubt the witch could have detected it, and it's nearly impossible to break a blood bond," said Reed confidently.

At least that had gone right. But he didn't want to wait until she was asleep to know if she was okay. And there was no guarantee she would be able to open that fucking door for them since they hadn't had a chance to test it. Callum took a deep breath and reached out for Ailia, trying to find that delicate thread that had been steadily growing stronger over the past couple of days. He nearly collapsed from relief when he felt the shimmer of their soulbond. She was alive. He would know if she wasn't.

He turned at the sound of footsteps behind them. The soldiers were still unconscious, strewn out across the beach. The Finfolk, however, were running toward them with a man Callum could only assume was his father trailing close behind.

"We couldn't make it in time, and the king's witch had warded the area so we couldn't use our magic," said the eldest Finfolk as they slowed their approach.

This could not be happening. This could not be fucking happening. Ailia could not be gone. Callum put his hands on his head and sank to a crouch.

"The king?" asked Reed. "Callum, what the fuck is going on?"

"The King of Elflaine took Ailia," he said quietly, wishing it wasn't true.

Reed turned, cursing soundly.

"What do we do? I should still be able to reach her with my stone if she has it," said Reed.

"They would just kill you," said Callum. "We will go after her. But we can't do it alone. The king is very powerful, and if that witch was the same witch that trapped Ailia in a vision and is practicing dark magic, we will be completely outmatched. We need to get to Elflaine." Callum looked up at his father. "And I think I am going to call in a favor to get us there."

Callum's father squared his shoulders and nodded his head once. Good, he understood.

"I will contact the Faerie Queen and explain that I have found Thomas Rhymer. She will let us back into Elflaine." If she didn't, he would rip a hole in the realm himself.

He was trying to stay calm, but was riding a knife's edge. He went over to Storm's too-still body. "Storm," he said gently. "Torneach—wake up," he said more forcefully. Callum ran his hands over the beast's body, and Storm finally twitched. Thank the gods for their bond. Storm lifted his head, sniffing, searching for a girl that was not there. "They took her, but we will find her," he whispered. Storm stood, looking as dejected as he felt. "Someone get me paper," he called out behind him.

The Finfolk conjured paper and a pen, handing it to him in silence. Callum quickly wrote a note explaining that he had found Thomas Rhymer, requesting to enter Elflaine immediately. He folded the note and gave it to Storm.

"Be swift, my friend," he said. He barely finished speaking before Storm was gone.

Callum stood again and began pacing. Why did the king want Ailia? He needed to wake up one of these bastards and get some answers—the ones that hadn't died from Ailia's blast of magic. The males that had accompanied the king were some of his more brutal, unruly soldiers, so he wasn't surprised that they were up to the task of kidnapping an innocent girl. He was, however, surprised that Alasdair was involved.

Callum walked over to where Alasdair was laying face first in the sand, not bothering with the other soldiers yet. He hoped they were dead.

"Wake up," he said, kicking Alasdair hard in the side to turn him over.

Alasdair grunted. Not dead, then.

"I said wake up!" he commanded.

Alasdair's eyes flew open, and he was immediately on the defense. "I can explain, Callum. Let me explain."

"That's the only reason you're still alive, you fucking traitor," Callum said through gritted teeth.

Alasdair took a deep breath. "The king told us that we were to retrieve a threat to the kingdom and bring her back for questioning. That was all we were told. If I had known you were involved, I wouldn't have agreed."

"A threat to the kingdom?" said Callum, barely controlling his rage. "Fuck me, Alasdair. Did she look like she was a threat to the kingdom?"

"Considering she took out seven of the most highly trained soldiers in Elflaine with a single blast of magic, maybe she is a threat, Callum," Alasdair said defensively.

"You know nothing about her," Callum seethed. His blood sang with the need for vengeance—for violence—that she had been taken from him. That his soulbound had been in pain, and he hadn't been able to prevent it. That the fucking King of Elflaine currently had her and he had no way to reach her. He turned away from Alasdair and methodically made his way to each of the soldiers—his soldiers—that he had trained with and fought with for centuries, and slaughtered them without remorse if they weren't already dead.

Covered in blood, he returned to Alasdair. "Did you partake in a blood oath with the king or can I trust you?"

"I didn't take an oath," replied Alasdair, his eyes hardening.

Callum took his dagger and slit his hand. "You will take an oath of loyalty to me right now or I swear to the gods, Alasdair, I will kill you."

Alasdair nodded, turning his hand up toward Callum. Callum swiftly sliced both of their palms, and they clasped hands, not needing to speak the ancient words of fealty aloud.

Callum turned from Alsdair before he changed his mind about keeping him alive and stalked back toward Reed and the Finfolk.

"So we have to wait for Storm to return?" asked Reed.

"Yes," said Callum. "But we will receive a quick response."

The Finfolk approached them. "Come with us. We had a temporary shelter built in anticipation of your visit. We will give you the bridle, and you can wait there."

Callum nodded his head, the adrenaline quickly fading and being replaced with an acute dread. Callum and Reed gathered their things, the sea salt and citrus scent clinging to Ailia's pack making Callum's heart ache, and followed the Finfolk to the path that cut into the cliff. So far, his father hadn't spoken to him, but Callum didn't really care.

They silently made their way up the steep path, Callum and Reed nearly collapsing into the chairs by the hearth once they made it to the tasteful cabin. He figured Reed was feeling the same things as him—hopelessness, fury, fear—so he didn't bother speaking to him before standing up and walking to the washroom.

He would find Ailia. And all of Elflaine better be prepared for the war he was about to wage to get her back.

REED

Reed had let his fury and panic simmer while he watched Callum slaughter the males that helped take Ailia from them. He knew there was nothing he could do. Maybe it was shock, or maybe it was that he couldn't believe that Ailia was actually gone, but he just sat, waiting for instructions.

Callum had walked stoically to the washroom, but Reed felt stuck. He had the stone that connected him to Ailia in his hand, and had been turning it over and over and over, trying to convince himself that Callum was right, and it would be suicide to go after her right now. He could feel the bond that demanded her protection vibrating within him, coaxing him to do something. Anything.

He had to stay away from the hopelessness that was threatening to consume him. The rage was much better suited for what they were going to have to do. They would get her back.

The Finfolk and Callum's father had not spoken to him or Callum since arriving at the cabin, but they were carefully guarding the male that Callum had spared. Callum had entered battlefield commander mode, and at this point, Reed was happy to let Callum take charge.

Reed knew this anger and panic wouldn't be sated until he had Ailia back, and he would gladly let it be a driving force until that moment.

Callum walked back into the room, the blood gone from his body but still staining his clothes. It was as if Callum had transformed in the past hour. He had always been formidable, but now, even his energy was buzzing with feral dominance.

Reed stood and walked over to him, clasping him on the shoulder. "Tell me what to do, and it will be done."

Callum nodded at him, acknowledging Reed's offer. Reed had known their journey to Elflaine would be difficult, but this—this was war.

CHAPTER SIXTY-FIVE

AILIA

It was dark. And cold. And silent.

Ailia tried to look around her, but the darkness was absolute.

Wake up, wake up, wake up. This must be a dream.

She tried to stand, but her ankles were shackled to the floor.

She pulled at the chains, the bite of the metal drawing blood.

Wake up, wake up, wake up. It must be a vision.

Tears streamed down her face, and she sat, holding her knees.

Then, she remembered. The beach. The cruel face sneering at her. The witch burning through her mind. Then nothing.

This was real.

Ailia took a deep breath. And she yanked and clawed and cursed at the chains. She would not let the darkness consume her. She would not be anyone's prisoner. She would not give up without a fight.

ACKNOWLEDGMENTS

First, I'd like to thank you, dear reader, for believing in my story.

Thank you to my husband, Jamie, who has inspired, supported, and encouraged me. When I told him that I thought I wanted to write a book, he said, "Of course you do. I always knew you would."

Thank you to my family (American and Scottish), Mama, Papa, Jake, Susan, and George, who have been my biggest cheerleaders, and my children who have taught me about love, joy, and dragons.

Thank you to my sister, Brooke, and my sister-in-law, Emily, for all the sister things, the many book discussions, and for being early sounding boards for my ideas.

Thank you to countless friends that inspired me to keep going.

Thank you to my critique partners, Aneka and Audrey, for all of the feedback and love, and my beta readers, ARC readers, and fellow authors for their support and kindness.

An endless thank you to my patient, funny, and kind editor, Courtney (@c.hanan.editing), for helping me bring this story life.

Thank you to my incredibly talented cover designer, Ida (@idatj_drawings), for translating my visions for the artwork into reality so beautifully. And of course to her sister and my dear friend, Kat, for all of the "behind the scenes" work.

Thank you to Nathan and his team at Softwood Books (@softwoodbooks) for producing this book with me, and answering my many emails with grace and kindness.

Lastly, thank you to all the storytellers that came before me. I hope I've done your legacy justice.

ABOUT THE AUTHOR

HALEY HAMILTON

Haley Hamilton lives in Georgia with her husband, Jamie, four children, and pup, Pippa. An avid reader, she was inspired by Scottish folklore to write her debut novel, which you currently hold in your hands. Follow Haley on Instagram (@haley.h.writes) for updates about upcoming books.

www.ingramcontent.com/pod-product-compliance
Ingram Content Group UK Ltd.
Pitfield, Milton Keynes, MK11 3LW, UK
UKHW021700030225
4426UKWH00010B/87